THE COMPLETE HAPPINESS SERIES

HOLLY MARTIN

THE LITTLE VILLAGE OF HAPPINESS

CHAPTER ONE

Willow McKay swerved across the road to avoid a pheasant and checked in the rear-view mirror to see it stumble safely back onto the grassy verge and disappear into the tall bushes that lined the road. What was it with this place? That was the fourth animal that had almost been squished under the wheels of her car. Maybe the animals round here were particularly stupid or they just weren't used to cars. She had been driving along this little country lane for what seemed like an hour, going up and down hills, and hadn't passed a single vehicle. The village of Happiness really was in the furthest corner of nowhere.

But that was exactly what she needed.

Six months ago she had proposed to her boyfriend of four years and he'd said yes. The very next day, he'd changed his mind.

In hindsight, she hadn't really wanted to marry Garry with two Rs, which was how he introduced himself to everyone. She'd just wanted something to change between them. They had stagnated for far too long. She'd kind of thought a marriage proposal would be the make or break of them. And in reality she wouldn't have cared too much if he'd said no, she just wished he'd done that before she had announced the news on Facebook and told all her friends and family. The texts and Facebook posts reporting the change in her status the next day were more than slightly awkward.

Although she and Garry with two Rs had parted fairly amicably, her friends and the people in her town couldn't seem to let it go. The looks of pity, the sniggers; she'd had enough.

She needed a fresh start and Happiness was just the place to make it happen. The illustrated poster on the advert had showed glittering seas and the little whitewashed Cornish village tumbling down the hillside. It had looked tranquil and inviting.

Brightly coloured flowers danced and bobbed on the roadside as she passed, the warmth of the sun seeped into the car like a cosy blanket and up ahead she could spot the sea sparkling like a turquoise-sequinned carpet spread out beneath her.

It filled her with hope.

The opportunity to move to Happiness had seemed too good to be true. The privately owned village lay nestled in the grounds of a castle and, in an attempt to fill some of the empty houses, the new owners had offered free accommodation for a year to anyone who could give something back to the village, either by taking over one of the closed shops, fulfilling a role in the community such as a doctor or teacher, or providing some kind of service. And while candlemaking couldn't exactly be described as something vital like being a doctor, she still felt that she had something to offer. And clearly so did the new owners of the castle, Kitty and Ken, who had practically snapped her hand off, offering her a place in the village within a few hours of her applying. She was excited about the change.

A jaunty little sign on the side of the road declared she had finally reached her destination.

Welcome to Harmony Castle and the Village of Happiness.

She couldn't help but smile as she swept through the gateposts and drove past the castle. It looked a bit tired in places and one poor turret seemed like it had crumbled away to nothing. It must be very expensive to maintain these kinds of places. She drove round the front of it and came to a row of four houses, though she could see the road wound away down the hill and included several more houses and shops. She had been allocated Sunrise Cottage but she had no idea where to look.

She pulled up on one side of the green and got out.

The four houses here were grey. There was no other word for it. These were not the whitewashed cottages she had seen in the poster. Some of the windows were broken, one house had its shutters hanging off and the flowers in the hanging baskets were dead. Two of the houses actually looked like they were sinking into the ground. The sun dipped behind the clouds, leaving a dullness that made the light in her heart go out. Was this what the whole village was like?

Why hadn't she visited before she packed up all her worldly goods and left the little town of St Octavia behind for the Cornish coast? Her mum always said she was too impetuous, the kind to rush in and ask questions later. That had been her trouble throughout her life. She made snap decisions and then often regretted them later. She was already second guessing this decision.

Her eyes scanned across the houses; they didn't even look habitable let alone like anyone lived there. In fact there didn't seem to be a single other person in sight. Was she literally going to be the only person to live in the village of Happiness?

A roar came from the castle and a man appeared on a quad bike. He was wearing a sky-blue baseball hat, a paint-splattered t-shirt, and faded cargo shorts. His dark curly hair stuck out in different directions from underneath his hat. He bumped down the hill towards her and came to a stop, flashing her a small cautious smile.

'Hi, I'm Andrew Harrington, I'm the estate manager here.'

She tried to recover herself from the shock of the state of the village. 'I'm—'

'Willow McKay, yes we've been expecting you. I'm sorry I wasn't here to greet you when you arrived, I would have stopped you from seeing that shambles behind you.'

'How would you have stopped me from seeing it, by blindfolding me?'

'It crossed my mind,' he grinned.

He had a nice smile. Although Garry with two Rs had a nice smile and look where that had landed her.

'Come on, hop on, I'll take you down to your cottage,' Andrew said.

'What about all my stuff?'

'I'll give you a hand with all that after, I'm sure you're dying to see your new home. I promise, it's nothing like this.'

Willow eyed the back of the quad bike dubiously and then climbed on.

'You might want to hold onto something, it gets a bit bumpy in parts,' Andrew said. 'Wouldn't want to lose you on the way.'

There was nowhere to hold onto except Andrew himself and from the smile on his face, he knew that.

'I normally insist on dinner before wrapping my arms around a man.'

'Well if you insist, I'll let you take me out for dinner later,' Andrew said.

She smiled. 'Any weird spellings to your name that I should know about?'

'Only the silent K in the middle,' Andrew said.

She laughed and wrapped her arms around him. Maybe life in the village of Happiness wouldn't be so bad after all.

CHAPTER TWO

They bumped down the little cobbled road, passing shops and houses that appeared not to have been lived in or used for years. A couple of the shops looked like they might be open during working hours but at the moment all the doors were closed and the lights were off.

'How many people live here?' Willow asked.

'Forty-seven in the village, well forty-eight now you've arrived. That doesn't include the housekeeper up at the castle or Kitty and Ken.'

'What are they like?'

'Lovely, really wonderful people. You'll like them,' Andrew said, loyally.

She would have to pop in and introduce herself properly.

'And how many houses are in the village?'

'Including the four where you parked your car, one hundred and twelve. Seventy-five of them are empty.'

That was a bit depressing.

'How many of the shops are in use?'

'Four at the moment, five when you open up yours.'

That really was a sad state of affairs. It wasn't the thriving village that she'd expected.

'That's the only pub in the village,' Andrew pointed at a tall stone building with a battered old sign swinging gently outside: *The Welcome Home*.

They took a right at a little fork off the main road and travelled down a tiny track lined with overhanging trees. There were a few more houses down here.

'That's my house,' Andrew pointed to a pale blue little cottage, hidden under a mountain of thatch. It was tidy and well maintained and the garden was blooming with flowers. 'Feel free to pop in at any time and if you have any problems, you know where to call.'

They passed a few other houses and then the trees fell away and Willow was treated to a glorious view of the sea. Andrew pulled to a stop outside a bright yellow house.

'This is Sunrise Cottage,' Andrew gestured grandly.

Although it was very small, it at least looked like it wasn't going to fall down any time soon, which Willow supposed was a bonus, and it had an amazing view. Her view from the front of the house she had shared with Garry had a view of the houses on the opposite side of the street and a graveyard from the back. It hadn't exactly been inspiring.

She climbed off the bike and Andrew rushed forward to open the little gate, which almost fell off in his hand as he did.

'I'll fix that,' Andrew muttered, as he tried to shove it back onto its hinges and failed.

The lawn had been recently mowed and there were a few flowers trying to bloom in the overgrown borders; there was potential here. And the newly painted bench, angled to take in the view, was a lovely touch.

'The door is open,' Andrew said.

Willow pushed it, feeling the tackiness of freshly painted wood. So tacky in fact, her hand actually stuck to the wood. She peeled it off, leaving a lovely handmark on the front door.

'Ah sorry, I thought that would be dry by now. Don't worry, I'll paint over the handprint.'

She walked in and was faced with a tiny lounge with a bright red two-seater sofa, a tiny coffee table and an old cube-shaped TV in one corner. There was also a little log burner. She could see the kitchen through an archway. There was a slightly tatty feel to the place, but it had obviously been cleaned and patched up and painted recently. Someone, probably Andrew, had tried to make it feel like a home. There was even a vase of freshly picked flowers above the fireplace.

She looked at him and he was watching her hopefully.

'It's lovely,' Willow said, truthfully.

'I'm glad you like it. Now the shower has just been grouted so I'm afraid you can't use it until tomorrow night to be on the safe side, but you're welcome to pop up and use mine if you want one before then.'

'You're inviting me to use your shower, that's very forward,' Willow teased.

He smirked. 'It's not like I'm offering to scrub your back for you. I'll be downstairs, with my eyes closed for good measure.'

Willow giggled at the thought of him sitting on his sofa with his eyes firmly closed just in case.

'Well that's very kind of you.'

He shrugged. 'Now, I wouldn't recommend bringing your car down here, the lane is too rocky for that and probably too narrow. So if you give me your keys, I'll hook the trailer up to the back of the quad bike, load your stuff into that and bring it down here myself. Why don't you go out for a walk, get to know the place, and by the time you get back, all your stuff will be here. I'll park your car in the car park behind the castle and leave your keys here too.'

'Wow, that is good service. Let me give you a hand loading the trailer, there's quite a lot of stuff.'

'There's no need. As many of the elderly folk say, I'm a big strong lad, I can cope with a few bags. Please, go and explore, meet the locals.'

'OK, if you're sure.' Willow couldn't deny that she wanted to see her new home.

'You can go back to the village the way we just came. Or if you follow the coastal path to the left along the cliff path, you'll come to some steps that will take you down to the beach. You can go left at the top of the steps and the path will take you to the bottom of the main high street. Keep following that and you'll come to the pub again. The village is kind of laid out in a big triangle so it's not too hard to find your way around.'

'Thank you,' she said, handing him her car keys.

He smiled and ducked back out the door. He really was rather huge. She watched him walk down the path, shaking his head at the gate as he passed through it, and then he climbed on the quad bike and roared away, giving her a wave as he disappeared up the lane.

She stepped outside and pulled the door closed behind her. She hadn't seen a key but she supposed Andrew must have that. As there was nothing of hers in the house and she was really in the back end of nowhere, she wasn't too bothered. She walked out of the gate and took the coastal path that wound its way past the cottage and along the cliff tops.

The view from up here was utterly spectacular, the sea a gorgeous turquoise green glittering with gold-crested waves. She could see the cliff tops and meadows that hugged the coast stretching out for miles ahead of her and, other than the rooftops of the houses from the village of Happiness, she couldn't spot a single sign of life as far as the eye could see.

The idea of solitude appealed to her but the isolation of Happiness meant it was just a bit too quiet. At least in St Octavia, she would pass people on the streets she had never seen before, she could walk into a shop without everyone knowing her name. She got the sense that here, in the village of Happiness, if she so much as sneezed the whole village would know about it.

Her phone rang in her pocket and she smiled when she saw it was her best friend Ruby. She answered it.

'Hey Rubes, how's it going?' Willow said as she walked along the little cliff path.

'Shouldn't I be asking you that question?' Ruby laughed.

'Well I've arrived in the village of Happiness.'

'And is it happy? Are there little lambs gambolling everywhere, children dancing round the maypole, flowers blooming from every surface?'

'Not quite,' Willow said. 'It looks pretty dead, some of the houses don't even look habitable.'

'Ah Willow. You know that famous expression?'

'Only fools rush in?'

'No, you're not a fool, you're an optimist. Which is a lovely thing to be. I was going to say, "Look before you leap." Maybe you should have checked this place out before you decided to move there.'

Willow sighed; she knew Ruby was right. She was definitely a fool.

'It's only for a year,' Willow said, trying to defend her decision. 'I have to start paying rent to the owners of the village after a year. I'm not staying if I hate it, but at least I can save some money while I'm here so I can buy or rent somewhere if I come back. But I think I need this. I don't think it was just mine and Garry's relationship that had stagnated, I had too. I want adventure and change and, while I've only met one living person so far and the village looks half in ruin, maybe Happiness is the place to find it. I've always wanted to live near the sea and now my house is right on the edge of the cliff. The view is startling.'

'Always the optimist,' Ruby said, fondly. 'You know you didn't need to run away just because of what happened with Garry.'

'I'm totally fine with what happened with Garry,' Willow said, with exasperation. 'We were never meant to be together. What I'm not fine with is the constant comments, giggles and looks of pity. I bought a cake from Linda's cake shop the other day and she asked if I was drowning my sorrows. It's been six months. Let them talk about something else for a while, maybe they will have forgotten all about it by the time I get back.'

'OK, OK,' Ruby sighed. 'I hate to say you probably made the right decision because I'm missing you already, but I think this could be good for you.'

'You can visit anytime,' Willow said as she approached the steps to the beach.

'I may hold you to that.'

Willow smiled as she imagined Ruby with her brightly coloured clothes. She would be just what Happiness needed to brighten the place up.

'You'd be very welcome.'

'Are there any hot men there?'

Willow thought about Andrew. He was good-looking and had those huge shoulders she liked in a man. He had wonderful Mediterranean-blue eyes, which seemed to sparkle with permanent amusement. He made her laugh too. She shook her head with a smile.

'Not for me, I think I need some time to find happiness on my own for a while, not fall into bed with a handsome stranger with a nice smile.'

'Ah, so there is someone?'

Willow laughed. Ruby wouldn't let it go if she thought there was even the remotest chance of romance in the air.

'Ruby, you're breaking up.'

'Don't you hang up on me.'

'The reception is really bad, I'll call you later,' Willow said, making some crackly noises with her throat for good measure and then she disconnected the call as Ruby gave another squawk of protest.

She slipped her phone into her back pocket and looked out over the view for a moment. The tide was out, leaving a long horseshoe-shaped beach at the bottom of the steps. Steps that seemed to go on and on down the side of the cliff. The beach was completely deserted even though it was a warm sunny day. Clearly none of the residents of the village fancied a long trip down the steps either or the journey back up. Maybe she'd leave that bit of exploring for another day.

She turned up the path and headed back towards the village. She passed a few houses that were no more than crumbly stone walls, probably hundreds of years old. She hoped the rest of the village fared better than this. It didn't take her long before she reached the bottom of the main high street where there were little houses either side of the cobbled road. Some of them were boarded up but, she noticed as she made her way further up the high street, even the ones that seemed lived in looked worse for wear with peeling paint, tiles missing from the roofs and broken fences.

She just felt so disappointed. Happiness was supposed to solve all her problems. She was going to start a new life here, and now that new life was looking bleak and dismal. She had been completely misled by the beautiful painting and she couldn't help feeling a little angry about that. But it was just an advert, of course it was going to try to show Happiness in its best light. A crumbly, broken old castle and a village in ruins was hardly going to make anyone want to come. And really, she was more angry at herself. She was an idiot. How could she not have checked this place out first? How could she let herself get so easily swayed by an advert? Could she really stay here and build a new life for herself amongst the tattered ruins? But then what was the alternative? There was no backing out now. She could hardly go back to St Octavia with her tail between her legs. The gossips would have lots to say about that.

She carried on up the high street and curtains twitched as she walked past. She gave the occupants a cheery wave. But other than that she didn't see another sign of life anywhere, the street was deserted. It was only half past six, was everyone really tucked up in their beds already?

She passed a row of shops that looked as though many years had passed since they had sold anything. One shop had an abandoned teddy in the window which looked sad and lonely as it stared out through the dusty glass.

She spotted the post office, the only splash of colour in what was otherwise an almost entirely grey affair. The front door was painted a bright red as was the sign above the shop window, the words *Post Office* painted in gold, written in a rather ornate handwriting. Someone clearly took pride in their place of work. In fact the three other shops that were clearly in use were all clean at least, their products ranging from cheese to paintings displayed cheerfully in the windows, even if the paint was peeling on the outside. There was hope here – not much, but some.

She decided to go to the pub, if it was still open. She was hungry and hopefully they might be serving food so she wouldn't have to cook. If she was lucky she might even find someone to talk to in this little ghost town.

CHAPTER THREE

She pushed open the door and was met with the kind of quiet you find in a library, so much so that for a moment she thought the pub might be closed. But there were people inside, a scattering of customers, maybe no more than ten, most of them sitting by themselves, a few talking quietly in small groups.

Ah, finally there was life here, after all. Albeit very quiet life.

Although what little conversation there was quickly died off to silence as everyone spotted her and gawped at her like a rare exhibit in a museum. She stood there awkwardly for a moment taking in her neighbours. Almost every one of them looked like they were over the age of ninety.

'What can I get you, love?' came a voice from the bar and Willow looked over at the barmaid who was at least in her forties. She was wearing a bright red polka-dot dress that matched the shade of her hair completely.

Willow cleared her throat and walked up to the bar with a

confidence she didn't feel as slowly quiet conversations resumed around her.

'Don't mind these guys,' the lady said. 'They're just curious and all completely harmless. I'm Tabitha and my husband Connor is around somewhere. We're newcomers too, although we've been here about a month now.'

'I'm Willow. How are you finding it here?'

Tabitha let out a big breath. 'Well, it's very peaceful and quiet, everyone keeps themselves to themselves.'

Willow smiled at Tabitha's attempt to put a positive spin on it. 'Can't be good for business.'

'We do OK, mostly because Connor is a demon in the kitchen and some of the residents prefer to come in here for their lunch or dinner than cook for themselves. But we're not exactly the social hub we hoped we would be.'

'I know. The place feels so tired. I just expected Happiness to be a bit more... happy,' Willow said.

'So what will you be doing here?' Tabitha asked, handing Willow a menu.

'I'm having one of the shops, I'm a candlemaker.'

'Ah that sounds nice,' Tabitha said, though she didn't seem totally convinced. Willow wasn't convinced either. People loved her candles, the scents and different shapes and sculptures she made from the wax, but it certainly wasn't going to bring anything great to the village.

Willow glanced down at the menu.

'I can recommend the curry,' Tabitha said.

'Curry it is,' Willow said. 'And a half of cider.'

Tabitha poured her drink and Willow paid and went and sat in the window so she could look out on the street.

No sooner had she sat down than she was joined by a lady of about seventy years old who plonked herself down on the seat opposite Willow. Maybe Willow's earlier assumption that everyone was over ninety had been a bit harsh.

'I'm Dorothy.' The lady stuck her hand out, her eyes shining with happiness. 'I'm the village's resident artist, I own the painting studio out on the high street.'

'Willow,' she said, shaking Dorothy's hand.

'Did I hear you say you were a baker?' Dorothy said, excitedly.

'No, sorry, I'm a candlemaker.'

She watched Dorothy visibly deflate. 'What good is that to the village?'

'I'm sorry,' Willow said, awkwardly.

'We used to have a wonderful baker here when I was a little girl. His name was Sam and he would have the most delicious cream cakes in the window, freshly baked every day. He would only have the best cakes on display and, if any of them got broken, he would take them off display and give them to the kids to take home at the end of the day. There used to be quite the queue of children outside his shop at five o'clock each night. Sometimes I think he used to break some of the cakes deliberately, just so he could give them to us at the end of the day. He made the most delicious apple cake too, great big slabs of it. We would have it every Sunday in our house throughout the summer and autumn.'

'You've lived here your whole life?' Willow asked, keen to distract Dorothy from the shortcomings of her being a candlemaker.

'Yes, born and raised.'

'What was it like here when you were growing up?'

'Oh, it was thriving. Neighbours would walk in and out of each other's houses, borrowing sugar or vegetables or just stopping for a chat. The children would play in the streets. Everyone helped each other out. We used to have dancing here in the pub or up at the castle. It was a wonderful place to live.'

'What happened?'

'The old lord of the castle, Rupert, was a wonderful man, as was his father before him. Rupert looked after everyone in the village and was very much part of the community. When he died, his grandson took over the castle and he was everything his grandfather was not. He was rude, arrogant, and had no time for the villagers. He partied away his inheritance, squandered it all on fast cars and alcohol until he was completely bankrupt. In a desperate attempt to get more money he tripled the cost of the rent of the houses and shops. Most of the people in the village couldn't afford to pay those kinds of prices and, within a few months, over three-quarters of the village had packed up and left.'

'That's so sad,' Willow said.

'The grandson sold the castle on then but we never saw the person that owned it after that, I'm not sure if he even came here. The place fell into ruin and more people left. We had some new people come, like Roger and his sister Liz from the cheese shop,' Dorothy nodded to an older couple sitting quietly in the corner. Roger had a splendid red flowery cravat knotted neatly at his neck. Liz had gold-rimmed spectacles that were balanced precariously on the very end of her nose and was wearing a blue fluffy cardigan despite the heat of the day.

'But most of the newcomers didn't stay long,' Dorothy went on. 'The castle and village passed through several hands over the last few years until Kitty and Ken bought it. They're trying to build the village back up again but I think they've bitten off more than they can chew.'

Willow sighed. The village needed people to make it thrive again, young families to breathe life into the shops and houses, but when most people came and saw the state of the place they wouldn't be stopping even if the accommodation was free.

The atmosphere, at least in the pub, was one of defeat. The villagers didn't care any more and she didn't know what she could do to change that.

A man who she presumed was Connor came over with her food and she picked up her knife and fork hungrily.

Just then the door was pushed open and Andrew walked in. He had changed into jeans and a clean white shirt that was rolled up at the elbows, revealing strong tanned arms. The sleeves around the shoulders were taut around muscles she hadn't really spotted before. His curly hair was a little damp at the ends, but it was a bit more tamed now it wasn't sticking out at all angles from underneath his baseball cap. She wondered idly what it would feel like if she were to stroke her fingers through it. He had those wonderful crinkles around the sides of his eyes when he smiled, clearly showing that he smiled a lot. She liked that.

Immediately, Roger stood up and came over to talk to him, obviously bemoaning some problem or other, pointing and gesticulating as Andrew listened intently. He gave the impression of taking Roger's complaints seriously and that he had all the time in the world to listen to him, despite it being already way past normal working hours. Clearly, whatever Andrew said made Roger visibly relax. Eventually, after Andrew had taken the time to reassure him, Roger went and sat back down with his sister. But Andrew had only taken two more steps to the bar before a lady approached him. But again Andrew didn't look annoyed, he was nodding thoughtfully as he listened patiently. Willow found herself smiling; it was clear he genuinely cared about the villagers.

'He's easy on the eye, isn't he?' Dorothy said.

Willow realised she had been blatantly staring at Andrew ever since he'd walked into the pub and Dorothy had noticed that. Willow's food had been forgotten.

'Oh no, I was just watching how much in demand he is. He's not... I'm not looking for a relationship right now.'

'You could do a lot worse than Andrew Harrington.'

'I'm sure he's lovely.' She had a feeling that was an understatement. 'But I'm quite enjoying being single at the moment.'

'Hmm.' Dorothy was clearly unconvinced.

Finally Andrew got served and Willow forced her attention away from him to focus on her food. The last thing she needed was the villagers to get the wrong idea and try to matchmake between them.

She looked up to see him striding towards her, a big smile on his face.

'How are you finding the village so far?' Andrew said, sliding into the booth opposite her, next to Dorothy.

'It's lovely,' Willow said automatically and then berated herself. She wanted to moan to Andrew about what a state it was and how she had been misled. But none of it was Andrew's fault and it seemed he had enough problems to deal with without listening to her complaints. Andrew smirked though, because it was quite obvious that the village wasn't lovely. Dorothy grunted; even she clearly thought otherwise. 'It will be lovely once it's finished,' Willow said carefully.

Andrew was staring at her intently, a small smile on his face. He really did have the most amazing blue eyes. She focussed on her food again and looked up to find he was still studying her. She glanced over at Dorothy who gave her a theatrical wink.

'I'll be up and out early tomorrow so if you want to come for a shower and I'm not there, just let yourself in and help yourself,' Andrew said. 'My door is always open and not just in the metaphorical sense.'

'Oooh,' Dorothy chuckled. 'You going to scrub her back for her?'

'You'd love that, wouldn't you, you saucy little minx,' Andrew laughed, nudging her. 'Dorothy here, and quite a few women in the village actually, have been trying to set me up for months with their daughters and granddaughters and friends' daughters. They all think I need a nice woman to look after me, when I'm more than happy on my own.'

'Oh come on, Willy's lovely,' Dorothy gestured towards her like she was showing off a prize cow.

Andrew smirked at Dorothy getting her name wrong.

'*Willow* is very lovely, but we're not going to get together just because we're the only two people in the village below the age of forty,' he said, gently. 'And I'm way too busy with the renovations of the village and getting ready for the open day to be getting involved with someone anyway. So you can stop your meddling.'

Dorothy held her hands up innocently as if she wouldn't dream of doing so. Willow smiled slightly at the not-so-subtle warning to her too. Andrew was simply sitting here chatting to her to be friendly and she wasn't to get any ideas that it was something else. She had received that message loud and clear. Well, that suited her just fine.

'What's the open day?" Willow asked, trying to change the subject.

'There's an open day in eighteen days, we've put invites out with all the local estate agents and renting agencies. We're hoping that loads of people will come and be encouraged to apply for one of the houses. So we're trying to get all the houses ready in time for that.'

'That's a big job,' Willow said, thinking of all the houses she had seen so far that looked like they had seen better days.

'It is,' Andrew said, frowning. 'Anyway, it's pub quiz night, want to make a team?'

'Oh, don't you have other friends here that you normally team up with? Don't feel you have to look after me.'

'I don't, and no, I just team up with whoever wants me.'

'Everyone wants Andrew to be on their team.' Dorothy rolled her eyes with amusement. 'The boy knows everything.'

'Is that right?' Willow laughed.

'I have a head full of completely useless facts. Are you in, Dorothy?'

'Of course, it'd be nice to win for a change.'

Tabitha came round with quiz sheets as Willow finished off her dinner. She looked around the pub as people shifted around to make up teams. One team seemed to be Liz, Roger and another man who had pulled out a huge magnifying glass to read the quiz sheet. There were two ladies on another team; one seemed to be having a little nap. No wonder Andrew always won if this was the competition.

'Shouldn't we wait for more people to arrive?' Willow said.

Andrew shrugged. 'We don't get a big turnout. Most of the villagers prefer their own company. So we need a team name, how about... Young at Heart?' He gave Dorothy a playful nudge and she giggled like a schoolgirl.

Willow thought about that name and what Andrew had said a few moments before. She looked around at the small scattering of villagers again. 'Are we really the youngest in the village?'

'Yes, by a mile,' Andrew said.

'No children?'

He shook his head.

There was something sad about that too. The village

needed children and young families to give it some energy and oomph. But what could they do to encourage families to live here?

There was no time to think about that as Connor suddenly switched on the microphone and tapped it a few times to get everyone's attention. 'OK, are we all ready for round one, question one?'

There were a few murmurs of assent but Connor ploughed on regardless of whether people were ready or not.

'Question one, who is the Prime Minister of New Zealand?'

'What's her name? Oh it's Jacinda, Jacinda something,' Willow said, desperately trying to find the name in the depths of her memory.

'Jacinda Ardern,' Andrew supplied helpfully.

'That's it.' Willow quickly wrote it down.

'Question two, continuing on with the head of countries theme, who is the King of Belgium?'

'That's King Philippe,' Andrew muttered.

'Are you sure?' Willow asked, pen poised over the page. He nodded and she quickly wrote it down.

'Question three, who is the Prime Minister of Canada?' Connor went on.

'Oh, I know this one,' Willow said. 'Justin Trudeau.'

'Are *you* sure?' Andrew said, a smile playing on his lips and she knew he was teasing her.

'OK smart-arse, I'm sorry for doubting you over the King of Belgium question.'

'You're forgiven.'

'That Justin Trudeau is a hot bit of stuff, isn't he?' Dorothy said. 'Clever too, he knows stuff about quantum technology that would blow your mind. I always think intelligence is a highly attractive attribute, don't you?'

Dorothy gave Willow a look and then gave a not-so-subtle nod towards Andrew, as if Willow would find him attractive simply because he'd answered two questions, well one and a half.

Willow turned her attention back to Andrew. He was an attractive man, there was no denying that, but she wasn't going to leap into a relationship with someone just because they had a lovely smile, strong arms and incredible eyes. And she meant what she'd said to Dorothy and Ruby: she wanted time to just find herself again and to find what made her happy.

CHAPTER FOUR

Willow stepped outside the pub and stared up at the starlit sky. It had been a good night during which she'd gotten to know Andrew and Dorothy a bit better. Even Roger and Liz had come over to say hello during the break.

As predicted, Andrew had known the answer to almost every question, even some of the most bizarre ones. Willow had known the answer to many of them but she had nowhere near the general knowledge that Andrew had. And Dorothy had been right, the fact that he was so smart was an attractive feature. He had a playful sense of humour too, which she really liked.

And despite his earlier protests, she had a feeling he quite liked her as well. The way he had stared at her as they had talked over the last few hours had been almost a bit... intense. He hadn't taken his eyes off her all night except to write down some answers on the sheet. There had also been quite a number of times when he'd glanced down at her mouth as she talked instead of into her eyes and she'd wondered if he was thinking about kissing her, which seemed a bit forward considering they'd only just met a few hours before. She wasn't entirely sure she wanted that. He seemed nice, sweet, and yes there were certain things she found very attractive, they got on well too, but she really wasn't looking for a relationship right now, with anyone.

Halfway through the last round of questions, an elderly man who Andrew had called Joseph had arrived in the pub, clearly in a bit of a state, and hurried over to Andrew to tell him of a leaky ceiling. It had been close to ten o'clock, Andrew had just bought himself another pint and still he'd rushed off to help poor Joseph as if he was a doctor attending a medical emergency. There had been no sign of frustration or annoyance from Andrew that his evening had been disturbed and she liked that too. He was clearly a very patient man.

She turned down the little lane heading back towards her cottage. Within a few minutes, the lights of the main part of the village fell away and she found herself walking in almost complete darkness, the only illumination coming from the moon. It picked out the houses, silhouetted in the darkness, a few of them with warm golden light pouring from the windows.

The trees swallowed her, the glow from the moon going out completely, and she fumbled in her pocket for her mobile phone, switched on the flashlight app and shone it around so she could find her way.

Dorothy had told her that there were fifteen people, including herself, who had grown up in the village and had spent their entire lives there. The other thirty-odd people had all moved there later on in their lives, but most of the villagers had been there while Rupert had been the lord of the castle, before it had all gone wrong. But they had stayed there regardless, this was their home. Although at some point along the way, they had stopped caring. The owners of the village hadn't cared for them or the houses and so the villagers hadn't cared either. They had withdrawn from the community way of life. Willow wanted to be able to give them back the village they fell in love with but she couldn't do that alone. The villagers had to start caring again and she wasn't sure what she could do to make that happen.

She cleared the trees and could see her little cottage on the cliff tops, the twinkly black sea behind it, seemingly stretching out for miles. Little solar stars and dragonflies dotted the bushes and trees around her house glowing gold in the darkness. It looked magical. This was her home now too, she wasn't going to leave because it hadn't turned out how she'd imagined in her rose-tinted view of the world. If she wanted it to be rose-tinted, then she was going to have to make it that way.

~

Willow woke the next morning to sunshine sparkling on her face. She got out of bed and went to the window. The sea stretched out in front of her before disappearing into an early morning pinky haze on the horizon. The water was an inky blue today, crested with gold. She could stare at that view forever.

She quickly brushed her teeth, got dressed and then gathered her shampoo and toiletries together so she could go and have a shower at Andrew's house. She felt like she had a lot to do today.

She walked up the track and waved cheerily to Joseph. He was tending to his garden, bending over to prune the bushes, and as he straightened up to wave, he stretched his back out to ease the discomfort from all the bending.

She passed another house and stopped, noticing that it had been painted all the way round the outside but obviously only as far as whoever lived there could reach. There was easily three foot of wall above the new paint that hadn't been painted, leaving the house looking like it was stripy. The top part of the new paint wasn't even in a straight line, it was wobbly and there were different levels to it. Willow almost wanted to laugh except it was just a little sad that someone had tried to paint their home but made such a bad job of it.

She carried on to Andrew's house and knocked on the door. There was no answer. She waited a moment or two then knocked again. Still no answer. She opened the door and called out to him but the house seemed to be utterly silent.

She hesitated for a moment, but he had said that if he wasn't there she was welcome to let herself in and use his shower. She walked upstairs to where there were only two doors. One was obviously the bedroom as she could see the bed, so the other closed door must be the bathroom.

She went into the bedroom and undressed, leaving her clothes on the bed. The bedroom was neat and tidy and smelt of his wonderful scent. There was a large photo of the aurora borealis on the wall over a snowy mountain range. It looked beautiful.

There was another photo in a frame on top of a chest of drawers and she moved to pick it up. It was of Andrew and a small girl of about five who had her face painted like a butterfly. They were both laughing with big grins on their faces.

She put the frame down just as there was a movement near the door. She looked up to see Andrew stark naked staring at her in shock. She registered a stunning phoenix tattoo in yellow, orange and red with hints of blue and purple flying over his chest and shoulder. It looked magnificent. She also noticed how strong his arms were and how broad his chest was. Her eyes drifted lower before she remembered they were both standing there naked. She yelped and turned away, clamping her hands over her eyes for good measure before realising she was now giving him a fabulous view of her arse. She dived onto the floor behind the bed.

'I'm so sorry,' Willow said, but there was no answer.

She heard him moving around and she peeked up over the bed. She watched him, still naked, pick up two small flesh-coloured bullet-shaped objects from the top of the bedside drawers. He saw her watching and scowled so she quickly ducked back down below the height of the bed. Her cheeks were burning with embarrassment. A few moments later she felt him lean over the bed.

'Here, put this on.'

She looked up and saw that he had placed a hoody on the bed for her to wear. She quickly slipped it on and peered over the bed again to check that he was now suitably attired. He was wearing a pair of knee-length cargo shorts although his fabulous chest and tattoo were still on display.

He didn't look happy at all.

'I'm so sorry, I did knock twice and I called out to you. Did you not hear me?' Willow said as she stood up, the hoody coming down to almost her knees.

'I was in the shower,' he muttered. 'I wasn't expecting you so early.'

'I thought you were out. I'm really sorry.'

He still seemed pissed off, which hardly seemed fair. 'You did say to just come in and help myself if you were out.'

'I know.'

She frowned. They had chatted for hours the night before, but now he could barely look at her. Why was he being all weird?

She scooped up her clothes and grabbed her soap bag. 'I think I'll leave the shower.'

She walked out of the room and down the stairs. She'd got as far as the front door when she heard Andrew running after her.

'Wait, just wait a moment,' he said, slamming the door shut just as she opened it.

She turned round to face him and he was right there in her space as he leaned against the door.

He stepped back and pushed his hair from his face. It was wet and curly and stuck out at all angles but it just made him look cute and dishevelled.

He sighed. 'I didn't hear you knock or call out because... I didn't have my hearing aids in.'

She stared at him. She hadn't been expecting that. 'You're deaf?'

'Yes, not completely. I can hear fairly well with my hearing aids in but without them I'm pretty much next to useless.'

'You're not useless,' Willow said, defensively.

'No, you're right. That's the wrong word. My therapist would crucify me if she heard me say that.'

'Your therapist?'

He stared at her for a moment as if deciding whether to talk to her about this.

'Yes, I had a therapist when I was a kid just because I was deaf. Or maybe she was some kind of motivational life coach, I don't know. She was supposed to convince me that I was just like everyone else, that I could do anything that all the other children could do. The ironic thing was I'd always thought I was just like everyone else, until I wasn't allowed to play outside with my friends every Saturday because I had to sit in my therapy sessions and listen to how my *condition* shouldn't hold me back. What kind of weird twisted logic was that?'

'It doesn't seem like the best way to convince you,' Willow said.

'My mum knew that there was a very good chance I would be deaf as her sister was, so she had me tested at a very early age and I had hearing aids fitted even before I could talk. I think having it diagnosed so early helped my speech to develop almost at the same rate as other children my age.'

He chewed on his fingernail for a moment and Willow realised that he wasn't exactly comfortable talking about this.

'You don't like people to know,' she said.

He shook his head. 'This *special needs* label followed me throughout all my education no matter what, so when I left school I decided I wouldn't tell anyone I was deaf. I can hear just fine with my hearing aids in and they are very discreet so there was never any need for anyone to know. Of course people find out and when they do they speak louder, enunciate their words, they try to mouth what they are saying more clearly so I can lip-read, when in fact that always makes it harder. Inevitably a lot of the people that find out always treat me like I'm stupid and I hate that.'

'You are far from stupid, you knew so much in that pub quiz.'

'I read a lot. You don't need to be able to hear to enjoy a book. I can take as much time as I need with a book and I don't need to be able to concentrate to keep up like I do with a conversation.'

'Books don't judge you.'

He smiled slightly. 'No. Look, I'm sorry. I've been here three months and no one knows and I was annoyed that you've not been here twenty-four hours and you've found out already.'

'I didn't find out, you told me.'

'You saw me pick up my hearing aids, you shouted out for

me and I didn't hear you – you would have figured it out. Besides, I wanted to tell you because I was annoyed at the situation, not at you. This isn't your fault. I'm sorry if I was an arse up there.'

'You weren't.'

'No?'

'Well, maybe a little.'

He smiled slightly.

'Look, I'm not going to tell anyone. Why should anyone be defined by the things we can't do? Your secret stays here,' Willow said.

'Thank you. I really appreciate that.'

She glanced down at the phoenix tattoo again and suddenly it made sense. He'd felt like he had to fight to prove he was good enough. The phoenix had risen from the ashes and Andrew must have felt that he'd done the same, that he'd fought to be something, to be accepted.

'I like this.' Willow gently touched the phoenix.

He stared at her and she watched his eyes cast down to her lips again.

A sudden realisation hit her, making her cheeks flame red. 'Oh god, you can read lips can't you?'

'Yes I can. I find myself studying people's lips when they talk even though I can hear perfectly well with my hearing aids in.'

Willow laughed in embarrassment.

'What?'

'Oh nothing.'

'I've just told you my secret, I think you can share yours.'

Willow sighed. 'Last night you kept looking at my lips and I thought…'

He smiled. 'That I wanted to kiss you.'

'Yes.'

Andrew grinned and looked down for a moment. 'There might have been an element of that.'

Oh god. Her heart leapt as the chemistry sparked between them, until he took another step back away from her.

'Please, go and have a shower. I promise, I'll stay down here the whole time,' Andrew said.

'With your hands over your eyes?'

'Yes, that too. And I'll even make you breakfast to sweeten the deal. How does a bacon sandwich sound?'

'Now that sounds like a plan.'

CHAPTER FIVE

Andrew had left Willow to finish off her breakfast with the excuse that he had work to do. It wasn't a lie, he had a list a mile long of things he needed to do to help turn the village around and a very short time to do it all. But mainly he'd left because Willow clearly wanted to talk some more about being deaf and he didn't want to go into that.

Willow was incredibly easy to talk to. He hadn't talked about his struggles with growing up deaf with anyone, preferring to leave that part of his life behind. He knew a lot of deaf people who would berate him, saying he shouldn't be ashamed of his hearing loss, and he wasn't, but he didn't exactly want to make a big deal of it either. It was a part of him, not who he was. He was someone who was deaf, not the deaf kid, which was how he'd always been labelled at school. To him, there was a big difference. But he'd known Willow less than twenty-four hours and already he'd found himself opening his heart to her, telling her about his childhood. And that bothered him a bit. While there was something lovely about being able to share that with someone, he had now closed that box back up.

He didn't want her sympathy, didn't want her to think of him as different. He didn't want to give that vulnerable side of him to her, or to anyone.

But he liked that she had treated him exactly the same after she had found out he was deaf as she had before. She had chatted to him as normal over breakfast about the village, the different villagers and about Kitty and Ken. She had not made her voice louder or tried to mouth the words more clearly like a lot of people did.

He really liked Willow, there was something about her that made him feel warm inside and he hadn't felt like that in a very long time.

He had a feeling life was about to change in the little village of Happiness.

~

After Willow had left Andrew's, she wandered into the village to explore some more. She felt a bit happier about it all now. The village might be in a state of disrepair and over half the houses empty, the locals might prefer to keep themselves to themselves and her candlemaking skills might not be totally appreciated by the villagers, but waking up every morning to the incredible view she saw from her bedroom today was going to be hard to top. She mentally started ticking off all the positives. Having the beach right on her doorstep was something she had dreamed about all her life. She now lived in a beautiful part of the world with rolling hills and pretty meadows as far as the eye could see. The villagers she had met – Dorothy, Liz and Roger – seemed nice. And then there was Andrew. He seemed to deserve a tick box all of his own. He was... lovely and he made her smile a lot. And although she stood by not wanting to have a relationship right now, she did think they could become very good friends.

But she had decided that if she wanted the village of Happiness to change then she was going to have to be that change. And while she could hardly renovate a whole village, she knew there must be something she could do to help make the village shine.

She looked at the cluster of little shops, which were already open and selling their wares. What was going to be her candle shop was standing on a corner opposite the pub and she smiled to see that it was painted in the same bright yellow paint that Sunrise Cottage had been painted in. Obviously Andrew had bought a job lot of paint and decided to go with the theme.

She didn't really plan to go in there today, she was waiting for more of her stock to arrive. She had a few bits and pieces here but as she had fulfilled all of her online orders before she'd left, she wanted a few days to explore the village and get to know the place before she settled into work again.

She pushed open the door to the post office and stepped inside. Andrew had already told her that she could pick up a few groceries here. She had brought a few bags of food with her, and she had a big grocery order being delivered in the next few days, but she needed a couple of things to keep her going. She hadn't quite been expecting the huge and eclectic range of things to buy. There were buckets and spades, mops, irons, picture frames, cuddly toys, sandals, cooking utensils, pyjamas, envelopes in every size, indoor fountains, paddling pools, cushions, blankets, disposable barbeques, outdoor lights, dog leads, board games and several aisles of groceries, all jammed into a shop that appeared so tiny and unassuming from the front. Willow had no doubt that whatever she needed or wanted at any point in her life, it would be found here.

'Hello, can I help you?' came a voice from somewhere in the depths of the post office emporium.

Willow moved forward through the overcrowded shelves. 'Hello, I was just... looking for something for my lunch.'

She would save the other groceries she needed to get for another time. The whole place was a little overwhelming and she felt sure if she stayed too long then she might come out with a jacuzzi and pet husky named Blaze.

A small elderly lady appeared round the end of one of the aisles. She had big puffy candyfloss-pink hair that seemed to shimmer and shake as she walked.

'Ah, you must be Willow McKay. I'm Julia Dalton, the postmistress. I've been waiting for you.'

Willow smiled. She didn't realise she had an appointment.

'Let me show you how the postal service works here,' Julia said, ushering her to the till. 'All the post for the village comes to me and I make a record of it here in this book, see. That way you can come in and, if I'm busy with customers, you can check the book to see if there is any post for you without having to queue up to ask me.'

Willow looked around the shop. There was not a single soul in there apart from her and Julia. It was hard to believe that Julia ever got busy in here or had even seen a queue.

'OK, that's good to know,' Willow said.

'When you collect any post, you'll have to sign to say you've collected it,' Julia went on, showing the signatures of all the villagers in her special book. 'I keep all the post locked in a cupboard out the back, so it's quite safe here if you can't get in to see me every day.'

Willow wondered if Julia was expecting her to come in

every day. She never got that much post at home so she wasn't suddenly expecting an influx here. 'OK.'

'Now,' Julia clapped her hands together loudly. 'What can I help you with today?'

'Well just something for my lunch, perhaps a sandwich or the means to make one. Maybe a bit of fruit.'

'There's a bakery in the next town that delivers a small selection of sandwiches here every day. Let's see.,' Julia gestured for her to follow her to a small open fridge. 'We have egg and cress and umm… oh yes, another egg and cress.'

Willow resisted pulling a face. 'Oh, how about those sausage rolls, they look nice. And I'll take a few bananas and some grapes if you have them.'

'Of course we have bananas. We have lots of fruit. We even had a pomegranate in here the other day. Didn't sell though, I had to throw it away in the end. This way, dear.'

Julia bustled off and Willow grabbed a packet of sausage rolls and followed her.

The fruit display was a bit sorry-looking. There was certainly a wide range, but most of it looked a little past its best. Willow picked up a banana that wasn't too freckly and a packet of grapes at least two days past its sell-by date.

'I think that's everything for now,' Willow said, hoping Julia wouldn't try to persuade her to buy the wrinkly kiwi fruit or the strange orange fruit that most definitely wasn't an orange.

'Are you sure there's nothing else I can help you with?' Julia asked, hopefully.

'This is fine, thank you,' Willow said.

She followed Julia back to the till and she rang up her purchases.

'Well, do pop in again,' Julia said. 'If I don't have what you need, I can get it.'

Willow had no doubt of that. 'Thank you.'

She turned to leave and walked straight into Andrew, literally headbutting him in his hard chest.

'Hello,' he said, gently, steadying her with his hand on her bare shoulder.

'Hey,' she said. He had such a lovely smile. He hadn't taken his hand from her shoulder and something about that touch, the heat of his skin against hers, did something inside her that she hadn't felt in years.

'Just getting some lunch for later,' Willow said, gesturing unnecessarily to her sausage rolls.

'So I see.'

This seemed a bit too polite for two people who had seen each other naked about an hour before. She blushed at the glorious memory. He had an amazing body. Her eyes cast down and caught the edges of the phoenix tattoo peeking out from underneath his t-shirt sleeve. She wanted to see that again. She caught herself and looked back up at him. He was smiling as if he knew exactly what she was thinking. But he couldn't possibly know. He might be good at lip-reading but not mind-reading. She comforted herself with that thought, although the spark of amusement didn't fade from his eyes.

'Well, must dash, there's lots to do, nice seeing you again,' Willow said and hurried off, her cheeks burning. She was so silly. They had chatted just fine over breakfast, so why was she suddenly embarrassed about seeing him now? She knew why. Because her mind was going to all the places it shouldn't with those memories and that simple touch.

She moved off down the main high street until the houses that were homes gave way to the houses that were most definitely not. She could see that Andrew had started work on some of these but there was still so much to be done.

She passed an old shed-type building. The doors were

open and inside were stacks of tins of paint amongst other things and she paused for a moment as an idea came to mind. Before she became a full-time candlemaker she used to buy old wooden shelves, chests, chairs and tables and give them a new lease of life, painting them pink or blue or sunshine yellow, some with flowers, butterflies, suns or stars, some with fish jumping out of the waves. She wasn't particularly skilled or artistic but the simplicity of her designs appealed to some people. She had stopped doing it after she had started going out with Garry. He always moaned that it took so much of her time and paid her so little, but the money had never been the reason why she did it. She just loved giving these old bits of furniture a second chance, to see what they could become with a little bit of love and care. Garry had insisted she focus on something that could actually pay the bills and she'd known he had a point. Initially it was a hobby instead of her main focus, but when her candlemaking business started to take off her hobby had soon stopped altogether because Garry didn't like their home cluttered with old bits of furniture. She did miss it though.

But maybe she could have a chance of doing that again here. Only not with furniture this time, but with the houses themselves. Maybe that was what the village needed. A little bit of love and a lick of paint could go a long way. Maybe that could be the thing she could give to the village, maybe she could help it shine again. Garry always said she was a fixer, a doer. If a bulb needed changing, a shelf needed fixing, a picture needed putting up, she would just get on and do it. She looked around the village and sighed. This was a bit bigger than a broken shelf or a chest of drawers that needed painting, but maybe she could help in some small way.

She stepped inside the shed and looked around at the tins of paint. It was mostly white paint but there were some colours there too. Andrew had started decorating large ceramic plant pots different colours – purples, pinks, greens. He had seen what she had seen, that the village needed a bit of colour to brighten the place up.

She could paint some flowers around the door of one of the houses, emerald-green leaves and curly stems with flamingo-pink roses. She could see it in her mind and she knew it would look great.

But would Andrew be annoyed with her for doing it? Should she go and find him and ask him if it was OK? Although seeing Andrew and imagining seeing him naked again was enough to veto that idea. If he hated it she would personally paint over it herself.

She grabbed a few pots of paint and some brushes and went back outside, excitement bubbling through her. She paused outside one of the houses that had already been painted white, although a quick look through the windows confirmed this particular house was a long way off being finished.

She popped open one of the pots of green paint, dipped a brush inside and painted a beautiful winding stem up the side of the door. She was surprised at the rush she got from that simple act. It had been too long since she had done something like this and she loved being able to do this again. She curled the stem over the top of the door and down the other side. The green paint gleamed in the sunlight. She added some curvy leaves at different places around the door and then stood back to look at it. It looked better already. It made the house come to life and, once she added the pink flowers, it was going to look really rather special.

It was such a tiny thing when the village needed so much work, but at least she was doing something to help. She only hoped Andrew would love it.

CHAPTER SIX

Andrew walked down to the end of the village. He had spent most of the morning trying to fix Joseph's leak. He hadn't been able to find the cause of it the night before so had just turned off the water after filling up a few saucepans so Joseph could still have his cup of tea. And he had now spent the last few hours trying to find the problem and then fixing it. Honestly, it was time he simply didn't have. With the open day coming up in just under three weeks, he knew that even if he worked every hour of the day he wouldn't get all the houses finished on time, so he really didn't need setbacks like this. He loved the villagers and he wanted to do everything he could to help them, but he really needed some help and he had no idea how to approach Kitty and Ken to ask them.

Although there was one man who always seemed to have time on his hands and who might be willing to come and help him for a few days.

He pulled his phone out of his pocket and gave his brother a call.

'Andrew, how's it going?' Jacob said.

'All good here, the sun is shining, the beach is glorious. Why don't you come and stay for a few days?'

'Well, isn't that sweet, my little brother wants to spend time with me,' Jacob said, sarcastically.

He knew very well Andrew had an ulterior motive. He and Jacob weren't exactly close. Jacob was sarcastic, interfering, confident to the point of cocky and quite honestly a pain in the arse, but he was also protective, loyal and generous with his time. If Andrew told him he needed his help, Jacob would be there, no questions asked. Although he might bitch and moan about it, Andrew knew he didn't really mean any of it.

'And what would I be doing on this little holiday of mine?' Jacob said. 'Picnics on the beach perhaps?'

'Well if that floats your boat, sure. But I'm sure there's plenty of inspiration here for your next *masterpiece*,' Andrew said, sarcastically. Jacob was a scrap metal artist and a very good one. But Andrew would never tell him that. 'And maybe you can give me a hand with a tiny spot of painting.'

'Well that sounds like a wonderful way to spend my holiday,' Jacob deadpanned. 'But as luck would have it, I do have a few days spare to come and get my brush wet.'

'If that's a euphemism, you've got no chance.'

'What about that new woman, Willow is it? The one who came to live there without even coming to see it? That shouts "woman trying to escape" if ever I heard it. I could be the fortress in her storm. What's she like?'

Andrew tried to find the words to describe Willow McKay. 'She's… nice.'

That was a gross understatement. *Nice* didn't even come close to describing what she was like.

'Oh, is she hideous?'

'You're so shallow. There's more to someone than just their looks.'

'Ah she is.'

'She isn't actually, she's…' Andrew trailed off because he didn't need to give Jacob any encouragement where Willow was concerned. 'She's off limits.'

'Oooh little brother, are you staking a claim? Because I definitely need to come and check her out if you've got your eye on her.'

'No, it's not like that.' It most definitely was like that. 'I just think she can do better than you.'

'Well, that's probably true. I'll be there in a few days and I'll see for myself.'

Andrew sighed as his brother said his goodbyes and hung up.

He thought for a moment about what Jacob had said. He wondered if Willow was escaping from something. He thought about how she'd been before in the post office, she'd practically run away from him when she'd seen him. He wondered if she felt awkward around him now she knew he was deaf, but that didn't seem to make sense when she had chatted to him just fine over breakfast.

He stopped suddenly and backtracked a few steps to the house he'd just passed. He stared at the flowers growing up the walls around the door which certainly hadn't been there yesterday. But as he stepped closer he realised they had been painted on. Who the hell had done that?

He looked around and saw three more houses, all with the same flowers growing up the sides of the door, and then he spotted the culprit working on house number five, only this one had stars of different sizes.

He stared at Willow as she painted. He didn't know whether to be angry that she had done this without checking it was OK, delighted that she wanted to help or frustrated that, of all the ways she could help, painting little flowers was not going to be anywhere near his top ten. He supposed the flowers did look quite nice, they gave the houses a bit of colour, but he couldn't believe she had done this without asking him. He marched over to tell her that this wasn't appropriate.

As he approached she looked up at him and he faltered in his stride because she had the biggest grin on her face he had ever seen on anyone in his entire life. She looked like a child whose Christmases had all come at once and to be angry at her felt like he would be kicking a puppy.

'Oh, I'm so sorry. I was just going to do one house and then come and find you to see if you liked it and if you didn't I was going to paint over it. But then I enjoyed doing it so much that I thought I would just do one more and now I've done five. I'm sorry, I just got carried away. If you hate it, I'll paint over them all myself. Do you hate it? Please don't tell me you hate it,' she laughed, nervously.

She had such exuberance and enthusiasm for what she was doing. He felt his anger just fade away.

He cleared his throat and looked again at the flowers. It really did help the houses to stand out and maybe even detract from any other little faults.

'It looks lovely,' Andrew said.

'Really? Oh god, I'm so relieved. I thought you might hate it or hate me for doing it.'

'I don't think it's possible to hate you, Willow McKay,' he said, softly.

'My old boyfriend, Garry, used to hate me doing stuff like this,' Willow went on. 'I used to paint old bits of furniture in bright colours and little designs like this. He said it was a waste of my time.'

'How can anything be a waste of your time if it makes you this happy?'

Her ex-boyfriend sounded like an arse. Christ, he'd let her paint the whole goddamn village with flowers and stars if it meant it kept that huge smile on her face.

'I did love it,' Willow said, wistfully.

'You shouldn't let anyone stand in the way of your happiness,' Andrew said.

She stared at him. 'I think you're right. Is it really OK, you don't mind?'

'I don't mind,' Andrew said, and he really didn't. It wasn't her job to paint or fix things in the village so he could hardly expect her to pick up a roller and start painting. The fact that she wanted to help at all was actually wonderful. Many of the other villagers had no interest in contributing to village life. And it did look lovely. The white houses looked smart and uniform but this added a little bit of character. 'Feel free to paint as many houses as you want.'

'Can I? Well, that's exciting.'

Her eyes lit up at the prospect of painting the whole village and he smiled. He'd definitely done the right thing.

'I can get more paint for you if you wish. Just let me know.' He paused as he watched her paint another star. 'Why does this one have stars?'

'Oh, I found this,' Willow said, picking up a broken name plate that had obviously hung outside at some point: *Starlight Cottage.*

'Very appropriate. I can fix that.'

'I bet you can, but why don't you leave that to me. I'm sure you have lots of other things to do.'

He nodded. 'And on that note, I really must crack on.' He took a step away and then turned back. 'Can I ask you something?'

'Sure.'

'Why did you run away before, when we were in the post office?'

He watched her cheeks flush bright red. 'You really don't want to know.'

He pursed his lips. 'Yeah, I really do.'

'But then you'll think terrible things of me.'

'Well now, I'm intrigued.'

'I was remembering what you looked like naked,' Willow blurted out.

He stared at her and then burst out laughing. 'I love your honesty, Willow McKay.'

'I couldn't help it, I headbutted your hard chest and your hand was on my shoulder and suddenly my mind was going to all the places it shouldn't. And just to be clear, I know you're not looking for a relationship right now and there's no way I'm looking for one, but it doesn't stop my filthy mind from wandering every now and again. But now you think I'm a pervert.'

'Oh no, I wouldn't think that.'

'No?'

'OK, maybe a little bit.'

She laughed.

'I really had better get on. I'll be over here if you want to perv over me again.'

She laughed again. 'Stop it. There'll be no more perving.'

'Good to know.'

He smiled and walked over to the shed to collect his tools and some paint. She made him feel warm inside.

~

Willow was feeling deliriously happy right now. Painting was such a simple thing but it did bring her so much happiness. And although it was such a tiny piece in the grand scheme of things, she really felt like she was doing something to help the village. She wanted to talk more to Andrew about the village, the open day and everything that needed doing, but she got the sense he just wanted to get on with his work today. She had stopped for lunch but Andrew didn't. She had offered him one of her sausage rolls which he gladly took but he didn't come and join her as she sat on the grass outside the latest house she had painted. He just carried on with his work, painting, hammering, fixing. He was diligent, that was for sure.

She stood back to inspect the latest house she had finished. This one was called Dragonfly Cottage so she had painted some dragonflies amongst the flowers that were winding and curling their way around the door. She hadn't done dragonflies before, but they were relatively easy.

She looked round as a voice called out for Andrew. Dorothy was hurrying down the hill towards them.

'Andrew!' Dorothy called, waving her hands to attract his attention. 'Andrew.'

Willow glanced over at Andrew and saw his shoulders droop the tiniest bit as he climbed down the ladder to come and talk to Dorothy.

'Andrew, all the lights have just gone out in my shop. I turned the light on in the kitchen to make a cup of tea and all the other lights went out. I didn't want to bother you, but I can't paint in the dark now, can I?'

'No, of course not,' Andrew said. 'I'll come and have a look for you. Did you happen to notice whether the other shops or houses still have lights?'

'All the rest of the shops seem fine, think it's just mine,' Dorothy said.

'Come on then,' Andrew said.

'Why don't I go?' Willow said, wiping her hands. 'And you can stay here and carry on with your work.'

Andrew looked at her dubiously.

'It's likely that the bulb has blown and it's tripped all the other lights. I can easily reset the switch on the fuse board and replace the bulb for her and if it's anything else then I can come and get you,' Willow said.

'OK, if you're sure,' Andrew said. 'Thank you.'

'No problem,' Willow said and turned to Dorothy. 'Let's have a look and after you can make me a nice cup of tea and show me all your wonderful paintings I've seen in your window.'

Dorothy blushed with pride as she took Willow's arm.

Willow looked over her shoulder to see Andrew watching them with a smile before he turned and went back to his work.

'I hate to disturb him,' Dorothy said as they walked back up the hill. 'He works so hard, always rushing from one job to the next. Everyone in the village thinks he's at their beck and call for every little thing. He never says no to anyone but he is stretching himself too thin. I try to do everything for myself but when the lights all went out, I didn't know what else to do.'

'It's OK. I'm sure Andrew would want you to come and get him, rather than standing in the dark worrying. I'm sure I can help you.'

'You're a good girl, Willy.'

Willow didn't have the heart to correct her. She walked with Dorothy back into the main part of the village. There was so much that needed doing, but a lick of paint could fix a lot of the village's problems. The shops especially could do with some bright colours on the signs above the doors. Maybe she could do them too. Or was she getting too carried away?

'Here we are, dear,' Dorothy said, gesturing to the painting shop as if Willow wouldn't be able to find it on her own.

Willow let herself inside and sure enough the place was in darkness apart from the light streaming in through the main window.

Luckily the fuse box was by the front door so she didn't have to hunt around for it. As she suspected, one of the switches was down and she flipped it back up again and all the lights came back on in the shop.

'Oh you are clever,' Dorothy said, clapping her hands together.

'Now, which light were you turning on when the lights went out?' Willow said, closing the fuse box door.

'The kitchen one,' Dorothy said, pointing to the little kitchenette out the back.

Willow followed her to the back of the shop. 'Do you have a spare bulb?'

'Oh yes, I always keep some in the cupboard. I can change the bulb myself, I always do,' Dorothy said, getting a wobbly-looking stool from behind the door.

'Why don't I do that for you this time,' Willow said. 'And you can make us both a cup of tea.'

Dorothy set about making a pot of tea in the limited light from the shop and Willow quickly changed the bulb.

'There we go,' she said, climbing down from the stool and flicking the switch.

'Oh thank you Willy,' Dorothy said as light filled the kitchen.

'No problem. Mind if I have a look around?'

'You go ahead, dear.'

Willow wandered out into the main shop area and started looking at all the paintings. There were some portraits of various members of the village but mostly they were of landscapes, hills, meadows, fields of flowers, beaches, the sparkling sea. They were all so pretty.

'Your paintings are lovely,' Willow said, as Dorothy came out with two pink china cups on matching saucers. 'I bet people come from all over to buy them.'

'Oh, not in here. I almost never get any customers in here,' Dorothy said. 'But I have a steady income from selling my paintings on Etsy.'

Willow wanted to laugh that this sweet little elderly lady, who couldn't even work out how to flip a switch in a fuse box, was a successful businesswoman on Etsy.

'Oh I sell my candles on Etsy too, amongst other online shops. In fact all of my business is online, I've never had a bricks-and-mortar shop before so that's a new step for me. Look at us, two young entrepreneurs of Happiness.'

Dorothy giggled.

Willow carried on moving around the shop and looking at all the paintings. Her eyes suddenly fell on a very familiar painting. It was the poster she had seen of Happiness, the little village, the thatched cottage on the cliff side, the sparkling blue of the sea, the little pink flowers around the sides. The only things missing were the inviting words, '*Start a new life in the village of Happiness*.'

'This is the picture they used for the advert,' Willow said.

'I know. Kitty and Ken asked me if I would paint something for it, make Happiness look warm and inviting. I based that little cottage on your Sunrise Cottage,' Dorothy said.

Willow stared at the painting. She didn't want to tell Dorothy that it was a complete misrepresentation of the village because, really, who in their right mind would uproot their whole life based purely on a painting? It was hard to believe this little painting had changed her life completely. She supposed only time would tell if that change was going to be for the better.

She moved the painting out of its stack to get a better look at it, revealing a portrait of Andrew behind it.

It was so realistic it was like looking at a photo. Dorothy had even managed to capture the little twinkle in his eye and the laughter lines around his eyes. He was laughing at something and the painting just captured his gentle, patient and mischievous personality perfectly.

If there was one person in the village who could help her make Happiness the vision of loveliness she'd seen in the painting, then Andrew was definitely the man for the job.

CHAPTER SEVEN

Andrew was just getting a cake out of the oven when there was a knock on the door. He gave a little sigh. He loved living here and he loved the villagers but his time never seemed to be his own. There was always something wrong, something else that needed fixing, something else to be added to the long list of repairs and maintenance he needed to do. There simply weren't enough hours in the day to do it all. Kitty and Ken were looking at hiring him an assistant and, honestly, it couldn't come soon enough. It was just starting to get dark now as well, so unless it was a real emergency, the problem would have to wait until the morning.

He plastered on a smile and answered the door. He was surprised to see Willow standing on his doorstep. Surely she hadn't found fault in Sunrise Cottage just yet?

'Hello. Have you come for another shower?' Andrew said, quickly clamping his hand over his eyes.

She laughed. She had this wonderful infectious giggle and he couldn't help smiling at the sound of it. There were many beautiful sounds in the world and sometimes he liked to close his eyes and just listen to the birds or the waves crashing onto the beach. He liked to commit them to memory. Willow's laugh was one of those he already wanted to play again in his head.

He peered through his fingers at her and she laughed even more.

'No peeking.'

'Sorry,' he put his hand back over his eyes again.

'I'm not really here for a shower. Just thought I'd come by and say hi.'

He lowered his hand in surprise. 'Not many people come by here to say hi. They come to me with a list of problems.'

'Well, I thought we could talk,' Willow said.

'That sounds ominous, you better come in,' Andrew said, stepping back to let her inside. She squeezed past him into the hall, she smelt of sunshine and holidays and coconut.

'Something smells amazing,' Willow said as she walked through into the kitchen.

He had to agree but then he turned his attention to what she was saying and realised she was talking about the cake.

'Rhubarb cake, it was growing in an abundance up at the castle, thought I'd make the most of it. Would you like a slice?'

'I've just had the biggest burger in the world, courtesy of the pub, so maybe a very small slice,' Willow said, sitting down at the breakfast table.

He smiled and cut off a big chunk of cake, placing it on the table in front of her. He cut himself a slice and sat down opposite her.

'I thought you might be there actually – at the pub, I mean. Not that I was waiting for you. Well, I kind of was but just because I wanted to talk. Not because I wanted to see you naked again.'

He laughed loudly. 'I'll try not to be offended that you don't want to see me naked again.'

'Oh no, don't be offended. I don't want to see you naked again purely because I really do want to see you naked again.'

She made him smile so much. 'Well, that's perfectly clear.'

Willow blushed and took a bite of cake, clearly as a distraction. 'Mmm, this cake is fantastic.'

He watched her for a while, tucking in. He'd never really considered himself to have a type. But his past girlfriends were all blondes so he supposed he must have. Willow was definitely not his type. She had this gorgeous brown wavy hair which seemed to shimmer with copper and bronze as she moved. He had never dated a girl with freckles before but Willow had them all over her nose and cheeks and, with her large green eyes, she was cute. She had this energy about her that made her shine. He straightened in his chair. But definitely not his type. In fact he wasn't looking for a relationship at all right now, so no woman was his type. And with everything else going on in the village, he didn't have time to start anything.

'What did you want to talk about?' Andrew asked.

'I don't know. This village, it's just…'

'Depressing, I know. I'm sure Kitty and Ken would understand if you've changed your mind.'

'I'm not leaving,' Willow said, defensively.

'Oh.'

'I just think it needs… something.'

'OK,' he said, slowly. He wasn't sure where she was going with this. By the look on her face he didn't think she knew either.

'How many people have taken Kitty and Ken up on their offer of free accommodation for a year?' Willow asked.

'Including me, you and Tabitha and Connor at the pub, seven.'

'You're new too?' Willow said in surprise. 'I've been hearing from all the locals how wonderful you are. From the sound of it, you've been here for ages.'

'Three months. I was the first. Kitty and Ken hired me as estate manager, maintenance man, Man Friday, odd-job man and the house came as part of the job. The whole free incentive was actually my idea. You can see how well it's working out,' he said, dryly.

'Are you getting lots of interest?' Willow asked, popping another chunk of cake in her mouth.

'Oh yes, but once they visit, they don't come back.'

'Those four houses near the entrance to the castle don't help.'

'No they don't,' Andrew admitted.

'You need to spruce them up.'

'They're not safe to live in – there's an old passage that led from the castle out to the beach and it's collapsed. Those houses are built right on top of it. The ground isn't stable, two of the houses are actually sinking into it. We've had the rest of the village checked out though, you're perfectly safe where you live, it's just up there that's a bit dodgy.'

'Well you need to either knock those houses down or tart them up, make them at least look pretty, even if they aren't available to rent. Or we could cover them up, put something in front of them so they can't be seen when we have visitors to the village.'

He thought of his friend, Morgan, an idea bubbling in his mind. But he pushed it away. There was too much else to do rather than worry about houses that no one was ever going to live in.

'You make it sound so easy,' Andrew said.

'No, I appreciate it isn't. Sorry, I didn't mean to imply you're not doing your job properly. I'm sure you have tons to do.'

'I have, there's so much that needs doing ready for the open day, so many houses need repainting or renovating.'

'You can't do all that alone.'

'They are going to get me an assistant.'

'You need a team. A big one.'

He sighed, because he had to agree with her. He was reluctant to ask that of Kitty and Ken because they were so generous with their money and he didn't want to take advantage of them. The free home incentive had been his idea and since then he'd felt like he was constantly asking them for money for one thing or another. But they had no idea how much everything was going to cost, how long it was all going to take. It was a massive project to overhaul the village and they had no idea how big it really was. He had been trying to do things on the cheap for them, but maybe that was worse than not doing anything. He needed to have a serious conversation with them and he had been putting it off for too long.

'They don't have any money, do they?' Willow said, misunderstanding his reluctance.

'They do, I just don't think they appreciate how much this is going to cost them and I feel bad because all of this was my idea.'

'But they must have wanted to do it,' Willow said.

'They've always talked about doing the right thing for the village, of making it like it used to be. I think they'd like to bring that kind of community spirit back to Happiness, but I'm not sure we'll ever get that back.'

'We have to try,' Willow said. 'This village has so much potential. It could be great again. I appreciate seventeen days is such a short amount of time to get everything finished but there's still a lot that can be achieved in that time. Do you have a list of everything that needs doing and an idea of how much it will all cost?'

He nodded. 'In my head. Although the list gets bigger every day.'

'You're thinking of the bigger picture, but in reality you need to think on a smaller scale. You just need to make the village look nice from the outside. Make, say, five houses look good on the inside and those can be our show houses for the open day. If we suddenly get an influx of people wanting to move here then we can hold them off for a month or two until we can get more houses ready internally. No one will expect to move in the very next day. They will need to sell their house or at least give a month's notice if they're renting. But if the whole village is aesthetically pleasing from the outside that's going to be a huge step forward in getting people to want to move here.'

He hadn't thought about it like that. He looked at his rhubarb cake; if he wanted to sell it, he needed to add some icing, put some pretty leaves and flowers on it. He had been trying so hard to get everything finished but he had to prioritise and Willow was right, getting the exterior looking good was the most important. No one ever needed to know that the village was falling apart on the inside because, by the time they moved in, all that would be taken care of.

'OK.'

'Well, let's work through the list together now, make it as detailed as possible and prioritise what needs doing before the open day. Then we can go to Kitty and Ken tomorrow and tell them what we need, including a team of builders and decorators.'

He smiled, slightly. Willow was clearly-the-take-charge-and-get-things-done type.

'We?'

'I need to meet them anyway and I'd like to help. I might not be good at any of the practical, renovation-type stuff, but I can help with a bit of the aesthetics, painting around the doors, painting the shop signs. I want this move to work, I can't go back. Everyone thought I was an idiot for packing up all my worldly goods and moving hundreds of miles away but then they all thought I was an idiot anyway so…' She shrugged as if she didn't care what anyone thought, but he could see straight through that bravado. 'I really want this to work. I want the village to be wonderful again.'

'I want this village to be a big success too,' he admitted.

'Then let's get started.' Willow shrugged out of her jacket, clearly meaning to stay for some time.

Andrew stared at her for a moment and, as he got up to get his notebook and pen, he wasn't sure whether to be pleased or annoyed that he'd opened the door.

Willow yawned and stretched her arms above her head.

'Well, I think we've made good progress,' she indicated the list.

Andrew nodded grudgingly. 'Yeah, it's quite extensive. But I know a good team who can help me if Kitty and Ken are willing. Thank you for your help.'

She smiled. She wanted to be able to give something worthwhile to the village. She loved making candles, she had a very successful online business and her candles made people happy so she wasn't going to give that up, but even she could see that pretty candles were not what this village needed right now. So she was pleased to be able to help in some small way. And decorating the houses felt like a step forward too.

'My pleasure. Right, I think I'm going to call it a night.'

She pulled on her jacket and was surprised to see Andrew slipping his on too.

He saw her surprise. 'I'll walk you back.'

She smiled at that gentlemanly gesture, but it was hardly necessary. She had walked home in the dark just fine the night before.

'I don't think I'm in fear of being attacked or mugged on my way home.'

'No, but it's pitch-black out there and the track is hardly smooth and bump-free. Plus I have a good torch.'

Willow nodded to concede that. She certainly didn't want to break her ankle and there were parts of the track back to her house that were in almost complete darkness.

'Oh, and take a cake with you.' Andrew offered her a large round cake, wrapped up in foil.

'I'm not going to eat a whole cake on my own.'

'Take it anyway, I always make too much. You can invite your neighbours round for coffee and cake.'

She took it, a great big heavy slab of a thing, and tucked it under her arm.

They left his house and she noticed he didn't lock the door behind him.

'No key?'

'Ah no, it's not really that kind of place. You have one for your door, but I don't think it's necessary for myself.'

He flicked on his torch and a silvery beam spread over the track in front of them. Without the lights of the city she was so used to, she could see millions of stars in the inky canopy above them, twinkling like tiny crystals.

'So what's your story, why are you here?' Andrew asked.

She didn't know what to say to that. She wasn't hung up over her break-up with Garry, she wasn't pining over him or nursing a broken heart. Breaking up had been the best thing that ever happened to her. But she had come here for a clean slate, to get away from the comments and looks of pity. She certainly didn't want to bring them with her.

'I guess I'm here for a fresh start. What about you?'

He shrugged. 'I suppose we all are.'

They walked on in silence for a while, probably both contemplating their own mistakes and experiences which had led them to being here.

'That's Elsie's house,' Andrew pointed to the little white cottage which was very badly painted. 'That's Joseph's and that's Dorothy's.'

Willow nodded, trying to remember where they all were so she could find them if she needed to in the cold light of day.

She shifted the large cake into her other arm. Then she had a sudden thought.

'Hang on a second.'

She turned and ran up the little path of Dorothy's house. It was in complete darkness so she was either tucked up in bed asleep or still in the pub lamenting the loss of her favourite baker.

She placed the cake on the doorstep and ran back to join Andrew.

'Didn't want my cake after all?' Andrew teased.

'I think Dorothy's need is greater than mine. She was telling me all about life in the village when she was growing up, especially how much she used to love the baker here and his amazing cakes. I take it we don't have anything like that amongst the shops that are in use?'

'We have a knitting shop, a post office, a cheese shop and an art-gallery-type shop. Not exactly huge, pivotal roles in the community. What is it you'll sell in your shop?'

The stars above them had disappeared as they walked

through the trees and Willow cringed a bit in the darkness. 'I'm a candlemaker. Sadly, nothing huge or pivotal, I'm afraid.'

'Ah, I didn't mean…'

'It's OK, I know what you meant.'

'Everyone has their role to play in the community, I'm sure you'll be a valuable part of it,' Andrew said, clearly trying to make her feel better about her contribution.

She didn't have time to think about what she could offer the village as just then she saw Andrew stumble, the torch smashed into the ground and everything went black.

CHAPTER EIGHT

'Andrew?' Willow said, frozen in the darkness.

Silence. It was completely and utterly black here, the moon and stars above them not penetrating through the trees.

'Andrew!' Her voice was higher, filled with anxiety.

A groan came from nearby and she quickly rushed over towards the source of the sound, and then went flying as she tripped over him and landed with a thud on her front.

'Crap, are you OK?' Andrew said and she heard him feel around with his hand for her before it landed on her bum.

'I'm OK, are you?' Willow asked, frowning slightly that his hand was still on her bum. Either he hadn't realised or he didn't care. She really hoped he wasn't the sort to try to take advantage of this situation.

'I'm fine, I think,' Andrew said, moving his hand around in what he probably hoped was a comforting way but he was now stroking her bum.

Suddenly he must have realised where his hand was because he snatched it away as if he had been burned.

'Sorry.'

'It's fine.'

'No it isn't. I would never—'

'I know, don't worry.' She rolled over and sat up. 'Can you stand?'

She heard him shuffle around and grunt and then, judging from the sound of his breathing, he was clearly standing up.

'Here, give me your hand,' Andrew said, from somewhere above her.

She reached out and quite obviously grabbed him in the groin.

'Ah sorry,' Willow said.

She heard him chuckle and then burst out laughing and she started laughing too. This whole thing was completely ridiculous.

She clambered to her feet herself and realised that she was standing just inches away from him. She could feel his warmth, smell his wonderful tangy scent. The laughter died in her throat.

He placed his hands on her shoulders, clearly needing some connection with her in the darkness.

'Sorry about all this, I just tripped over. I think we still have quite a way to go to get to your house, so we really need to find that torch. Unless you have one of your candles stashed about your person?'

'And a means to light it,' Willow said. 'Sadly I don't but if we can find our way to mine I can provide you with a lantern to get you back home. I don't even have my phone with me as I left it to charge. I think that torch is probably ruined, it looked like it smashed before the light went out. Look, there's a clearing up ahead, it's a lot brighter there and I can hear the sea so we can't be that far away. We can make it.'

'OK, hold my hand,' Andrew instructed and her heart leapt

a little as the warmth of his hand enveloped hers. They moved forward tentatively together, feeling around the ground with their feet for anything else that might trip them up as they inched towards the clearing. Finally they made their way out of the trees, and they could see Willow's little cottage standing on the cliff tops ahead of them, glinting in the moonlight.

She smiled as Andrew continued to hold her hand as they picked their way down the rest of the track.

Andrew walked her right up to her door.

'Here, let me get you a lantern to get back home,' Willow said, letting go of his hand to push open the door. She flicked on the light and went to one box, pulling out a small copper lantern with a large white candle inside. These were very popular with her online customers, having that antique feel. She lit the candle and then closed the little glass door, before returning to Andrew who was still waiting on her doorstep. In the light of the house she could see he had a leaf in his hair and, without thinking, she reached up to remove it.

He stared down at her and, for the briefest of seconds, there was this… spark between them before he stepped back into the shadows.

'Thanks for this,' he held up the lantern.

'No problem,' she said, watching him as he walked out the gate. 'And Andrew?'

He turned back to face her.

'You might want to add some kind of lighting down that track to your massive list.'

She watched him smile and nod and then he disappeared into the darkness.

~

After a shower followed by breakfast outside in her garden the next day, Willow went off into the village to have a look at her new shop.

At the fork in the road, just outside the pub, there seemed to be quite the gathering of villagers, huddled together, with Dorothy holding court in the middle.

'It was just there this morning when I got up, no note, no explanation. And let me tell you, it was the most delicious rhubarb cake I have ever tasted. Tangy and moist and fresh.'

'Who do you think left it there?' Julia asked, her pink candyfloss hair wobbling as she talked.

'I'm not sure,' Dorothy said smiling, although she looked like she had a fair idea.

'Maybe it was Connor,' Liz said. She nodded her head towards the pub. 'He knows his way around the kitchen and some of his puddings in there are divine.'

'Why would Connor leave me a cake?' Dorothy said, rolling her eyes at the stupid suggestion. 'I'm old enough to be his mother.'

Willow wondered if she should step forward and admit it was her but Dorothy seemed so excited by the mystery of it all that maybe she should keep her guessing for a bit longer.

'Why does it have to have anything to do with age?' Roger said, today sporting a dashing yellow polka-dot tie.

'Because I think it was a token of love,' Dorothy said, her face beaming.

Willow couldn't help but smile at this wonderful optimism.

'Maybe it was one of the newbies,' Julia said, practically, clearly dismissing the love theory.

'Maybe it was Andrew,' Liz suggested. 'I saw him carrying a load of rhubarb from the castle yesterday.'

'Maybe Andrew is in love with you,' Roger teased.

'Andrew is not in love with me,' Dorothy snapped.

'Look, there's Willow,' Julia pointed in her direction. 'She lives in Sunrise Cottage near you. It could easily be her.'

All eyes swivelled in Willow's direction.

'It wasn't her, I know who it was,' Dorothy insisted.

'Ask her,' Liz said.

Dorothy huffed. 'Fine, I'll ask her. Willy, Willy dear. Did you make me a cake?'

Willow moved closer to the group, ignoring the fact that Dorothy had got her name wrong again. She didn't like lying but she could answer that question with complete honesty. 'God no, I'm shocking in the kitchen. I couldn't bake a cake if Jamie Oliver was standing next to me and telling me how to do it.'

'Oooh, I like that Jamie Oliver,' Liz said.

'Give me Gordon Ramsay any day,' Julia said, fanning herself.

'I prefer that Paul Hollywood, with his twinkly eyes,' Roger said.

'See, it wasn't Willy,' Dorothy said, trying to bring the conversation back round to the mystery cake.

'Who do you think it was?' Willow asked.

'I think it was Joseph,' Dorothy said, dreamily.

'Joseph?' Julia said in surprise. 'Why would Joseph leave you a cake?'

'Because we grew up here together. He moved away, I got married, he got married, but I think he's always had a thing for me. Now he's back and we're both young, free and single again, maybe he's decided to make his move.'

'Well, not exactly young,' muttered Roger, which Dorothy clearly heard and decided to ignore.

'His house is just opposite mine, so it would be very easy to leave the cake there. And I think he's been giving me the eye.'

'That's probably cataracts,' Liz said and Roger snorted.

'Plus his grandfather owned the bakery here, I bet Sam must have showed him a thing or two about cakes growing up,' Dorothy carried on regardless.

'I still think it was Andrew,' Liz said. 'Everyone knows how kind he is. He probably heard you moaning on about wanting a bakery in the village and decided to make you the cake.'

'I was not moaning,' Dorothy snapped.

Right on cue, Andrew roared into the village on his quad bike. Willow wondered how the villagers would react to him ruining their tranquil little haven with the noise of its engine but he had clearly already won them over with his charm and likeability. If this was a cartoon, love hearts would be coming from all of their eyes.

'Why don't we ask him?' Willow said, hoping he would play along.

Julia waved him down and he came to a stop and cut the engine.

'Andrew dear, how are you?' Liz fussed around him, removing imaginary bits of fluff.

'I'm fine, thanks Liz.'

'Did you have company last night?' Julia said, her eyebrows wiggling mischievously. 'I was walking my Colin and Rufus down the little lane behind your house and I could hear you laughing and talking with a girl.'

Willow frowned slightly. That was a little creepy.

'Yes, I did,' Andrew said, vaguely.

'A friend or someone *special*?' Julia asked.

He grinned at the digging; clearly he was used to this kind of attention.

'I think I'd have to say both.'

Willow smiled at that.

'Andrew,' Willow said, meaningfully. 'Someone left a cake

on Dorothy's doorstep last night. Do you know anything about it?'

Andrew hesitated for a fraction of a second before he shook his head.

'No, sorry, as Julia already pointed out, I was entertaining my guest until late last night.'

They all collectively *oooohed.*

'That kind of night, was it?' Roger laughed, clapping Andrew on the back.

'It was a good night, but I definitely didn't have time to go about the village leaving cakes on people's doorsteps,' Andrew said.

'See, I told you it wasn't Andrew,' Dorothy said.

'Dorothy hopes it was Joseph,' Julia said.

Andrew smiled. 'Really?'

'I think it's his subtle way of letting me know he has feelings for me,' Dorothy said, knowledgably.

'Well maybe you should subtly let him know that you have feelings for him too,' Andrew said.

'Oh, I couldn't do that,' Dorothy said, suddenly blushing.

'Maybe you could leave *him* a gift,' Willow said, loving the way this was unexpectedly going.

Dorothy clearly thought about this. 'Maybe I could.'

Willow smiled. A glimmer of an idea was forming in her head. She needed to talk to Andrew about it but maybe this could be the very thing that Happiness needed.

~

Andrew drove his quad bike towards the castle. He had agreed to meet Willow at the entrance at one and they were going to meet Kitty and Ken together. He was glad she was coming with him, he was a little nervous about asking for so much money in one go, but if this open day was going to be a big success then it had to be done. As he rounded the corner and came up to the castle entrance, he smiled when he saw that Willow was waiting for him.

He didn't know what mischief she was up to with the cake she had left for Dorothy and then pretending she didn't know who had left it there, but there was one thing for sure: this girl was going to be trouble.

He liked her. Willow was sunshine personified. She sparkled with her over-the-top exuberance. He liked her honesty too.

He pulled to a stop in front of her and she climbed on behind him without any hesitation, wrapping her legs and arms around him. The warmth from her spread inside him like drinking a hot cup of tea on a cold day.

'Have you had a productive morning in your shop?' Andrew asked, raising his voice slightly to be heard over the noise of the engine as he drove through the castle gates. 'Or have you been too busy causing mischief and mayhem?'

'How dare you,' she laughed. 'I am a very righteous and upstanding member of this community.'

'Of course you are,' Andrew said, dryly.

'You'll be pleased to know, I've been in my shop all morning and not spoken to anyone since you roared off on your quad bike after that impromptu village meeting. I've cleaned the shop from top to bottom and this afternoon I'll be ready to move some of my stock in.'

'Do you have a lot of stock?'

'Not with me, it's on its way. I have enough to make an impressive window display but it won't take me long to start making some more, once the rest of the stock arrives. It's exciting really, this is the first time I'll have my own shop. Everything I've sold before has been online so I've never had to think about displays before. But I thought the main attraction of my shop could be that tourists might want to watch me work. Some of the candles are quite elaborate to make and I thought any visitors to the village might be interested in seeing the process. So I'm going to set up a workshop area in the middle of the shop to make my candles and visitors can browse the shelves and watch me work too. If nothing else, I will have a proper area to work in to sell my online stuff. Before I came here I made all my candles in a shed in the back garden.'

He smiled. She had so much energy and enthusiasm. He didn't know whether to burst her bubble now or later. Maybe he'd start the ball rolling.

'We don't get too many visitors here.'

'Yeah, Dorothy was saying she doesn't get many customers in her painting shop. But I find that hard to believe. That big old castle, the cute little village, no one wants to see that?'

'The village isn't that cute right now.'

'True,' Willow said. 'But it could be. And I know the castle is crumbling away but I bet people would still want to come and see it. Castles are big draws. Is it open to the public?'

'No, not really.'

'Well, maybe that's another thing I can talk to Kitty and Ken about. Bringing visitors to the castle would also bring them to the village, and if nothing else it would be good custom for the pub, even if it doesn't bring any visitors to my shop.'

He marvelled at her spirit – it would not be dulled no matter what.

'The castle is not in a good shape. Kitty and Ken are basically living in the old servants' quarters and the rest of the place is falling into ruin,' Andrew said.

'But people love castles. Kenilworth Castle in the Midlands

is largely just a few old walls and turrets, it hasn't been lived in for hundreds of years, and people still flock there in their thousands. If they open it to the public, regardless of the state it's in, people will come.'

He pulled the quad bike to a stop next to Ken's Range Rover and turned off the engine.

'You really are a glass-brimming-over kind of girl, aren't you?'

She clambered off the back and he climbed off too.

'Better that than be the glass-half-empty kind. What type are you?'

He thought about that for a moment. 'Probably three-quarters full. All the good stuff is still there, but room for a little improvement.'

'I'll take that.'

She looked up at the castle, and he wondered what she saw. Up close it really was in a sorry state but she certainly didn't seem to be put off by it.

'So what was going on this morning with Dorothy and the cake?' Andrew asked. 'Why not just tell her that you left it for her?'

'Did you see how excited she was about the mystery of who it could be? I didn't want to take that away from her,' Willow said.

'But now you've encouraged her to think that it was Joseph.'

'She was thinking that before I came along and a little harmless matchmaking won't hurt.'

'It will if Joseph doesn't feel the same way. She'll end up embarrassed,' Andrew said.

'Dorothy doesn't seem the type that would embarrass that easily. I have an idea, actually. Maybe you can help me with it.'

Andrew pulled the huge five-page list from his pocket. 'I'm a bit busy with the last idea you wanted help with.'

She laughed. 'Oh shush, as if all of that was my fault.'

'Go on then, tell me your wonderful idea,' Andrew said, dryly, as if he was less than thrilled about anything she was going to suggest. But the truth was he could listen to her talk all day and not get bored of it.

She didn't take him remotely seriously.

'I'll tell you later, it'll be something for you to look forward to. Besides, I want to meet Kitty and Ken.'

She moved off towards the door and he rolled his eyes as he shoved the list back in his pocket. But an idea suddenly sparked to life. 'Wait, before we go in, you need to know that you're expected to curtsey to them.'

She turned to look at him in shock. 'Are you kidding? You said they were lovely.'

'They are but you know, they're royalty, and they're a bit old-fashioned like that.'

'They're royalty? I've never heard of a Princess Kitty before,' Willow said, doubtfully.

'Kitty is actually Lady Katherine, the Queen's third cousin and I believe thirty-fifth in line to the throne.'

She stared at him. 'Are you serious? Oh my god, I've never met royalty before.' She looked down at what she was wearing in horror. 'Why didn't you tell me, I would have got changed.'

He bit his lip. 'It's fine, they really are rather normal.'

'Apart from that they live in a castle and like people to bow and curtsey to them.'

'Well, yes, apart from that. Come on, let me introduce you to them.'

He opened the door and let her go ahead into the large kitchen. He stepped inside after her, ducking his head to get through the door. Willow held back for a moment.

Kitty and Ken were both sitting at the table reading. Ken looked every inch the royal lord with his splendid red waistcoat and walrus moustache. They both looked up as they entered and smiled at him.

Ken spotted Willow and shot out of his seat to greet her.

'Kitty, Ken, this is Willow McKay who arrived a few days ago.'

Ken held his hand out to greet her and Willow took it and duly bobbed into a perfect curtsey. She was going to kill him for this.

'My Lord,' Willow said, clearly having watched films like *Pride and Prejudice* too many times.

Ken looked flummoxed for a moment. Kitty stared in shock, and Beryl, the housekeeper and cook, let the mug she was washing up clatter back into the bowl, sending little bubbles flying through the air.

Andrew's shoulders were shaking from suppressed laughter as Kitty stood up and came round the table towards them.

'Oh you rogue, Andrew Harrington,' Kitty said, shaking her head fondly. She turned her attention back to Willow. 'Did he tell you that you had to curtsey to us?'

Willow straightened, dropping Ken's hand in confusion. 'Yes, on account of you being royalty.'

Ken chortled. 'Royalty, eh? Now that would be nice.'

'You're not Lady Katherine?' Willow said.

'Oh no, although that does have a nice ring to it. Beryl, I might start getting you to call me that from now on,' Kitty said.

Beryl snorted. 'You know what you can do if you think I'm going to start walking round here with airs and graces.'

Willow looked up at Andrew. 'You were winding me up?'

The laughter burst out of him and he wiped his eyes. 'I'm sorry, I couldn't resist.'

Willow's cheeks flushed bright red and then she smiled and started laughing too. 'Oh, is that how it's going to be? I'm going to get you back for that.'

Andrew couldn't contain his laughter. 'Of that, I have no doubt.'

'Willow, let's start again, I'm Kitty and this is my husband Ken, it's lovely to finally meet you.'

'Would you like a cup of tea?' Ken asked, going to the kettle.

'Oh yes please,' Willow said, as Kitty held a chair out for her to sit down at the table.

'And Beryl made a delicious chocolate cake this morning, would you like a slice?' Kitty said.

'I can see I'm going to get fat while living here,' Willow said as Andrew sat down opposite her. 'I had a slice of Andrew's rhubarb cake last night and it was amazing. But I've always got room for chocolate cake.'

Kitty removed the cake from the tin and cut off a big slice as Ken made a pot of tea. Andrew smiled as he watched them; they were about as far removed from royalty as you could get.

'What do you think of Sunrise Cottage?' Kitty asked, placing the plate in front of Willow as she sat back down at the table.

'It's lovely,' Willow said, taking a huge bite. 'Very cute, small but the perfect size for me and that view is incredible.'

'Andrew worked so hard on the house to get it ready for you,' Kitty said, smiling at him.

'And what do you think of the village?' Ken asked, hopefully, as he brought the tea to the table.

Willow glanced briefly at Andrew, obviously wondering what she should say. 'It… has a rustic charm.'

He smiled at her. You couldn't just walk into someone's home and start insulting their back garden and she knew that.

Although Kitty could see right through that. 'It's a bit sad and tatty right now, but it has potential.'

'Oh, it has so much potential,' Willow said, sitting straight, her eyes lighting up. 'It could be a wonderful place to live again. It just needs a bit of TLC. Well OK, a lot.'

She glanced over at Andrew again and gave him an encouraging nod.

He took a deep breath. 'That's what we wanted to talk to you about actually. We have sixteen days until the open day and we want this place to shine. I can't do everything that needs to be done on my own.'

Kitty nodded. 'Of course, we're going to be placing an ad in the local newspaper this week to get you an assistant.'

Andrew cringed inwardly. 'I'm afraid it needs more than that.'

Kitty and Ken exchanged glances. 'How much more?'

Andrew smoothed out the list of jobs on the table and then spread the sheets out so they could see the sheer quantity of it all.

'Quite a lot.'

'But we also have some ideas to help you and the village, financially,' Willow said, excitedly.

Andrew smiled at her enthusiasm. He kind of felt like they were playing the roles of good cop, bad cop. He would upset them with the list of everything that needed doing and the expense and she would temper that with her sparkly infectious exuberance.

Ken leaned over to look at the sheets of paper. 'Come on then, let's see what we've got.'

CHAPTER NINE

'And you know someone who can do all of this?' Ken said as he glanced again at the total figure of what it was going to cost.

Willow felt bad for Kitty and Ken. It was quite obvious they had clearly underestimated how big this project was when they took it on.

'Yes, I know a good team that can take care of the bulk of it,' Andrew said. 'I can see what their availability is like. I know they've just finished one project. But they may have other jobs lined up. To complete the whole list will take several months, but if we can get Jack and his team to come in and spend a few weeks doing the surface-level stuff, at least it will help the village look good for the open day, even if the underneath isn't quite so shiny. I know a good landscape gardening team too. Oli and Tom can take care of the aesthetics on that side of things.'

Ken sighed and then nodded. 'OK, we'll let you take care of arranging all that. Let me know if you need any money up front.'

'I will.'

Ken looked utterly deflated and Willow wanted to come round the table and give him a big hug.

'Why did you buy the castle and village?' Willow asked gently, wondering if living in a castle had been the lure and the village had been this millstone around his neck.

'My dad was born and raised here, lived here until he was around twenty-five and he always used to tell me these stories of how wonderful it was, the cosy community spirit. Later, when he got older, he talked about how he wanted to move back here. We brought him down not long before he died and he was just so happy as he reminisced about his life here, but he said how everything had changed now and how it wasn't the same place any more. But I could see how much potential it had, how it could be great again.'

Kitty smiled with love for her husband. 'Ken has always had a kind heart and a soft spot for underdog projects.'

Ken smiled at her. 'Me and Kitty, well, we've been very fortunate in our life. We've made some very good business decisions over the years, made the right deals with the right people and in some cases just got very lucky. When we heard that the village and castle were for sale at a ridiculously cheap price, considering what we were actually getting, well, we wanted to help. We wanted to bring the village back to life again, to how my dad remembered it. There were a number of companies that wanted to buy the land and probably raze it to the ground and build a bunch of faceless identical red-brick houses or great big blocks of flats. We couldn't let that happen. Although it's safe to say we didn't realise the extent of the renovation project when we took it on. But I guess we'll do whatever it takes.'

Willow smiled at his determination to make it work.

'I had an idea about how you could bring some money in, maybe help cover the costs in some small way.'

Ken brightened a little. 'I'm listening.'

'I thought you could open the castle to the public.'

Ken's smile fell off his face. 'I don't think that's a viable option, it's in quite a state. Plus it has no historic significance, it didn't belong to any royalty. In fact I would be very surprised if any royalty or nobility even visited, there were no great battles or anything important that happened here. I don't think any of the historic organisations would be interested in managing it for us.'

'But it's a castle, people love castles,' Willow said, not to be deterred. 'Even the old tatty ones. Would you give me a tour?'

Ken stared at her for a moment, weighing it up, before getting to his feet. 'Come on then. I think you'll change your mind when you see it.'

He'd clearly decided that the easiest option would be to go along with Willow's suggestion, at least for now.

Willow shot to her feet, eager to explore. 'Andrew, you coming?'

'Oh yes, I haven't actually seen much of it yet. I've been too busy down in the village. I'd love to have a look.'

'You see, people will be interested in it,' Willow said.

Kitty got up too and linked hands with her husband.

'It's quite small really, despite its stature,' Ken said, pushing a door open on the other side of the kitchen and Willow followed him into a stone corridor. 'I think it was more of a folly than used for any kind of fortification purposes. As far as I can tell it's only a few hundred years old, which is very young in comparison to other castles. And this one wasn't built to last.'

'Do you know a lot about its history?'

'Not really,' Kitty said. 'The first mention of it we can find is in the mid-1700s, although it was possible it was around before that. It changed names many times over the years, almost as many times as it changed owners. The first owner, we think, was Charles Archer but we don't know anything about him and it wasn't passed down through his family.'

Ken pushed open a large wooden door. 'This is the great hall.'

Willow eagerly followed them in but felt her excitement deflate a little when she saw a gaping hole in one of the walls. In fact there were several holes and walls falling down. There was no furniture or pictures or tapestries on the walls – the room was no more than a shell. *Great* hall was a bit of an exaggeration.

'The previous owners stripped out and sold anything of value,' Ken said. 'There's not a lot left. There are also places where they tried to make renovations, very badly, and then either ran out of money or patience. That far wall with the majority of the holes in, I think the owner wanted to make the hall into a large garage for all his cars and figured he'd just knock down the outer wall so he could park in here.'

'What?' Willow said incredulously.

'Yes, the previous owners were less than respectful,' Ken shook his head, sorrowfully.

'Are all the rooms like this?' Willow asked.

'Some of them are not this bad, but yes, pretty much the whole place is in disrepair. The north tower has completely collapsed.'

'Come on, show me the rest.'

They walked from room to room with Ken reeling off some historical fact or nugget about the architecture or how the rooms were used. It was just as he had said though, the building was in a terrible state.

They walked back to the kitchen and Willow sat back

down at the table again.

'Still think we can open it to the public?' Ken said.

'Yes, I still see potential here. Kids love climbing over ruins, they will enjoy running from room to room pretending they are a knight or a king or queen, regardless what state it is in. I think the first thing is to get some people in to assess how safe it is and there may be some places, like the north tower, that you have to close off to the public for safety reasons. You'll also need some public liability insurance. And a website advertising your castle, but a good website designer could come up with something snazzy. You could even run some Facebook adverts fairly cheaply. Again, someone internet savvy could set them up for you.'

Kitty and Ken stared at her with wide eyes.

'I also think, even though you don't know a lot about the castle's history, you do know quite a bit about the architecture of the place and some great general historic knowledge that you've been telling me as we've been walking around. You could spend some time writing up these little facts and putting them on display cards around the castle to provide a little historical context of each room. The stuff you told me about the still room was fascinating. While the kids are running riot around the castle, the parents might find those little snippets interesting.'

'Oh, no one is going to be interested in my waffle,' Ken tried to shrug it off.

'Of course they will,' Kitty said, defensively.

'Kitty's right, people will love it, and I bet you could do a bit more research for some of the other rooms too.'

Ken nodded. 'I could do that.'

'Bringing visitors to the castle would bring in a small amount of money to help with the restoration of the village but also it would bring life to the village and much-needed custom to the shops and the pub too. Andrew is taking care of the village for you, I think the castle could be your new underdog project.'

Kitty and Ken exchanged glances and Kitty gave her husband an encouraging nod.

'OK, we'll look into it,' Ken said.

Willow smiled, pleased that she had done something good for the village and hopefully for Kitty and Ken too.

'Well, I better go, I need to sort out my shop,' Willow said.

'I'll give you a lift back,' Andrew said.

'Andrew, would you mind just holding on for a second?' Kitty said.

'That's OK, I can walk, it's not far,' Willow said. 'It was lovely meeting you.'

'Pop by and see us again,' Ken said. 'There's always cake here, Beryl makes sure of that.'

'I will, thank you.'

She stepped outside and started walking down the driveway. The sun was high in a cloudless turquoise sky. Something positive had been achieved today. Now she just needed to create a visually stunning window display, so the tourists would flock into her shop in their droves.

She laughed to herself; that might be a bit too optimistic.

There was a roar behind her as the quad bike came tearing down the drive. Andrew stopped by her side and she climbed on, wrapping herself around him.

'Everything OK?' Willow asked.

Andrew nodded and grinned over his shoulder at her. 'They think you're magnificent.'

Willow laughed. 'What?'

'I'd have to agree,' Andrew said, and then roared off down the drive.

Willow smiled at that and rested her cheek on his back.

Maybe coming here was the right thing for her after all.

The next day was equally as hot as the day before with the weather showing no signs of change. Willow had the door of the shop open, letting in the warm summer air as she made her candles. The radio was on softly, playing some old tunes she could sing along to. As summer was well and truly here she wanted the candles she was making to reflect that, which would be especially useful when it came to keeping her website updated and fresh.

The night before, she had cut several large oranges in half, scooped out all the flesh and then baked the peel shells in the oven overnight, making her whole cottage smell of oranges which wasn't a bad thing. She had also baked and dried orange slices, whole raspberries and strawberries cut in half too. The orange halves were now dried out and hard which meant they were unlikely to rot and go mouldy. She was going to use these as the candle holders.

Melting gently on the little camping stove was a large pot of parasoy wax. It consisted of paraffin wax and soy wax. Paraffin wax had a much better scent throw than the soy wax, but the latter was much nicer to work with, so over the years she had opted for a blend of the two.

As she danced over to the stove to take a peek, another truck trundled past. There had been a steady stream of vehicles coming and going all morning – the renovation work was clearly starting with a vengeance. She had spent a few hours painting a few of the empty shopfronts the day before, as she had run out of freshly painted houses to add her flowers to. With only fifteen days now until the open day, she felt a bit guilty for wanting to spend a few hours making some candles.

But this was her business and her regular customers were always coming back to her website to look for new candles, so she didn't want to leave it too long before she updated it. The most successful businesses were always fresh, always offering new things. And she promised herself she would squeeze in a few more hours of painting that afternoon, so she didn't feel too bad.

The wax looked like it might be ready, so she slipped on her oven glove and lifted the metal jug out of the saucepan of boiling water. She gave it a stir to check the consistency and, when she was happy that it felt OK, she started adding the orange and yellow colouring and the tangy orange-scented oils, giving it another stir to ensure the colour and scent were distributed evenly throughout the wax. She decided to leave the wax time to cool slightly as it was always better to pour if it wasn't really hot.

She turned her attention to the glass jars she was preparing for the clear gel wax. She loved working with this wax as she could get some beautiful effects, making candles that were almost too good to burn. She had already poured an inch of the blue parasoy wax in the bottom of the jars and the wick was sticking up out of that. As the wax was still cooling down and hardening, now was the perfect time to add the decorations. She sprinkled a bit of gold glitter for the sand in each of the jars and then glued some sea shells in different sizes and colours, pressing them gently into the wax so they were secure. She sprayed a clear glue over the top to set it all in place, then took the liquid gel wax off the stove and poured it on top of the shells in one jar slowly to try to decrease the amount of bubbles. She filled it almost to the top. She secured the wick between two bits of masking tape to make sure it was in the centre of the jar while the gel solidified and then she moved on to the next jar. The gel wax would harden almost completely clear but it had a shimmery quality that sparkled in the sunlight.

Once that was done, she moved back to the orange candles. She carefully glued the metal disk at the bottom of the wick inside the orange halves and then, checking the orange wax was cool enough, she poured it into the oranges. The smell was wonderful.

Next on her list was to make some candles that looked like glasses of Pimm's, champagne and other cocktails.

Willow scooped out some more gel wax and put it in the jug for melting. She opened up a box of champagne glasses and placed them on the table.

'Bit early in the day for drinking, isn't it?'

She looked up to see a paint-splattered Andrew leaning against the door frame.

She smiled, her heart leaping a little at the sight of him. OK, a lot.

'Ah, my old granddad used to say, "It's over the yardarm somewhere in the world." Although he died from liver failure in the end so probably not the best person to take drinking advice from.'

'I'm sorry,' Andrew said, moving into the shop.

'Oh, it was a very long time ago, I think I was only seven or eight. I didn't really know him that well, he just turned up at the odd family gathering and got drunk in the corner. Me and my brother used to find it hilarious.'

'Ah, you have a brother too. Older or younger?'

'Older.'

'Same. Older brothers are the worst, aren't they?' Andrew said.

Willow smiled as she thought of hers. Luke had teased her mercilessly growing up, used her as target practice when he had joined a fencing club, stole her toys, drew willies on her

My Little Ponies, arranged her Care Bears into rude sexual positions and thrashed her in every single board game, card game or computer game they had ever played together. But he had also beaten up Richard Blake after he had deliberately trashed a model bridge that Willow had spent months making for a science project. He had walked her home from school every night instead of hanging around with his friends, he had cooked her dinner before Brownies every Monday when her mum had to work late. He had persuaded his best friend, David, to go on a date with her when she had confided in her brother she had a crush on him. He had held her tight when she had found her pet rabbit dead one morning. They had become very close as they grew older; it was just a shame he now lived in Australia and she rarely got to see him.

'I think I got one of the good ones,' Willow said.

'Lucky you,' Andrew said.

'Do you not get on with your brother?'

'Oh, I suppose me and Jacob get on much better now than we used to. I think he's a bit of an arse sometimes. He'll be here in a few days so you can judge for yourself. We used to fight endlessly when we were growing up, I'm sure I still have the bruises to prove it.'

'You're not supposed to get on with your older brother when you're young. There's kind of a rule against it,' Willow said.

'Ah, that's OK then.'

'Any other brothers or sisters?'

'A younger sister, Lottie,' Andrew said. 'She has a little girl called Poppy who's also deaf, although a lot more than I am. She barely speaks right now, but we all communicate with her using sign language.'

'Is Poppy the little girl in the photo in your bedroom?'

'Yes she is.'

'She looks very happy.'

He paused as if he expected her to say something else. 'She is. She's a very happy, bubbly little girl. Very bright too. Her world is almost completely silent but she doesn't know any different so it certainly doesn't get her down.'

'Kids are resilient creatures, far more so than adults. You've given her the tools to communicate, albeit in a slightly different way, but that's all she needs. Well that and a ton of pink sparkly toys.'

He stared at her for a moment. 'You know, when I tell people my niece is deaf, their first reaction, every single time, is to say, "I'm sorry." Like it's some terrible affliction or disease and they feel sorry for me and my family for having to put up with this curse. And you've picked up on the one thing that hearing people miss. Is she happy? That's the single most important thing for a child, surely. She is healthy in every way and as long as she's happy then we're happy.'

'Sounds like you have that balance exactly right.'

Andrew smiled. 'Apart from that she probably needs more pink sparkly toys?'

'A girl can never have enough.'

He paused for a moment. 'I want her to be proud of who she is. I want her to know she can do anything. Be who she wants to be. I don't want her to ever think, "I can't do this because I'm deaf."'

'It sounds to me like she has an amazing uncle who will make sure she knows that.'

He cleared his throat and frowned. 'So, are you going to tell me what you were really doing with these champagne glasses?'

He was obviously changing the subject, as if suddenly regretting going down that line of conversation with her, but she decided to let it go.

'I'm making cocktails,' Willow said, innocently, as if that explained everything. 'Would you like to watch?'

'Do I get to try them after?'

Willow wrinkled up her nose. 'You might not like these cocktails so much. Here, I'll show you the champagne ones. Will you put a small blob of glue on the bottom of those wicks for me and stick them to the bottom of the glasses?'

Willow went to check on the gel wax, which seemed to be OK, so she lifted it off the heat. She turned to watch Andrew and saw how carefully and precisely he was doing his job. She waited patiently for him to finish his six glasses.

'Is that OK?' he asked.

'That's perfect. So I'm now going to add a few drops of this honey colour. We don't want to lose the translucency of the gel wax, so we'll only add a tiny amount. I'm also going to add a few drops of this champagne scent.'

Andrew watched her avidly as she did what she said and stirred it into the gel wax. She poured a little bit into a spare glass jar so she could see the colour. 'What do you think, does it look like champagne?'

'Sure,' he said, doubtfully.

Willow laughed. 'It will.'

She put a blob of glue on the bottom of the dried raspberries and pressed them into the bottom of the glass to cover up the metal disk of the wick. She gave the yellow-tinted gel wax another stir and then poured it as fast as she could into the champagne glasses. Whereas with the seaside-themed jars she had made a short while before, the fewer bubbles she had the better, but with these candles she wanted loads of bubbles in them to look like champagne.

'Ah, now it looks like champagne,' Andrew said as she secured the wicks in place in the centre of the glass.

'Once this gel wax has cooled and set I'll add another thin

milky layer of gel wax on the top which will look like the froth.'

'These are really clever.'

'Even if they aren't a valuable contribution to the village,' Willow teased.

'But they are. They're something different which will help in the long run to attract visitors to the village. And you're making a valuable contribution in other ways. Many ways in fact. The shops look great, I presume that was your doing?'

'Oh yes. I don't know what those shops will be so I didn't do any writing. I just left the signs blank but at least that part of those shops is finished.'

'Thank you. You never did tell me what your big idea was,' Andrew said.

'I haven't seen you. You're always rushing off to save the village.'

He laughed. 'Maybe I need to start wearing my underpants on the outside.'

'You'll probably need a cape too, otherwise you'll just look odd. But if you're not too busy tonight, why don't you come round for dinner and I'll explain everything. It's spaghetti bolognese, my speciality.'

He narrowed his eyes. 'Are you trying to butter me up for something?'

'I wouldn't dream of it,' Willow said, feigning innocence.

Andrew smirked, clearly not buying any of this. 'How does seven o'clock sound?'

'It's a date.' Her heart leapt. 'No, not a date, definitely not a date.'

'It's OK, I got it,' Andrew said, smiling. 'I'll see you later.'

He gave her a wave and left the shop.

She frowned. It definitely wasn't a date.

CHAPTER TEN

Willow had just finished unpacking her clothes in her bedroom that evening when there was a knock on the door. If that was Andrew he was a half hour early. She quickly went downstairs and answered the door to find Andrew standing there with bags of grocery shopping.

'Delivery,' he said, holding the bags up.

'Oh no, I forgot that was coming today. I ordered this before I came here. Did the delivery van come all the way down here?' Willow said, looking up towards the track.

'No, it can't come down this way. But not to worry, I just loaded it up on the trailer.'

'I'm so sorry, I'll make sure I'm there to meet the delivery driver next time.'

'It's no bother, just let me know in future so I can look out for it.'

'Let me give you a hand unloading the trailer,' Willow said.

'It's OK, there's just two more bags,' Andrew said, placing the ones he was holding just inside the door and turning back to the trailer to collect the rest. He came back a few moments later.

'Are you off the clock now or do you still have work to do?' Willow asked.

'I'm never really off the clock but I'm not doing any more tonight.' He narrowed his eyes suspiciously. 'Why, what do you have planned?'

She laughed. 'No need for the shifty eyes, I don't plan on getting you back just yet for that stunt you pulled at the castle yesterday. Just the dinner is ready, it's keeping warm in the oven and I could open a bottle of wine while we wait for the pasta to cook.'

In her mind, it even sounded like a date. Good job she hadn't gone the whole hog and decided to light some candles too.

'That does sound good.' He closed the door and carried the bags through to the kitchen.

Willow followed him in with the rest of the bags. She picked up a packet of pasta shells and tipped some of it into the saucepan.

'Whoa, what are you doing? Andrew asked in shock.

'Putting the pasta on,' Willow said in confusion.

'You promised me spaghetti bolognese, that doesn't look like spaghetti.'

Willow laughed. 'I'm not really a fan of spaghetti, will pasta shells do instead?'

'You can't go around changing the rules like that. I think the trades description people would have something to say about pasta shells in spaghetti bolognese.' Andrew shook his head in mock disappointment at her standards. 'Next you'll be telling me that you don't actually put toad in toad in the hole.'

Willow laughed. 'Wait, is that a euphemism?'

'I hope not,' Andrew protectively cupped his manhood. 'I could think of many names for it but toad isn't one of them.'

'Well,' Willow quickly decided to change the subject, 'I've never had toad before, although I did eat frogs' legs in Paris once, so I guess that counts. Normally I use sausages in my toad in the hole.'

Andrew shook his head, sadly.

'Glass of wine?'

'Well, just the one, I am driving,' he indicated the quad bike out the front, his mouth twitching in a smirk.

'Yes, of course, you don't want to be decapitating any of Dorothy's gnomes on the way back. And obviously you don't want to be caught by the police on that long drive home.'

'No, I'm a respectable member of the community.'

She poured out two glasses and sat down at the table. He joined her.

'So a successful meeting yesterday, and I see the crew have already arrived and been hard at work,' Willow said, then she held up her glass. 'Here's to bringing Happiness back to its full glory.'

Andrew chinked her glass with his own. 'Thanks to you.'

'Oh no, I was just... driving the car, you're the one that's going to do all the heavy lifting and co-ordinating. It's a big job and I've just made it bigger for you.'

'You just got me a ton of help so thanks for that. Jack and his team are here for two weeks which will take us right up to the open day. They've got other jobs to do after that but they'll come back and finish the rest off at the end of August. That will help massively in getting all the empty houses ready for potential owners, at least on the outside, and like you said, we are aiming to get at least five houses ready on the inside too. Our show houses. Oli and Tom are going to come along and help with making the place look pretty with flowers and plants. They're going to make us a load of hanging baskets and pots ready for the big day so that's good too. Hopefully people will be distracted by the flowers and not look too closely at some of the other issues.'

'We just have to grab their attention, let them see the potential of the place. A little window dressing wouldn't hurt,' Willow said. 'I'll try to paint all the houses with flowers or butterflies around the doors too. Every little helps.'

'I agree and I've also contacted a friend of mine who creates backdrop screens for plays and theatres. She's going to create one for us to put up in front of those houses near the castle entrance. There's no point really doing up those houses when no one's ever going to live in them, so I took your advice and decided to cover them up. Morgan is going to paint a screen with a medieval castle on the front, similar to Harmony Castle, with knights and jousting going on in the foreground. I thought the visitors to the castle would enjoy that.'

'That sounds like a lovely idea,' Willow agreed, getting up to give the pasta a quick stir.

'I'm feeling positive about this project for the first time since I got here,' Andrew said. 'Thank you for that.'

'Ah, I'm glad I could help.' Willow sat back down again.

'So are you going to tell me more about your bright idea that involves Dorothy and the cake?' Andrew said, taking a sip of wine.

'Well, I've been thinking about this a lot today and there was so much excitement over who had left Dorothy the cake.'

'I have to say that was the most excitement I've seen from the villagers for the last three months.'

'Exactly. They seemed so happy. From what Dorothy and a few others have told me, nothing has happened here for years and everyone seems to have withdrawn from the community.

But yesterday they were all out on the street talking to one another.'

'I haven't ever seen that from them.'

'I wonder about trying to give that back to the village. Bring happiness back to Happiness.'

'OK, what do you have in mind?'

'Well if one mystery cake could bring so much happiness, I was thinking about maybe giving a few more people a mystery present.'

'Really? How many more?'

'All of them,' Willow said, quietly, suddenly realising that was a big project in itself.

'That's a lot of cake,' Andrew teased.

'It won't all be cake,' Willow laughed.

'In all seriousness, getting forty-seven presents, well forty-six since you don't need to include me, could be quite costly.'

'Forty-five now, Dorothy has already had her gift. And it doesn't necessarily need to be bought gifts – and if I do buy presents, they only need to be cheap. But maybe I can make some of the gifts or do nice things for the villagers. Like Elsie's house, have you seen that she's only painted the bottom half?'

Andrew rolled his eyes. 'Yes, she's been on at me to paint it for her and I promised her I would, but it just wasn't a priority. Getting the houses ready for the new people was more important. She clearly decided to take matters into her own hands and now it looks even worse than it did before.'

'I could do the rest for her.'

'How do you intend to do that without being seen? I'm presuming the secrecy of the gifts is going to be a big part of this plan.'

'I could do it at night,' Willow said.

He cocked his head. 'Have you really thought this through?'

'Probably not. I always rush into things without thinking about it first.'

He smiled. 'You'll need a ladder to reach the apex of the house, and probably the eaves. I know it's a bungalow but you're not going to reach much higher than she did without a ladder or some kind of extendable roller. And you'll need lights if you're going to paint in the dark. It's really a two-man job during the day, let alone at night.'

'Well fortunately for me, I'm on quite good terms with the sexy estate manager,' Willow said and immediately regretted using the word sexy.

'Oh no, you're not getting me involved in this madness and...' he paused.

Good, he hadn't noticed the compliment.

'Did you just say I was sexy?'

Crap.

'Well flattery goes a long way,' Willow tried to brazen it out. 'I could think of lots of lovely things to say about you if you agree to help me.'

He leaned his head back as if looking to a higher being for strength. He let out a theatrical groan.

She waited patiently but knew he was going to say yes.

'I'll even throw in a present for you to sweeten the deal.'

He looked back at her and shook his head with amusement. 'Fine, but it better be a bloody good present.'

She laughed. 'It will be, I promise.'

'Very well.'

'I thought we could come up with a list of everyone in the village and maybe you could tell me a little about each person, what they like and dislike, so I can start to come up with some ideas for their presents.'

'Another list.'

'I love a list,' Willow said, not taking his complaints remotely seriously.

'Clearly.'

'But as I'm nice, I'll let you eat first.'

'So kind.'

She got up to dish up the dinner. She glanced over her shoulder to see if he was still cursing his decision to come here tonight and found he was watching her with a huge smile on his face, which he quickly swapped for a scowl when he realised she had spotted him. She turned back to the oven with a smile. This project was going to be fun and working with Andrew was going to be a huge part of that.

CHAPTER ELEVEN

Andrew drained the last mouthful of wine from his glass.

'I think we have a good list there,' he gestured to the piece of paper between them.

'I think it stopped being a good list about half hour or so ago.' Willow picked up the empty bottle of wine and held it up to him as proof. They'd also started on a second bottle.

'You might be right there, but I think we came up with some good stuff at the beginning of the evening.'

'Let's hope so.'

It had been a good night. In between coming up with ideas to surprise the villagers, they had chatted and laughed like old friends. He really bloody liked this girl.

'Well, I better go,' Andrew said.

'No driving home, you'll probably drive straight off the cliff.'

'I'm not that drunk, it'll take a bit more than a few glasses of wine to get me in that state, but to be on the safe side, I'll walk. I've got a torch on the quad bike.'

'Just don't drop this one,' Willow said. 'I don't like the thought of you stumbling around in the dark again.'

'Anyone would think you cared about me,' he said, standing up.

'I do.'

Andrew hesitated for a moment as he stared at her, his eyes locked on hers. He was in trouble here. He felt like he needed to walk away, clear his head, before he said or did something he would likely regret.

He moved to the door and she followed him.

'Thanks for dinner.'

She opened the door for him. 'Thanks for the help with the list.'

He stepped outside feeling like he should say something but he didn't know what. Something sparked in the air between them.

'Goodnight Willow.' He bent his head to kiss her on the cheek but as she moved towards him he caught her on the very edge of her mouth. He saw desire flicker in her eyes as he pulled back. He turned towards the gate, his heart thudding in his chest. It was a beautiful night, the sea was mirror calm, the stars twinkling in the inky sky. The chill of the night seemed to wipe away any fuzziness in his head and he suddenly had this moment of clarity. He looked back to see Willow was still standing there watching him and he had never felt so sure about anything in his entire life. He walked back towards her, cupped her face and kissed her.

She immediately kissed him back, wrapping her arms around his neck. The taste of her slammed into his gut. Her lips were so soft. He moved his hands down to her waist, feeling her warmth against him. When she slid her tongue into his mouth it was the single most sexy thing he'd ever experienced. The kiss turned urgent and desperate and he knew he should stop. He pulled back slightly and she moved her lips to his throat, her hot mouth there sending all clarity and sense from his brain.

He picked her up and she wrapped her legs around his waist. He kicked the door closed behind them as he carried her back inside.

~

Willow landed with a thud on the sofa with Andrew on top of her. They barely stopped kissing for a second as they caught their breath at the sudden jolt on their bodies. The weight of him pinning her to the sofa was divine. This kiss was everything, this was what had been missing from her life for the last four years.

She hadn't planned for this tonight, in fact she hadn't planned for this when she came to Happiness, but right now there wasn't a single part of her that didn't want it.

She ran her hands down his back, feeling the strength in his shoulders. He was there, surrounding her with his scent, his kiss, his touch, his warmth, it was almost too much all at once.

He must have felt the same as he pulled back slightly to look at her, his breath heavy as he took her in.

She stroked his face. 'That was one hell of a goodnight kiss.'

'It's important to do these things right.'

'Well you did that.'

'I should go,' Andrew said.

She frowned slightly at this sudden about-turn.

'Not because I want to go,' he was quick to reassure her. 'But because I really don't want to.'

'I'm glad we cleared that up,' Willow said.

He smiled and leaned his forehead against hers for a second before standing up. He held out a hand for her and helped her to her feet as well.

'Let's try this again,' he said, still holding her hand as he walked to the door and opened it. 'Goodnight Willow.' He bent his head and this time gave her a brief kiss on the lips.

He walked to his quad bike and pulled a torch from the compartment under the seat. He gave her a wave and disappeared into the darkness.

Willow went back inside and closed the door. She ran her fingers over her lips, still tasting his kiss. What the hell had just happened? And more importantly, what was she going to do about it?

~

Willow got up the next morning, poured herself a bowl of Cheerios, made a cup of tea and took it outside to sit on the bench so she could enjoy the spectacular view.

She hadn't been able to stop thinking about that kiss all night. She couldn't say she regretted it, because it had been incredible, but she also stood by what she'd told Ruby a few days before. It was way too soon to be getting involved with someone, she wanted time to find herself first.

She had no idea what she was going to say to Andrew either. She didn't want it to be awkward between them and she certainly didn't want to hurt him. She wondered how he felt about it this morning and whether he was now plucking up the courage to face her.

She looked down at the notepad that she and Andrew had been working on the night before. After one or two glasses of wine, they had decided to call themselves 'The Secret Society of Happiness'. She liked that. He had a wonderful silly sense of humour that was very attractive.

She picked up the pad. Andrew had drawn her a very detailed map, showing where everyone lived in the village, which was going to be a big help in delivering the presents to the right people and ticking everyone off. She looked at the list. There were some silly suggestions there, clearly they had come in the latter part of the night. She decided to circle the ones she could do now as that seemed like a good place to start.

Mary, from the pink cottage near to the pub, had recently lost her watch and had scoured the whole village looking for it. Though Willow couldn't do anything about returning the lost watch to her, she did have a replacement. She had a thing for buying things at car boot sales and she was like a magpie for anything antique-looking, unique and sparkly. Generally she bought things and then sold them on eBay for a small profit, although she hadn't got round to selling the last lot before she moved. She had been going to donate them to a charity shop rather than bring them with her but she hadn't got round to that either. Upstairs, in her bedroom, she had a small box filled with jewellery and watches. She knew just the watch she wanted to give Mary. She would put it in a gift box and deliver it under the veil of darkness later that evening.

Then there was Ginny, who constantly had fresh flowers delivered every few weeks, so Andrew had told her. Ginny would display the flowers in a big vase in her front window. There were tons of wild flowers growing alongside the track leading from the village down to Sunrise Cottage; roses, violets, sunflowers, poppies and cornflowers seemed to be growing in abundance and there was even a big forsythia bush which she could cut a few stems off. Willow was sure the bouquet that she planned to pick and arrange for Ginny wouldn't be anywhere near as good as the professional shop-bought bouquets but she hoped, as a flower lover, Ginny would still appreciate the gesture.

And she and Andrew had planned to try to paint the rest of Elsie's house that night so, with Ginny and Mary too, that felt like a really good start to the Secret Society of Happiness List.

She placed the pad down and wrapped her hands around her mug for warmth.

'Hi.'

She looked round to see Andrew hovering awkwardly at her gate and her heart went out to him.

'Hello.'

'I... just came to collect the quad bike.'

She smiled and patted the bench next to her. He sighed in relief and came and sat down next to her.

They sat in silence for a while, before eventually Andrew spoke.

'You think last night was a mistake, don't you?'

'No, I think last night was lovely. Actually it was incredible. I've never been kissed like that and there is a huge part of me that wants to explore this wonderful connection between us and say to hell with it and take you straight up to my bedroom now and test the springs on my brand-new mattress.'

He laughed. 'That sounds like a plan.'

'But I think what happened last night was too soon. At least for me. I came down here for a fresh start. I was in a relationship with my last boyfriend for four years and I kind of lost sight of who I was, of what I wanted. I drifted along in this mundane relationship and it sucked the life out of me. Since it ended, in let's say a fairly embarrassing way, six months ago, it has been such a relief to be on my own again. But I couldn't get away from feeling like a laughing stock and the looks of pity I was getting from everyone, and I needed a break from all of that. I've been part of Garry and Willow for so long that I need to find out what it's like to just be me for a while.'

'I understand,' Andrew said.

'You do?' Willow was surprised by this as she wasn't sure she totally understood it herself.

'Yeah.' He squeezed her hand and placed a kiss on her cheek. 'I've had a string of bad relationships and I swore I wasn't interested in having another, at least not for a while. And I'm not sure what came over me last night, I don't think I can even blame the alcohol. The only thing I can say in my defence is that you're really bloody lovely and I just got carried away. You have my word, it won't happen again.'

She smiled and leaned her head against his shoulder. 'I think you're pretty wonderful too.'

Which made her wonder, why was she so intent on holding back?

'How about a pact?' Willow said, suddenly feeling like she didn't want to draw a line under her relationship with Andrew completely. 'Six months from now, if I haven't annoyed you too much with all the lists I'm going to make you write, and you're still single and not married with babies on the way, we revisit that kiss and see where the night takes us when you don't have to rush off.'

He smiled. 'Have you just booked a date for us to have sex six months from now? That's a bit too organised if you ask me.'

'Is that a no?'

'Hell no.' Andrew got out his phone and she laughed as she watched him enter a new event into his calendar. *Hot sex with Willow.* 'I'll look forward to it.'

She smiled. She liked the sound of that plan.

CHAPTER TWELVE

Willow had decided that she needed to do some more painting in the village that day. With only two weeks now until the open day, she wanted everything to be perfect. She had spent a good deal of time the day before updating her website so that was done and until any new orders came in she had some hours to spare. It was hot already and it was still early in the morning; it promised to be another sweltering day so she didn't want to waste the good weather sitting inside her shop.

She wandered down to the far end of the village, thinking about Andrew. She just hoped that, after their kiss and their agreement that nothing should happen between them, it wouldn't be awkward for them to work in such close proximity to each other.

As she got closer she was surprised how much had changed in just a day of Jack and his team working here. But a quick head count revealed that Jack's team included at least twelve people so it was no surprise they had got so much done already. She counted at least four more houses that had been painted since she had last been down here, although she hadn't been down this end for a few days as she had been focussing her attention on painting the shops in the main part of the village.

She headed for the shed and grabbed some tins of paint and brushes. She looked around. She wanted to make sure she wouldn't be in the way of any of the work that was going on and she didn't want to start painting on a house that might still have wet paint. There was no sign of Andrew, though there was clearly work going on inside one or two of the houses.

She saw a man who looked like he might be in charge as he gave directions to two other men and she heard one of them call him Jack. He had stripped down to his shorts, as many of the men had. He had the body of someone who did a lot of manual labour. As he finished talking, she walked over to speak to him.

'Hello,' Willow called to get his attention.

He turned round and flashed her a winning smile. 'Hello,' he said, his eyes appraising her. 'Can I help?'

'Yes, I'm the one painting the flowers and designs around the doors. I just wondered—'

'Oh, you're the artist.'

'I wouldn't go so far as to say that, it's just a few simple flowers.'

'They look great. I hope he's paying you.' He jerked a thumb to one of the cottages, presumably where Andrew was busy working.

'Oh no, I live here in the village, I'm just trying to help.'

'Well, that's very kind, but don't let him take advantage of you,' Jack said.

Willow frowned. Andrew would be the last person in the world to do that. 'I was just wondering which houses I could work on, I don't want to be in your way.'

'I don't think you could ever be in my way.'

She resisted rolling her eyes. Jack was smooth and this method of flirting had probably worked very well for him in the past. She waited for him expectantly.

He eventually realised he wasn't going to get far with her. 'You can start on those two and when you've finished you'll probably be able to do that one.'

'Thanks,' Willow said and moved over to one of the houses he'd pointed at.

She started painting the curly green stem and leaves again but this time she painted bright yellow roses around the door. It looked cheery. She moved on to the next house where there was evidently work going on inside as she could hear lots of drilling and banging taking place. She peered through one of the windows just in time to see Andrew stripping off his t-shirt. God he really was glorious. Seeing his body affected her in ways that seeing Jack's didn't. Maybe it was because she had been pinned underneath that body the night before, or maybe it was because it belonged to such a wonderful man.

To her shame, Andrew saw her gawking at him through the window.

She quickly moved away but a few seconds later he came to the door.

'Are you perving at me again, Willow McKay?'

'No, I was just looking through the window to see what work was going on.'

He was smirking at her, clearly not believing a word of it.

She shrugged. She might as well be honest. 'And it came with the added bonus of this marvellous view.'

Andrew laughed. 'Well, I like to keep the workers happy. I take it you're here to do some more painting?'

'I am.'

'It's really appreciated, thank you.'

His genuine smile made her feel warm inside in ways that a simple payment for her services could never achieve.

'It's OK.'

'It really helps Happiness to look good from the outside and with our secret project maybe we can help the villagers feel better on the inside. Talking of which…' He looked around to make sure that nobody was listening. 'Are you ready for our Secret Society shenanigans tonight?'

'Yes, I can't wait. Shall we do Mary and Ginny first before we go to Elsie's house to do the painting?'

'That sounds good. We can stop at my house after we've done Mary and Ginny to pick up the paint and the ladders. Should we be wearing black with camouflage paint on our faces?'

Willow laughed. 'Wearing black might not be a bad idea but let's leave the camouflage paint for now. I think we'll certainly look suspicious if we're caught walking around looking like we've come fresh from a war zone.'

Andrew looked a bit disappointed that he couldn't go full-on commando but he soon recovered himself. 'Do you think we need a secret handshake or a special password for all those that are in the Secret Society?' he teased.

Willow smiled, she loved his silly sense of humour. 'I think we'll have to come up with one.'

'So shall we meet after dinner?' he said.

'Yes.' And then because he looked like he might be about to invite her to have dinner with him she decided to make up a prior arrangement. 'I promised my friend Ruby that I'd have pizza with her tonight.'

'She's coming here?'

'No, we're having dinner together over Skype.'

She immediately felt bad for lying to Andrew but there was no point in turning down a relationship with him in order to find herself if she was going to spend every night with him anyway. She might as well enjoy the other aspects of the relationship if that was the case. She had given herself six months to just be Willow rather than part of a couple but she honestly didn't think she would last that long. She enjoyed his company so much that it felt like a slippery slope to then spend all her time with him as well. Dinner every night could then easily lead to breakfast every morning and it would only be a matter of time before they decided to fill that gap in between.

'I was going to say that I have darts tonight down the pub so it will have to be after eight anyway,' Andrew said.

Oh god, she'd got it all wrong and the way he was looking at her suggested he knew she was lying about her plans too.

'Why not come round to my house when you're done with darts and then we can do our Secret Society business together,' Willow said, knowing that now she would have to have dinner with Ruby just to prove him wrong and would deliberately still be talking to her on Skype when he arrived.

'Sounds like a plan.'

He held his fists out as if he wanted to bump fists with her. She frowned in confusion but copied the gesture. He bumped it on the top, the bottom and either side and she laughed as she realised he was trying to do a secret handshake.

'What?' Andrew said. 'Does it need a bit more work?'

'Just a smidgen.'

'I'll keep practising,' Andrew said as he turned to go back inside the house.

'On your own?' Willow called after him.

'I have two hands, don't I?'

Willow giggled as she imagined him practising the secret handshake by himself. He waved goodbye and closed the door.

God, she really liked this man.

CHAPTER THIRTEEN

'This is not a bad idea, you know,' Ruby said, gesturing to the Chinese she had in front of her, the noodles she was eating dripping with some kind of red sauce. 'Having dinner together. It's almost like you're really here.'

When Willow had told Ruby she needed to have dinner with her that night over Skype, Ruby had leapt at the idea, although she hadn't followed the instructions to the letter when she turned up with sweet and sour chicken. But Willow had pizza so she didn't think it mattered that much.

'It's lovely to see you. It's silly, I've only been gone a few days and I'm missing you already,' Willow said.

'It's not silly at all, I am rather fabulous,' Ruby said, tonight sporting a t-shirt with Rudolph on the front with a glittery red nose. Ruby loved Christmas so much, she lived and breathed it all year long.

Willow smiled. 'Yes you are.'

'So tell me why we're doing this?' Ruby snapped a prawn cracker in half and popped one piece in her mouth.

'Because I miss you.'

Ruby let out a bark of a laugh. 'You're such a lying toad. Want to tell me the real reason?'

Willow sighed. 'Because I lied to a rather lovely man to avoid dinner plans for tonight and he wasn't even going to invite me to dinner after all. And now I feel horribly guilty and he'll be coming round shortly to help me with something and I want him to see I wasn't lying even though I was.'

Ruby laughed. 'Oh what a tangled web we weave. If the man was so lovely, why did you not want to have dinner with him?'

'Because…' Willow really didn't want to tell Ruby about the kiss because then she'd make it into a thing and it wasn't going to be a thing, definitely not. Although she knew she had to tell Ruby some of it. 'Because I like Andrew.'

'And?'

'And I'm not looking for a relationship right now.'

'Who says it has to be a relationship? Just have some fun. That's just what you need to get over your relationship with Garry.'

'I am over it,' Willow said, with a sigh.

'Yes, I didn't mean that,' Ruby said. 'I just meant passion and excitement has been missing from your life for the last four years. Why not have a bit of that again? Get out there and enjoy yourself. It doesn't have to be anything serious.'

'Andrew is too lovely for that.'

'So you're just going to avoid him in a village that's smaller than my pokey little flat.'

'I'm not going to avoid him, we're working together on a project right now. I just think that I don't need to spend every night with him too. He came round here for dinner last night, and it was… really nice.' It had been a hell of a lot more than nice. 'I just think if we end up having dinner together every night then it could so easily turn into something more.'

Ruby shook her head affectionately. 'Well at least I get to meet him.'

'Ah god,' Willow said. She hadn't thought this through. 'Don't say anything.'

Ruby crossed her heart and zipped her lips. 'I promise.'

'How's everything going with you anyway?' Willow asked, keen to change the subject.

'Oh, OK I guess,' Ruby said, with a sigh. 'I've been thinking about you and how you've just packed up everything you own and started over somewhere new. I kind of wish I could do that too. Everyone knows *everything* about me here and that's not always a good thing.'

Willow thought about Ruby and her past. Although Willow had met her when Ruby was in her early twenties, a few years after she had her heart broken in the worst possible way, Willow knew that, even ten years later, the people of St Octavia would never let Ruby forget it. But Ruby was normally so upbeat, it wasn't like her to get down. Although her elderly neighbour, Maggie, had died two months before and Willow knew that Ruby had been upset by that. She wondered if that had anything to do with Ruby's change of mood.

'Has something happened?' Willow asked.

'I don't know, life just drifts on, doesn't it. Nothing ever changes unless you make the change yourself. I sit on my little market stand every week and I see the same people come and go. Bill and Connie come into the market hall every Tuesday to get four slices of ham from the deli stand and *some of that nice cheesy bread* from the bread stall. Thomas comes and looks at the model trains on the next stand every evening after he leaves work. He never buys any of them. Sally and her son Noah come in every Saturday to get a chocolate milkshake *with extra sprinkles* and I get the impression that's the only quality time she has with him. I don't know, I just feel I need a change.'

'Is this to do with Maggie?' Willow asked.

Ruby shrugged. 'Maybe. You know she had the same job her entire life, working in the local chemist since she was sixteen, right up to when she died. I was talking to her a few weeks before she died. It was her seventieth birthday and I asked her about her life and what she had achieved, what she was most proud of – and, beyond having her kids, she couldn't think of a single thing she had achieved or done that she was proud of. She tried to laugh it off and said people would remember her for being a fantastic chemist and I just thought it was a little sad, that that was the only thing she would be remembered as. My brother is a bloody Paralympian for goodness sake and what have I done with my life? I've lived here in St Octavia almost my whole life apart from when I went to university. What will people say about me after I'm gone: "She had great baubles"?'

Willow smiled at the unintentional euphemism. Ruby made her living selling Christmas decorations all year round. She loved it and Willow didn't think she'd ever give that up.

'So what are you going to do?'

'I don't know.'

'Go travelling?'

'I'm not sure I'm the sort of girl who would travel alone. I just feel like I need a change. I need a new routine, new faces.'

'Well what's stopping you?' Willow said. 'You could do what I did. Hell, you can even come here. Open up a Christmas shop in the village.'

'You make it sound so easy.'

'It is. You have no job to give notice to, you hate the flat where you live. Free accommodation and rent for a year. If you hate it after that, you can always move back to St

Octavia. At least come and visit and see the place for a few days.'

Ruby smiled slightly as she thought about it.

'And to be honest, I could really do with your help and expertise,' Willow said, knowing Ruby couldn't say no to her little plea.

'My Christmas skills?' Ruby asked.

Willow thought about it for a moment and then found herself nodding. 'Actually yes. Christmas lights, the white ones. We need them in abundance. We have this big open day coming up in a few weeks and it needs to look magical. White lights could help with that. And you're just the person to know where to hang them.'

She hoped Andrew wouldn't mind that she had suddenly made this executive decision, but who didn't love fairy lights?

'I could do that. I have a ton of that stuff in storage, I could lend them to you for a few weeks. You know what, I will come and visit. If nothing else, I want to meet this lovely man who you've fallen in love with in person.'

'I have not fallen in love with him,' Willow protested, just as there was a knock on the door. 'Now shush.'

Ruby sat forward on the edge of her seat eagerly as Willow went to answer the door.

Andrew was standing there, dressed all in black. He looked sexy, like the Milk Tray man.

'Oh hey, Andrew,' Willow smiled. 'I won't be a moment. I'm just finishing my conversation with Ruby. Come in for a second.'

She stepped back so Andrew could come in and she watched him clock the open laptop with Ruby's grinning face on the screen. She felt like saying, 'See, I wasn't lying after all.' But she had been and this suddenly felt like a double lie.

'Ruby, this is Andrew. Andrew, this is my best friend Ruby.'

'Hi.' Ruby waved inanely.

Andrew smiled as he bent over to get closer to the camera. 'Hello.'

'Are you taking care of my friend?' Ruby said and Willow rolled her eyes.

'I'm making sure she is well looked after,' Andrew said.

'Right, I think we better go,' Willow said, before Ruby said something too cringey. 'Lots to do tonight. I'll be right with you, Andrew.'

She ushered him back to the door and turned back to the laptop. 'Bye Ruby.'

'He's hot,' Ruby mouthed.

Willow made a noise in her throat that was a vague agreement.

'Sleeping with him would definitely put a huge smile on your face,' Ruby whispered.

'Bye Rubes.' Willow slammed down the lid of the laptop and turned back to face Andrew who was looking like he hadn't heard anything. She gave a little sigh of relief.

'How was darts?' Willow said, pulling on her boots.

'Fine, our team lost, but it was fine. Ruby seems nice, very smart.'

'She is.' Willow frowned in confusion. 'What do you mean, smart?'

'The things she said.'

Willow flushed. 'You heard her?'

'I lip-read, remember?' Andrew chuckled. 'She speaks a lot of sense.'

'Oh shush.' Willow laughed.

She picked up the gift-wrapped watch and the hand-tied bunch of flowers she had prepared earlier that day. She slipped the watch into a bag so no one would see her holding the box and put two and two together the next day. The flowers were a little harder to hide.

'These look wonderful,' Andrew said, gesturing towards the flowers.

'They looked a lot better in my head but they'll do.'

They stepped outside together and Willow closed the door behind her.

'We'll take the coastal path I think, less likely that we'll be seen that way and Ginny's house is quite near the bottom of the village so we can do hers first,' Andrew said.

'Sounds like a plan,' Willow said.

Andrew flicked on his torch and they set off down the little path. It was completely dark here – although the moon was shining brightly above them, it wasn't giving off enough light to allow them to see where they were going. The path was slightly uneven in parts and she found herself linking arms with Andrew, but purely for safety reasons. She certainly didn't want to trip and go flying over the edge of the cliff. He didn't seem to mind.

'So can I ask you something?' Andrew said.

'Anything,' Willow said.

'Did you lie about your plans with Ruby tonight and then feel like you had to go ahead with those plans to prove to me that you weren't lying?'

Willow felt her cheeks burn red in the darkness. 'Well when I said ask me anything, I didn't mean that.'

'You don't have to answer,' Andrew said.

He was being so kind. She had lied to him and he knew it and he was still being lovely.

'Well I do now, because silence is a guilty omission and if I answer then I can at least try to defend myself.'

'Please go ahead,' Andrew said.

'I thought you were going to invite me to dinner.'

'OK.'

A rabbit leapt out of a nearby bush and darted up the hill away from them, its white tail flashing in the light of the torch.

'I enjoyed having you round for dinner last night immensely, you are wonderful company and I'm very happy to do that again. I just thought if dinner was going to become a regular thing, like every night, then…' she trailed off.

'Then we could end up testing out your bed springs a lot sooner than our prearranged six-month date,' Andrew finished for her.

She laughed. 'Something like that.'

'I understand. But if I invite you to dinner and you don't want to come, you can just say no.'

'I didn't want to hurt your feelings.'

'I'm a big boy. I can take it.'

They walked on in silence for a while and, because they were veiled in the darkness, she felt like she could say this and it wouldn't really count.

'I could fall for you Andrew Harrington. I mean I haven't, but I feel like I really could. I have a feeling that six-month embargo will come to a spectacular end a lot sooner than we think but I'd at least like to finish unpacking before I leap into bed with the first man I met.'

There was silence from him for a moment and she wondered if she had scared him with her half declaration of love. She was kind of scared of her feelings for him herself.

He pulled her to a stop, put the torch on the ground and turned to face her in the darkness. He pressed a kiss to her forehead.

Her heart erupted in her chest and she found her hands going to his waist and leaning into the warmth of his body.

'I think, sometimes, you meet someone who is worth

breaking all the rules for.' He pulled back slightly to look her in the eyes. 'And sometimes you meet someone who is worth waiting for however long it takes for them to realise it too.'

Oh god. This man.

She was in trouble with him and there was nothing she could do about it.

CHAPTER FOURTEEN

'Come on,' Andrew said, breaking the moment. He picked up the torch, grabbed her hand and carried on walking across the cliff tops. He didn't know whether to kick himself or give himself a bloody medal for walking away from that. There she was, bathed in the moonlight, looking magical and breathtakingly beautiful, staring up at him like she wanted to kiss him, and instead of grabbing her and kissing her again, he'd walked away. But as much as he liked her, he wanted to respect her decision to wait. He totally understood where she was coming from, things were moving way too quickly between them.

She jogged to keep up with his long-legged stride and he forced himself to slow down. He glanced down at her and she smiled up at him.

'Stop smiling.'

This made her smile even more. It lit up her entire face. He quickly looked away.

They reached the top of the steps to the beach and he

turned off up the little path towards the village. They soon passed the stone ruins of the first houses in the village.

'They say these houses are thousands of years old.'

'Surely they can't be that old,' Willow said.

'I don't know. Apparently they had some historians digging round here many years back and they found evidence that pointed to several hundred years BC. They think it's haunted too.'

'What?' Willow said, suddenly walking a lot closer to him.

'You scared?' Andrew said.

'I wouldn't say scared but not exactly thrilled. Have you seen anything?'

'No. I don't come down this way that often. I go for a swim in the sea from time to time but I haven't seen any ghostly apparitions whenever I've walked past. But if you believe the gossip in the village – and I'd take a lot of that with a pinch of salt – some of the locals have seen something. Most people seem to think it was a story told by the older folk of the village many years ago to scare the children who grew up here from coming near the place. Although if I grew up here and heard those kinds of stories, it would be more likely to make me come down here and investigate than stay away.'

'So what kind of ghosts are we talking about?' Willow linked arms with him. 'Headless horsemen, cloaked figures, that kind of thing?'

'Vampires that suck your blood,' Andrew said, pulling her close to him and playfully biting at her neck.

'Stop it,' Willow laughed, batting him away.

He carried on walking, wishing he hadn't done that because he could now taste her on his lips. 'I don't know really, depends who you speak to.' The lights of the village twinkled ahead of them. 'Some say it's the ghost of the woman who walks the cliff tops looking for her lost love,' he said.

Willow laughed. 'That's a bit tragic. Maybe she fell in love with the handsome estate manager but kept giving him the run-around and in the end he went off and married someone far better and she wandered the cliffs weeping. And because she had tears in her eyes, she fell over the edge and died a tragic and senseless death.'

Andrew smiled. 'Maybe. But I don't think we have any fear of history repeating itself there.'

'Me falling over the cliff in my grief?'

'Me running off with someone else.'

'Ah, you're a true gent.'

He smiled. 'Actually there is also an old wives' tale that the apparitions are really fairies.'

Willow laughed. 'I think I believe that even less than the ghosts.'

'The fairies apparently help the villagers when they are in need.'

'Well that's nice of them. They haven't done much for the village in its current state.'

'Sshhh! You don't want to anger the fairies. Maybe you have to ask for help.'

Willow stopped and turned back to face the ruins. 'OK, fairies, we could really do with your help with the village. It's looking a bit tatty and we need it to be ready for the open day in two weeks. Also we need some help with the presents we're giving to the villagers, so any help you can give us there would be great.'

She turned back to look at Andrew. 'How was that?'

'Fine. But you have to make an offering.'

'What?' Willow laughed.

'Hey, I don't make these rules.'

'It sounds to me like you're making them up on the spot. What do you suggest?'

Andrew thought about this for a moment, because while he had heard rumours of fairies, he was making up the stuff about giving the fairies an offering.

'How about a dance?'

'You want me to dance for the fairies?'

Andrew nodded. 'I think the fairies will love it.'

'On my own?'

He shrugged. 'You're the one doing the asking.'

She clearly thought about this for a moment and he honestly expected her to tell him where to shove it but after a few seconds she started to sway and swing her arms from side to side, then she started bouncing her shoulders and banging her knees together. It wasn't like any dance he'd ever seen before. He wanted to burst out laughing and he also wanted to gather her close and kiss her because this bloody woman had got right under his skin. She had captured his heart and he didn't think he would ever get over that.

He cleared his throat and she looked at him. 'That was amazing.'

'Do you think the fairies will be suitably impressed?'

'Well, I know I was.'

She smiled and linked arms with him again as they carried on walking towards the village. 'I don't believe any of this for one second.'

'You still danced though.'

'This village needs all the help it can get. If that means I have to dance naked next to a fire at midnight, under a full moon, then I'll do it.'

'Oh yes, the dancing naked part. That's what I forgot,' Andrew said, turning them back around. 'Let's do it again, this time naked.'

Willow turned them back to face the village. 'Only at a full moon.'

'Damn it.'

He smiled as they walked along in the darkness. She made him really happy.

They were approaching the first houses in the main part of the village now and luckily for them Ginny's house was one of the first they would come to. The lights were on and the noise of the TV could be heard from inside.

'OK, it's this house here,' Andrew said. He looked around to see if anyone else was around but the street was completely deserted.

He watched Willow glance around too. 'What if someone else takes the flowers?'

'That would be a pretty heartless thing to do.'

'Maybe we should knock on the door?' she said.

'And then what, run and hide? I didn't take you for the *knock door, run* type.'

She flashed him a mischievous look and walked over to the door. She placed the flowers on the doorstep and then, to his surprise, she raised her fist to knock on the door.

'Wait,' he hissed. 'We need a plan, where are we going to hide?'

'I'll leave that to you,' she said, knocking three times loudly on the door.

Crap.

He looked around frantically as he saw the shadow of Ginny get up behind the curtains. He quickly snatched Willow's hand and yanked her into the space between two houses on the opposite side of the street. He pulled her back into the darkness just as the door was flung open. His heart was beating out of his chest as Willow stifled a giggle. He watched Ginny look up and down the street and then glance down and spot the flowers. She bent down to pick them up and he saw her whole face light up with happiness.

He felt a warm glow spread through him as she looked around once more and went back inside with a big smile on her face.

He glanced down at Willow and saw she was smiling too. They had done something wonderful tonight, well Willow had, but it felt amazing to be a part of it. This tiny gesture had just made a lonely old woman incredibly happy.

Willow looked up at him, her eyes shining in the light from the street. She was incredible.

He touched her face, grazing his thumb down her cheek. 'I think I'd wait an eternity for you Willow McKay.'

She pressed a gentle kiss to his palm. 'I don't think you'll have to. Come on, we have lots to do.'

With a quick check out on the street, she stepped out of the shadows and into the light. There was suddenly a big part of him that felt like he was doing the same. He smiled and shook his head and then followed her out on to the road.

Willow could not stop giggling. Andrew's stepladder was the squeakiest, creakiest thing she had ever heard as he carried it the short distance from his house to Elsie's. Surely everyone in the village would be able to hear it. Andrew was theatrically creeping along the little track, walking on his tiptoes, and that was making her laugh so much too.

'Could you be any louder?' she giggled.

He turned to stare at her incredulously. 'Do you want to carry this?'

'Oh no, I'm fine with carrying the paint and the brushes. I take it back, you're doing a splendid job.'

He muttered something under his breath that didn't sound too polite.

They approached Elsie's house and stood surveying it for a moment. There was still quite a lot to do, but it was a very small house so Willow didn't think it would take them that long.

'Let's start round the back first. We can do the front last as we're more likely to be seen there, and the later we're painting that the better,' Willow said.

Andrew nodded his agreement.

They walked through the gate and crept round the back. The house was in darkness, which in some ways was worse because if Elsie was asleep then she could be woken. If she had been watching TV then she would at least be distracted by that and the noise would drown out any squeaks and creaks.

The back and front would be quite easy as even Willow could reach the top of the thatch with the paint roller. But the sides would be trickier as Andrew would have to go up the ladder to reach the apex of the house.

Andrew laid the torch down on the ground, not pointing it directly at the house probably in case the light woke Elsie up. He poured some paint into the tray; luckily Elsie had started the house in white so they didn't have to worry about matching the colours up. They both began painting the wall with their rollers, starting in the middle and working their way out to the edges of the house.

Once that was done, they picked up their paint and ladder and moved round to the side. They were just propping the ladder up against the wall when Julia walked past with her Jack Russell and, to Willow's surprise, a ginger cat on a lead. Julia didn't see them but unfortunately the Jack Russell did. He started yapping immediately as Andrew quickly pulled her to the ground.

'What is it, Colin?' Julia said. 'Did you see a rabbit or something? Oh, I bet it's that nasty fox that's been after my poor chickens.'

Frustratingly, Julia decided to try and see herself, coming right up to the fence and dragging an unwilling Colin and the angry ginger cat with her. Willow was glad for the foresight Andrew had shown in his suggestion they wear black, but she wished she'd taken his advice on the camouflage paint right now. Willow wondered if Julia could see the ladder – she was certainly taking her time with looking over Elsie's fence and Colin was still barking. Luckily the torch was still round the back but Julia could probably see the extra light coming from Elsie's back garden.

Eventually she gave up and left, taking a still yapping Colin and the angry ginger cat with her.

Willow and Andrew lay there not moving for a while longer.

Andrew sat up. 'I think she's gone.'

'She's probably creeping round the back of your house trying to spot you with a *girl*,' Willow said, clambering up. 'And are we not going to address the fact that Julia was walking a cat on a lead?'

Andrew shrugged as if it was perfectly normal. 'Rufus, apparently he likes it.'

'He didn't look very happy to me.'

'Come on. We need to be quick, she'll be back shortly,' Andrew whispered, scrambling to his feet too.

This whole project was going to be quite stressful. If they could deliver the presents to all the villagers over the next few weeks without getting caught it was going to be a bloody miracle.

Andrew followed Willow through her gate, which he still needed to fix, and she let them into her house. He was bone-tired. After spending most of the night before lying awake thinking about that incredible kiss and then getting up early to help with the renovations in the village, and now spending the last few hours painting Elsie's house, he was exhausted. Julia had been back along the road three times, either because she suspected something was going on or she just wanted to give Colin and Rufus a good walk, but it held them up considerably. Julia wasn't the only one on a late-night walk either. They'd seen Connor from the pub walking his Labrador and Dorothy out for a random stroll too. Who knew that Happiness village was such a social hub for late-night activity?

He flopped down on Willow's sofa for a moment.

'I'll make you a coffee,' Willow said, disappearing off to the kitchen.

He felt his eyes droop closed and leaned his head on the back of the sofa. He wondered what the rule book said about him spending the night on Willow's sofa because right then he didn't have the energy to make it back home. He didn't want her to feel uncomfortable with him staying but maybe she'd let him have a kip for a half hour or so. He felt himself dropping off as he heard her move around in the kitchen. After a few minutes, he heard her come back in and place the coffee cup on the table. He couldn't even open his eyes. He felt a blanket being draped over him but the next thing he felt her snuggling in by his side, resting her head on his shoulder and wrapping an arm round his stomach. He opened one eye to look at her but her eyes were closed now too.

'I really like you Andrew Harrington,' she whispered.

He put an arm around her and kissed her head. 'I really like you too.'

She looked up at him. 'Are you planning on staying here tonight?'

'Just for a little while,' Andrew said, closing his eyes again.

She got up out of his arms and he felt a bit bereft. 'Then let's go to bed.'

Both eyes snapped open to see that she was holding out a hand for him. Good god. Of course he wanted that but he also respected her decision to not get involved in a relationship right now. He didn't want her to do something she would later regret. He must have looked like a startled rabbit because she laughed.

'To sleep, you pervert.'

He smiled with relief because he wasn't sure sex would be a good idea for two people who didn't want to get involved. Although sleeping in a bed with her probably wasn't a good idea either, it would make things very complicated. But the thought of going to sleep with her in his arms... well, there was no way he could walk away from that. He was respectful but he wasn't a saint.

He stood up and took her hand. 'I can think of nothing I'd like more.'

'Oh, I'm sure you could think of something,' Willow said, a mischievous glint in her eyes.

'I'm not sure I'm up to anything else.'

He followed her up the stairs and sat down on her bed to take off his boots. He stripped down to his boxer shorts and got into bed, closing his eyes so Willow could get changed in private. He felt her slip into bed and cuddle up to him again, with her head on his chest. Yep, definitely complicated. He slid an arm round her shoulders.

'Thank you for helping me tonight,' Willow said.

'It was my pleasure,' Andrew said, honestly. 'I really

enjoyed it. Seeing Ginny's face when she saw those flowers, that was pretty special wasn't it?'

'It really was. There'll be lots of talk in the village tomorrow. We should get our stories straight about what we were doing.'

'I'm going to tell everyone that I spent the night in bed with an incredible woman,' Andrew said and she laughed.

They fell silent for a while and he knew she was dozing off. Normally he would wait for the woman he was with to fall asleep before taking out his hearing aids, he hated drawing attention to his deafness, but he didn't have to do that with Willow. She already knew and he liked that. He still felt a little self-conscious about it but he felt so at ease with her, nothing seemed to faze her.

'I'm going to take my hearing aids out now,' Andrew said. 'So don't talk to me if you want an answer or at least make sure you're facing me. And if there's a fire in the middle of the night, you'll have to give me a big nudge.'

'What do you do in your house to protect yourself from a fire?'

'I have my smoke alarm linked to a strobe light and a vibration pad under my pillow.'

'Oh, OK. Well, I promise not to let you die.'

He smiled and took his hearing aids out, his world going almost completely silent, so he couldn't hear her breathing any more and that bothered him more than anything else. She lay on his chest, her head propped up on her hands, just watching him, a smile on her face. He popped the hearing aids on top of her bedside drawers. He looked back at her to see she was still staring at him, a big smile on her face. He stroked her hair, needing to be connected to her in some way now he wouldn't be able to hear her.

She started to talk and he focussed on her lips so he could see what she was saying.

'So lip-reading, how accurate is it?' she said.

'Not very accurate, a lot of it is guesswork based on the context, plus other facial features, body language and the expression in someone's eyes. Even the best lip-readers in the world can only read about thirty to forty percent of what is being said. And that's only if the person talking is well lit and looking face on. Facial hair is also a bit of a problem. So don't grow a moustache. There are also many words that look very similar or identical on the lips, like "I love you" looks the exact same as "olive juice" and "elephant shoes".'

She laughed and he hated that he couldn't hear that either. It was just an echoey noise, like being underwater.

She looked back at him. 'OK, just so there's no confusion, I'm going to stop talking and do this instead.'

And with that, she leaned forward and kissed him.

Christ, there could be no misunderstanding this. He stroked down her hair, tasting her lips, inhaling her scent, all of his other senses coming alive. She was magnificent and she made him feel utterly spectacular. He had kissed quite a few women in his life, but it had never felt like this. This was different, better in so many ways, and he had no idea why.

She pulled back slightly and smiled.

'Well thanks for clearing that up,' he said.

Her smile grew and she gave him another brief kiss on the lips. 'Goodnight Andrew.'

She reached up and turned off the light but the moon outside poured through the windows, bathing everything in silver. She lay back down and snuggled into his chest where he knew she would feel his heart hammering against his ribs. Sleep would be very far away again tonight.

CHAPTER FIFTEEN

Willow woke the next morning to an empty bed and, judging by the silence in the rest of the house, Andrew wasn't there either. She sat up and looked around. Next to her on the pillow was a note and a yellow rose. She picked it up and stroked the soft petals as she read the note.

My lovely Willow,

You are quite honestly the most incredible woman I have ever met and I could quite easily have stayed in your bed for the rest of the day, holding you in my arms and maybe even enjoying more of those glorious kisses. But I'm not sure where we are, whether that wonderful kiss last night was just a temporary reprieve or a step forward, and I thought if you woke up this morning and regretted the kiss, I would save you the awkwardness of having that conversation again. If you still don't want a relationship just yet, then I'm happy to wait until you do. But if last night was you throwing caution to the wind and you'd like to do this thing properly, then I'd like to ask you round to dinner tonight as our first official date. I make a mean chicken tikka masala and there will be candles and flowers and definitely more kisses. If you don't want that just yet, you don't need to worry. I can freeze the extra curry and I promise you it won't be awkward if you say no. But if it's a yes, then I look forward to seeing you at seven.

Yours hopefully
Andrew x

Oh god. She couldn't help but smile at this wonderfully sweet note. This man, it was ridiculous how much she felt for him already. And while there was a part of her that still wasn't sure whether running head first into a relationship mere days after arriving in Happiness was a good idea, there was a part of her that wanted to see where this incredible connection would lead.

She wondered what her mum would say if she knew Willow was falling in love just a few days after she had arrived in her new home. She didn't really have a close relationship with her mum. After her parents divorced several years before, her mum had moved to Scotland rather than stay near her dad and Willow had moved to St Octavia, where Ruby lived. But Willow had never been close to her mum. The overriding sense she got from her mum was disappointment. '*Oh Willow*' was one of her mum's favourite phrases, followed by a sad shake of the head every time she heard what Willow had done or said. When Willow had announced she was moving to Happiness, '*Oh Willow*' must have been used three or four times in the same conversation. Willow certainly didn't need her mum's approval or most likely disapproval when it came to matters of the heart.

Ruby, however, would probably go to completely the

opposite end of the spectrum and tell Willow to stop messing around and go for it. They had known each other since going to university together and had shared a room in their halls of residence. Ruby was definitely more the throw-caution-to-the-wind type.

No, if she was going to make a decision like this, she would have to do it on her own. And what she really wanted to do and what she *should* do were probably two very different things. But when she next saw Andrew, she would simply listen to her heart and then she'd know what she should do.

~

Willow got down to her shop just before nine and the street was almost deserted. She waved at Tabitha who was opening the pub for breakfast. Maybe news hadn't spread about the Secret Society's deliveries the night before.

Just as Willow pushed open the door she saw Mary running down the street, waving at Tabitha.

'I got one, Tabby, I got one.'

'Mum, are you OK?' Tabitha asked. 'What did you get?'

'A secret gift!' Mary said excitedly as Willow watched from inside her shop.

'Really? What was it?' Tabitha asked as she put the menu board outside the door.

Willow watched Roger walk out of his cheese shop with Dorothy and his sister Liz.

'What's going on?' Roger said.

'Mary got a present too,' Tabitha said.

Willow wanted to wander over and join in the chat but she was a terrible liar and she wasn't sure she'd be able to withstand the inquisition, should any questions come her way.

She decided she would clean the windows so she could at

least listen. She quickly filled a bowl with soapy water, grabbed a cloth and stepped back outside.

Mary was showing off her new antique watch to anyone who was passing and there was quite the gathering now.

'There was a knock on the door late last night and when I went to answer it, no one was there,' she said. 'But there was this beautifully wrapped box there instead and this watch was inside.'

Willow glanced around as she started scrubbing. Dorothy looked a little put out that Mary had received a mystery gift too. Of course, if Mary had received a gift too, then Dorothy's gift was less likely to be from Joseph.

'Who do you think it's from?' Tabitha asked. She'd now been joined by her husband Connor, Julia and several other villagers Willow hadn't met yet.

'I don't know, maybe Kitty and Ken,' Mary said.

'Lord, I think they've done enough for us,' Julia said, her pink candyfloss hair styled in a beehive today, wibbling like jelly on top of her head. 'This whole village could probably be a contender for some best-looking village award by the time all the renovations and improvements have been made. I don't think they're roaming the streets late at night giving presents to us all as well.'

'Well who is it then?' Dorothy asked.

'Well you thought your gift was from Joseph. Maybe he's giving presents to everyone,' Liz said.

'It's not Joseph,' Dorothy said, protectively, as if Liz was trying to steal Joseph from her.

'Well who is it?' Connor asked, admiring the watch.

'Are you sure it's not that lovely Andrew?' Liz asked.

'I don't think it's Andrew,' Julia said, quite proudly, as if about to impart some great pearl of wisdom to exonerate him. 'I was walking Colin and Rufus past Sunrise Cottage early this morning and who should walk out of there but the man himself. His hair was all dishevelled and he hadn't shaved. He had the biggest grin on his face. I think it's safe to say he stayed the night at our young Willow's house last night, which meant he had other things to occupy himself than giving out secret gifts in the middle of the night.'

Everyone turned to stare at Willow and she found her cheeks flushing bright red. Here was the perfect alibi for both of them – but at what cost? By the way they were all looking at her with excitement in their eyes, this was probably the biggest piece of gossip the villagers had heard since the invention of sliced bread.

Oh god, what should she say? If she lied and said that he'd just popped round that morning then they would know instantly that she wasn't telling the truth and then their alibi would go straight out the window.

Fortunately, she was saved from any more embarrassment or questions by Ginny's arrival.

'What's going on?' Ginny asked the happy throng. 'Did you all get a present too?'

'Did you get one?' Dorothy asked, incredulously.

'Yes,' Ginny beamed. 'Someone left a beautiful bouquet of flowers on my doorstep. They knocked on my door and—'

'When you answered, there was no one there,' Roger said. 'Yes, we got the picture.'

Another man joined the group then. 'Are you talking about last night's activities?'

'Did you get a present too, Pete?' Liz asked.

'No, but Elsie's house was painted.'

The little crowd collectively *ooohed*.

'Oh, it's definitely Andrew then,' Liz said, knowingly.

All eyes swivelled in Willow's direction to see if she would say otherwise.

'He came to my house straight after he'd finished playing darts,' Willow said honestly. Telling the truth was far easier. 'And we spent the rest of the night together.'

Good lord, now it sounded like something far more wonderful than what had actually happened.

Everyone looked so delighted by this piece of news, it was as if they had just won the lottery. They all leaned forward eagerly to hear the next bit of gossip. Oh to hell with it, there was no going back now.

'And let me tell you, he was definitely far too *busy* with me to go out painting houses in the middle of the night.'

There were gasps and squeals of excitement and Willow wanted the ground to swallow her up. She'd just practically declared to the whole village that she and Andrew had had sex the night before.

'Well, must get on, lots of work to do.' Willow quickly scuttled into her shop and closed the door.

She sat down and let her head fall into her hands. It was safe to say that when Andrew heard that piece of gossip, their date would be well and truly off the table, and she didn't blame him at all.

~

Willow had been busy working in her shop all morning, keeping her head down, not getting involved in the gossip that continued to be bandied about outside on the street. She was so embarrassed that she'd said that about her and Andrew. Of all the things to say to preserve their alibi, why did she have to come out with that? And what would Andrew think when he heard? He seemed like a private person, he wouldn't want that kind of gossip spread around the village even if it was true, let alone when it was false.

She busied herself with the ice candles she was making. She draped the wick inside the paper cup and attached the other end to a lollipop stick which she rested on the top of the cup. She grabbed the jug of small ice cubes she had just taken from the freezer and started pouring it out into the paper cup, either side of the lollipop stick, until the cup was half filled with ice. She took the jug of melted bright yellow wax off the heat and gave it a stir.

There was a noise at the door and she looked up to see the silhouette of Andrew leaning against the door frame. The sun was blazing behind him so she couldn't see his face and whether he was angry or not.

She quickly ran over to him and wrapped her arms around him, burying her face in his chest in embarrassment. God, she needed to apologise, to explain why she did it. She realised he wasn't hugging her back. He really was pissed off.

'Well this is a lovely greeting, although I don't think my brother would be too impressed,' Andrew said, sarcastically, except it didn't actually sound like Andrew at all.

She frowned in confusion and looked up. This was a man who looked like Andrew but was definitely not. It looked like someone had tried to copy Andrew's face but not got it exactly right. It was the eyes that were so different. There was no warmth or kindness there.

She yelped in fright and stumbled back, tripping over a box of wax on the floor. She would have fallen over if the doppelganger hadn't reached out and grabbed her arm.

She stepped back out of his touch to look at him some more and suddenly what he'd said made sense.

'You're Andrew's brother, Jacob?'

'Yes, good to meet you, although I wasn't expecting a welcome as warm as that.'

'God, I'm so sorry. I thought you were Andrew. I don't normally go hugging strange men.'

'No, just kissing them and sleeping in the same bed as them.'

She frowned; she didn't like his tone. 'If you're talking about me and Andrew then that's absolutely none of your business.'

'He's my little brother, it comes with the territory,' Jacob said.

'Sticking your nose in?'

'Looking out for him. You're all he's been talking about all morning. And I wanted to come and meet the woman my brother has fallen in love with.'

Willow swallowed. 'He said he's fallen in love with me?'

'No, but the huge grin on his face speaks volumes.' He cocked his head to look at her. 'So what's your story, Willow McKay?'

He'd come here to see if she was good enough for his brother. She didn't know whether to be incensed by that or find the whole thing hilarious.

She turned her attention back to the yellow wax, gave it another stir and slowly poured it into one of the paper cups covering the ice cubes, then moved on to the next cup and did the same.

'What would you like to know?' Willow said, her eyes on the wax the whole time.

'Well, Andrew said you're not interested in a relationship after not long coming out of a crap one. Yet you've kissed him, slept in the same bed as him and, he says, he's asked you out on a date tonight and he has no idea if you're going to turn up. So what I'd like to know is, are you just playing some weird little game with my brother?'

Holy shit. Put it like that and she did sound like a complete bitch. God, she didn't want to play games with Andrew. That wasn't what this was. But in trying to decide whether it was best to avoid having a relationship or just to go for it, she was messing him around and she hated that. He was so utterly lovely and he deserved better than that. He was being so sweet and patient but she *had* kissed him and slept in the same bed as him. No wonder the poor guy was so confused. And just because she wasn't ready to have these feelings didn't mean they would go away. Working with Andrew on the Secret Society business, spending time with him, those feelings were only going to intensify. It was crazy to try to deny how she felt any more and it wasn't fair on him either.

She carefully filled another cup with wax, listening to the ice crack and hiss a little as it came in contact with the hot liquid. 'You're right. I had no intention of coming here and falling straight into a relationship. And then I met your brother with his kind eyes and his beautiful smile and his silly sense of humour. I love how easy he is to talk to and his patience and warmth. I really like your brother. And yes, I have been overly cautious because it scares me how much I like him, but it was never my intention to hurt him, that was the very last thing I wanted. Truth be told, I think I've fallen a little bit in love with Andrew Harrington and that terrifies me.'

Jacob was completely silent and she looked up at him to find he was staring at her like she was a complicated puzzle he was trying to work out.

She carried on pouring the wax into the remaining cups, wondering if he was waiting for more from her.

Jacob moved to the table and picked up the first paper cup she had filled which had probably gone hard already. He carried it over to the towel she had laid out on the other side of the table and started ripping the paper cup carefully away from the wax. 'I made these with my niece a few weeks ago, she loved doing them.'

Willow watched him. 'Poppy?'

He looked up. 'Yes, did Andrew tell you about her?'

'Yes he did. She sounds like a lovely little girl.'

A smile appeared on his face, the first one Willow had seen. 'Yes she is.'

Willow watched him remove the candle carefully, letting the water drain out onto the towel. She wasn't sure what was going on. He seemed to have completely moved on from the subject of her and Andrew already.

'You'll have to bring her here one day, she can help me make some candles.'

His smile grew. 'This place would be like heaven for her, she loves making candles.'

'Then I'd definitely like to meet her. Although I don't know any sign language so maybe you could stay and help her.'

'I could do that. Although Andrew knows sign language too and I'm sure you'd rather spend the day with him than his grumpy older brother.'

Willow smiled. 'I don't think you're half bad.'

He smiled at this, then he frowned.

'He told you Poppy was deaf?'

'Yes.'

She could see he was mulling this over.

'I know he's deaf too, if that's what you're wondering.'

His eyebrows shot up. 'That does surprise me. He doesn't tell anyone that, especially not so soon into a relationship.'

'I sort of caught him out and he explained he was deaf.'

He picked up another candle and started tearing the paper away.

'He's really sensitive about it, I wouldn't expect him to go into too much detail about it.'

She nodded. 'He told me a bit about his childhood, how your mum made him have therapy.'

'Wow, you really have got under his skin. He never discusses that. In my mum's defence she was trying to do the best for him. My aunt had a tough time growing up deaf in the sixties, there just wasn't the support that we have now. There wasn't that much support when Andrew was growing up, but there was a lot more understanding and awareness of it. My aunt didn't even learn sign language until much later on in her life as it wasn't something that was encouraged and I think Mum felt so useless in not being able to help her. Mum decided that Andrew's upbringing would be different. The whole family learned sign language so we could communicate. She was determined he would be treated the same as any other children, but sometimes I think she went too far in trying to prove to him and to everyone else that he wasn't different.'

Willow was quiet, wondering if there would be more.

He sighed. 'As we grew up, Andrew always thought he had to show that he was as good as everyone else, because my mum was always fighting to prove it. She had to fight to put him into a mainstream school because it was thought he should go to a special school that could cope with his needs, whatever they were. So he worked hard, studied long hours, made sure he always did his homework on time to prove he deserved to be there. It wasn't easy for him.'

Willow thought about this; she knew Andrew had only shared the tip of the iceberg when it came to that side of him. She wondered if she could get him to open up some more, rather than keeping it bottled up inside.

'You're not what I expected, Willow McKay. When Andrew told me all about you, well I was expecting…'

'A manipulative bitch?' Willow supplied.

'I don't know if I would go that far but I didn't exactly have high hopes. Andrew has had his fair share of crappy girlfriends and I think it's put him off anything serious. Over the last few years every girl he has been with has been very casual and I suppose it's safer that way for him. Don't fall in love, don't get hurt. He certainly hasn't been in love for a very long time. To see him floating around on cloud nine this morning, well I wanted to make sure he wasn't falling for someone crappy again.'

Willow picked up one of the other cups and started tearing the cardboard away. 'And do I meet with your approval?'

'I wouldn't go so far as to say that,' Jacob said, a mischievous smile on his lips. 'But you'll do.'

Willow laughed.

Jacob walked to the door and then turned back. 'Are you going on this date tonight?'

Willow hesitated for just a second before nodding. 'Yes I am.'

Jacob nodded. 'Good. I'll be here for a few days so I'm sure I'll hear all about it tomorrow, so keep it clean for my sake.'

'I can't promise that.'

Jacob rolled his eyes and walked away.

Willow smiled. Andrew was right, his brother was an arse, but she liked Jacob nonetheless.

She turned her attention back to the candles and then her heart leapt. Shit. She had a date that night.

CHAPTER SIXTEEN

Willow went to the pub at lunch, deciding she couldn't hide away from the villagers forever. It was nice to see that it was a bit busier today than it had been on her first day. There were several tables or large groups all talking in excited tones. She had no idea whether it was the Secret Society business that was keeping them entertained, or her non-existent sex life with Andrew, or something else entirely, but it was still good to see.

She went up to the bar and Tabitha greeted her with a smile.

'What do you recommend for lunch today?' Willow asked.

'The fish and chips are good. The fish was fresh off the boat this morning and Connor makes all his own batter.'

'That will do,' Willow said. 'And can I have a glass of lemonade too?'

Tabitha picked a glass from under the counter and half filled it with ice. 'So the mystery presents have been the talk of the village all morning. Would you happen to know anything about it?'

'Me? No,' Willow said, the lie coming that little bit more easily.

'It just seems a little convenient that the first gift appeared after you arrived here.'

'As you heard, I was with Andrew last night,' Willow said.

'Well he was here earlier and he seemed very surprised by the news that you two had slept together.'

Willow cringed. 'I never said that.'

'You implied it,' Tabitha said.

'I just said we were busy all night.'

'Doing what?'

Willow blushed.

'Aha, so you are sleeping with him?' Tabitha seemed even more excited by this than the prospect that Willow was the secret gift-giver.

'We're… getting to know each other,' Willow said.

'Ah, is that what the kids are calling it these days?'

Willow smiled to herself. Tabitha couldn't be more than ten years older than Willow. She decided to change the subject slightly. 'So if it wasn't me and Andrew that delivered the presents, as we were both *getting to know each other* all night, who is the most likely suspect?'

'Well, there's lots of ideas. Dorothy is still insisting that Joseph gave her the cake, so maybe he's trying to woo all the ladies in the village,' Tabitha said, handing over her glass of lemonade.

'Ha, maybe he is.'

'My money is still on Kitty and Ken,' Tabitha gestured to the other side of the room. Willow looked round to see the couple in question tucking into their fish and chips in one of the booths. 'What would anyone else have to gain from it?'

Willow frowned slightly. 'Why do you think it's being done for some kind of gain?'

'People don't just give presents to other people for no reason.'

'Of course they do, sometimes people do things for other people just to be nice.'

Tabitha shook her head. 'Maybe you're right but my gut says there's some other reason for this.'

Willow didn't like that. When it inevitably got out that it was her and Andrew who were giving the gifts, would the other villagers think she was doing it for some ulterior motive too?

'I'll be over there with Kitty and Ken,' Willow said, taking her drink. She walked over to their table and they looked up. 'Do you mind if I join you?'

'Not at all, dear,' Ken said, patting the seat next to him.

She slid onto the bench. 'Beryl not cooking for you today?'

'Ah, it's her day off. Besides, Connor's fish and chips are the best for miles around,' Kitty said.

'Well, if we get any visitors to the castle, if you decide to go down that path, maybe we can encourage people to go to the pub after. We could print the pub name on the back of the castle tickets, "Try the best fish and chips in the world, five percent off with this ticket", or something like that.'

Ken nodded as he chewed his fish. 'That's not a bad idea.' He looked around and lowered his voice. 'Though personally, as much as I love Connor's fish and chips, I think he could do so much more with fresh fish, different sauces, different dishes. I think he could attract more visitors to the village if he offered something a bit more than great pub grub.'

'Oh shush, the food is lovely.' Kitty waved her hands at her husband, protectively.

'It is, I'm not saying it isn't, Connor is a great cook,' Ken said. 'I just think he could up his game slightly.'

'Well, if we start to get more outside visitors maybe that's something we can gently encourage with him,' Willow said.

'Oh, I wouldn't want to interfere,' Ken said.

Willow smiled. 'I look at it more like positive suggestions or constructive feedback. And as they are renting the property off you, albeit for free, you are technically their boss.'

Ken clearly thought about this. 'Maybe you're right.'

'For now, the locals seem happy enough and we don't get too many outside visitors, and probably won't unless we give them something to come here for,' Willow said, carefully. She tapped her chin thoughtfully as if thinking about ways to bring people to the village. She didn't want to push them into opening the castle to the public – having people traipsing all over their home was not going to be everyone's idea of fun.

Kitty smiled, seeing right through Willow's attempt to be vague.

'We've been seriously thinking about your idea actually,' Ken said. 'There's a man that's coming out tomorrow to see whether it's safe or which areas we can open to the public. I've looked into getting a website designed and spoken to someone I know about marketing. I've looked into insurance too. But everything hinges on tomorrow. We have to make sure it's safe for the tourists above everything else. It might be that we need to do a few repairs here and there, or it might mean we can't open it to the public at all. *But* if the man gives us the OK, at least for parts of it, we thought we'd try to coincide the big opening of the castle with the open day of the village. There's a nearby battle re-enactors group, and we've asked them if they would come along on the day and teach the children how to be knights. We might even get a jousting group in. I mean, the castle isn't medieval, not even close, but I don't suppose the little kids will care too much about historical accuracy when they have a wooden sword and a shield in their hands.'

'I think that sounds like a wonderful idea,' Willow said, excitedly.

'Try to rein in that excitement for a bit longer,' Kitty said, practically. 'I think we've all been getting carried away with the idea but the castle is in a bad way. And although I agree with you about the children loving the ruins, we won't be able to open at all unless we're given the all-clear tomorrow.'

Willow nodded. 'OK, no excitement. I'm not really that bothered at all.'

Kitty laughed. 'You're a terrible liar. Anyway, do you know anything about these gifts that everyone has been receiving? It's quite exciting actually to think someone is doing this for all the villagers.'

Kitty and Ken were the last people she wanted to lie to, and it was their village, so maybe they should be kept apprised of what was happening inside it. Although she didn't know if she could trust them to keep the secret if she told them, and the secrecy of the gifts was key to making them a success.

However, by the looks on Kitty and Ken's faces, they'd already guessed it had something to do with her.

'I… may know something,' Willow said, quietly.

The smile on Kitty's face grew.

'We think it's a wonderful idea. Do you know if the plan is for everyone to get a gift?'

'Yes, that's the idea. I believe,' Willow quickly added.

'Well, if you think whoever is responsible might need any help with it, then let us know,' Ken said.

'I'll… pass that on, thank you,' Willow said.

Kitty finished her lunch, wiping her lips with her napkin. 'Now, more importantly, we want to hear all about you and Andrew.'

Tabitha walked over at that point with Willow's fish and chips and she deliberately hovered for a few minutes, laying out the napkins and the knife and forks then getting salt and pepper and sauce for the table. It was quite clear she was hoping to hear more gossip. Willow busied herself with eating and waited patiently for Tabitha to go away. Eventually she did, but only because she had to serve someone.

'Andrew is such a lovely boy,' Kitty gently pushed.

'He is. I really like him. I'm not sure what you've heard but we haven't… we're not… We've kissed a few times and we've got our first official date tonight. So we'll see how it goes,' Willow said, wanting to be honest with Kitty and Ken, at least about that. 'It's very early, and really I've only just met him.'

Ken nodded. 'I think in life, you can meet people who you like and you can meet people you fall in love with and sometimes, very occasionally, you meet someone who is your soulmate. It was like that for me and Kitty. We knew, from the very first moment we met, that we were going to spend the rest of our lives together. I asked her to marry me after one week and everyone thought she was crazy for saying yes. We've been together forty-six years now. I'm not saying that's going to happen for you and Andrew but don't let the time you've known him put you off. When you know, you know.'

Willow stared at him. That was very wise advice. There was no right time to fall in love, the heart decided that and there was no point in fighting it. She wasn't sure if she believed in the whole soulmate thing but it was definitely time to see where this connection between them would lead.

~

Andrew dipped his roller in the tray of paint and then spread it across the wall, smiling to himself at how much fun it had been the night before doing this with Willow. He had been exhausted, they had nearly got caught too many times, but they had been giggling and laughing the whole time about the ridiculousness of painting a house in the dark. He had been by the house earlier and they hadn't done the best of jobs, although it certainly looked better than it had before.

'Are you thinking about Willow again?' Jacob said, dipping his roller in the tray and painting his section of the wall.

Andrew grinned. 'What gives the game away?'

'You have that big stupid smile on your face again,' Jacob said. 'I haven't seen you like this about a woman in... well, forever. It's kind of a bit creepy, like my brother has been possessed by something.'

'Ah shut your face, you're just jealous.'

'I met her earlier. When I went into the village, I kind of... bumped into her.'

'You met her, why didn't you say?'

'We only chatted for a few seconds, I just forgot. She seems nice. Not my type, but nice.'

'What does "not my type" mean?' Andrew said, feeling suddenly very protective of Willow.

Jacob smiled. 'She's... soft and sweet and lovely. Definitely not my type.'

Andrew liked that description of her, Jacob had summed her up perfectly.

'Look, I know she's important to you and quite honestly I can see why,' Jacob said, in a rare moment of seriousness. 'Just... try not to fall in love with her, not yet anyway. Tread carefully.'

Andrew stared at him. 'Are you seriously trying to give me advice about matters of the heart?'

'I know. Trust me, I hear myself and it sounds ridiculous even to my own ears, but... I don't want you to get hurt.' Jacob said the last bit so quickly, Andrew wasn't sure he had even heard him correctly.

'Christ, are we going to start hugging soon? I'm not sure we're ready for that,' Andrew said.

'Let's not go that far,' Jacob muttered. 'And remind me again why I'm here helping you paint when I'm supposed to be on holiday?'

Andrew noted the change of subject and decided to let it go. Jacob could be an arse sometimes but he had always looked out for him. It seemed that habit had never gone away, despite them both being grown-ass men now. 'Because you have nothing better to do with your time.'

'I could go on long coastal walks, look for inspiration for my sculptures,' Jacob said.

Andrew laughed. 'You're not really the outdoorsy, coastal-walk sort of person. You're more the sitting-in-the pub, faffing-about-on-your-phone type.'

'Wow, you make me sound such a catch,' Jacob said, dryly.

'I'm simply saying, living in a tiny village by the sea isn't really your thing. You're a townie through and through.'

Jacob carried on painting for a moment. 'I don't know about that. This place has a certain… charm.'

'Could you really see yourself living in a place like this?' Andrew said. He wasn't sure he actually wanted his little haven taken over by his brother.

Jacob shrugged. 'I lived in London for several years and hated it. And living in Penzance now is… it's nice but it doesn't feel like home. This would be a good place to settle down and raise a family one day.'

Andrew stared at him in shock, paint dripping from his roller. 'What the hell is going on with you? You suddenly care about me getting hurt, you want to get married and have kids.

This is not the Jacob I know. You've never had a serious relationship in your life.'

'Maybe it's time that changed.'

Andrew resumed his painting. He wasn't sure if he was ready for that change, especially not on his own doorstep.

CHAPTER SEVENTEEN

Willow looked down at her black dress despondently. It had taken her over an hour to decide what to wear for her date with Andrew. She had no idea what people wore on dates any more. In fact, it had been way too long since she'd been on one. She'd never even been on a date with Garry. He had been her flatmate and it had slowly turned into something more. By that time she'd already been to the pub with him as a friend on several occasions with other friends or just the two of them. So there had never been a time when he'd actually asked her out on a date.

She had tried on multiple outfits for tonight and nothing seemed to be right. In the end she had settled for her trusty black dress, but now she was standing on Andrew's doorstep she was doubting that decision. Black wasn't her colour at all. She liked sparkles and bright patterns. Maybe she had time to go home and change. But she didn't want to be late for the date, she hadn't seen Andrew all day to confirm she was coming and she hated the thought that he would be sitting there feeling disappointed that she wasn't.

She spotted a sunshine-yellow rose growing near the front door. She quickly snapped it off the branch and threaded it into the thin braid she'd done at the side of her head. There, that was a little bit of colour at least.

The door was suddenly flung open and Andrew was standing there, dressed smartly in a pale blue shirt that was open at the collar and had the sleeves rolled up to show his strong, tanned forearms. He was smiling at her.

'You thinking of coming in or running away? I've been watching you hovering for the last five minutes.'

'Oh no, I was just thinking I'd go home and change.'

'Why? You look lovely,' Andrew said, stepping back to let her in.

'I look like I'm going to a funeral. Or an interview. Or an interview at a funeral parlour.' Willow pulled at her dress as she stepped up in front of him.

'Willow, you're beautiful,' Andrew said, softly. He stroked one hand down her cheek and kissed her.

All doubts and fears disappeared from her head instantly. She was on a date with a wonderful man. That was the only thing that mattered.

'Thank you for coming,' Andrew whispered against her lips before kissing her again.

'I'm happy to be here.' She held his face, staring into his eyes which were filled with so much warmth for her.

He took her hand and started leading her off to the kitchen. 'Come through, dinner's nearly ready.'

'Hang on a minute.'

He turned back to face her.

'I'm sorry for messing you around.'

He frowned. 'Are you going already?'

'No, I just meant, over the last few days, kissing you, putting that ridiculous six-month hold on our relationship, lying to you, kissing you again, inviting you to share a bed with me. I've been sending you some very mixed messages and I'm sorry.'

'You don't need to apologise.'

'I do. I was with Garry for four years and, even after we split up, he stayed in the flat for a while until he found somewhere else. Which was hard given… given how we broke up. After that humiliation, I just wanted a break, just some time for me. But then there was you and I quite honestly have never felt this way about anyone before. I would be crazy to walk away from what we have. I want to explore this connection with you and even if it all fizzles out to nothing after a few weeks, I don't want to regret not giving this a chance.'

He stared at her for a moment and she realised she'd gone too far with her apologies.

'I'm sorry. I haven't had a first date for a very long time. I turn up here in this hideous funeral dress and practically declare my undying love for you. I bet you're desperately trying to come up with some excuse to cancel the whole evening.'

He smiled and came back to her. Sliding his large hands round her back, he kissed her again.

'I don't do dates either, not really and not for a very long time. But I can tell you that this is shaping up to be one of the best dates I've ever been on.'

Willow frowned in confusion and her heart melted a little when Andrew kissed her frown away.

'Why is this a good date?'

His eyes were locked on hers. 'Because it's you.'

Oh god, it was crazy to feel this way about him so quickly. She leaned up and kissed him, cupping his lovely face between her hands. He ran his hands up her back and she suddenly liked this dress a whole lot more when his fingers grazed her bare skin. The dress had a deep V cut into the back which always left her feeling a little chilly but right then she was red hot. His fingers danced gently across her skin, tracing her spine all the way up to the top of her neck.

'I really do like this dress,' Andrew said against her lips.

She smiled. 'I do too.'

'Now, as much as I'd like to stand here all night and kiss you, dinner will be ruined if we don't dish it up soon and I'd hate for you to miss out on the world's best curry,' Andrew said.

'The world's best? Now that's a bold claim.'

'Well, certainly the best in Happiness.'

'I think Connor might have something to say about that. You better lead the way then and I can judge for myself,' Willow said.

Andrew took her hand and she followed him into the kitchen. The table was laid with a beautiful silver candelabra that looked like it was made entirely from forks. Three tall white candles were burning happily away in the middle of it.

'That's an interesting piece,' Willow said.

'It's one of Jacob's. That's his thing, he makes sculptures from old bits of metal. He buys forks and spoons and things like that from charity shops and makes them into the most incredible things. Although don't tell him I was singing his praises, it will go to his head.'

Willow laughed. 'I met him today.'

'Yes, he said he bumped into you.'

Willow thought about that for a moment. 'Bumped into you' made it sound so much simpler than it was. Jacob had specifically come looking for her to warn her off his brother, something he had clearly not told Andrew. But despite that, they had parted on good terms and she certainly didn't want to stir up any bad feelings between the two of them. So if Jacob hadn't mentioned the true reason for his visit then she wasn't going to either.

'Did he tell you I hugged him? I thought it was you and I threw my arms around him and hugged him before I realised it wasn't.'

'He didn't mention that,' Andrew said, as he retrieved a big dish from the oven.

'I think he found the whole thing a bit embarrassing, I know I did,' Willow said. 'Oh, talking of embarrassing, I'm so sorry for letting people assume we'd had sex last night. Everyone was talking about who had given the mystery gifts and because Elsie's house was painted they all thought it must be you. So I tried to cover for you and said we'd spent the night together and everyone just assumed that meant we'd had mad passionate sex. And to be honest, the alibi was such a good one I might have played up to it a bit.'

Andrew grinned as he dished up white fluffy rice onto two plates. 'I kind of liked it, everyone I met today was clapping me on the back as if I was some kind of stud. I've never had that reputation before. Jacob has always been the one who had women falling over themselves to go out with him. When we were teenagers, Jacob had a different girlfriend every week. I didn't even lose my virginity until I was eighteen. Besides, the villagers will find out about us sooner or later. The village is so tiny, everyone knows everyone else's business. I wouldn't be surprised if they have this place bugged. And Julia saw me leaving your house very early this morning, so word would have got around anyway. We did need an alibi. A lot of people will think it's you as it all started happening after you arrived.'

'Kitty and Ken have already guessed. And though I didn't

admit it to them, I didn't lie to them either. It didn't feel right, it is their village.'

Andrew scooped out some of the amazing-smelling curry on top of the rice. 'I was going to suggest telling them, they should know what's going on down here.'

'We'll have to induct them into the Secret Society,' Willow said.

'Only if they're prepared to learn the secret handshake.'

Willow laughed as she watched Andrew bend down to retrieve the nan breads, admiring his gorgeous bum as he did so.

'You checking out my bum Willow McKay?'

She laughed loudly. 'You caught me. Would you like any help?'

'You can open a bottle of wine, I have one chilling in the fridge.'

Willow retrieved a bottle of sparkling wine and unwound the cage around the cork. She tried to ease the cork out but it seemed to be stuck fast. She grabbed a tea towel and wrapped it round the cork and tried to wiggle it from side to side. She felt it give slightly, rising up out of the bottle, but when she tried to ease it out some more it seemed to be stuck again. She took the tea towel off so she could prise it out of the bottle. Just as she did so, the cork shot out, up in the air like a missile, and took out the light bulb with a smash, plunging them into semi-darkness, the only light coming from the flickering candles.

Andrew stood there in shock with the two plates in his hands. Fortunately, the light bulb was far enough away from him that none of the glass could have gone into the food.

'I'm so sorry. I can't even open a bottle of wine.'

'It's OK, makes the room more romantic.'

'Where's your dustpan and brush, I'll clear it up.'

'Honestly, don't worry about it,' Andrew said, putting the plates on the table.

'Please, I feel awful about it.'

'Well, we can't have you feeling awful. It's under the sink but leave it until after we've eaten.'

Willow retrieved the dustpan and brush anyway and bent to sweep it up, while Andrew poured out two glasses of wine. Luckily, the bulb seemed to have smashed into several big chunks rather than tiny smithereens and she was able to clear it all up relatively quickly.

She sat back down with Andrew who was patiently waiting for her.

'I'm really sorry.' She took her seat and Andrew sat down opposite her.

'It's just a light bulb, no big deal. Here's your wine, shall we make a toast?'

'OK.' She let out a deep breath, as she tried to refocus on their date. She rose her glass in the air. 'To us.'

He smiled. 'To... getting to know each other, to lots of wonderful kisses, to cuddling in bed and to making love under the stars.'

'That's much better than my toast,' Willow said. 'I like the sound of that very much, especially that last bit.'

'Well the beach is very secluded, no one ever goes down there because of the number of steps. I often swim naked down there. We could make love down there in broad daylight and no one would ever see us. But there's something magical about going down there at night.'

Now that was a wonderfully delicious thought. She was half tempted to suggest they go down to the beach for their *dessert*, but there was still a cautious part of her that wanted to go slow with him.

He must have read her mind because he linked hands with

her. 'There's no rush though. I'm very happy to just spend some time getting to know you.'

She smiled and decided to change the subject slightly.

'You swim naked?'

He grinned. 'Yeah. There's something very liberating about that.'

The image of him naked, his glistening wet body powering through the water, was not something she was going to be able to erase from her mind very easily. And this wasn't helping her forget the idea of making love on the beach either.

She cleared her throat and took a bite of the curry. It was wonderfully tangy, creamy, the spices dancing on her tongue.

'This is amazing,' Willow said.

'Told you, the best curry in all the lands,' Andrew said.

'So tell me, what brought you to Happiness?' Willow asked.

Andrew focussed his attention on dipping his nan bread into the sauce for a moment, clearly giving himself time to answer. He looked up and frowned.

'It's OK, you don't need to answer,' Willow said. He was clearly uncomfortable with the question.

'No, it's not that. You, erm… have a caterpillar on your forehead.'

Willow let out a little squeal as she felt around her head, found the offending critter and flicked it off. It landed with a splat in Andrew's curry.

Andrew looked down as the caterpillar struggled against the sauce and burst out laughing. He grabbed a piece of kitchen towel, carefully scooped it out and then gently wiped the curry sauce off before taking the bug to the back door and probably releasing it with a pat on the head.

Urgh, what if there were other creepy crawlies in that rose, which was where the caterpillar had evidently come from? She grabbed the rose and yanked it from her head, but the braid was wrapped around one of the thorns and it got stuck in her hair. No amount of pulling would free it, in fact she was pretty sure it was getting more tangled and knotted the more she tried to yank it out.

Andrew came back from releasing the beast and watched her struggle for a moment.

'Here let me help,' he said.

He gently tried to untangle the rose.

'God this date is turning out to be—'

'Memorable,' Andrew said, fondly. 'If we get married one day, this is the story I'll tell in my wedding speech.'

'You'll do no such thing,' Willow laughed. 'You'll tell everyone how you fell in love with my magnificence.'

'Well that too. But they also need to know the dark and murky truth. I'm sorry, I can't get this out. I think I'm going to have to cut it, it's knotted up pretty bad.'

'This is what I get for stressing too much over what I was wearing, a bloody caterpillar on my face and a massive knot in my hair.'

Andrew pulled out a pair of scissors from the drawer and carefully cut the rose out of her hair.

'There, all done.'

'Well now you have a lock of my hair, you can keep it in a box by the side of your bed,' Willow said, as Andrew sat back down.

'Creepy. Although I could use it to clone you.'

'And that isn't creepy?'

Andrew laughed.

'Sorry about throwing a caterpillar into your food.'

He shrugged and carried on eating, seemingly not bothered at all.

She watched him with a smile. 'Nothing really fazes you, does it?'

He thought about this for a moment. 'I think there are quite a few things that faze me but the big stuff, not any of this. I'm enjoying spending time with you and caterpillars and smashed light bulbs aren't going to change that.'

She smiled as she watched him. She could really fall in love with this man.

CHAPTER EIGHTEEN

As Willow lay on the sofa with Andrew kissing her, she knew she couldn't be happier. There were no longer any doubts and fears about whether she should or shouldn't be doing this, or whether this was moving too fast. She had never been so sure in her life that she was doing the right thing.

'What are you smiling about?' Andrew said, pulling back slightly to look at her.

'You. Us.' She stroked his face. 'This is...'

'I know...' His eyes were soft as he looked at her.

'And the crazy thing is, if I'd stuck to my silly rules, we wouldn't be doing this for another six months.'

'I'd have waited,' Andrew said, rolling onto his back and bringing her onto his chest. 'And I don't want to rush anything with you. We'll go as slow as you want. And if you think it's going too fast, we'll stop and we'll just go back to being friends again – well, friends who kiss. I'm not sure I could give this up.'

She smiled and rested her head on his chest as he stroked her hair.

'So what was so awful about your last relationship?' Andrew asked. 'I want to make sure we don't make the same mistakes.'

'It wasn't awful, but we didn't love each other, never did. We were flatmates and we got on well. We had the same friends, and all our friends assumed we were a couple long before we were. He was nice, good-looking and my friends couldn't understand why we weren't together. Even his friends were egging him on. I guess in the end I thought, are they all seeing something that I'm not. Before Garry, I had two boyfriends that cheated on me and I knew I could trust Garry. But you need more than that in a relationship. We had zero chemistry. Sex was nice, he was a nice kisser. I don't know. So many of my friends were desperately trying to find a man and the men they did date, well, a lot of them would turn out to be arseholes. My friends all said that I was so lucky to be going out with Garry that I started to think maybe they were right. He was nice, he used to cook for me, he always took the bins out.'

God, even to her own ears it sounded so dull.

'I started to think maybe this is what being in a relationship was like. That maybe the books and films over-romanticised everything and that as long as you got on with the man you were with, he didn't cheat or treat you badly, maybe it was better than being alone. When actually, being single for the last four years would have been far better. We just drifted along, never rowed because we simply didn't care enough to get angry or upset. We had sex once a week, always on a Saturday morning, before he'd bring me breakfast in bed. It was boring and neither of us could be bothered to do anything about it. Well, that was until I asked him to marry me.'

'What? You've just described the most mundane relationship ever, where you clearly weren't happy, and you decided marriage would fix that?'

'I don't know what I was thinking actually. I was desperate for change and I wasn't entirely sure breaking up was the answer. I guess I wanted to see if he did love me, whether we had anything worth fighting for. I think I was kind of hoping he'd say no, just so I knew it was really over.'

'And did he?'

'No, he said yes and for a few hours I got swept away with the excitement of a wedding, of wearing that dress, the champagne, the special day. I'd already picked out the bridesmaid dresses in my head. I announced it on Facebook and texted all my friends and family. All the ones that were married said it was about time, Ruby went mad at me and said I'd be a fool to marry him and I did start to panic and wonder if she was right. Next day, he told me that he'd changed his mind, that although he loved me, he wasn't in love with me and that he didn't want to spend the rest of his life with me. It was a bit of a kick in the teeth but I was relieved more than anything. Except that I then had to tell all my friends and family that the wedding was off not even twenty-four hours after it had been on. Slightly embarrassing.'

'And what was everyone's reactions?'

'"Oh no, I'm so sorry, this is so sad." I tried to tell them that actually it was a good thing but no one really believed that. They just thought I was putting on a brave face. Anyway, after we broke up, I felt like I was stepping out into the light. I vowed then that I didn't need a man to make me happy, I was just fine on my own.'

'And now?'

'Well, I still don't *need* a man to make me happy, I'm perfectly fine without one, but I'm also very very over the moon with one too,' Willow giggled, knowing she wasn't really making a lot of sense. 'I think in reality swearing off all men was a bit ridiculous. What I should have said was that I didn't want a relationship with a man unless he set my world on fire.'

Andrew chuckled. 'And I tick that box for you?'

'Oh god yes.'

'Well that's good to know.'

'What about you, why were you not interested in a relationship? You said you'd had some crappy ones.'

Andrew sighed and he didn't speak for a while. 'I think my biggest issue with being deaf is people's reactions to it. It's something different to what they know and some are scared of it.'

Willow frowned. 'Really?'

'I had one girlfriend, thankfully we hadn't been going out that long, maybe a month, she was horrified when she found out I was deaf, saying I should have told her because she could catch it.'

'I don't know whether to laugh or cry at that,' Willow said.

'You can laugh, I did.'

'People can't seriously be that stupid,' she said.

'Don't forget we live in a world where thousands of people still believe the earth is flat. Trust me, there are lots of stupid people in the world.'

'That's depressing.'

'I know. I've had quite a few similar issues over the years. I think a lot of hearing people don't understand what it really means to be deaf.'

Willow thought about this for a moment. She could never really comprehend what it was like to be deaf. She could stick earplugs in and walk around like that all day but that was very different from living with that for the whole of her life. And dealing with people's prejudices and opinions on it would be something else entirely too. She'd never had to cope with being labelled as different. Would this lack of understanding on her part eventually be a sticking point for them as it had been for his other girlfriends?

'When one girlfriend found out I was deaf, she said things like, "But you look just like a normal person, you talk like a normal person," without realising how offensive that was. It was a big novelty to her, she'd ask me to lip-read what people were saying, she'd ask me to teach her sign language, but only the swear words. It didn't last long.'

'I think I'd rather know how to sign cake or biscuit or the kinds of things that we are most likely to say in bed when you've taken your hearing aids out. Things like "Kiss me" or "Make love to me."'

He grinned. 'Trust me, you're never going to have to ask for those things.'

She smiled and then reached up and stroked his cheek. From what Jacob had said, Andrew had his heart broken in the past. And though these women he'd dated didn't sound like they were the best, it didn't seem like any of them had broken his heart.

'Did you love any of these women?' she asked carefully.

He nodded. 'None of the ones I've mentioned, but there was one woman, Sophie. I loved her. Looking back, I'm not sure why. She had this perfect image of what her life was going to be. I don't think she was over the moon when she found out I was deaf, it didn't fit in with her perfect ideals, and I thought for a while we might break up but we didn't. We were together for about two years and I thought we were happy. We talked about marriage, kids, buying a house together. When my niece, Poppy, was born, it was clear from very early on that she was deaf. And Sophie just couldn't get her head around that. She asked me if we were to have children would our kids be deaf too. I told her that statistically more deaf children were born to hearing parents than to deaf parents but yes there was a chance, especially as there seemed to be a gene in our family. She said she didn't want to have deaf children and we broke up. I was… heartbroken.'

'Oh Andrew, that's horrible.'

'I think that was the first time in my life that I didn't feel good enough. It was even worse that I was made to feel that way by someone I loved.'

'No, don't ever think like that. That was more her issue than it ever was yours.'

'I know, I do realise that. And in many ways I do feel like we'd had a lucky break.'

'What kind of person doesn't love their child unconditionally regardless of whether they can hear, see, talk, read, write, or even walk as well as their peers? I understand having a child who is deaf or blind could be a challenge, but having children *is* a challenge. Those sleepless nights, potty training, settling a child at night, is the car seat fitted properly, are they getting enough milk, is the bath water hot or cool enough for them. As they get older the responsibility of teaching them right from wrong, teaching them about different cultures and beliefs, how many sweets is too many, how much screen time is too much, their friends, their boyfriends and girlfriends, are they happy, are they safe. All of that is bloody hard work. But I would love my child, completely and utterly, regardless of any condition they might have.'

Andrew smiled, giving her a kiss on the forehead. 'I think that is the right answer.'

'Please, please don't take that on your shoulders. You are an incredible man and any woman would be very lucky to raise their child with you,' Willow said.

He stared at her for a moment and then bent his head and kissed her. But this was very different to their other kisses. This was sweeter, more tender, filled with love.

He pulled back slightly. 'I think I better take you home now.'

'Oh.' Willow felt a little disappointed that their date had come to an end already but a quick glance at the clock showed that it was approaching midnight.

'Not because I want to, but because I really want to take you upstairs and spend the rest of the night making love to you—'

Willow opened her mouth to speak but Andrew quickly carried on talking.

'And before you say that's a good idea, I'm going to remind you that we're supposed to be taking this slow.'

'I'm not sure I agreed to that.'

Andrew groaned and stood up. 'Come on, let's get you home.'

He pulled his boots on as Willow tied up her own shoes and then he quickly bundled her out of the house.

Willow giggled at his haste. She couldn't help feeling a little disappointed that his plan for the rest of the night wasn't going to happen but there was a large part of her that was quite relieved. A few days earlier she hadn't even wanted a relationship; it made sense to take things slow, at least for now. She'd never slept with a man on a first date before and, although it felt like she'd known Andrew for a lifetime already, she still thought it was probably a good idea for her to go home.

He linked hands with her as he switched on his torch. The path wound away from them, disappearing into the trees, the bushes either side of them casting odd shadows in the torchlight.

'You can give Jacob a call now and tell him the coast is clear,' Willow said.

'He's staying in the pub actually, they have a few rooms there. There really isn't enough room in my house for the two of us. There really isn't enough room in this village for the two of us, but he's thinking of moving here.'

'Really? Is that so he can keep an eye on you?'

'I hope not. But he can be a bit overprotective at times, he's been like it all his life. He says he wants somewhere quiet to settle down and raise a family. Those are honestly words I never thought I'd hear coming out of his mouth. I mean, it'll be nice that I get to see him a bit more often but I kind of wish his settling down wasn't happening right on my doorstep.'

'Do Lottie and Poppy live nearby?'

'Not too far away so I guess it'll be nice for Jacob to be closer to them too. He adores Poppy. We all do.'

'I can't wait to meet her.'

He looked down at her. 'She will love you. You pretty much have her dream job.'

Willow smiled. 'It's my dream job too.'

There was a screech of an owl nearby which made her jump, though Andrew didn't seem bothered by it at all.

'Did you always want to be a candlemaker when you were growing up?'

'Oh no, I changed my mind weekly about what I wanted to be. A vet, a dancer, an astronaut, a scientist – which I thought would involve dealing with lots of potions – an actor, an archaeologist… I've always been very crafty though, and when I got older I knew I wanted to run my own business. I took business studies at university which is where I met Ruby. Making candles was something I enjoyed and it just sort of turned into my job while I was looking for something practical to do with my degree. What about you, what did you want to be when you grew up?'

'Batman.'

Willow laughed. 'Now that's a great goal.'

'I think the anonymity appealed, no one knowing who he was. Everyone knew who I was at school. I could have had my own persona, "Deaf Kid". Except I'm not sure what my superpowers would have been. I was pretty crap at most things.'

Willow frowned. His childhood would have been very different from hers in many ways.

'What was it like growing up with that label over your head?'

He was silent for the longest time. 'It was fine really. All kids have issues growing up, don't they? Anyway, I heard there was a lot of interest in the mystery gifts today.'

He had changed the subject again. Every time he started opening up to her, he slammed that door closed before she could see inside. She didn't know whether to push it, but if he wasn't comfortable talking to her about that, what could she do? It did hurt a little that he didn't want to share that with her. If they were going to be in a proper relationship they needed to be able to talk to each other about the good, the bad and the ugly. Still, it was very early days for them, maybe that level of trust would come later. She decided to let it pass for now.

'Oh yes, the whole village was talking about it, who it could be, who is going to be next, why they are doing it. Everyone is very excited.'

'So who's next on our list of Secret Society gifts?' Andrew asked.

'Well, a lot of people think it's Kitty and Ken giving the presents so I wondered if we should give them one so people would stop thinking it was them.'

Andrew clearly thought about this for a moment. 'If people think it's them, let them carry on thinking it for a while. It takes the attention off us.'

'That's a good point. What about Joseph? That way, if Dorothy still thinks the cake is from him, Joseph getting a gift will make it clear that it wasn't before she embarrasses herself with her declarations of undying love for him.'

'Good idea,' Andrew said. 'Any ideas what you're going to give him? I can't remember much from the night we compiled that list, other than that was the first time we kissed and that was pretty bloody memorable.'

'Mmm, most heated first kiss ever,' Willow said. 'I do have an idea for him, but I think it's something that will need to be made.'

She looked up at him with hopeful puppy dog eyes.

Andrew laughed. 'Don't look at me like that. I have a whole village to renovate.'

'How is that coming along?' Willow asked as they walked past Joseph's house and into the trees.

'It is actually coming along a lot faster than I thought it would. Jack and his team are doing a great job and, although there will still be a lot of work that will need to be done at the end of August, there are now twelve houses that are painted on the outside and four that are ready to move in.'

'That's good.'

'Yeah, I'd done a few before they started and they've been working on the ones that didn't need too much doing to them. Some of the houses that need a lot more work we are just going to paint the outside so it at least it looks good for when we have the open day. If a lot of people suddenly want to move in, we will have to stagger their arrival so all the houses are finished in time. I'm not sure how much interest we will have but hopefully we'll get a few more people who want to move here.'

'We just need to make sure the open day goes off with a bang. Oh, talking of which, I was thinking—'

'Here we go again,' Andrew teased. 'More bright ideas.'

'Hey!' Willow laughed. 'You love my ideas.'

'Go on then, tell me your idea.'

'I think we need to have stuff going on in the village that will encourage people to stay for most of the day. The longer people are here, the more likely it is they will fall in love with the place. If the castle opens, that could take care of entertainment during the day, but I wonder if we should do something on the night, a firework display perhaps, maybe over the castle or at the end of the village overlooking the sea. We could do a lantern parade where everyone will carry a lantern down to the cliff tops, show everyone who visits this thriving community spirit. I could make the lanterns very easily. We could make it a big family day.'

'It's not a bad idea,' Andrew said. 'Although firework displays can be very expensive. I have a friend, Leo, who runs his own firework display company. He owes me a massive favour actually, maybe he'd do it on the cheap. I'll speak to Kitty and Ken about it tomorrow and then I'll give Leo a call. Anyway, back to Joseph. This thing you want making for him, is it big, small, metal, wood?'

'I'm not sure,' Willow said. 'He loves gardening and I saw him on his knees the other day, doing some weeding, and it was a real struggle for him to get up. I kind of thought we could make him some kind of knee cushion that had a frame around the outside so he could use that to help him get back up.'

'That sounds like it should be made from metal. If it's wood, it could rot if it gets wet and muddy. Jacob would be your best bet for something like that. He's a whizz with any kind of metalwork. I'll ask him tomorrow.'

'OK.'

They cleared the trees and Sunrise Cottage gleamed in the moonlight that sparkled over the sea.

'If Joseph's gift is going to take a few days, I'll have to think of someone else to give the gift to tomorrow,' Willow said as they walked up the path to her house. 'Maybe even a few people like we did last night.'

'Why don't we meet for lunch tomorrow, in the pub and you can tell me what the plan is for tomorrow night,' Andrew said.

'OK. Is lunch going to be our second date?'

Andrew grinned. 'Yes, why not.'

'OK, I'll see you tomorrow.' Willow leaned up and kissed him and he wrapped his arms around her back, holding her tight.

He pulled back. 'Goodnight Willow McKay. Sweet dreams.'

She smiled. 'Oh, I'm sure they will be.'

He gave her a sweet kiss on the nose and then walked off into the darkness.

She watched him go and then went inside. Her dreams were going to be very nice indeed that night.

CHAPTER NINETEEN

Andrew woke up with a huge smile on his face. The night before had been wonderful and it was safe to say he was completely smitten with Willow McKay. He was going to see her again at lunch and he couldn't wait.

Also his friend Morgan was coming today with the screens for the backdrop to cover the houses at the entrance to the village. She'd be here for a few days painting the screens and erecting them.

He got up and quickly washed and dressed. He made himself some toast, wrapped it in a piece of kitchen towel and left the house.

He automatically looked down towards Sunrise Cottage in the hope he might see Willow, and was surprised to see Jacob walking up from that direction.

'I'm guessing I'm not who you were hoping to see,' his brother said.

'Your ugly mug versus Willow's lovely face, hmm tough choice,' Andrew said, as Jacob fell in at his side and they started walking towards the village.

'I've just seen her,' Jacob gestured over his shoulder.

'You did?' Andrew looked back towards Willow's house but sadly couldn't spot her.

'She was sitting on the bench in her front garden with a big happy grin on her face. I didn't talk to her, I didn't want to interrupt whatever daydream she was in. She didn't see me anyway. I'm sure she was too busy thinking about you.'

Andrew smiled at that, although the smile fell off his face when Jacob swiped a slice of toast from the paper towel.

'Hey!'

'I'm hungry.'

'Then go to the pub for breakfast.'

'Oh I'll do that too, this is my starter.' Jacob took a big bite.

Andrew rolled his eyes. 'What were you doing down there anyway?'

'I was just out for a walk.'

'Really?' Andrew asked, dryly.

Jacob laughed. 'Genuinely. I thought I'd explore a little. It's a nice place.'

'Don't start that again. This place is too small for you and your ego.'

'My ego would fit in perfectly here, thank you very much.' Jacob munched on his toast. 'OK, maybe the walk had the added bonus of seeing if you spent the night at Willow's house again.'

'Ha. I knew it. Actually I was the perfect gentleman.'

Jacob snorted. 'You mean she turned you down.'

'No, we're taking things slow.'

'And I bet that's killing you.'

'Like you wouldn't believe,' Andrew said and his brother laughed.

Jacob finished his slice of toast and then went to take another but Andrew held it out of reach.

Jacob shrugged. 'So it went well, last night?'

'Yes, it was wonderful. I know you're going to give me hell over this but I don't care. I honestly think I'm going to marry this girl.'

'Christ!' Jacob muttered. 'I told you not to fall in love with her.'

'I haven't. Yet.'

'I thought you were taking it slow.'

'We are but... she's pretty bloody special.'

'You've been on one date; do you know how ridiculous you sound?' Jacob said.

Andrew couldn't help smiling as he nodded. 'I'm well aware how it sounds, there's just something different about this girl. We even talked about having children last night.'

Jacob groaned and Andrew laughed, having only added that little titbit to wind his brother up.

'In the general sense, not "Let's make a baby now." Just... I told her about Sophie and she was horrified.'

'Well, most decent human beings would be. I never knew what you saw in Sophie anyway. In fact, most of your girlfriends have been questionable. Remember that one, the over-enunciator?'

'Tammy, yes that did get annoying,' Andrew said as he remembered how she would carefully pronounce each word for him and overexaggerate all of her lip movements to help with his lip-reading. He did try to explain that with his hearing aids in it was unnecessary, and that when he had them out her excessive lip movements actually made it a lot harder, but she didn't seem to comprehend.

'And the one that shared her bed with hundreds of cuddly toys,' Jacob said.

Andrew laughed as he remembered Beatrice. The cuddly toys had gotten everywhere which always made having sex a bit of a challenge. She had been a sweet girl but not someone he could hold a decent conversation with.

'And Saskia, she was into all that kinky stuff, wasn't she?' Jacob said.

'Trust you to remember *her* name.'

'Why did you let her go?'

'If I'm honest, she was more than a little scary,' Andrew said.

'You couldn't handle her, you mean?'

'Something like that.'

They approached the crossroads with the pub and he smiled to see Willow's shop window filled with all manner of candles in different colours. She certainly brightened up the place.

'And then there was Morgan,' Jacob said, scathingly.

'Morgan was never my girlfriend. Not really.'

He'd known Morgan for a long time. Her brother was deaf and Andrew had been friends with him. Morgan sort of came with the package. They'd kind of grown up together and then lost touch over the years. They'd bumped into each other a couple of years before and somehow ended up in bed together. Neither of them had wanted something serious, although they had slept together four or five times over the next few months. But it had never been more than just sex between two friends. He hadn't seen her for nearly a year now and last he'd heard she had been dating a pilot. She had seemed delighted to hear from him when he'd called her a few days before to ask her to do the screens. He just hoped she wasn't coming here in the hope of rekindling their *friendly* arrangement.

'And why do you say her name like that?' Andrew asked.

'I always felt she used sign language around hearing people

because she loved being in this secret club they weren't privy to.'

Andrew didn't agree with that. Sign language had always been such a big part of Morgan's life. With her mum and her brother being deaf, sign language had been Morgan's first language so she would often lean towards that in a conversation.

'Morgan doesn't switch to sign language to annoy or exclude hearing people. She constantly flicks between the two in the same way that a person who is raised in a bilingual family might switch between the two languages in a conversation,' Andrew said, feeling the need to defend her.

'No, I get that,' Jacob said. 'But I always got the feeling that wasn't what it was for her. She had a bit of a nasty side sometimes. I never liked how she would use sign language to take the piss out of hearing people, knowing full well they wouldn't understand what she was saying. There was something a bit cowardly about that. And I've never liked bullies.'

Andrew suppressed a smile. Jacob had been like a bodyguard when they were at school, standing up for him against anyone who would dare say anything derogatory about him. Jacob had landed himself in detention many times after getting into fights. He wasn't the only person his brother had stuck up for, it was safe to say he was champion of the underdog. But Jacob was right, Andrew hadn't really liked that side of Morgan either. After being on the wrong side of insults and jokes growing up, he didn't like to see other people being exposed to that, whether they knew it or not. But whenever Andrew stopped her from doing it she always insisted she was only joking. And Morgan did have a lot of good qualities; she raised a lot of money for charity, spent a lot of time fighting for more accessibility for deaf people, and Poppy adored her.

Morgan was great with his niece, she always had a lot of time for her.

'She's coming here today actually, so try to be nice,' Andrew said.

'Whoa, why is she coming here?'

'She's doing a big backdrop for the entrance to the village.'

'Your old girlfriend and your new girlfriend together, is that wise?'

'Morgan was never my girlfriend. She dated other people while she occasionally came to me for no-strings-attached sex. We're friends. I'm sure it's going to be fine.'

Jacob didn't look so sure. 'Does Willow know?'

'Yes. Well, no. She knows Morgan is coming here to do the backdrop. She doesn't know that we…'

'Were friends with benefits?' Jacob helpfully supplied.

'Yes, if you like. She doesn't need a detailed rundown of all the women I've been with just like I don't need to know a potted history of all her ex-boyfriends.'

'OK, you keep telling yourself that. Personally I think if you want this to work with Willow then you need to be honest with her.'

'OK, OK. I'll tell her. Jeez, I just hadn't given it any thought. It's been a year since I've seen Morgan, she's not exactly been uppermost in my thoughts.'

'Just tell Willow. I'm going for breakfast, I'll catch you later.'

Andrew nodded and watched Jacob disappear inside the pub. Well that was a conversation he wasn't really looking forward to. Suddenly his day looked a little bit duller.

Willow was busy working in her shop when Liz and Roger came in.

'Hello,' Willow said in surprise. Apart from Andrew and Jacob, they were the first visitors in her shop. Although something told her they weren't there to buy anything. 'Are you here to buy or...'

'There were more presents delivered last night,' Liz said, almost bursting at the seams with the exciting news.

'What?' Willow asked in confusion.

'Kitty came down to the village this morning to buy some milk and she said she had been left a parcel last night, a beautiful hand-knitted pink scarf. Kitty loves scarfs and this one had lovely little flowers all over it,' Liz said.

'Well who left that for her?' Willow asked. Were there secret members of the Secret Society that she didn't know about? Seeing that her and Andrew were the only members, that was unlikely.

'Well that's the question, isn't it?' Roger said, bouncing on his toes and fixing Willow with a look.

'It wasn't me,' Willow laughed and for the first time she could be completely honest about it.

'Julia did say she saw you and Andrew eating in his kitchen when she walked Colin and Rufus past the back of his house early evening,' Liz said.

Willow made a mental note to close the curtains whenever they were in Andrew's house or hers from now on, especially at night time.

'Well there you go, we were busy. It was actually our first date,' Willow said, trying to deflect the conversation away from their possible guilt.

'Talk about shutting the stable door after the horse has bolted,' Roger muttered.

'I'm sorry?' Willow said.

'Well, you've already slept with him, seems a bit late now to have a first date.'

'We haven't slept together. We've been—'

'*Getting to know each other*,' Liz and Roger echoed.

'Umm yes, exactly. Anyway, it wasn't us, we were together all night and then Andrew walked me home.'

'Aha, so you could have delivered the scarf then. Or Andrew could have done it after he dropped you off,' Liz said.

'It was very late and we were both very tired. Andrew has been so busy helping with the renovation of the village. I doubt he went home after dropping me off, hand-knitted a scarf and then walked all the way up to the castle to deliver it.'

Liz and Roger looked at each other as if they might actually believe her.

'There was another present too,' Roger said.

'Oh my god, who?' This was getting more and more bizarre.

'Joseph. He found a book about roses this morning on his doorstep. It was gift-wrapped.'

At least Willow had a good idea who that might be from. Dorothy had probably left it there to thank him for the cake she was so convinced he had left. But did that mean that she had left the present for Kitty too?

'Well this is getting a bit mysterious,' Willow said. She certainly needed to talk with Andrew about it over lunch. What did this mean for her list if Joseph and Kitty had already received a present? 'Maybe it's the fairies.'

'Hmm, we've got our eye on you, young lady,' Roger said, which sounded a bit too stern considering her only crime was to give presents to people.

Willow smiled. 'I'll keep that in mind and if I see the fairies, shall I give them a message?'

'Yes, tell them we don't like it,' Liz said.

'Aw Liz, I bet the fairies will give you a present too, I'm sure they will make sure everyone gets one,' Willow said.

Liz snorted her disapproval and left the shop. Roger watched her go and then turned back to Willow with a glint of excitement in his eyes.

'Chocolates, she loves chocolate,' Roger said. 'Just in case you are in contact with the fairies. Or tea. Liz loves flavoured tea. She has hundreds of different flavours in our kitchen. I gave her some cheese-flavoured tea once, she wasn't so keen on that but most flavours she loves.'

Willow grinned. 'I'll be sure to pass that along… if I see them. And is there anything in particular that I should tell the fairies that you would like? No guarantees of course.'

'Ah no, I'm fine. A calendar with half-naked men or that Chris Hemsworth, or a half-naked Chris Hemsworth. Something like that would go down a treat.' He winked at her and left the shop.

She smiled. Well this was getting interesting.

CHAPTER TWENTY

Andrew leaned against the door frame of Willow's shop as he watched her engrossed with her work. She looked like she was doing a very weird version of KerPlunk with this latest candle, sticking kebab sticks into a large paper cup at different angles so their ends came out the other side.

He approached her from behind and slid his hands round her waist, placing a little kiss on her neck. She immediately turned round and wrapped her arms around his neck, kissing him deeply. He gathered her close as the kiss continued. God, he could keep kissing this woman all day.

'Hello,' she whispered against his lips as she pulled back slightly.

'Well that's the nicest greeting I've had in a very long time,' Andrew said.

'Let me just finish this and I'm all yours,' Willow said, turning round in his arms to face her candle. His hands, which had been at her hips, were now resting on her bum. He didn't move them away and she didn't seem bothered by it either. In fact as he stroked his thumbs down her bum, she gave a little wiggle against him that drove all sense and any coherent thought from his mind.

He cleared his throat and tried to focus on something else instead.

'What are you doing?' he asked.

'It's a bit of an experiment really. I kind of wanted a Swiss cheese effect with these holes all the way through the candle. Once it's hard, I'll take the sticks out and the holes should still be intact. If it works, I'll try thicker sticks to make the hole bigger. The only problem I have is the wax might seep out of the holes in the cup so I'm going to use this melted wax which has been cooling for a while and I'll pour a little bit into the cup first to try to seal the holes around the sticks.'

His hands were still on her bum and he was having trouble concentrating on anything she was saying. He decided to step away so he could listen to her properly. She flashed him a smile.

He watched as she poured a bit of the wax into the cup and rotated the cup in her hands so the wax sloshed around its sides. Once she was happy, she poured the rest of the wax inside and filled the cup to the top.

'There, that should do it. We'll see how it turns out later,' Willow said, turning back to him. 'Now I'm all yours.'

'Well, would you like to accompany me to lunch?' Andrew said, offering out his arm.

'I'd be delighted. Are you taking me some place grand?' Willow said, locking the door behind her and linking her arm through his as they left the shop.

'Yes, the finest eating establishment in the whole of the village.'

Willow giggled. 'Oh, I have some interesting news. There were two more presents delivered last night.'

'What?'

'I know, that was pretty much my reaction. Have you been sharing that secret handshake with other people?'

He laughed. 'No, I promise, you're the only one I'm… shaking hands with.'

She grinned up at him. 'Glad to hear it.'

'So go on then, spill. Who got the gifts?'

'Kitty got a scarf and Joseph got a book about roses.'

'Well, that is interesting.'

'That's what I thought.'

'People who have received the gifts are trying to pay back the people who they think gave the presents to them,' Andrew said.

'Yeah, maybe. Or, they are paying it forward: "I've received a nice gift, I want someone else to have a nice gift too."'

'Yeah, it could be that.'

'Although personally I think Joseph's gift was from Dorothy,' Willow said.

He nodded. 'I was thinking that.'

'Great minds.'

He pushed open the door of the pub which was a lot busier than normal. There was a steady hum of happy noise as people sat and talked. Andrew and Willow walked up to the bar where both Tabitha and Connor were busy serving.

'What's going on?' Andrew asked Connor.

'I don't know, but it's been like this ever since those gifts have started to appear. They all want to come here and catch up on the latest news surrounding the gifts. Of course the two of you getting together has also added to the excitement. So for god's sake, don't break up,' Connor said.

'We'll try not to,' Willow said, looking up at Andrew with a smile.

Andrew gave her a kiss on the forehead and to his surprise there was a little cheer of appreciation from behind him. He looked around to see that almost the whole pub was watching them. Small communities were not all they were cracked up to be.

'What do you have on the menu today?' Andrew asked.

'We have lasagne.'

'That sounds great.'

They ordered their drinks and took them over to a small booth.

Willow looked around to see if anyone was listening to them, but they were all too busy with their own conversations to bother with them any more.

'So what do we do about Joseph and Kitty now?' Willow asked quietly. 'Do we go ahead and give them a present anyway, which will mean they get two presents, when everyone else will get one? Or do we cross them off the list now they have received a gift, regardless that it wasn't from the Secret Society?'

Andrew thought about this carefully. It didn't seem right that some people in the village didn't get a present from the Secret Society, but they had at least received a present, even if it wasn't from them. 'I think, for now at least, we cross them off the list. It will look suspicious if they get two, like you said, and lots of people haven't even had one yet.'

Willow nodded. 'OK. So who should we do next?'

Andrew looked around. 'How about Tabitha and Connor?'

'Excellent idea. And I have just the thing for Connor too.'

'Oh yes?'

Willow leaned across the table. 'Ken was saying the other day that he wished that Connor was a bit more adventurous with his cooking, especially with his fish. I have a huge fish cookery book my brother bought for me when I was on a bit of a fish health kick a while back. I never made any of the dishes, it pretty much sat untouched on the shelf in my kitchen for the last few years, but I brought it with me as it was from Luke and it seemed wrong to throw it out. Now I think it would be much more appreciated by someone else.'

'Great idea,' Andrew said, taking a sip from his drink. He watched her pull the list out from her pocket and flatten it on the table.

'What should we give Tabitha?' she asked.

'What did we put down on the list?'

Willow pulled a face. 'I think hers was one of the ones we filled in towards the end of the night. We put chocolates, but that's a bit lame.'

That *was* a bit rubbish. 'The Secret Society can do better than that.'

'Well, you know her better than I do. What kind of things does she like?' Willow asked.

'Cliff Richard.'

'Really?'

'She loves him,' Andrew said.

'Yeah, I can't see us getting Sir Cliff to come down here for a pint,' Willow said.

'No.' Andrew thought about this for a moment. 'But there's a young lad who lives in the next town. He does a tribute act of Cliff Richard. Apparently he's really good. Looks like him too, in his younger years. He used to do all the local pub gigs over the last few years. I think he's stopped lately because he's at university, but he did a gig a few weeks ago for charity. Maybe we could convince him to come here and do a small set in return for free fish and chips.'

Willow broke into a smile. 'That's a great idea.'

'OK, let me see if I can make a few phone calls, see if he's willing and what his availability is like.'

Tabitha came over then with their food. She didn't linger though, they were a bit too busy for that, which was nice to see. Their hard work was already starting to pay off in terms of getting the community to socialise more and that filled Andrew with a warm buzz of encouragement.

'A live act would also be great business for this place too. And if it does well maybe Tabitha and Connor might be persuaded to do it more often.'

Andrew nodded as he tucked into his food.

'Have you seen Kitty and Ken today?' Willow asked, waving her fork around. A bit of lasagne flew off and landed on his plate. 'Oh god, sorry.'

Andrew pierced the errant piece of pasta with his fork and ate it. She giggled. She had the most wonderful-sounding laugh.

'No I haven't, why?' he said, bypassing her faux pas.

'Ah, I'm desperate to know what the surveyors think of the castle. They're coming today to see if it's safe to open up to the public. But I don't want to go up there and ask, it would be too pushy.'

'They know you're pushy, I don't think there's any point pretending you're not.'

Willow laughed in mock outrage. 'I'm not pushy.'

He cocked his head. 'What would you call it?'

She smiled as she chewed on a piece of garlic bread, clearly thinking it over. 'Passionate.'

He laughed. 'OK, I'll give you that. And I have to say, I do love your passion.'

He watched her carry on eating, smiling to herself.

He stared at her. This really wasn't like any date he'd ever been on before, this was two people who got on really well, just chatting as if they'd known each other for several years. There was this ease between them that he'd never had with any of his previous girlfriends. There was no need to try to impress the other because it seemed both of them were already sold.

She looked back up at him. 'I've just realised we've spent the whole time talking about the gifts and the castle, we haven't talked about anything… dateish.'

'What counts as dateish topics?' Andrew said.

She grinned. 'I don't know, what was the name of your first pet? Who was your favourite teacher? That kind of stuff.'

'It kind of feels like we've bypassed all of that. But in the interest of keeping this dateish, first pet was a rabbit called Muffin, favourite teacher was Mrs Gillespie.'

'Why was she your favourite?' Willow asked.

Andrew didn't want to tell her that Mrs Gillespie understood what it meant to be deaf more than any other teacher, that she always discreetly sat him at the front so he could lip-read more easily, made sure she was always facing him when she spoke to the class, used visual aids wherever possible and gave him handouts at the end of each lesson to go over what had been taught. He had found it hard to concentrate in class, his hearing aids picking up a lot of background noise, but for some reason her class was quieter, which made listening so much easier. He didn't want Willow to know any of this. He didn't want to appear less in her eyes.

He shrugged. 'She gave me sweets.'

For a second he saw a flash of hurt in her eyes. She knew he was lying.

'My favourite teacher was Mr Ray,' Willow said after a while. 'He loved drama and always had us dressing up to play different historical characters.'

She was going to let him off the hook. She knew he didn't want to talk about it and she was just going to let it go. He felt a bit bad but mostly he just felt relief that he wasn't going to have to talk about that side of his life with her. Well, not now anyway.

She looked up at him and he leaned over the table and kissed her briefly on the lips, something that was met with a resounding cheer from the other villagers. He didn't even care.

'What was that for?' Willow asked.

'Just because, I really like you.'

'Well I really like you too but you know you're just stoking the fire here,' she gestured to their little impromptu fan club and he shrugged.

'They'll get used to it soon enough.'

'I suppose it is a bit surprising for them. We are moving quite quickly.'

He frowned slightly. 'Are you having doubts?'

'No, god no. This thing between us, it feels so right and maybe we don't need to follow proper conventions. We need to do what feels right for us and to hell with anyone else. Did you know Ken proposed to Kitty after only a week?'

He cleared his throat. Was that how Willow saw their relationship? If so, that was suddenly moving a lot quicker than he imagined.

Willow laughed. 'I'm not expecting a proposal from you. Hell, if you did propose now, I honestly don't know what I'd say but I don't think I'd be booking the church just yet. My point is, I'm very happy with how things are going right now, we don't need to speed things up but I certainly don't want to slow down either. In fact, I would love it if you came for dinner tonight. If three dates in twenty-four hours is not too fast for you.'

He smiled. 'That would be perfect.'

'And we can deliver Connor's gift after dinner and maybe

we can give a gift to someone else if there's something easy we can do tonight.'

'Good idea.'

'I've ordered a few things online for a few of the other presents, so that might take a few days to arrive,' Willow said.

'Well keep checking at the post office, you won't get post delivered to your door here. Julia keeps a good log of everything that comes in so it won't take her long to check if you have any deliveries.'

'Yes she showed me the log, she was quite proud of it.'

Andrew smiled; Julia was definitely proud of her post office.

Willow finished her lunch and stacked her plate on Andrew's already empty one. Then she took his hand.

'Thank you for lunch, but I better be getting back, I have a number of orders I need to package up and take to the post office this afternoon. Come round about seven?'

Ah crap. The date was over and he hadn't mentioned Morgan. Although was a date really the right time to bring up an ex in the first place? But he knew he needed to tell her. He wanted to be nothing but honest with Willow.

'Listen, I wanted to talk to you about something for a moment. I mean it's not something, I mean it was. Well I wouldn't exactly call it something even back then,' Andrew started.

Willow looked at him in confusion. 'Are you going to spit it out or shall we play charades and I can guess it?'

He smiled, slightly. He watched her across the table, this funny, brilliant, dazzling woman. He was enjoying himself way too much with her to want to throw a spanner in the works so early on. His semi-relationship with Morgan was in his past and there was no reason to bring it up now. To draw attention to what he'd had with Morgan would make it seem like her coming to the village was a much bigger deal than it was. She was here to do a job, there wasn't anything more to it than that, so why did he need to upset Willow with something that was nothing?

'Do you know what, it can keep.'

'Are you sure?' Willow said.

'It's not important.' And it really wasn't.

'OK, I'll see you later.' She stood up, kissed him on the cheek and then left him alone.

He watched her go but he couldn't help the uneasy feeling in his gut that he'd just made a terrible mistake.

He pushed that thought away. Jacob was making him doubt himself, a man who had never had a serious relationship. Why would Andrew take advice from him?

It was going to be absolutely fine, he was sure of it.

CHAPTER TWENTY-ONE

Andrew rode his quad bike up towards the entrance to the village so he could meet Morgan. He'd left it to the last possible minute to go up there. He certainly didn't want to be waiting for her to arrive as that would seem like he was keen to see her, but he also didn't want to keep her waiting as that would be rude. Morgan was his friend and, although he had no intention of picking up where they had left off, he didn't want to be horrible about it.

He shook his head as he drove along. She probably didn't have any interest in him in that way at all. After all, she had stopped calling him, she had been dating a pilot for several months. It was rather arrogant of him to assume she was coming here to have sex with him. Just because she had sounded delighted that he had called, it didn't mean anything. It could simply be because she was looking forward to catching up with an old friend. Although it had been a long time since they'd had that kind of relationship.

He left the main high street and manoeuvred round the

slopes leading up to the castle. He could see Morgan's little van parked outside the four houses, where she was unloading her stuff, and he pulled up behind it.

She straightened from unpacking a large bag and her face broke into a huge smile when she saw him.

He climbed off the quad bike but the next thing she ran towards him, slamming into him and wrapping him in a huge hug.

He hesitated. He wouldn't think twice about hugging any of his female friends but this somehow felt different because Morgan *was* different to his friends. He had history with her. He had seen her naked, made her scream in the throes of passion. There was a reason why men and women couldn't really stay friends after they'd slept together because it was awkward as hell. Although was it only awkward because he was with Willow now? Would it be this awkward if he wasn't thinking of her the whole time? But, not wanting to hurt Morgan's feelings, he gave her the quickest of hugs in return.

'Andrew, how are you?' Morgan stepped back to look at him, her hands still on his arms.

'I'm good, really good actually. I live here now and I love it. I have a lovely girlfriend, Willow, I'm sure you'll meet her later, but yes things are great.'

He cringed a little at mentioning Willow. He knew it would seem as if he had deliberately shoehorned her into the conversation to make his status clear, which in many ways he had.

'A girlfriend?' Morgan seemed surprised at this, although she didn't relinquish her hold on him. 'I thought you didn't really do girlfriends.'

'Willow's different. I *really* like her.'

'So it's serious?'

'Yes it is.'

'And she knows that you're…' she trailed off but signed the word '*deaf*'. She knew he didn't really like to tell anyone.

'Yes she does,' Andrew said.

'Wow, that is serious.'

'Ah, things change. I suppose we grow up. I'm thirty-two next month. Maybe it's time I settle down.' He refrained from saying that when you met the right person then it was worth giving a proper relationship a chance, because he didn't want it to sound like Morgan wasn't the right person for him. He didn't want to be mean. 'You must feel the same, you're with that pilot bloke, aren't you? What's his name, Jim is it?'

'Yes. We broke up. He was sleeping with one of the air hostesses.' She shrugged as if she didn't care but he could tell that she did. 'I guess not all men are ready to grow up.'

'I'm sorry to hear that,' Andrew said.

She suddenly switched to sign language but he was used to the change with her.

'Oh, I'm not the settling-down type,' Morgan signed, trying to pull off an air of nonchalance she didn't quite achieve. *'I'm much more the having-fun, no-strings-attached type. That way no one can get hurt. You used to be so much fun, Andrew.'* She ran her hand down his chest in a gesture that didn't need any sign language to understand. 'Are you still fun?'

Andrew stepped back slightly out of her reach. Her question was crystal clear and he wanted to be as direct with his answer so he didn't reply with sign language as he normally would.

'I'm very very happy with Willow. This is something serious for me and I can't imagine being with anyone else but her. So if your question is am I still up for no-strings-attached sex then I'm afraid my answer is no.'

Morgan stared at him for a moment. 'Jesus Andrew, I was only joking. I'm happy for you, really I am.'

She moved back to the van and grabbed a few more things and he could tell that he'd hurt her by his rejection. He felt horrible. But he knew she hadn't been joking either.

He cleared his throat and decided to move on to safer subjects. 'So, what are your thoughts about the screens?'

She paused for a moment as if she hadn't been expecting the sudden change of direction in conversation, then she turned back to face him. 'Well I'm going to use four separate screens, I simply can't get screens that big to cover all four of the houses. But the picture will run across the screens so it will be continuous. I've ordered screens with a hilly background and I'll paint the picture on top of that.'

He nodded. 'How can I help?'

'Well I need to peg the screens open next to each other on the ground so I can ensure the continuity of the paintings and drawings across all four of them.'

'OK, I can help with that.'

'I'm only going to draw the castle and characters today and then I'll start painting each screen separately tomorrow. Fortunately the weather is lovely and warm so I can leave the paint to dry in the late afternoons, early evenings, before putting the screens away overnight. The whole thing will take me a few days but we're not in any great rush, are we?'

'Not really. But the open day is in twelve days so it needs to be finished and erected by then.'

'That's no problem. It shouldn't take me longer than a week.'

'That's great,' Andrew said, but inwardly cursed that she would be here that long. This whole thing was uncomfortable and he didn't know what Willow was going to make of it either.

~

Willow closed the shop door and locked it. She glanced down the high street towards where she knew Andrew was working, but there was no sign of him.

She looked up the high street and saw Kitty coming towards her. She waved and headed over to meet her.

'I hear you got a present last night,' Willow said.

'Yes, a beautiful scarf, thank you.'

'Ah, I can't even take credit for that. It seems there really are mystery gift-givers in the village.'

Kitty looked confused. 'So who was it?'

'I have no idea,' Willow said. 'Maybe it was the fairies.'

Kitty laughed. 'Anyway, enough of that for now. I came down as soon as we heard. The surveyors have approved the castle to be opened to the public. Two of the towers are out of action – well we knew that one of them certainly would be, and in actual fact we need to block off part of the gardens immediately surrounding that tower – but other than that we are free to let people in.'

'Oh my god, that's great news,' Willow said. 'I really think this will help the village.'

'There's loads to do, paperwork and websites and advertising, but we might just be ready for the open day.'

'Well I'm not sure what use I will be on that side of things but whatever I can do to help, just let me know.'

'Thank you. I better go, I feel like we have a mountain to climb, but I just wanted to let you know as all this was your idea,' Kitty said.

'I hope it makes a difference, I really do.'

Willow waved Kitty off and then did a little excited bounce on the spot. This would make such an impact on the village in a good way. She decided she would go and find Andrew and tell him the good news.

She moved off down the road, heading in the direction of where all the work was taking place. She saw Jacob coming towards her and she waved to say hello.

'Have you seen Andrew?'

'He said he was going for a swim before your hot date tonight.'

Willow smiled and then a thought occurred to her. Andrew said he swam naked.

'Thanks Jacob. I think a swim sounds a lovely idea.'

'I bet it does,' Jacob grinned and sauntered off to the pub.

Willow made her way down through the village until the houses fell away and she was left with only fields and the old ruins. It was a gloriously warm summer's day and the sea was a gorgeous turquoise green as it sparkled in the sunlight.

She reached the top of the steps to the beach and quickly went down them, although there were a lot more steps than she'd thought. The beach was completely deserted, beautiful golden sands stretching right around the cove. It seemed such a waste that no one from the village came down here.

She spotted Andrew out in the sea straight away. He wasn't too far from the shore but, as she had hoped, he was completely naked. She could see his strong arms powering through the waves, the water glistening off his back and his bum, the occasional glimpse of that spectacular tattoo. For a few minutes she just stood and watched him; it was a dazzling sight.

She noticed his pile of clothes and walked over to them, wondering whether she should wait there for him to come out or take off her clothes and go out and join him.

Suddenly she had an idea. She had sworn revenge on him

for making her curtsey to Kitty and Ken and this seemed like the perfect opportunity.

She started picking up his clothes and then hesitated for a second. He wouldn't be swimming with his hearing aids in and she didn't want to take them away from him. They would probably be in his clothes somewhere. Unless they were in his boots. She grabbed the boots and put her hands inside. Sure enough, she found a handkerchief inside one with the hearing aids wrapped up carefully inside. Putting them back inside the boot, she scooped up the rest of his clothes and his towel and quickly ran back to the steps.

'Oi!' Andrew yelled as he started wading out the water.

She gave him a little wave and ran as fast as she could up the stairs. Sadly she wasn't that fit and reached the top panting and heaving. She stopped for a few seconds to catch her breath before moving off towards her cottage, not running – she was too worn out for that – but walking quickly.

She turned round to see if Andrew was in hot pursuit and saw him reach the top of the steps and start chasing after her. Finding a new lease of life, she broke into a run and raced back to the cottage, giggling so hard she could hardly catch her breath.

She got back to the house and shoved his clothes in a cupboard, knowing it wouldn't be long before he arrived to claim them back.

She couldn't stop giggling as she imagined him dashing stark naked along the cliff tops wearing only his boots. He was going to be furious.

It only took a few moments before he was bursting into her lounge in all his magnificent naked glory. It was clear he had been running as his chest was heaving slightly and he was still wet from his swim, little water droplets pouring down his chest.

'You took my clothes,' Andrew said, incredulously.

'Consider it payback for the curtsey debacle.'

He arched an eyebrow in amusement. 'Oh I see. You want to play that game?'

'I think we're even. There is no need for you to get me back for this.'

'You think one little curtsey is equal to making me walk naked along the cliff path?'

'I left you your boots. I'm not completely heartless.'

He clearly thought about this for a moment as he caught his breath and she used the moment to enjoy the view some more. He really was spectacular… in every way.

'See something you like?'

'Oh yes, very much,' Willow said.

'I think you better give me my clothes back.'

'Or what?' Willow said, unable to keep the smug smirk from her face.

'Or… I'll take all of yours.'

It was a nothing comment, a threat plucked straight from the air. But the thought of him stripping her out of her clothes was suddenly all she could think of. And clearly he was suddenly thinking of that too as all amusement faded from his eyes.

Right then, there wasn't a single fear or doubt that this next step for them wasn't the right thing to do.

She swallowed and stepped up to him, feeling bold. 'I'm not going to give your clothes back.'

He stared at her, not moving, not saying a word. He was barely even breathing.

'So you better take my clothes,' Willow said, raising her arms in the air so he could take her dress off more easily.

His fingers twitched at his side and then he stepped forward and pulled at the hem of her dress. Sliding it slowly upwards and over her head, he let the dress slide to the floor.

He stared down at her standing in just her bra and knickers. 'You did say you'd take *all* of them,' Willow said.

'I'm working on it,' he muttered.

His hands moved around her back, gently stroking up her spine until he reached the clip of her bra. He slowly unhooked it and then slid the straps down her arms, until her bra landed neatly on top of her dress. He ran his fingers down her sides until they reached the waistband of her knickers. She quickly toed off her sandals as he started sliding her knickers down her legs, kneeling down on the floor to help her out of them. He stood back up, tossing her knickers onto her small pile of clothes.

'I think you better take your boots off too,' Willow said and Andrew practically kicked them across the room. 'What are you going to do now you have all my clothes?'

He cleared his throat. 'Well my first thought was to run away with them, but now I'm having other ideas.'

'Want to show me what those ideas look like?'

He hesitated for the longest moment and she wondered if he was going to talk himself out of it.

'Or I could show you my ideas,' Willow said, placing a gentle kiss on his chest and then another on his tattoo.

'I think our ideas are very similar,' Andrew said.

He cupped her face and kissed her hard. Her heart exploded in her chest, this desperate need for him bubbling through her.

He hauled her close to him and she could feel he wanted this as much as she did. Without taking his lips off hers, he bent and scooped her up into his arms. She giggled against his lips as the kiss continued and he carried her upstairs.

He laid her down on the bed and he was right there over

her, kissing her, stroking, touching everywhere. He tore his mouth from hers to kiss her throat, her chest, before kissing her breast, making her shout out a whole load of noises she had never heard herself use before. His mouth dipped lower, trailing his tongue across her stomach and then even lower still until he was kissing right at the top of her thighs. She ran her fingers through his hair as every coherent thought went straight out of her brain. This man knew exactly what he was doing. That wonderful tingling sensation spread out through her whole body before she was screaming and shouting and writhing with the most glorious orgasm she'd ever had.

He moved back over her body, pinning her to the mattress with his weight as he kissed her again.

'Please tell me you have a condom,' he said.

She smiled. 'I do have condoms. Lots of them in fact.'

'Thank god for being prepared,' Andrew said.

'They're in the bedside drawer. I would get them myself, but I seem to be trapped under this big, beautiful man.'

He grinned and leaned over to grab one. He gave her a brief kiss on the lips before sitting back on his knees to put it on. She sat up too, kneeling up on all fours, leaning over to kiss him as he dealt with the condom. He kissed her, running his hands down her back. Then suddenly he hauled her on top of him so she was sitting on his lap, her legs wrapped around his back. With his hands tight on her hips, he pushed inside of her.

'Oh god Andrew.' Willow let her head fall back as he kissed her throat, moving inside her harder, deeper, holding her tight against him with his large hands around her back.

He kissed her breast, taking her nipple into his mouth, and she clung onto his shoulders, feeling the strength in his back.

That feeling was building in her already and she looked back at him, lifting his chin so she could kiss him again.

This man, this wonderful, kind, glorious man, it was ridiculous to have these feelings for him so soon. She wanted to tell him, to shout it out, but she wouldn't do that. She pulled back slightly so he might see what was in her heart as she fell over the edge, clinging to him. His eyes were locked on hers as he watched her fall completely and utterly in love with him. Did he know? Did he feel it too? But before she could catch her breath, he kissed her hard, gasping against her lips, holding her tight as he lost all control too.

CHAPTER TWENTY-TWO

Andrew stared at the ceiling as the pink glow of the sunset danced across the waves. Willow was lying snuggled up against his side, peppering soft kisses across his chest. They had dozed a little and kissed a lot. But they hadn't really spoken since they'd made love. Quite honestly he had no idea what to say to her and now it was getting a little awkward.

Because what do you say to someone you've fallen in love with? Should he tell her? But that felt way too soon. They were supposed to be taking it slow and, although they had broken that rule by jumping into bed with each other, to suddenly declare his love for her felt like he'd be smashing that rule into smithereens.

But then not telling her felt like a lie. It was as if the next words out of his mouth would be deceitful somehow if he didn't tell her the truth.

He honestly hadn't expected this. Yes he'd really bloody liked Willow and he'd told Jacob that he might even marry her one day. That day had felt very far away but now…

He hadn't been in love with anyone for many years. Every woman he'd been with he'd kept it casual, something fun. And while he knew that being involved with Willow was always going to be something much more than that, he hadn't expected to fall so hard so quickly.

No, this was lust, pure and simple. No one falls in love during sex. Sure he was very fond of her, she made him smile a lot and he cared about her deeply, and he was definitely attracted to her, but it wasn't love. He simply wasn't ready for that yet.

She stroked a hand down his stomach and then pressed a gentle kiss right over his heart.

Christ, he was in trouble.

She looked up at him, her eyes so filled with tenderness and affection, and the words nearly fell from his mouth right then and there.

He ran his hand through her hair, stroked his thumb down her cheek.

'Are you OK?' Willow asked.

He nodded, swallowing down the lump in his throat.

'You're very quiet.'

'I'm just… that was… I didn't expect… I've never felt…' He trailed off because he couldn't find the right words to even begin to describe what was going on in his head, to explain what had just happened for him.

She smiled as if she understood but he didn't think she did. Not really.

She kissed his heart again and then slid her hand lower. As it slipped beneath the sheet that was covering his hips, his body responded to her touch instantly. God, he needed her again.

She looked back up at him with that beautiful mischievous smile. 'Want to do it again?'

He quickly rolled her, pinning her to the mattress and she let out a little shriek of surprise.

'Hell yes,' he said, kissing her hard.

This was easy, he could do this. Amazing, uncomplicated sex. He ignored the little voice at the back of his head that told him it was way more than that.

She gasped against his lips as his hand moved between her legs. She clung to him as she let out a groan of pure ecstasy. He kissed her again, capturing it on his lips.

He leaned over and grabbed a condom, he slid it on and moved inside her, barely taking his lips from hers for a second. Passion and need for her drove him beyond insanity. This was lust, that's all it was. He moved against her faster and harder, desire sending him close to the edge.

It was her gentle touch that made him pause, a caress over his shoulders, a hand sliding up round the back of his neck and cupping his head. He pulled back slightly to look at her and it was her expression that floored him: trust, happiness, this complete blissful serenity like this was where she belonged and amongst all of that was this look of complete adoration.

He started moving against her slower, gentler, taking his time. She wrapped her arms and legs around him, holding him close, and the whole time he just watched her, their eyes locked together. He felt the change in her body, heard the hitch in her breath as he drove her closer and she reached up and held his face.

And just before she tumbled over the edge, he heard her whisper, 'I think I'm falling for you Andrew Harrington.'

Then she was shouting out all manner of words and noises that didn't seem remotely recognisable but it was those first words that made him lose control, kissing her hard as he trembled in her arms. He collapsed down on top of her, his heart thundering against his chest.

Christ, she was falling in love with him and, even worse than that, he knew he was falling in love with her too – if he hadn't already fallen. He could deny it all he wanted but this was so much more than lust.

~

Willow looked across the table at Andrew and smiled. She had relented and given him his clothes back. Well, some of them. Well, his tight black boxer shorts. Everything else was still in the cupboard. There was not a finer sight in the world than Andrew Harrington sitting across from her wearing next to nothing as he finished his very late dinner or in reality a very early breakfast.

Willow would have been more than content to spend the rest of the night in her bed with this wonderful man but their rumbling stomachs had driven them to go in search of food, even if the planned meal of chilli con carne had gone out of the window. They had settled instead for a chicken sandwich and a bowl of chips which Andrew seemed equally happy with.

They still hadn't spoken a great deal, other than to discuss food options. She frowned as she ate the last chip from her plate. Was he regretting what had happened? She didn't believe that. Not after the way he had looked at her while they'd been making love.

But something had changed between them. She just wasn't sure what.

'So are we just doing Connor's present tonight?' Andrew said, carrying on as normal as if they hadn't just spent the last few hours having the best sex of her life.

'Yes, I think so. We need to have a think about some of the others and come up with some ideas. Right now, I'm a little bit too exhausted to have to think about that list too much. I kind of want to just climb back into bed again.'

He flashed her a mischievous grin.

'To sleep,' Willow laughed. 'God, I've created a monster. No more sex for you.'

He smirked. 'That seems a bit harsh. You seemed to be enjoying yourself.'

'I absolutely enjoyed myself. I'm not saying no sex ever, but no more sex until… tomorrow morning.'

He looked outside at the twilight sky of the dawn. The sun hadn't risen yet but it wouldn't be long before it arrived.

'I can wait that long,' Andrew said, with a grin.

She shook her head. 'You're an animal.'

He smiled, then leaned over and took her hand, circling his thumb around her palm in soft sweeps. It was such a gentle gesture, he was barely touching her, but it did things inside her that made her breath hitch. He must have realised what he was doing because his smile grew.

'So no regrets?' he said.

'No, definitely not,' Willow said, without hesitation.

'Good.'

'Do you have any regrets? You've been fairly quiet since we…' she gestured to upstairs.

He copied the gesture with a smirk. 'Since we?'

'Since we… had sex,' Willow said.

'Since we made love, you mean,' Andrew said.

Her heart filled with love for him because he was right, *having sex* just didn't seem to cover what had happened between them.

'Look, I know you didn't come here looking for a relationship but this thing between us…' he shook his head as if he didn't quite believe it. 'I have never had a relationship that has felt so completely and utterly right. I don't regret it for one second. Tonight was incredible and I just wasn't expecting that.'

She smiled with relief. 'I thought so too.'

She wasn't sure what was going on here but she really liked it. Maybe it was moving too fast, maybe she was a fool for letting herself fall for him so soon, but she really wanted to see where this was going to go.

'Come on, we should go and deliver Connor's present before the village wakes up,' Willow said, changing the subject because with the way he was looking at her right then, she wanted to take him straight back to bed. 'And then maybe we can squeeze in a few more hours' sleep before morning.'

'OK, sounds good. Just one little problem.'

'What's that?'

'I'm going to need my clothes.'

~

The sun was merely a whisper on the hazy pink horizon when they left Sunrise Cottage to deliver Connor's present. It was ridiculously early and not even the birds had woken up but it was light enough for them to see.

Andrew slipped his hand into Willow's as they walked up the track towards the village. She looked up at him and smiled. There was this peace between them now, like they both knew they were unbreakable. Maybe it was too early to think stuff like that, but he meant what he'd said earlier: this felt so right.

'My friend Ruby is coming tomorrow,' Willow said. 'Well, later on today.'

'Ah wonderful, we can tell her we took her advice.'

Willow laughed.

'Where is she staying?' he asked.

'At the pub. She can keep Jacob company.' She paused. 'I'd really like her to meet you.'

'I'd love to meet her. I'll be a bit busy during the day but we could all do dinner tomorrow night in the pub. I have arranged for the Cliff Richard man to come so that will be entertainment for us all.'

'Ah, that will be brilliant. Ruby will love that and hopefully Tabitha will too. And thank you for wanting to meet her. She's important to me and so are you, so…'

'It will be my pleasure,' Andrew said.

'And I'd like to meet your friends too. Morgan, for instance, I must pop along and meet her.'

'Ah, Morgan isn't really a friend…' Andrew trailed off because that felt mean. Morgan was a nice girl and they had been friends in the past when they had been much younger, before it had become more than friendly. Even the day before, after her offer of sex had been turned down, they had worked alongside each other for a few hours to get the screens ready. And actually it had been easy between them, as if that moment had never happened. 'I mean, we haven't seen each other for so long now that we've kind of drifted apart. Of course she's still my friend but I wouldn't say we were close any more.'

'Oh, I see.'

'But you'll meet Leo at the open day, he's agreed to do the fireworks for us in the evening.'

'Oh, that's going to be fantastic, such a great celebration of our open day. And it'll be great to meet Leo too,' Willow said.

'He'll be bringing his wife and son along. Well, technically his stepson… well actually it's a bit more complicated than that, but yes he'll be bringing his family with him so you can meet Isla too.'

'I look forward to it.'

They arrived at the pub and Andrew checked up and down the high street to make sure there was no one around. He gave Willow the nod and she took the gift-wrapped book for Connor from her bag and left it on the doorstep.

'Come on, let's go,' Willow said. 'Before anyone sees us.'

They were making their way back down the lane when they saw Mary come out from a little alleyway that led from the main part of the village. Andrew grabbed Willow and they ducked behind a large bush to watch her. What was she doing out this time of the morning? Over the last few months he'd gotten to know the villagers pretty well, and they were mostly creatures of habit. Julia was a night owl, walking her Colin and Rufus around the village at very odd times of the night, but Mary stayed up late watching TV and was rarely seen out and about before nine in the morning.

She was carrying some kind of large box or tin as she made her way up the lane towards them.

'What's she doing?' Willow whispered.

'I'm not sure,' Andrew said.

They watched her walk up the little path to Eileen's house, look around to make sure no one was watching and then leave the tin on the doorstep, before hurrying back the way she had come and disappearing up the alleyway again.

Willow looked up at Andrew with excitement. 'She just left a mystery gift. Do you think she had anything to do with Kitty and Joseph's presents last night?'

'I don't know, but shall we go and see what she left?' Andrew said, more curious about that than anything else.

Willow looked around and then nodded. 'But let's be quick.'

They quickly moved over to Eileen's doorstep, giving another look over their shoulders, and then Andrew carefully lifted the lid. It was a cake tin and inside was the most amazing-smelling apple pie.

Willow smiled at him, clearly bubbling over with excitement.

He carefully placed the lid back on and they hurried off back down the lane towards Willow's cottage.

The sun was well and truly up now, this glittering golden orb in the cloudless sky blanketing the sea with ribbons of fire.

They walked into the lounge and Willow closed the door behind them and then turned to face him.

'I love this, I love that the villagers have taken our lead and are now leaving each other gifts as well,' she said.

'I do too, we've inadvertently created something amazing,' Andrew said, then gathered her in his arms. 'This is all you, you know, this was your idea. You've given something wonderful to the village.'

She smiled and he kissed her and then the kiss quickly developed into something more.

'No more sex,' Willow said, pulling his t-shirt over his head.

'But it's morning,' Andrew said, not really feeling the conviction of her words as she was already busily undressing him.

She smiled. 'OK, fair point.'

He lifted her and carried her to the sofa where they fell in a tangle of kisses and arms and legs and discarded clothes. They didn't move from there for a very long time after that.

CHAPTER TWENTY-THREE

Willow made her way up to the village entrance the next morning with a huge smile on her face. Everything seemed so completely perfect at the moment, nothing was going to ruin her mood today. She had spent the entire night with Andrew, kissing, cuddling, making love, sleeping in each other's arms. It was safe to say she was completely smitten by him.

She couldn't wait to see Ruby today and tell her all about him. Ruby had stayed in a hotel a few hours away the night before, halfway between St Octavia and Happiness, but she had phoned Willow not long before to say she was only half hour away now. It hadn't been that long since Willow had seen her but she couldn't wait to catch up with her again. She was up to speed with everything she needed to do in the shop so she could take the day off and spend it with Ruby. The sun was out so Willow thought they could spend a few hours down on the beach.

As she approached the village entrance Willow spotted a

woman on her hands and knees as she painted a large screen just in front of the four old houses. This must be Morgan.

She hurried over to say hello to Andrew's friend.

Although the screen was still in the initial stages of being completed, she could see how brilliant it was going to be when it was finished.

'This looks amazing,' Willow said and Morgan looked round and smiled.

'Thanks, it will be. It's not there yet, but thank you.'

Morgan turned back to her work but Willow wanted to introduce herself properly. 'I'm Willow.'

'Oh, Andrew's girlfriend,' Morgan said.

'Yes.'

Morgan stood up, wiping her hands down her denim shorts. 'It's lovely to meet you.'

'I wanted to come and say hello,' Willow said. 'I know you and Andrew are friends.'

'Oh, you don't need to worry about me and Andrew.'

'Sorry?' Willow was confused.

'It's fine, I get it.' Morgan smiled as she waved her hand dismissively.

'No, I'm not—'

'We go way back,' Morgan interrupted her. 'We were friends growing up. I think for him, I was always someone he could talk to about being deaf because I understood. My brother is deaf too. I know how hard it was for Andrew sometimes and I was the only one who didn't treat him differently. I think you're naturally drawn to someone who understands the significant things in your life, that's why work colleagues always end up together. Andrew has always had a bit of a soft spot for me, I get him like no one else can.'

Willow found herself chewing on her lip. She hadn't been worried about Andrew and Morgan before but she certainly was now. It sounded like Morgan was staking a claim on him, which was odd. They were just friends, weren't they?

'Andrew's talked a lot about you, he says it's something serious?' Morgan went on.

'You sound surprised.'

'No, I mean... a little,' Morgan laughed. 'He doesn't really do serious relationships.'

'Yeah, I know he was hurt in the past,' Willow said.

'He was? I mean, yes he was. I'm surprised he told you about... *that*,' Morgan said.

'Well... yes, we've told each other everything,' Willow said.

'Oh, he just doesn't really talk about that... Wait, are we talking about the same thing here?' Morgan said.

'I don't know, I was talking about... Sophie.'

'Oh that,' Morgan waved her hands dismissively. 'I thought you meant the other thing.'

'What other thing?' Willow asked.

'Oh, nothing, I probably shouldn't say. Andrew should probably tell you about the time he really had his heart broken.'

Willow frowned. Why hadn't Andrew told her that when he'd told her about Sophie?

'So things are going well between you?' Morgan asked.

Willow smiled slightly to herself. Things were going very well between them for two people who had only known each other for around a week. 'Yes they are. I don't think either of us were looking for a relationship but when we met we just sort of clicked.'

Morgan nodded. 'I've always thought Andrew would make a great boyfriend, he has all those wonderful qualities you would look for in a husband. That's if he can stay with one woman longer than a few weeks, he has a very small attention span when it comes to women, he gets bored easily. But I'm sure that's not the case for you two. How long have you been together?'

'Umm, about a week.'

'A week?!' Morgan was incredulous. 'From the way he was talking I thought you two had been together for a lifetime. Ah, you're still in that lovely honeymoon period where you both think the other person is completely perfect. Soon enough you'll start to get annoyed about him leaving his boots everywhere or that he never takes the rubbish out.'

Willow cleared her throat uncomfortably. 'I'm sure there will be things we both do that will piss the other person off but I suppose as long as the good outweighs the bad that's all that matters.'

'Oh yes, totally. No one ends a relationship over smelly socks and bad breath.'

'Andrew doesn't have bad breath,' Willow said.

'Oh, I didn't mean Andrew.'

Willow was mortified. Did Morgan mean she had bad breath?

'I didn't mean you either,' Morgan quickly said. 'I was just talking generally, you know. That's not why people break up. There are much more serious reasons to break up with someone. Why am I talking about breaking up? You two are clearly head over heels for each other.'

'Right,' Willow said. This whole conversation was making her feel just a little uneasy.

'Why would you break up with him over boots or socks when he is that amazing in bed, who would ever walk away from that?' Morgan nudged her with a wink. 'I mean, I have never had multiple orgasms with anyone else, but Andrew… that man has a gift for them.'

Willow's heart sank. 'You and Andrew used to be a thing?'

'Yes. Oh god!' Morgan's hands went to her mouth. 'You

didn't know. I'm so sorry. I just assumed he would have told you, as you've told each other everything.'

Willow wondered why Andrew hadn't told her.

'It was nothing, just a casual fling,' Morgan went on. 'I mean, it didn't last longer than six months, nine months tops, so it wasn't anything serious.'

Willow stared at her. Nine months sounded pretty bloody serious to her.

'It was just sex really,' Morgan tried to rectify the situation but only succeeded in making it worse. 'I guess you could say we're friends with benefits.'

And why the hell was Morgan using the present tense?

Willow swallowed. 'You mean you were?'

'Yes, yes, that's what I meant,' Morgan quickly reassured her. 'I'm making a right balls-up of this. Andrew really likes you, please don't pay any attention to my inane ramblings.'

Willow had no idea what to say. Knowing Andrew had kissed Morgan, touched her where he had touched Willow, whispered things in Morgan's ear as they made love made her insanely jealous. Which was ridiculous, Andrew was thirty-one. Of course he had a history, they both did. But why hadn't he told her that Morgan was one of his exes?

Fortunately Willow was saved from having to think of something to say by the arrival of Ruby's custard-yellow Mini and Ruby tooting cheerfully on the horn as she spotted Willow.

'That's my friend, she's here to stay for a few days so, umm... I'll guess I'll see you later.'

'Yes, look forward to it,' Morgan said, smiling before returning her attention to her painting.

Willow moved away from her to greet Ruby, a million thoughts swirling through her mind. She tried to push them all away to concentrate on her friend.

Ruby scrambled out of the car and threw herself at Willow, wrapping her in a big hug. Willow felt the lump in her throat as she held her friend tight.

'I've missed you,' Willow said.

'You daft lump, it's only been a week,' Ruby said.

'I know, but I've got so much to tell you.'

Not least that she had stupidly fallen for someone who she probably didn't know at all.

'Well, let's get all this stuff stowed at the pub and then you can tell me all about it,' Ruby said.

'This Morgan sounds like a complete bitch if you ask me,' Ruby said after Willow had told her everything about her and Andrew and her conversation with Morgan.

Willow wiggled her toes in the sand as she stared out over the gold-crested waves.

'I don't think that Morgan was saying those things to be mean. We were just chatting about Andrew and of course it would come up in conversation that she used to date him or whatever kind of arrangement they had that involved him giving her multiple orgasms.'

Willow swallowed the bitter taste in her mouth.

'You're right, it would come up in conversation that they dated, but not that she had amazing sex with him. Who would say that to their ex's current partner? Morgan was deliberately trying to stir up trouble,' Ruby said.

Willow knew Ruby was right. That was not a normal conversation topic.

'And what about all that other stuff about you having bad breath?' Ruby said, slathering sun cream onto her shoulders.

'She didn't say *I* had bad breath.'

'You were just chatting about people in general having bad breath?' Ruby said, sceptically.

'Yes,' Willow said, although now she was starting to doubt herself. She cupped her hand in front of her mouth and breathed into it.

'Oh my god, you do not have bad breath,' Ruby said. 'Believe me, I would tell you if you had.'

Willow sighed. Why was she suddenly doubting everything?

'And what about that stuff about Andrew having a short attention span when it comes to women? It was almost like she was telling you this thing between you two wouldn't last.'

Ruby was right, about everything. The whole conversation had made Willow feel uneasy. She had wanted so much to like Andrew's friend that she had tried not to see what was staring her in the face. Morgan was a bitch and for reasons Willow wasn't entirely sure about, Morgan wanted to cause trouble between her and Andrew.

But Willow wasn't only angry at Morgan.

'I just feel a bit let down by Andrew more than anything else,' Willow said. 'Why did he invite his ex here in the first place? I wouldn't want to invite any of my exes to come and do a job for me. That's a little weird, right?'

Ruby shrugged. 'I suppose it depends how well you get on with them.'

'Is it wrong that I don't want him to get on well with someone he gave multiple orgasms to?'

'I think there would be something wrong with you if you weren't bothered by that.'

'I think the thing that bothers me the most is that he didn't tell me that he and Morgan had history. I mean, it's not something you can forget.'

'No, quite.'

'So did he deliberately hide that from me? And what is the big thing that broke his heart if it wasn't Sophie? We lay together and talked about our life and he told me how devastated he was over what happened with Sophie but Morgan said there was something far bigger than that, so why didn't he tell me about it? I mean, I don't need to know all of his romantic history, just like he doesn't know all of mine, but if it was as significant as Morgan says, do you not think he would have mentioned it to me then?'

'I think you need to talk to Andrew about all of this,' Ruby said.

'I'm such an idiot Rubes, I've fallen for this man after one week and I really don't know him at all.'

'You're not an idiot, you're just… rose-tinted. There's nothing wrong with seeing or hoping for the good in this world.'

'But then there's always the disappointment when you're wrong.'

'I think I'd much rather hope for the good than expect the bad, it's a much nicer way to live your life,' Ruby said.

Willow sat up and took a swig from her water bottle. She decided to change the subject as this whole conversation was making her a little bit fed up.

'Tell me something about St Octavia to cheer me up,' Willow said.

'Why, are you missing us?'

Willow thought about that for a moment as she lay back down. She had only moved there after she had left university and her parents had split up and moved to opposite ends of the country, but for a while St Octavia had been her home. Although beyond Ruby she hadn't made any lasting connections. Many of her friends had been Garry's friends and, when they broke up, their mutual friends hadn't really known how to act around her. She didn't really miss any of them.

'Not really. I know I rushed into this decision to move here, but I don't regret it. Regardless of what happens with Andrew, I do love it here.'

Ruby paused for the longest time before she spoke. 'There is something. I didn't know whether to tell you or not.'

'Just tell me.'

'St Octavia is such a small town and I know you're still Facebook friends with a lot of people there, and many of them would take great pleasure in telling you all the gory details. And I kind of wanted you to hear it from me first.'

'God Ruby, what is it?'

'Do you want the bullet points or the unabridged version?'

'I guess the unabridged.'

'Garry's engaged.'

'What?' It was safe to say Willow hadn't been expecting that.

'To that new girl who moved into the town six months ago.'

'Imogen?' Willow asked.

'Yes. Apparently they've been seeing each other for around four or five months now, not long after you two broke up. Garry wanted to keep it quiet out of respect for you. He said he didn't want to rub it in your face after he'd broken your heart by turning down your proposal—'

'Wait, he didn't break my heart,' Willow said. 'I was more relieved than anything.'

'I did try to say that to everyone, but as you did propose to him, no one believes me.'

Willow rolled her eyes in defeat. 'I can't believe he's engaged.'

'He's really excited, I've never seen him excited about

anything. I didn't even know he had that emotion as part of his repertoire. He's head over heels for her too. He's giddy. Now you're gone he wants to tell everyone he meets how much he's in love. He's even been caught a few times around town having sex outdoors. He can't keep his hands off her.'

Willow thought about this for a moment. Garry didn't do excited and giddy, or at least he never did with her. They'd never had sex anywhere but the bedroom and he certainly hadn't been the touchy-feely tactile type. God that was depressing. When they had broken up, she had felt like she had escaped from four years of mundane hell, but had he been bored out of his mind too? He had never proposed to her, never wanted to, she hadn't been enough for him, but four months of going out with Imogen had made him a changed man. The kind of man who wanted to shout his love from the rooftops.

Ruby watched her for a moment. 'Ah Willow, I should have done the bullet-points version. Are you OK? What are you thinking?'

'Just feeling a little bit inadequate. Garry never did any of that for me.'

'Would you have wanted him to? Would you really want to be married to him?'

'No of course not, but clearly I wasn't the sort of person that invoked those kinds of feelings in a person.'

'Not in Garry maybe, because you two were completely wrong for each other in every way, but when you meet the right person you will. And even if Andrew isn't that person, it sounds like things got pretty passionate between the two of you, that Andrew got *pretty excited* about being with you.'

Willow laughed as she blushed.

'What's going on with you anyway?' she asked, changing the subject again.

'Would it surprise you to know I've put my flat on the market?'

Willow sat bolt upright. 'Oh my god, that's amazing. What are you going to do?'

'I don't know. Maybe travel for a little while. Maybe I could move here for a year and save up some money if I don't have to pay any rent, then use that money to travel the world. I just need a break, to do something different.'

'I would love it if you moved here,' Willow said, delighted. 'Even if it is only for a year. And Happiness needs more unusual shops to attract different visitors so I'm sure Kitty and Ken would be thrilled to have you. And who knows, you might even be tempted to stay after you've been here a few months.'

Ruby smiled. 'I don't think I could live here for the rest of my life, but it would be lovely to live here for a short while. Especially if that hot bit of stuff we saw in the pub lives here too, he would be just the sort of distraction I need.'

Willow laughed. 'That guy you spoke to for all of five seconds at the bottom of the stairs?'

'Yes, he was yummy.'

'That was Jacob, he's Andrew's brother. And he doesn't live here so I wouldn't go getting your hopes up of falling in love and having a happy ever after.'

Ruby laughed. 'You know me, Willow, I'm not really the happy-ever-after and sunshine-and-sparkles kind of girl. I'll leave that up to you. And if I intend to go travelling in a year's time, I hardly want to put down roots with anyone, even if it is with Hottie McHotFace.'

Willow laughed. She had really missed this, and although it was all very much pie in the sky, she couldn't think of anything nicer than living in the same place as Ruby again.

CHAPTER TWENTY-FOUR

Andrew had just finished repairing a fence when he saw Willow coming towards him with what must be her friend Ruby. Willow looked sun-kissed, her hair damp probably from a swim in the sea, her face clean and a little shiny from where she'd overdone it slightly with the sun cream. She was beautiful. He caught Jacob looking at him and rolling his eyes. Andrew knew he probably had a loved-up grin on his face.

He threw down his hammer and stood up to greet them but, as he moved to wrap his arms around Willow, she put a hand out to stop him.

He frowned in confusion.

'I spoke to Morgan this morning,' Willow said, with no preamble.

'Morgan?'

'Yes, the girl you gave multiple orgasms to, does that ring a bell?'

Ah crap.

Jacob cleared his throat awkwardly. 'I think I might go and see what the pub has on for lunch.' He put his tools down.

'I think I'll join you,' Ruby said and they both walked off up the hill together.

Andrew stepped back and shoved his hands in his pockets. 'I should have told you.'

'Yes you should have. All morning, I've been thinking, why wouldn't you tell me? We've told each other so much.'

He sighed. 'I didn't want you reading something into me inviting her here. Why upset you over something that doesn't mean anything to me? It wasn't anything serious.'

'She says you were seeing each other for nine months, that's sounds fairly serious in my book.'

He shook his head. 'It wasn't like that. It was just sex. I suppose from the first time we slept together up to the last time it might have been a nine-month period, but we had sex probably no more than five times in those nine months. It was a very casual arrangement. She'd ring me occasionally and we'd meet up. We haven't seen each other for a year. We're friends on Facebook but, other than the odd comment on each other's posts now and again, we've not been in touch either. As I said to you before, we're not close any more. We were friends growing up and then we drifted apart. We met up again years later, had sex a few times. She's a nice girl but we didn't date or have any kind of relationship.'

'Yet you've shared things with her,' Willow said.

'What have I shared with her?' Andrew asked. Other than his bed.

'You told her about Sophie and—'

'She does not know about Sophie. I don't talk about that with anyone.'

Willow seemed to stall at this but then she carried on. 'And what about the other time you had your heart broken?'

Andrew stared at her in confusion. 'What other time?'

'She said there was a time that was much worse than Sophie.'

He shook his head. What had Morgan been telling Willow? Had she deliberately been trying to stir up trouble between them by making up these lies or had Morgan got him confused with someone else? Or had Willow got the wrong end of the stick completely?

'Willow, I'm not sure what Morgan told you but before I came here there was only one person that I had been in love with, one person who broke my heart, and that was Sophie. There has been no one else before or after. I have not shared anything personal with Morgan. We were friends who had sex, nothing more. There is no reason to be jealous.'

'I'm not jealous,' Willow said.

He resisted arguing with her on that. He had to pick his battles.

Willow let out a huff of breath.

'OK, when she talked about how amazing in bed you were, how you gave her multiple orgasms…' she trailed off.

He could feel himself getting angry. Why the hell would Morgan discuss that with Willow?

'Yes. I was jealous that you had touched her in the same way you had touched me, that you made love to her—' Willow went on.

'Sex,' Andrew corrected her. 'Willow, me and Morgan had sex. There's a big difference between sex and making love and what me and you shared was something I've not shared with anyone before, not even Sophie.'

She stared at him with wide eyes, then she let out a big sigh.

'I know we both have pasts, boyfriends, girlfriends, things we've done or said, good and bad. Those experiences are what shape us, make us who we are now. Sure, I wouldn't exactly invite my past to come and hang out with me. Garry would be the last person I'd want to see now, despite the fact that we parted on fairly good terms. Yes, I'm not exactly thrilled that you want to hang out with your ex but she's your friend and I don't want you to stop seeing your friends because of me. But you should have told me.'

'I don't… that's not… she was just the best person for the job, I didn't think of anything beyond that. You were the one who suggested covering the houses up.'

'And your first thought was Morgan?'

'Because that's her job. It's quite a specialised thing we're asking for here, it's not like looking for a plumber or a painter.'

Willow nodded. 'No, I get that.'

'I don't have feelings for her,' Andrew said, quick to reassure her. But by mentioning that, he felt like he was drawing attention to something that hadn't even been considered. 'I've barely given her any thought at all since the last time we met up.'

Now he was making it worse.

'Then we don't have a problem, do we?' Willow said.

Although by the tone of her voice he guessed it was a bit more of a problem for Willow than she was letting on.

'You should catch up with her properly while she's here. Go to dinner tonight with her, rather than me and Ruby,' Willow said.

He smiled at that. He could imagine how well that would go down if he decided to spend the night with his ex rather than Willow. And quite honestly, if Morgan was trying to cause trouble between him and Willow, she was the very last person he wanted to hang out with. Furthermore, faced with a choice of spending time with Willow or Morgan, there was absolutely no contest.

He reached out and took her hand. 'There is no place in the world I would rather be tonight than with you. This thing between us, I'm enjoying it way too much to want to stop.'

She smiled slightly.

'Morgan is... an acquaintance. I don't need to catch up with her. She is here to do a job. That's it.'

She was quiet for a moment. 'OK.'

'OK?' He dipped his head to look her in the eyes. He could see the affection for him return and the anger fade.

She nodded. 'I'm being an idiot.'

'No, not at all. If one of your male friends turned up here, someone you'd had *amazing sex* with, I wouldn't exactly be over the moon either. But for the record...' he lowered his voice. 'Sex with her wasn't amazing, not like it is with you.'

She smiled and shook her head. 'You're too smooth Andrew Harrington.'

'It's true.' He gingerly pulled her into his arms and after a few seconds she wrapped her arms around him and leaned into him. He breathed a sigh of relief into the top of her head.

She pulled back to look up at him. 'So no more secrets?'

'None at all,' Andrew said. 'I promise.'

'OK. What time does Cliff arrive tonight?'

'I think about seven.'

'Is he bringing loads of gear with him? That kind of thing is hard to keep hidden.'

'No, just him and his guitar,' Andrew said.

'OK, cool. Are you coming for lunch?'

'No, I really must finish here.'

She nodded and then reached up and kissed him. She leaned her forehead against his, holding his face between her hands, then she looked up at him, frowning slightly.

'What did you mean when you said, *before* you came here you had only been in love with one person?'

He thought about the words he had chosen to use. He had said that, which implied that there had been someone he had been in love with since he had moved here. Whereas before he'd just *thought* he might be falling for Willow, it now seemed his brain had already made the decision for him. But he certainly wasn't going to say those words now. If he was going to tell her he loved her then it wouldn't be in the aftermath of an argument. Those words were important and he wasn't going to use them to win opportune brownie points.

He smiled and kissed her on the forehead. 'Maybe that's a conversation for another day.'

She grinned. 'No secrets, remember.'

He laughed. 'In that case you should know, I adore you Willow, I think what we have could be something amazing.'

She smiled. 'I'll take that.'

She kissed him briefly on the lips and gave him a little wave as she walked up the hill.

He watched her go, unable to take the smile off his face. He really was in trouble with this one.

CHAPTER TWENTY-FIVE

Willow sat in the pub watching Ruby and Jacob flirt with each other as they got the drinks at the bar. It was quite an interesting thing to watch, two people who obviously liked each other a lot go through the motions of attracting the other. Ruby twisted a strand of hair round her finger, Jacob touched her hand, Ruby laughed at all of Jacob's jokes, Jacob licked his bottom lip. Willow had watched a nature documentary a few weeks before on mating rituals and this was like watching that. The only thing was that after mating with Jacob, Ruby was likely to eat him for breakfast just like the praying mantis.

She wondered what people would make of her and Andrew's mating ritual. Whether outsiders looking in would see a couple that were going to stand the test of time or just survive a few weeks. Her relationship with Garry had lasted four years and that had been a disaster. None of her other relationships had lasted longer than a few months. Maybe she wasn't long-term relationship material. Maybe she *was* boring or just wasn't enough for people to want a long-term commitment from her. After all, the thought of marrying her had been so horrifying to Garry he had turned her down the day after he'd said yes. Would Andrew get bored of her too? In terms of the nature documentary she had watched, would they be like swans and mate for life, or be like dolphins who quite often mated for pleasure and then moved on to another willing partner?

'Hey!' Andrew said, sliding into the booth next to her and placing a kiss on her forehead. 'What are you thinking?'

Willow leaned into him; he smelt clean and zesty like limes. 'Whether we'd be swans or dolphins.'

'Oh, swans definitely,' Andrew said, without missing a beat. 'Have you ordered food yet?'

She sat up and looked at him in surprise. 'Did you just get my obscure nature reference?'

'Swans mate for life, right?' Andrew shrugged as if it was obvious.

She smiled with love for this man and she cupped his face and kissed him.

'Oi! None of that,' Jacob said, sitting down opposite them and placing the tray of drinks for them all on the table. 'This is a respectable family establishment. We don't want any canoodling going on here.'

'No, that should be kept for behind bedroom doors,' Ruby said, eyeing Jacob as she sat down too.

'Agreed,' Jacob said.

Willow suppressed a smile.

'Ruby, we haven't properly met. I'm Andrew and I see you've already met my no-good brother.'

Ruby smiled as she looked at Jacob. 'He doesn't seem all that bad.' She turned her attention back to Andrew. 'It's nice to meet you, Willow hasn't stopped talking about you since I arrived. She's obviously completely smitten.'

'The feeling is very mutual,' Andrew said.

Willow smiled.

'Just don't hurt her or you'll have me to answer to,' Ruby said.

Andrew clearly wasn't fazed at all. 'Duly noted.'

'So there were more presents delivered last night,' Willow said, trying to be as vague as possible in case there were ears flapping nearby. The pub was packed so anyone could be listening. There were several groups of people in the pub that Willow hadn't seen before – maybe the young Sir Cliff had spread the word about his performance that night. 'Eileen was delighted to receive an apple pie, and Connor received something too, but he has been out all day so Tabitha doesn't know what his present was. I've just seen him come in about half hour or so ago so I guess we'll soon find out what he got.' Or, more to the point, what he thought of it.

Andrew looked at his watch and Willow knew he was looking to see what time Tabitha's present would arrive.

She looked at him expectantly.

'About ten minutes,' he said, quietly.

'What is going on with all these presents?' Ruby asked.

Willow hadn't told her about her involvement in the Secret Society of Happiness. Although her friend could be trusted to keep big secrets, she wasn't so good at keeping the smaller ones. But Ruby had already been there while Willow picked up some of the presents she had ordered from the post office earlier and when she'd opened them back at her cottage, Ruby had been intrigued over why Willow had bought such an array of things. She had especially loved the calendar of half-naked men holding up bits of cheese to preserve their modesty. It had taken Willow ages to find that but she was hopeful that Roger would love it. She was sure Ruby had put two and two together after seeing the presents and hearing the rumours.

She wasn't sure how much Andrew had told Jacob either and what Jacob had told Ruby.

'People in Happiness have been receiving mystery presents and no one has any idea who is delivering them,' Andrew said.

'Oooh, that's interesting. I wonder who it could be,' Ruby said, giving Willow a look that said she knew exactly who it was. 'Have you two had any presents yet?'

'Not yet,' Willow said, suddenly realising that if she was going to go undetected as the present-giver she would have to give herself one too.

Willow spotted Connor up at the bar and decided to change the subject. 'Shall I go and order the pizzas? There's three different kinds, shall I just get one of each?'

There were nods around the table and Willow hurried up to the bar.

Connor came over to take her order.

'Can we get one of each pizza for our table please.'

'Sure,' Connor said, ringing it through the till.

'So I hear you had a mystery gift last night? Everyone is dying to know what it is,' Willow said.

Connor made a noise of disapproval. 'A fish cookery book.'

Willow hesitated. 'You don't sound too pleased?'

'My fish is good, everyone loves my fish. But someone clearly doesn't think so. It's offensive is what it is.'

Her heart sank. 'I'm sure it wasn't supposed to be offensive.'

'And how would you know how it was intended?'

'I... I don't. I just think all the gifts so far have been... thoughtful, nice gifts. I'm sure the mystery gift-giver just thought about what kinds of things you liked and knew cooking was one of them.'

'Someone is trying to tell me how to do my job. How

would you like it?' Connor said as he gathered together cutlery for her.

Willow thought about it for a moment. 'I love making candles, I love playing with wax and creating different results. If someone got me a candlemaking book, I'd be over the moon. Even if most of the candles in the book I'd already made before, I'm sure there would be one or two ideas in there that I hadn't tried or at least could adapt, put my own spin on. I wouldn't be offended, I'd be thrilled that someone had taken the time to give me a book about something I loved.'

Connor grunted. 'That's a very rose-tinted outlook.'

Willow shrugged. 'It's normally better to see the good in things than to try to find the bad.'

She took cutlery and napkins back to the table and then flopped down next to Andrew.

'What's up?' Andrew said.

'Connor didn't like his present.'

'Why? What did you get him?' Ruby asked and Willow smiled and rolled her eyes.

'*He was given* a fish cookery book. He thinks it's offensive.'

'That's a bit small-minded,' Jacob said. 'I don't think you ever stop learning, in any profession.'

'And most people are gracious enough to say thank you for a gift whether they like it or not,' Ruby said.

'I hate the thought of upsetting anyone though,' Willow said, quietly.

The door of the pub opened and Willow sat up as a man with a guitar walked in.

She nudged Andrew. 'Is that him?'

Andrew looked over. 'Yes.'

'Tabitha Butler?' the man called out, addressing the bar at large. Willow was actually really impressed, he really did look like a younger Cliff Richard.

Tabitha looked up from where she was serving a customer and gave an uncertain wave.

Cliff smiled. 'I'm your mystery gift.'

And with that he launched into 'Summer Holiday', strumming away on his guitar. He sounded so similar to Cliff too.

'Oh wow,' Tabitha said, running round the bar and pulling up a stool in front of him. Cliff sat down next to her and carried on singing, seemingly just for her, not aware of all the other villagers and guests staring in their direction. Tabitha looked ridiculously happy as she stared at him, bobbing along with the music.

Other people started joining in, singing and clapping along. 'Summer Holiday' finished and Cliff launched into 'Devil Woman' and Tabitha laughed and started joining in too.

At least Tabitha was happy with her gift.

Connor came over with the pizzas just as Cliff started 'Living Doll'.

'Great,' he said, sarcastically. 'The mystery gift-giver has given my wife a hot young man to drool over. This day keeps getting better and better.'

Willow sighed. There really was no pleasing some people.

CHAPTER TWENTY-SIX

'I hope Connor isn't too upset,' Willow said, as she wrapped one of the gifts they were going to deliver that night in tissue paper.

'I still think that Connor sounds like an ungrateful sod,' Ruby said, sticking ribbon on one of the wrapped gifts now that she and Jacob had been enrolled into the Secret Society of Happiness.

Willow chewed on her lip. She kind of agreed with Ruby a little but then Ruby didn't have to live alongside Connor. At some point it was sure to come out who the mystery gift-givers were and what would happen then?

'Do you think we should get him another gift?' Willow asked.

'Absolutely not,' Andrew said, as he pulled Sellotape off the table to wrap his present. 'This is not a shop where you can take the gifts back if you don't like them. This is something nice we are doing for the whole village and it's Connor's problem if he doesn't like his present.'

'Remind me again why you are doing this?' Jacob said, curling the ribbon expertly with a pair of scissors.

Willow blushed. It sounded saccharine even to her own ears. 'To bring happiness back to the village,' she said, quietly.

'Wow you really are sweet, aren't you?' Jacob said, but not like it was a bad thing. 'Although, I can understand why this is bothering you. You want everyone to be happy and you can't tick that box in Connor's case. But I have to agree with the others, a fish cookery book was really thoughtful and I think he's been a bit of an arsehole about it. If it's any consolation, I did see him singing along to some of Cliff's songs tonight, so maybe Cliff could be considered a gift for both of them.'

Willow smiled slightly at that thought. Cliff had been brilliant that night. It seemed he had worked his way through almost the entire repertoire of Cliff Richard's back catalogue, even singing songs that Willow had never heard before, although Tabitha had sung along to every one. The whole pub had loved the live music and she had seen Connor take Cliff's card at the end of the night with a view to booking him again. Maybe he wouldn't take the fish cookery ideas on board, but it seemed he liked the idea of having live music, so something good had come out of that night.

'So if the goal is to make everyone happy by giving them presents—' Jacob started.

'It's not just trying to make them happy by giving them presents, but by providing them with a mystery to get excited about,' Willow said. 'It's all everyone is talking about at the moment, it's pulled them all together.'

'Yes I can see that, but what happens when it ends? What happens when all the villagers have received a present? What happens when the mystery has been solved and they all know it's you and Andrew?'

Willow hadn't thought about that.

It would be really sad if the village reverted to their old ways, keeping to themselves with none of the lovely community spirit that had started to blossom over the last few days.

'Do you have to be so negative about everything?' Andrew said.

'I'm not being negative, I think what Willow is doing is lovely. I'm just not sure that you're going to get out of it what you want. These villagers are set in their ways and, while this is all new and exciting for them now, what will they have to keep them happy and excited once the presents stop?'

Jacob had a point.

'I suppose that I was hoping the presents and the excitement would bring them together and that camaraderie would last. But I guess you're right, when all this is done, it may just fade away,' Willow said. If that was the case was there really any point in carrying on?

'You need to do something that will make this community spirit continue and you can't keep giving presents away to people for the rest of your life,' Jacob said.

'You need to get the rest of the villagers involved too,' Ruby said.

'Some of the villagers have been giving gifts as well, I think either to say thank you to the person they believe gave them their gift or in some attempt to pay it forward to someone else. That's been one of the lovely unexpected side effects of this mystery gift-giving: some of the villagers have really embraced it,' Willow said.

'Maybe we can get the villagers to embrace the whole spirit of the gift-giving going forward. Mowing lawns for each other, taking neighbours' dogs for walks, doing nice things for each other. That's what all of this has been about, just generally being nice to our neighbours,' Jacob said.

Willow thought about this for a moment. 'How do we get people to want to mow each other's lawns?'

'I don't know but surely everyone in the village will see the benefits of helping each other out. This is just the catalyst, but they are going to have to want to continue with this frame of mind if it's going to work,' Jacob said.

Andrew passed his present to Ruby to add the ribbon. 'I suppose for me, I really want all the people that visit us on the open day to see this wonderful village spirit, the kindness and our big hearts, and then people are going to be more likely to want to move in here. Hopefully seeing that generosity as the baseline will make them want to be part of that too.'

Willow finished wrapping the last present. 'Andrew's right, it's not enough that people will see nicely painted houses or that the shower has lovely new tiles and the gardens look pretty. The village has to feel like a home. It's going to be the villagers themselves that are going to be the big selling point on the open day, it's the villagers who are going to be the neighbours of the new people, the newcomers need to see them in the best light. Maybe we can show the visitors our generosity by getting the villagers to give little presents to anyone who comes to the village that day. We can have cakes, knitted toys, wooden ornaments, plants, candles, and each visitor can go away with a little gift of happiness to remind them of their day and of the wonderful village which might be their new home.'

Andrew smiled at her. 'I like that idea.'

She wondered how the villagers would take to the idea. She had only been here just over a week and it didn't seem right that she should start dictating to the villagers what they should be doing or coming in here with her bright ideas about how to change the place. The villagers might be really happy with how the village was now. Besides, announcing her idea of how to extend the mystery gift-giving to the village would be outing her and Andrew as the gift-givers and she wasn't sure if she was ready for that yet, especially not after Connor's reaction to his gift that night.

'OK, are we all done with the presents?' Willow asked and everyone nodded. 'Shall we go out and deliver them?'

'Why don't me and Ruby take the ones nearest to the pub? I'm knackered and I'd like to get into my own bed sometime before midnight,' Jacob said.

'Me too,' Ruby said. 'My bed that is, not yours.' She laughed nervously. 'I feel like I spent the whole day yesterday driving, I could do with a good night's sleep as well.'

Willow eyed the two of them. There was definitely something going on between them.

'Good idea, these three are the nearest to the pub,' Andrew said, handing them over. 'Stephen has a red front door, Suzanne has the big hanging basket and Coral has a gnome in a red hat sitting on her doorstep.'

Willow smirked at the fact that he knew all that.

Jacob took the presents and then practically bundled Ruby out of the house.

'God, the chemistry is almost tangible between those two,' Willow said, slipping on her jacket.

'I know. I hate to say bad things about my brother, but he's not the settling-down-and-happy-ever-after type. I hope he doesn't break Ruby's heart.'

'She's not the settling-down type either, not any more. She had her heart broken many years ago and hasn't looked for a serious relationship since. Maybe they'll be well suited to each other,' Willow said. She opened the door, grabbed her bag of presents and stepped outside. Andrew closed the door behind them.

'So, I heard you talking to Ruby earlier in the pub about

Garry's engagement. You don't exactly seem happy about it,' Andrew said, slipping his hand into hers as they walked along the darkened lane, lit only by Andrew's torch.

Willow had brought it up again with Ruby. It had been niggling away at her, but she hadn't meant for Andrew to overhear.

'I'm not unhappy because I'm jealous if that's what you're thinking,' Willow said.

Although there was an element of that, not because she wanted to be married to Garry, nothing could be further from the truth. But because he had never made love to her out in the open, he had never told anyone how much he loved her, he had never been giddy with excitement over being with her and he had never wanted to marry her. She had to ask herself if there was something wrong with her.

'Well I wasn't thinking that, but now I am,' Andrew said.

'Oh no, don't feel like that. If Garry turned up here now and asked me to marry him the answer would be an immediate and emphatic no. I just feel like…' She had no idea how to describe it without sounding jealous. 'I feel like, I wasn't enough for him. By all accounts he is a completely changed man now, he's happy and head over heels in love, but I didn't give him that. He was as miserable with me as I was with him. And I just feel a little bit sad that I didn't give him what he needed or what he wanted.'

'He didn't give you what you wanted or needed either. It takes two people to fail at a relationship.'

'I know.'

'By the sounds of it you two were completely wrong for each other.'

'We were, we drifted together because it was easy. We knew each other, I liked him and that felt like enough. I trusted him. I suppose I knew I could never get hurt with

Garry probably because I just didn't love him enough to be hurt if it ended.'

That was an awful thing to say. Poor Garry deserved more than that and now he'd found it.

'So why are you letting this get to you?' Andrew asked, shining his torch on an owl that suddenly took flight from a nearby tree.

Willow thought about it for a moment. 'What I have with you is different. It's something I've never had with anyone before. I suppose I'm just scared that…' she trailed off. 'I don't want to lose you.'

'You're scared because you think you weren't enough for Garry and that maybe you won't be enough for me?'

He'd hit the nail right on the head.

'You have no idea how completely and utterly you've captured my heart, Willow McKay. What we have is something incredible. I'm not going anywhere.'

She smiled and leaned against him, he wrapped an arm around her shoulders.

'Sorry for being an idiot.'

'Don't apologise. I'd rather you tell me your feelings and worries and then we can talk about them together. I want us to be completely honest with each other, I think that's the only way we will work. I had this huge feeling of inadequacy too after it ended with Sophie, that I clearly wasn't enough for her. I think I did exactly the same as you when I dated after that: I chose people who were uncomplicated choices, people who I knew I wouldn't get hurt by. I'd known Morgan for a long time before we got together. We grew up together. Her brother is deaf and he was a good friend of mine so I knew her very well, we had a lot in common. We drifted apart but when we bumped into each other years later, it just felt so easy and like the natural progression in our friendship.'

If this little pep talk had been designed to make her feel better, it was having the complete opposite effect. She didn't want to hear how easy and uncomplicated it was with Morgan when Willow seemed to come with a lot of baggage.

'Why do you think it didn't work out between you?' she asked.

'That wasn't what it was for Morgan. She wanted no-strings-attached casual sex, she made that very clear. Let's cut through here,' Andrew indicated the little alleyway they'd seen Mary use the night before to deliver her apple pie to Eileen.

They followed the darkened lane, the moonlight barely penetrating through the trees above them.

'And if she'd wanted more, do you think things would have been different?'

Andrew was silent for a moment as if really considering that option. 'I suppose if she wanted more we would have dated, but we never really did that. We never talked about our past or our hopes for the future. It was never that kind of relationship.'

'Did you want it to be?'

Willow knew she was opening up a whole can of worms here. She was asking questions she didn't want to hear the answer to.

'When we were together, having sex…'

Oh god, she really didn't need this level of honesty.

'… it was… empty. There was no connection there and I've never had that before. Even with the women I dated casually there was some emotion involved, but I didn't get that from Morgan. It really was just sex to her. And it did leave me feeling a little flat afterwards. So yes, I would have liked more from her.'

Willow was quiet. She had no idea what to say to that.

'But regardless of whether we had dated a bit more

conventionally, I didn't love her. It was never going to be a forever thing with her. Maybe she knew that and maybe that's why she didn't give more of herself to me. Maybe subconsciously I set the tone of the relationship and she only took what I was willing to give, or maybe it was always just sex for her and I had nothing to do with it. But either way it was never going to last between us.'

Willow tried not to think about what could have been if Morgan had been a bit more emotionally available.

He pulled her to a stop, stroking his thumb down her cheek as they stood in the muted darkness.

'What we have, I've never had with anyone, not even with Sophie. *This* is what a relationship is supposed to be. This is everything I've ever wanted. Don't ever doubt that.'

She leaned up and kissed him just as someone cleared their throat nearby.

Willow looked around and saw Julia out walking Colin and Rufus.

'Don't mind me, dears, I didn't see anything,' Julia said, giving them a theatrical wink as she squeezed past them.

Andrew laughed as he took Willow's hand and carried on walking up the alley. 'I'm sure that will be the talk of the village tomorrow.'

'I was hoping we wouldn't bump into her tonight, as one of the presents is for her. It's going to look a bit suspicious that she left her house and there was no present and when she comes back after seeing us walking towards her house, there is a present,' Willow said.

'Well, suspicious yes, but not exactly concrete proof. But Jacob's right, we probably won't be able to keep it a secret for much longer anyway, especially if we want to talk to the villagers about how they can contribute,' Andrew said.

'True.'

They emerged from the alley slowly and looked around the village to see if there were any more prying eyes but no one was around, most of the houses lying in darkness.

'Come on, let's get this done quickly,' Willow said. 'Before Julia comes back.'

They left the box of chocolate-flavoured tea on Liz's doorstep and the calendar on Roger's. They then crossed over the street to leave a book about quilting on Julia's doorstep, which they'd chosen after Andrew had overheard her talking about making one for her grandson. They left two other presents nearby and, with the three that Jacob and Ruby were delivering, that was eight people who would get surprise presents that night.

'It's a beautiful night. Let's take the cliff path back to your cottage,' Andrew suggested.

'OK.'

They followed the road out of the village and down towards the cliff tops. The moon glittered over the water, making the whole evening seem enchanting and magical.

'You know, if we're going to keep our identity as the gift-givers secret, we should probably give each other presents too so it doesn't look too suspicious that we're the only ones in the village not to receive one,' Willow said. 'What would you like?'

'I have everything I want,' Andrew smiled at her in the moonlight.

She smiled. 'Smooth.'

'Well apart from you turning up at my house stark naked, wrapped in a big bow, that would be a pretty spectacular present if you ask me.'

Willow laughed. She was sure she could think of something.

They passed the ruins of the old houses.

'No more stories about fairies and ghosts then?' she said.

'Actually I do have a story. Well, not really a story, more like a little nugget of information. This house here was known as the honeymoon house.'

'Really, why?'

'Apparently when a couple in the village got married, they would spend their wedding night here. The villagers would come out and decorate it during the day, get it all ready for them, but it was considered to be a very lucky place to consummate the wedding.'

'Blessed by the fairies?' Willow said.

'Something like that.'

In the light of the torch she could see Andrew's mischievous smile.

'Are you telling me this for some particular reason?'

He shrugged. 'Well if it's a lucky place to…'

'Have sex?'

'Yes. I think we could…'

'Consummate our relationship here?'

'Yes,' he grinned in the darkness.

'It's a bit bloody late for that if last night was anything to go by,' Willow said.

'Yes but that wasn't blessed by the fairies.'

'I'm not sure I want the fairies to watch us having sex.'

'I tell you what, we'll turn the torch off so the fairies can't see,' Andrew said, snapping the torch off and plunging them into darkness.

A thrill of excitement burst through her. She couldn't even see Andrew but she could feel his warmth as he stepped closer to her. He was still holding her hand and he placed a sweet kiss on her forehead before he stepped away and led her inside the four walls of the house.

Impossibly, it seemed even darker in here – though the

house didn't have a roof and she could see the moon above them, the stone walls blocked out any further light.

Andrew cupped her face in the darkness and kissed her, gently. She ran her hands down his shoulders, feeling the muscles there, taut and strong. He slipped her jacket from her shoulders and, as it fell to the floor, he placed a kiss on her collar bone. God, that simple touch from him was enough to have her climbing the walls with need for him. He placed another warm kiss on her shoulder. There was something so incredibly sexy about being kissed in the darkness, not knowing what he was doing, just feeling his hot mouth on her body.

She could see his shadow, looming large in front of her, but she couldn't see anything else. She felt her way down his sides until she found the hem of his t-shirt and slid it up over his head.

She ran her hands gently down his chest, caressing across his stomach, and heard his breath hitch. This was heaven. She had enjoyed seeing Andrew naked but this was a whole new level of intimacy, like she was truly exploring him for the first time. She felt the slight bumpiness of a scar just under his ribcage, she felt the contours of his broad chest and placed a kiss right over his thundering heart.

He pulled down the top of her dress, exposing one of her breasts to the cool night air, but she let out a groan as his hot mouth was suddenly on it, kissing her, teasing her with his tongue.

'Christ Andrew,' Willow whispered in the darkness.

She needed this man right now.

She stepped away slightly.

'What are you doing?' Andrew said.

'Taking my knickers off,' Willow laughed.

'Planning ahead, I like it.'

'Not too far ahead, I hope,' Willow said, feeling his warm hands at her waist.

He shuffled her back gently against the wall, kissing her hard. She moaned against his lips and wrapped one leg around his hips. He didn't take his mouth from hers as suddenly his hand was right there between her legs, caressing, stroking until she was shouting out all manner of nonsense.

She felt him fumble around in his pocket, heard the tear of the foil packet as it glinted in the moonlight. The next thing he lifted her and she wrapped her legs around his waist. He kissed her hard as he slid perfectly inside of her. She wrapped her arms round his neck, pulling herself tighter against him as he moved deeper inside her. His hands were underneath her bottom, pinning her to the wall with his wonderful body.

Her heart roared against her chest, that incredible feeling building inside her again.

'Can you feel this connection between us?' Andrew said.

'Yes,' Willow moaned, teetering right on the edge.

To her frustration, Andrew stopped and that feeling started to fade away.

'I don't mean amazing sex, although sex with you is always amazing. I mean this incredible connection, this spark between us. This is what it feels like when you're in a proper relationship, when the person you're with is so incredible, so brilliant and kind and warm, it feels like this passion is impossible to contain. Tell me you feel that too?'

'I feel it,' Willow said against his lips. And so much more.

He kissed her again and started moving again and that feeling started to build inside her again, spiralling out to every part of her body as he took her higher and higher.

God she loved this man. It was utterly ridiculous to feel like this after such a short amount of time but she knew that she loved him. She wanted to tell him, to shout it out for everyone to hear, but something held her back. Those three little words were so big and so important and so terrifying and she didn't want to casually throw them out during sex. But maybe she could tell him without saying it.

And just as that feeling burst through her she whispered against his lips. 'Elephant shoes.'

She felt him still as she fell apart around him and then he was kissing her passionately, moving against her faster and harder, holding her tight as he fell over the edge himself.

CHAPTER TWENTY-SEVEN

Andrew stroked a hand down Willow's hair as she slept on his chest. He was exhausted himself. It was already approaching nine in the morning and he had to get up and go to work. He was loath to wake Willow, and he would much rather spend the rest of the day sleeping off the night before with her wrapped in his arms, but he had a ton of stuff to do.

After making love in the honeymoon house, he'd practically marched her back to Sunrise Cottage, tumbled through the door onto the sofa and made love to her again. Then they'd kissed for what felt like hours, just kissing and stroking and touching, before he'd taken her up to her bed and made love to her again.

Christ this woman. He was never ever going to have his fill of her.

And she loved him, this incredible, smart, amazing woman loved him.

He remembered telling her that when deaf people lip-read a lot of words look the same on the lips. And that 'I love you' looks exactly the same as 'elephant shoes' or 'olive juice'.

Those weren't just two random words she had uttered in the throes of passion, she had deliberately chosen 'elephant shoes'.

To hear her say those words the night before, those two words that only he would understand, well he couldn't keep his hands off her after that.

He had never felt so complete in his life before, like there had always been something missing and now she had filled that hole so it was completely overflowing.

He ached for her, which was ridiculous when he barely had the energy to open his eyes.

He'd wanted to say the words back, but when had been the right time – when his mouth was on her breast, when his hand was between her legs, when he was buried deep inside her? The words were too important for that. And he didn't want to say them now when he had to rush off for work. But equally he didn't want to go another second without telling her how he felt. She deserved to know. He would wake her and tell her now. He smiled as he pictured how heated that conversation could get. He looked at the clock again, wondering if he could spend another half hour in bed with her. Although that wouldn't be enough. He sighed; realistically he was already running late and with only ten more days before the open day, there was so much to do.

He gently rolled her onto her back and she stirred slightly, her eyes flickering open for just a few seconds. She smiled when she saw him and then seemed to drift back off to sleep again with a big contented grin on her face.

That smile was going to get him through the whole day.

He slipped from the bed and quickly got washed and dressed, watching her sleep the whole time. He loved this woman so much.

He bent down and kissed her on the cheek and then whispered in her ear. 'I love you.'

She didn't even stir this time, although she was still smiling as she carried on dreaming.

He smiled and left the house.

~

Willow woke to an empty bed. She sat up and looked around. It was quite clear Andrew wasn't in the house. She looked at the clock and saw it was already half past nine so he must have gone to work.

She hoped his absence didn't have anything to do with sort of telling him she loved him the night before. Although the way he hadn't been able to stop kissing, touching and making love to her throughout the whole night was a good indication that he either wasn't bothered by her words or he hadn't heard them.

He'd never said the words back but then what did she expect, she hadn't properly said them either. And to be fair, it had only been a week since they'd met. Just because she had crazily fallen in love with him, she couldn't expect him to feel the same so early into their relationship.

She needed to get up and go and see Kitty and Ken about the next part of the plan from the Secret Society of Happiness. She also needed to get to the shop – more orders had come through yesterday while she took the day off and she needed to go in and sort those out, quickly. Then she needed to do some more painting and help Ruby with the fairy lights. She felt bad because, although Andrew had agreed the fairy lights would make a lovely touch to the village, it was creating more work for him as he was the one would have to hook up the power to all of them. She only hoped that all of this effort was going to pay off on the open day.

~

Andrew came out of the castle on his quad bike after talking through a few renovations with Kitty and Ken. He spotted Morgan on her hands and knees as she continued to paint the screens. She hadn't been there when he'd gone into the castle earlier. He wanted to talk to her about what she'd said to Willow. He was less angry today. After the wonderful night before that had happened in spite of Morgan's meddling, he was finding it hard to wipe the smile off his face, but Morgan still needed to know it was inappropriate.

He pulled up his quad bike behind her van and climbed off. She smiled at him as she looked up from her work. She stood up and came over to talk to him.

'How's it going?' Andrew asked, although from what he could see it looked fantastic.

'Great actually. I'm really enjoying this one. I've finished two of the screens so if you've got a spare few minutes you can help me erect them.'

'Sure, whatever you need.'

'OK, give me a moment, I need to clear these paints out the way.'

He watched her put the lids carefully back on the pots and tubes of paints.

'You were late starting today.' He cringed as soon as he said it. He didn't want to sound like the big boss, but the open day was fast approaching and the screens had to be finished by then. Although she was clearly making good progress.

She grinned at him. 'Sorry boss, it won't happen again.'

He'd known she'd take the piss as soon as he'd said it.

'I had a hot date last night,' Morgan said. 'We were at it all night and he was amazing. Very good with his hands if you know what I mean.'

Morgan was more of a bloke than he was when it came to talking about her sex life. When they had been friends, before they'd got together, she had always given him the intimate details of whichever man she had slept with the night before. He didn't really want to know.

He must have pulled a face because she laughed.

'You're not jealous, are you?'

Jealous? Nothing could be further from the truth. He had spent the night making love with the most magnificent woman he had ever met. Why would he be jealous of Morgan having no-strings-attached sex with someone else?

'No, I'm not.'

She laughed louder. 'Oh my god, you are.'

He sighed. 'I'm really not.'

'What we had was great, Andrew, but I've moved on now, to bigger and better things.'

He stared at her and laughed out loud at that one. 'Bigger and better things?'

She laughed too. 'Well I don't want to go into too much detail...'

'But I'm sure you're going to.'

'Zeus, my date from last night, he is the biggest I've ever seen. I never really thought size was important before, but it really is, and let me tell you he knew exactly what he was doing with it.'

'Zeus?' Was she actually making it up?

'He's from Greece.'

'I'm sure he is,' Andrew said, dryly. 'Anyway, while we're on the subject of sex, would you mind not discussing our sex life with my girlfriend?'

She switched to sign language.

'Oh I feel awful about that, I thought she knew about us. There she was saying that you'd told each other everything and I just

presumed she knew. I did wonder why you hadn't told her. It made me feel like a sordid little secret.' She grinned mischievously. *'I liked it. I don't mind being your sordid little secret.'*

'You told her I'd given you multiple orgasms.'

She laughed and continued signing. *'Well you did.'*

He signed back. *'And you needed to share that level of detail with her?'*

'I was just trying to be all girly with her. You know I'm rubbish with women. I have far more male friends than female ones. That's what girls do right, they talk about the sex they've had, compare stories. I thought we could bond over a common interest.'

Andrew sighed. *'And what was all that stuff you told her about me having my heart broken with some woman? We've never talked about anything like that, why would you make out that we have?'*

'You went out with that girl Amy, she broke your heart,' Morgan went on.

'I've never been out with a girl called Amy.'

'Oh, must be someone else I'm thinking of.' Morgan shrugged as if it was no big deal, but he got the sense she had completely made it up to upset Willow, although he couldn't exactly call her a liar.

Morgan stopped signing.

'Was she jealous that we had shared that?' she asked incredulously. 'Jesus, if she's getting jealous over stuff like that, it's not exactly a healthy start to a relationship. And she's been staring at us for the last two or three minutes so I guess she's not too happy about you chatting to me either.'

He turned round and sure enough Willow was standing at the end of the road leading from the village watching them.

Crap. Why did he immediately feel guilty?

She waved and made her way over and he moved away from Morgan a little to greet her. He cupped Willow's face in his hands and kissed her. God, how could the taste of her turn him on so much?

'You were fast asleep when I left you this morning, you looked so beautiful sleeping with this big smile on your face,' Andrew said.

She stroked his cheek and smiled. 'I was dreaming of you.'

He kissed her on the forehead and then took her hand and led her back to where Morgan was standing.

'I was just on my way to see Kitty and Ken,' Willow said as she smiled at Morgan. 'And I saw you two signing, it's so interesting to watch.'

Morgan started signing to him. *'Oh I'm glad sign language is so entertaining for her.'*

Andrew ignored that. He turned his attention back to Willow.

'What were you two talking about?' Willow asked. 'I was trying to work it out from the gestures but it moves so fast.'

'What we did last night. Sex, you, multiple orgasms,' Morgan supplied, rather unhelpfully but honestly.

He watched Willow frown. She hadn't seemed to be annoyed or jealous that he'd been talking to Morgan before but she definitely seemed pissed off now, not surprisingly.

Willow dropped his hand. 'Well, I need to go and see Kitty and Ken.'

She turned and walked up the hill towards the castle.

Andrew glared at Morgan. 'What the hell?'

'I was just being truthful.'

He shook his head and ran up the hill after Willow.

'Willow, wait.'

She didn't and he didn't catch up with her until they were inside the castle walls. He grabbed her arm and she rounded on him.

'I can't believe you. I woke up this morning thinking that

last night was one of the most incredible, amazing nights of my life and the whole time you're down here laughing about it. Was it really that bad?'

'God, no, I wasn't laughing about you.'

'I saw you.'

'That was something else entirely.'

'But you boasted about us, you came down here to tell your mate all the gory details about how you gave me multiple orgasms. Last night was something beautiful and private between us and you couldn't wait to get down here and tell Morgan all about it.'

'You've got the wrong end of the stick completely,' Andrew said, angrily. 'She was telling me all about her hot date last night with Zeus who apparently has the biggest penis in the world. That was what I was laughing at. And then I told her that it wasn't exactly appropriate for her to tell you all about my sex life with her.'

She stared at him.

'And why would you think so little of me? What kind of arsehole would I be to share that wonderful night with you and then tell all my mates about it after? Do you even know me at all?'

'Maybe I don't. Maybe you'd be better suited to someone like Morgan,' Willow said. 'You said yourself you have tons in common with her.'

'Maybe I would,' Andrew snapped.

'Fine.'

'Fine.'

Willow stormed off up the hill and Andrew stared after her in shock. What the hell had just happened?

CHAPTER TWENTY-EIGHT

Willow carefully poured the melted wax into ten different containers and then opened up the new box of scents she had bought. These ones were all named after different feelings. She wasn't sure what a feeling should smell like but she was intrigued enough to to give it a go.

It was raining outside right now, reflecting her mood perfectly. It had been raining ever since she had left Kitty and Ken so she hadn't seen anyone out in the village to hear about the gossip from last night and what everyone thought of their presents. But she suspected she would find out soon enough. Kitty and Ken had loved the idea of the gift-giving for the open day and now she just had to get the villagers on board. Kitty was going to call a village meeting in the pub that afternoon and Willow was going to talk through the idea with the villagers then. She guessed that most of them would realise she was behind the gifts after that.

She had planned to paint some more of the houses and help Ruby with the lights that day, but the rain had put a stop to that for now. However, it wasn't meant to last, so she was hopeful she might be able to get a few hours of village work done before the meeting. She'd texted Ruby and told her to come to the shop if she was bored, but her friend had texted to say she was busy doing online stuff for work and would catch up with her later.

Willow picked up the scent called Sadness and poured a few drops into one of the cups. Holding the wick to one side, she gave it a good stir and then leaned over and gave it a sniff. Sadness smelt a bit like honey, which wasn't a scent she would really associate with that emotion.

There wasn't any scent in the collection to reflect the other emotions that were churning through her gut: embarrassment for acting like a complete idiot, anger with herself for jumping to the wrong conclusion, regret over all the things she had said.

There had been no sign of Andrew when she'd come out of the castle and Morgan had packed her stuff away to escape from the rain.

Willow picked up the scent marked Happiness. She could do with a healthy dose of that right now. She poured a few drops into a different container and gave it a good stir. It made her smile. It smelt of summer holidays and sunshine and that wonderful coconut smell too.

'It smells nice in here.'

She looked up at Andrew hovering uncertainly by the door and she let out a breath of relief. He was here. After all the things she'd said, he was here. He was soaking wet though and she grabbed the towel she had used earlier and passed it to him.

'That scent is Happiness apparently,' Willow said as he dried his hair and stepped closer. She held the container up for him to take a sniff. 'All of these scents are different feelings and emotions. What do you think of Happiness?'

He smelt it, his eyes on her the whole time. 'It smells of you.'

She couldn't help smiling at that. She picked up another small bottle of scent and tipped it into another container of melted wax. She gave it a stir and then held it up for him to smell. 'This one is Passion.'

He sniffed it and his eyes darkened slightly. 'This one definitely smells of you.'

She smirked and quickly grabbed another bottle, adding a few drops to a different container.

He sniffed it. 'I like that one.'

She swallowed. 'Does it smell of stupidity?'

'No, is that what it is?'

'No, this one is Love.'

He stared at her.

'Because love makes me do some crazy stupid things, it makes me overreact and it makes me scared and it makes me say things I don't mean. I'm sorry.'

He stroked his thumb down her cheek. 'Willow—'

'I am jealous of what you have with Morgan and I don't mean sex and multiple orgasms. I mean that you grew up together, she knows what it was like for you growing up as the "deaf kid". She would have seen her brother struggle with it too. I don't feel I know that part of your life at all. I want to be there for you, for all of it, the good and the bad. But I do understand that you don't want to share or relive all of that.'

She didn't totally understand but she did respect that he might not want to talk about his childhood.

'I love you,' Willow went on. 'I know we've known each other for such a short amount of time and I don't expect you to feel the same way but I do, I love you. I held Garry back from finding happiness for so long, he was miserable with me and I don't want that for you. I want you to be happy even if you find that happiness with someone else.'

He frowned. He opened his mouth but she quickly spoke.

'Personally I don't think you would find happiness with Morgan either. You said sex was empty with her and sex should never be like that. Sex should be magnificent. I've had some good sex and some great sex and some pretty crappy sex in my life and I never knew that really it should be magnificent. Not until I came here and you set the bar so impossibly high that I don't ever want anything less than magnificent from now on. And you should aim for that too. Happiness is the most important thing in a relationship, but a part of that is sexual compatibility.'

She was waffling now.

'I'm sorry that I thought you had been boasting about us behind my back. I know you wouldn't do that, I don't know why I would think that.'

'Because Morgan deliberately made it sound like that. It sounded bad to my ears and I knew what we had been talking about. I think she has a bit of a twisted sense of humour, she likes winding people up. And you're right about one thing, Morgan is not someone I could be happy with. Sex should be magnificent, just like it was for me last night. But you're wrong about something else you said.'

'What's that?'

'I do feel the same way.'

Her heart exploded to life in her chest.

He signed something, pointing to his chest, holding his hands over his heart and then pointing at her.

Her breath was racing like she'd just been for a run. She didn't know any sign language but even she could work that out.

'Just to be clear, that means I love you,' Andrew said.

She let out a heavy wobbly breath and he moved closer, wrapping his large hands round her waist. She looked up at him as he bent his head to kiss her. 'I love you Willow McKay.'

She reached up and kissed him and he wrapped his arms around her and held her tight.

She pulled back to look at him. 'You really do?'

'Yes.'

'Do you know how utterly ridiculous this is?'

He laughed. 'Yes, it's crazy, but I suppose love does that to you.'

She kissed him again, laughing against his lips as tears ran down her cheeks.

The kiss turned very heated, very quickly, as they grabbed at each other with greedy hands. He lifted her and sat her on the table, standing between her legs as he started kissing her neck, and she suddenly realised that they were in full view of anyone walking past.

'Wait,' Willow said as Andrew pulled down the strap of her dress, trailing kisses down her shoulder.

He looked up at her in confusion.

'Not here. I have a storeroom out the back. It even has a desk.'

'Works for me,' Andrew said, lifting her off the table.

She wrapped her legs around him and laughed against his lips as he carried her straight into the storeroom and kicked the door closed behind him. He placed her down on the desk and this time he wasn't slow as he'd been the night before when he'd made love to her in her bed. This was just a desperate need and it turned her on so much to know she had this effect on him. He made very quick work of her clothes as she struggled to get him out of his. He was kissing and touching everywhere, pausing for just a second to tear open a condom, and then he was inside her, his hands tight on her hips, her legs wrapped around him as he moved against her faster and harder. That feeling started to build inside her already as she clung to his shoulders. He rolled her back gently so she was lying on the desk as he kissed her.

'I love you,' Andrew said.

'I love you too,' Willow said as her body trembled in his arms. He watched her fall apart and then he kissed her hard, groaning against her lips.

~

Willow was just finishing painting some flowers in the corner of a shop sign that was now painted a beautiful shade of royal blue when Ruby came sauntering down the high street towards her, carrying a large bag. The sun was out and Ruby was wearing a bright turquoise dress but she had the biggest smile on her face. It seemed that the effect of Happiness had already cast its spell on her friend.

'Hey, Rubes, how was your morning?' Willow said, climbing down the ladder. She felt bad that her friend had been stuck in the hotel room all morning because of the weather, but Ruby didn't seem too bothered by it.

'Oh it was fine, I had stuff to do, so it's been good,' Ruby said, vaguely.

Willow looked at her friend wondering what she *wasn't* saying. She was just about to ask her when Ruby spoke.

'How was your morning?'

Willow let out a heavy breath. 'Well, I had a stupid row with Andrew, spoke to Kitty and Ken about my idea that the villagers should make gifts for the open day, had amazing make-up sex with Andrew, made some candles, painted some shopfronts, so it's been a busy day.'

Ruby laughed. 'That does sound like a busy morning. What on earth did you row with Andrew about?'

'Oh, it was nothing really, but mainly it was down to Morgan causing trouble again.'

'I haven't even met this woman yet and I don't like her,' Ruby said.

'I don't particularly like her either,' Willow said. 'But I think a large part of that is jealousy that she has all this history with him and not just sexual history. She's Andrew's friend and he might want to keep in touch with her once she finishes her work here. If that's the case I'm going to have to try to be friends with her too.'

'So you have to play nice?'

Willow thought about it. 'Nice might be pushing it, but I certainly don't want to be nasty.'

'Well fortunately for me, I don't have any such scruples or restrictions on the way I should behave around her,' Ruby said.

'Rubes, I don't need you to fight my battles for me. Don't make things worse.'

Ruby clearly thought about it.

'OK, but if you want her disposed of, I could make that happen, just say the word.'

Willow laughed at the sudden gangster approach to solving the problem. 'Anyway, did you bring the lights?'

'I did, well these are some of them, I have two more bags in my car. But we can make a start with these. What kind of effect are you looking for?'

'I think just strings of lights draped over the top of the high street, kind of zigzagging over the road between the houses and shops. We don't want it to look Christmassy, more… like a party.'

'Are you asking me to be subtle with the lights, because I'm not sure I have that skill. You know I'm a throw-everything-at-it kind of girl when it comes to decorations.'

Willow laughed. 'I'm asking you to rein it in slightly.'

Ruby sighed theatrically. 'Well, as it's you, we'll try to keep it...' she swallowed as if she was going to say something difficult '... low key.'

'I think low key might be a bit much, but maybe we could stretch to... medium key.'

Ruby visibly brightened and plonked the bag on the floor. 'Let me show you what I've got.'

~

Willow sat next to Kitty and Ken in the pub nervously watching all the villagers arrive. Kitty had told her there had only been one village meeting since Kitty and Ken had taken over the castle and that had been purely for the purpose of introducing themselves. The villagers were probably wondering what was going on.

She watched them all, a hum of excited chatter as people talked about the mystery presents that had been delivered the night before.

Andrew came back from the packed bar with drinks for them all.

'Have you decided what you're going to say yet?' he asked, taking a sip of his beer. 'Are you going to out us as the mystery gift-givers?'

'No, I don't think so. There are still quite a few villagers who haven't received a present yet. It would be a shame to spoil the mystery for them, although most of them have probably guessed by now.'

Ken stood up and tried to do a head count although people

were milling about so it was pretty hard to do. He turned back to Kitty. 'I think everyone is here.'

Kitty stood up and banged her spoon against her coffee mug to get everyone's attention. The pub went silent as everyone looked over in their direction.

'Thank you all for coming today.' Kitty spoke in a clear confident voice. She was obviously someone used to public speaking. 'I know some of you have been the lucky recipient of a mystery gift. I myself was given the gift of a lovely scarf and I'd like to personally thank whoever left that for me. I know some of you have your suspicions over who the gift-giver is, but I also know that the gifts haven't just been given by one or two people. Lots of you in the village have embraced this idea and given gifts of your own. Over the last few days, this village has grown into a community, filled with people who care about each other, and it's been a lovely thing to see.'

There were murmurs of agreement around the pub, people smiling at each other, and, for the first time, Willow could really see that she had achieved what she had set out to do. Even if this spirit only lasted a few weeks, she had brought happiness back to Happiness. She felt a warm glow inside at that thought.

'I'm sure you are all aware that we have the open day coming up very soon and Willow has had an idea to help the visitors see this wonderful camaraderie and see Happiness as a home. Willow, would you like to say a few words?'

Andrew gave her hand an encouraging squeeze as Willow got to her feet.

'The gift-giving has been a great success so far and those of you who have given gifts to your friends and neighbours, thank you for embracing the spirit of this.'

'Is it you?' Julia blurted out. 'Are you the gift-giver?'

Willow stalled, not having expected to have questions shouted out at her.

'Are we all going to get a gift?' someone at the back of the room shouted.

'How do we thank our gift-giver if we don't know who it is?' someone else called out.

'What's the reason behind the gifts?'

'I, erm... I do know who some of the gift-givers are. And I do know that the gifts were only given with the best intentions. I also know that all of you will get a gift. We had an idea for the open day,' Willow hurriedly tried to get the conversation back on track. 'We thought that as you are enjoying the gifts so much that the visitors on the open day would enjoy receiving a Happiness gift too. And we would like you all to get involved. We thought that you might like to make little gifts for our visitors, maybe some knitted things, or wooden toys, plants, sweets, cakes. I will be making little candles to give away on the open day. It doesn't have to be something big or time-consuming, but we were hoping you might want to contribute twenty or so little gifts each. We thought that the visitors could all be given a voucher as they arrive, which they could exchange for one free Happiness gift of their choosing. We could have tables near the main entrance to the village and people can take their gift before exploring the village and the castle.' She paused. 'What do you think?'

There was silence for a few moments and then everyone started shouting out questions and comments all at once. Willow had no idea if they were good comments or not.

Kitty stood back up and quietened everyone down with a wave of her hands.

'We want to hear your thoughts and ideas, we really do, but can we just start off by taking a quick vote? There is no point discussing it further if most of you don't want to do it. Can you raise your hand if you think it's a good idea and you would like to contribute?'

Willow smiled at Kitty's no-nonsense, get-straight-to-the-heart-of-the-matter attitude.

There were a few murmurs and whispers and then slowly hands started to rise. Willow quickly started to count, hoping at least for a majority even if it wasn't unanimous. One, two, three… she stopped as the hands were being lifted faster than she could count until everyone in the village was raising their hand. Every single person.

She couldn't help smiling at Andrew in relief.

'That's fantastic, thank you,' Kitty said. 'Let's start off with the basics first then we can get a bit more specialised in a moment. If we can start taking down some names then my able assistant will start to make a list.'

Ken cheerfully waved his notebook and pen and the villagers laughed.

'So cakes are always going to be popular – cupcakes would be good rather than big giant slabs of cake. Who would like to make those?'

A few hands shot up and Ken wrote them down.

'Cookies anyone?' Kitty prompted and again a few more hands shot up.

'OK, kids' toys next, we want all the children to have something too. Any ideas?'

'I could make some wooden shields and swords for the boys,' Joseph suggested.

'And girls,' Kitty said. 'We don't want any gender stereotypes here.'

'No,' Joseph cleared his throat. 'Of course not. My granddaughter is a right little tomboy. She loves playing knights as much as she loves being a princess. But maybe I could make some glittery magic wands too for those girls and boys that like a bit of sparkle in their role playing.'

'That sounds like a wonderful idea.'

'I could make some knitted bears,' Mary piped up. 'In non-gender-stereotype colours of course.'

Everyone laughed.

Pretty soon everyone was piping up with suggestions and Ken was having a hard time writing it all down.

Willow couldn't help smiling as she sat next to Andrew. This was really going to work.

CHAPTER TWENTY-NINE

Willow sat on her sofa that evening unpacking some supplies she had ordered for the shop. Ruby had gone out to see a comedy act she'd seen advertised and, while Willow had thought about going with her, apparently Jacob wanted to see the comedy act too and Willow hadn't wanted to play the third wheel if something did happen between them. She hadn't seen Andrew for the rest of the day. During all the furore of organising the villagers' gifts for the open day, he had kissed her on the cheek and told her he had to get back to work and that he'd probably be working late that night to try to finish one of the houses off, but to come by his house later if she wanted. The open day was coming round far too quickly now and she knew Andrew was starting to worry about getting everything finished on time. She was probably a bit of a distraction too.

Willow had eaten dinner alone, which had actually been quite nice as she'd got to spend the time reading a book. She hadn't decided whether to go and see Andrew that night, he might prefer an early night. He had been working so hard lately and he certainly wasn't getting a lot of sleep in the evenings he was with her.

Willow thought she might watch a little TV, have a bath and then have an early night herself. Although after the big declarations of love earlier that day, she'd quite like to curl up and fall asleep in Andrew's arms if nothing else.

She unpacked some gift baskets and a large spool of satin ribbon. She remembered what he'd said the night before about her turning up at his house naked wearing only a bow and she grinned at the thought of surprising him in that way.

She quickly undressed and then unwound the ribbon from the spool. How should she go about wrapping herself in a ribbon? It was not something she had ever contemplated before. She tied it round her waist, but if she was going for the gift-wrapped-present look, then she hadn't quite achieved that. She slipped one length over her shoulder and the other between her legs, hoping that wouldn't chafe too much on the walk to Andrew's house, twisted the two lengths together round her back and tied it in a big bow round her belly.

She looked down at herself. It wasn't quite the sexy look she was going for but she thought Andrew might get a big kick out of it. Although there was no way she was walking up the lane dressed only in a ribbon. She grabbed her coat and pulled that on, buttoning it up to the collar, which frankly looked ridiculous in this warm weather.

She quickly left the house before she changed her mind.

Willow was hopeful she might be able to make the short distance to Andrew's house without meeting someone, although that hope was dashed when she saw Dorothy and Joseph walking towards her. To her delight she realised they were holding hands. She was so happy with this turn of events and the thought that she might have played some small role in it that she momentarily forgot that she was completely stark naked underneath her coat and hurried over to say hello to them.

'Hello, where are you two off to?' Willow asked, unable to stop smiling at their joined hands.

'We thought we'd go for a sunset walk along the cliffs,' Joseph said. 'It's such a beautiful night.'

'Yes it is,' Willow agreed, dying to ask if they were actually dating now.

'So why are you wearing a coat?' Dorothy asked, eyeing Willow's bare legs with interest.

'Oh, I just thought it might be a bit chilly later when I'm walking home,' Willow said, pulling the coat down a bit. It was quite a bit shorter than she'd realised.

Dorothy smirked as if she didn't believe a word of it. 'Yes dear, of course. Well, we better let you get on.'

They walked away with Dorothy giggling like a schoolgirl. Willow smiled as she watched them go but the ribbon really was starting to chafe a bit now and she wanted to get to Andrew's house before she met anyone else.

She hurried up his path and knocked on his door.

He opened it and his face lit up in a huge smile when he saw her. She quickly stepped inside and closed the door behind her. She was aware that the TV was on in the lounge, so obviously he'd just been chilling out before she got there.

'I'm so glad you're here—'

She stepped up and put a finger on his lips. 'I have a surprise for you.'

He frowned in confusion and she quickly unbuttoned her coat and let it fall to the floor.

His eyes bulged and he swore softly under his breath.

Suddenly there was a puppy standing in the doorway, yapping excitedly at the new visitor.

'Andrew?' came the sound of a woman's voice followed by footsteps from the lounge.

Willow looked at Andrew in confusion.

'My sister, quick in here,' Andrew muttered, opening the pantry door and bundling her inside before slamming it closed and plunging her into darkness.

'I thought someone was at the door,' said the woman's voice. His sister, Lottie.

'There was, it's nothing,' Andrew said.

'Oh, I thought we were going to meet the wonderful Willow then,' Lottie said.

Christ, no. The first time she was going to meet his sister and she was standing in the pantry wearing nothing more than a squashed and battered ribbon, the end of which had got trapped in the door. She didn't even have her coat to hide her dignity as that was somewhere in the hall. She looked around the darkened pantry for something to cover herself up but it was filled with food. There was a potato sack at the bottom of the pantry, filled with filthy potatoes. She wasn't sure if meeting his sister for the first time dressed in a potato sack would actually be worse than what she was wearing now.

Her cheeks flooded with embarrassment.

OK, it was fine. Lottie had no idea she was there and Andrew would hopefully be able to get rid of his family as quick as possible or at least smuggle her upstairs without them knowing. It wasn't like she would be here for hours with a ribbon stuck between her bum cheeks.

'Are you coming in, we're just about to put *Tangled* on,' Lottie said.

'Umm...' Andrew said.

'Poppy has been so looking forward to watching it with you. It's her new favourite.'

Through the tiny crack in the door Willow saw a little girl, presumably Poppy, come out and sign something to Andrew. He signed back and she took his hand and led him off to the lounge.

Crap. She would be here for hours.

OK, she just had to wait for the movie to start and then sneak out. Her coat would probably still be in the hall and she could put it on and get out the house without anyone noticing. It was going to be fine.

She noticed movement outside the door and she held her breath, not daring to move at all. She realised it was the puppy and that to her horror he had found the end of the ribbon and was pulling at it with all his might, yapping and growling at it as the ribbon between her legs started getting tighter. She tried to pull it back but the dog's barking and growling got louder as he put up the fight of his life.

'Max, what on earth are you doing?' Lottie was back.

Oh god.

'What have you got there?' Lottie said. Removing the ribbon from Max's mouth, she opened the pantry door to see what it was attached to.

For the longest moment no one moved, no one said anything. They just stared at each other.

The next thing Poppy came running out of the lounge. Lottie slammed the pantry door shut but Poppy had already seen her.

Willow wanted to curl up and die.

Through the crack in the door, she saw Poppy sign something to her mum.

Lottie signed back while speaking at the same time, probably for Willow's benefit. 'No honey, I have no idea why there is a naked woman in your uncle Andrew's pantry. Why don't we ask him?'

Andrew came running out into the hall looking stressed.

For a moment it was clear he didn't know what to say but then decided on some honesty.

'The woman in the pantry is Willow, she came round to surprise me and didn't realise you'd be here.'

'Evidently,' Lottie said, dryly. 'Well, why don't me and Poppy go in the lounge and you can let her out the pantry. Then she can go upstairs and put some clothes on and we can meet her properly?'

Really? She had to endure meeting Andrew's sister and niece after all this? Couldn't she just run away and hide?

Lottie and Poppy moved away and Andrew opened the door for her.

She put her face in her hands, her cheeks burning with shame, and Andrew moved forward and hugged her.

'I'm so sorry,' he whispered. 'I had no idea they'd be here tonight.'

She looked up at him. 'I'll just go home, I'll meet them properly tomorrow.'

He shook his head. 'Come and meet them now. I've told Lottie all about you. Just go and grab some of my clothes and come down and say hello. You might as well get the embarrassment over with now.'

Willow groaned and quickly ran upstairs. She ripped the stupid bow off, grabbed one of Andrew's shirts and pulled that on, then found a pair of his shorts. They were way too big but she used one of his belts to cinch them in at the waist. She looked ridiculous but at least it was a step up from wearing nothing.

She quickly washed her face to make some of the redness calm down, took a deep breath and went back downstairs.

Andrew was waiting for her at the bottom of the stairs and took her hand, leading her into the lounge. Lottie and Poppy were sitting on the sofa, Poppy clutching a doll with one eye, while Max was curled up fast asleep after he had exhausted himself with outing her.

'This is my lovely sister Lottie and my niece Poppy,' Andrew said, signing at the same time for Poppy's benefit. 'And this is my girlfriend Willow.'

'Hi Lottie, nice to meet you,' Willow said.

Lottie smiled but she didn't seem too thrilled. So much for first impressions.

'Hello Poppy,' Willow tried with Andrew's niece but, unless she could lip-read, she probably didn't understand what Willow had said.

Andrew signed for Willow and Poppy signed back. Andrew laughed. 'She says, why were you naked?'

Willow blushed. Whereas she and Lottie were steadfastly trying not to address the nudity, Poppy had no such scruples.

'I was… playing a silly joke on Andrew,' Willow explained lamely.

Andrew signed for Poppy what Willow had said and Poppy just stared unblinking at Willow.

Eventually she signed something back. Andrew laughed again. 'She says she doesn't think the joke was very funny.'

'I agree,' Lottie said, quietly.

Willow wanted to say something else, anything that might make Poppy laugh, but she felt so woefully inadequate right then. She knew no sign language, not even enough to say hello.

'Well, shall we put the movie on?' Lottie said, turning her attention to the TV.

'I should go,' Willow muttered to Andrew.

'No stay, watch *Tangled* with us.'

Right then, Willow couldn't think of anything she'd like to do less.

But Andrew sat down and pulled Willow down on the sofa

next to him. Poppy immediately climbed up on Andrew's lap and she signed something at Willow, clearly expecting her to understand.

'I'm sorry, I don't understand sign language.'

'You're going out with a man who's deaf and you can't be bothered to learn any sign language?' Lottie said, her tone as disapproving as her words. 'What will you do when he loses his hearing altogether?'

'Lottie!' Andrew said.

Willow blushed. She felt awful. Even though just over a week wasn't enough time to have learned much sign language – and Andrew had hardly tried to teach her – she had to admit that she'd totally taken for granted that Andrew could hear her when he was wearing his hearing aids. But what about the times he wasn't? And what did Lottie mean, "when he loses his hearing altogether"? Of course she should learn sign language so she could communicate with him at all times and with his niece too. She felt embarrassed that she hadn't thought of it.

Even Poppy's one-eyed doll seemed to be looking at Willow judgementally.

Andrew turned his attention back to Poppy and signed to her. *'What did you say to Willow honey, I missed it.'*

Poppy signed the same gestures she'd signed before.

'She wants to know who your favourite *Tangled* character is,' Andrew said.

'Oh, I've never seen *Tangled* before,' Willow said and Andrew signed her answer back.

Poppy stared at her as if she had three heads. In Poppy's mind not having seen *Tangled* was clearly a hell of a lot worse than not knowing any sign language.

Andrew put the movie on and Poppy made herself comfortable with her back against Andrew's chest, watching the screen avidly as subtitles played along the bottom of the film.

'How's Morgan doing?' Lottie said. 'It was so nice to see her again today.'

'She's fine,' Andrew snapped.

'I like Morgan, such a lovely girl. I always thought you two were so good together.'

'We were never together, not in that sense. We had a fling, that was it,' Andrew said.

Poppy was watching the film with wide eyes, clearly with no idea about the conversation that was happening over her head.

'Oh, it was so much more than that, anyone could see the chemistry you two had,' Lottie went on from the other side of Andrew. 'I really thought you were going to marry her.'

'Stop it,' Andrew said. 'I love you, I love seeing you and spending time with Poppy, but don't come in here and try to ruin what I have with Willow. She's the best thing that's ever happened to me. You're being a bitch and that's not who you are.'

That shut Lottie up. Willow had no idea what to say to make this awful awkward situation better. She decided she would just focus on the movie, just in case Poppy asked her questions about it later. She stared at the screen, not really taking in any of it, but after a few moments, Andrew slipped his hand into hers and they stayed like that throughout the whole film.

CHAPTER THIRTY

The film finally finished and Lottie started gathering her things ready to go.

'We're staying at the pub for a few days so we'll see you tomorrow,' Lottie said, deliberately not looking at Andrew or Willow. She was clearly still upset by what Andrew had said to her earlier.

'I have to work for a few hours tomorrow morning but maybe between me and Jacob we could take Poppy for a bit tomorrow afternoon,' Andrew said.

'I'm sure she'd like that, thank you,' Lottie said, giving him a weak smile.

Andrew got down on his knees to address Poppy. *'Goodnight beautiful, I'll see you tomorrow,'* he signed.

Poppy signed something back and he gave her a hug.

'It was nice to meet you,' Willow said to Lottie.

'No it wasn't,' Lottie said. 'I was a complete cow and I'm sorry.'

Willow was surprised by this sudden about-turn. 'It's OK,

we didn't exactly meet under the best circumstances. Maybe we can try again tomorrow.'

Lottie nodded. 'I'd like that.'

Willow turned her attention back to Poppy. 'It was lovely meeting you too.'

Lottie signed what Willow had said.

Poppy's hands flashed at an incredible speed as she spoke.

'She wants to know who your favourite character in *Tangled* was,' Lottie said.

'Oh, the horse,' Willow tried as she hadn't really paid attention to much of the film.

Lottie signed her answer and, to Willow's surprise, Poppy launched herself at Willow for a hug.

'Good answer,' Lottie said, 'Maximus is her favourite too. The dog is named after him.'

Little Max gave a bark of approval at hearing his own name.

Lottie gave Andrew a hug and with a little wave from Poppy they all left.

Andrew turned to her and let out a big sigh of relief.

'I'm so sorry,' he said as he pulled her into a big hug. She held him tight, stroking down his back.

'For what?'

He pulled back. 'Are you kidding? For my sister's terrible behaviour, for your embarrassing introduction to my family. For being forced to watch *Tangled* for the last two hours. For not being able to ravish you as soon as you walked through the door, which believe me was what I would much rather have spent my night doing.'

'It's OK.' She stroked his face; he looked exhausted. 'Let's go to bed.'

Andrew nodded and took her hand, leading her up to his

bedroom. He got undressed and into bed and Willow did the same, snuggling into his side. He wrapped an arm round her shoulders and she slid her arm across his stomach.

'You looked amazing tonight, best present ever,' Andrew said, yawning.

It was quite clear there would be no ravishing tonight. Willow smiled because cuddling Andrew in bed was more than enough.

They were quiet for a while and she looked up at him to find he was staring at the ceiling.

'What did Lottie mean when she said about you losing your hearing completely?'

He frowned. 'Nothing, she's just being a drama queen.'

She bit her lip. He really didn't want to share that part of his life with her and she didn't know how to feel about that. She couldn't say that their relationship was surface level because they had talked in depth about many things, but if he wouldn't share something that was such a big part of him, did they really have a future together? If she couldn't be that person for him, was she really the right woman for him?

She lay in silence for a while but Andrew broke it.

'Poppy's dad walked out on them about a year ago.'

Willow looked up in shock. 'What?'

'Things hadn't been great between them for a long time. Alex got a job offer in New York and he took it. Just told them he was going and a week later he was gone.'

'So he doesn't have any part in Poppy's life any more?'

'Not really. I think he did Skype her for a while but every time he did, Lottie cursed him for everything under the sun and it dried up after that. Alex really struggled to learn sign language and as his daughter grew up he just couldn't really communicate with her. I think it drove a wedge between him and Lottie, because there was a clear bond between Poppy and Lottie and he felt like an outsider in his own family. I mean, of course there were other things that went wrong in their relationship too, it wasn't just about Poppy. They were always bickering and fighting years before Poppy was born and I always wondered why they stayed together. So I don't think she was the reason that things didn't work between them, but I suppose it added to the strain in their relationship.'

'That's awful.'

Andrew was quiet for a while. 'My dad walked out on us when we were kids. Apparently he'd had affairs with multiple women. I kind of grew up wondering if it was my fault. Of course I don't think that now but I don't want Poppy to have that feeling too. I think Lottie's been struggling with it ever since. Being a single parent is hard and I think, despite it all, she still loves Alex and misses him terribly. I'm not excusing her attitude to you tonight, but she's had this prickly outer shell since Alex left, but inside there is still this wonderful woman. Just be a little patient with her. Once you get to know her, you'll really like her.'

'Of course. Maybe tomorrow, Poppy can come and help me make some candles in the shop. Give Lottie a break for a while. Although I'll need you or Jacob to interpret for me.'

'That would be great. I have so much work to do, but I'll bring her along and then hopefully Jacob will stay with her. I think Poppy will love you.'

Willow cringed a little. 'I'm not great with kids, I always say the wrong things. I make inappropriate jokes which they never find funny. I taught my brother's kids how to burp the alphabet. My sister-in-law was furious and rightly so.'

Andrew laughed. 'Yes, please don't do anything like that with Poppy, I want her and Lottie to fall in love with you as much as I have. But you don't have anything to worry about. You've already won her over with your love of Maximus. I'll give you one tip, she has this doll, Gertrude. It has no hair, one eye, one of the ears has melted off after she left it too close to the fire. It is the most hideous thing I have ever seen in my life and quite frankly gives me nightmares. She *loves* this thing and carries it around everywhere. Just don't insult it or look horrified if she asks you to hold it.'

'I'll tell her Gertrude is beautiful.'

'That's a great idea.'

'Will you show me how to sign that to her?'

Andrew hesitated.

'I want to learn it.'

'Ah, don't do this because Lottie gave you a hard time.'

'I'm not. This is part of who you are, I want to know this part too.'

He clearly thought about this some more. Then he sat up and slowly signed something. *'Your doll is beautiful.'*

Willow stared at the hand gestures feeling suddenly daunted. There was no way she would remember that.

He signed it again, breaking it down into little chunks. She copied each action as he did it and then tried to put all the chunks together into a sentence.

'That's it,' Andrew said, lying back down.

She practised it again, feeling like everything was hinging on these tiny little movements.

Andrew pulled her back down on top of him. 'This doesn't need to be a big deal. If you can't do it, just get me or Jacob to sign for you.'

Willow lay there listening to his heartbeat for a while. Don't be rude about the doll, don't say anything inappropriate, teach her about candles, make Poppy fall in love with her, all through Jacob or Andrew interpreting everything she said. No pressure then.

She thought about Alex, Poppy's dad, and how hard he had found it to communicate with his own daughter and how utterly heartbreaking that must have been for him.

'Is sign language hard to learn?' Willow asked.

'Yeah, it can be. I learned from a very early age so it was a lot easier for me. It's much harder to learn it when you're an adult. And as with the English language where there are many similar words, there are also many similar signs. There are also several signs that mean the same thing.'

Unease swirled in her gut. She had learned French and Spanish at school and had been awful at it. She had got an E in French in her GCSE and a U in Spanish. She couldn't even remember a single word of either language now. What if she struggled to learn sign language too? What if she spent her whole life having to have everything translated to Poppy for her? What if she had children with Andrew and they were deaf, what if she couldn't learn enough sign language to communicate with them? Would that drive a wedge between them?

No, she couldn't think like that. She would learn it. She had to if she was going to be a part of Andrew's life.

She looked up at him. 'I want to learn it.'

He stared at her for a moment. 'OK, I will teach you but try not to get frustrated with it, it's hard to pick up at first. We'll start off small.'

'OK.'

'I'm going to sleep now.'

He gave her a sweet kiss on the lips and she watched him take his hearing aids out and pop them on top of his drawers.

Then he signed something. '*Goodnight*,' he said.

She smiled and copied the gesture back.

'Perfect,' he said.

She stroked his face. 'I love you.'

He smiled and closed his eyes. 'Elephant shoes.'

She put her head back on his chest with a smile. She was going to do this, she had to.

CHAPTER THIRTY-ONE

After hot shower sex and breakfast, Andrew had rushed off to work with the promise to bring Poppy by Willow's shop later that afternoon. Willow had gone home to get changed into her own clothes and then decided to see if she could find Ruby before she went to work. She felt a bit guilty that her friend had come down to see her and she'd only spent one full day with her so far. Although Ruby seemed happy enough, so she didn't feel too bad.

Willow went through the back door of the pub which led straight upstairs to the bedrooms. She knocked on Ruby's door but there was no noise from inside. There was, however, laughter coming from one of the other bedrooms that sounded suspiciously like Ruby. Willow wandered down the corridor a little and listened outside the door. She had been sure Ruby was in room number six but that definitely sounded like Ruby inside number three.

Suddenly the door was flung open and Ruby walked out giggling.

'Ruby, I thought you were in number six...' Willow started.

The door opened wider and Jacob was standing there dressed only in a towel.

'I was, I mean I am. I was just borrowing some sugar from Jacob,' Ruby said, not in any way embarrassed at being caught in what was clearly the morning after the night before. She also didn't have any sugar with her.

Willow smirked. 'So good night last night? The comedy show, I mean.'

Ruby flashed Jacob a grin. 'It was a great night.'

Jacob smiled. 'I'll catch you later Ruby.'

'Oh Jacob,' Willow said. 'Andrew is bringing Poppy to my shop later this afternoon so she can make some candles with me. I know Andrew is crazy busy at the moment, would you be able to stay with her and interpret for us?'

Jacob frowned. 'Poppy's here?'

'Yes, I think Andrew was a bit surprised last night as well. They're here for a few days and Andrew said he'd have Poppy this afternoon but I don't think he really has the time so I said I would make some candles with her. Would you have the time to stay with her?'

'Of course, she'd like that. I'll see you later.' Jacob gave Ruby a wink and closed the door.

'Fancy having breakfast?' Willow said.

'Sure, that sounds good.'

They started walking down the stairs. 'Who's Poppy?' Ruby asked.

'Jacob and Andrew's niece.'

Ruby was quiet for a moment and Willow cringed a little that Jacob hadn't spoken to Ruby about Poppy.

'Why does Jacob need to translate for the two of you?'

'Poppy's deaf and she only really communicates through sign language.'

'Oh god, how awful,' Ruby said.

Willow cringed even more. 'I think Poppy's totally fine with being deaf. I don't think she would think it's awful at all.'

'But it must be, not being able to hear music or people chatting or birds singing or a child's laughter.'

'But Poppy has never heard any of those things so she doesn't think she's missing out at all. She's a very happy little girl.'

'It must be so terrible for her family though, for her parents and for Jacob.'

'What's so terrible about it? Poppy is a healthy, happy, bright, energetic little girl. Besides, I suspect her family are quite used to it. Andrew's deaf too.'

'Andrew's deaf?!' Ruby said incredulously as she pushed the door open to the pub and all eyes swivelled in their direction, including those of Lottie and Morgan who were having breakfast together with Poppy.

Ice settled into her stomach. Andrew didn't want anyone to know he was deaf and now in Willow's attempt to play down how *awful* it was for Poppy to be deaf, she'd let it slip to Ruby and her friend had inadvertently just told the whole pub.

'I can't believe Andrew's deaf,' Ruby went on, completely oblivious that she was making the situation worse.

'Sshhh,' Willow hissed. 'For god's sake be quiet. Go and grab a menu. I'm just going to say hello to Lottie and Poppy.'

'Is that them?' Ruby said, staring over at them like they were animals in the zoo.

Willow winced. Ruby was a lovely person but she was as subtle as a low-flying brick.

'Will you just go and sit down, over there?' Willow snapped. 'I'll be over in a second.'

Willow walked over to Lottie and Poppy's table. Neither Lottie or Morgan looked happy to see her. Although Poppy waved madly.

'Morning,' she addressed Lottie and Morgan. 'Hello Poppy.'

Lottie signed for Willow.

'Poppy, Andrew is going to bring you to my shop this afternoon. I make candles and we thought you might enjoy seeing how I do it.'

Lottie smiled slightly. 'Oh she'll love that.'

She signed what Willow had said and Poppy practically burst out of her seat in excitement.

'Did you just tell the whole pub that Andrew is deaf?' Morgan asked, clearly not in the mood to play nice.

Willow flushed with embarrassment. She was really hoping they hadn't heard, although Ruby had been loud enough.

'I, erm, I was just telling Ruby and…'

'And I bet Andrew specifically told you not to tell anyone?'

Morgan was right. He had told her he didn't want anyone to know and she had promised him she wouldn't tell a soul. Christ, this was all kinds of awful.

Willow looked round the pub. No one seemed to be taking an interest in their conversation and no one seemed to be excited about this latest bit of gossip like they had been over the presents or her relationship with Andrew. There were lots of little conversations going on but none of them seemed to be about Andrew.

'He's really sensitive about people finding out, he's going to hate this,' Morgan went on.

'Maybe he's a little more relaxed about it here,' Lottie said. 'This is his home.'

'I doubt it. He's tried to hide it his whole life. He doesn't talk about it with anyone. He trusted Willow and she's just let him down.'

'I think you're overreacting. Maybe it's time he embraced it,' Lottie said.

'I think that's probably Andrew's decision,' Morgan said. 'Not yours or Willow's.'

Willow had no words to defend herself. It should be her protecting Andrew not Morgan. But Morgan would never do anything so indiscreet as to out Andrew to the whole pub.

Willow cleared her throat. 'I'm going to go and have breakfast with my friend. Poppy, I'll see you later.'

Lottie signed for her and Poppy waved goodbye.

Willow returned to her table where Ruby was still watching Lottie and Poppy with evident interest.

'God, what have I done?' Willow said as she sat back down. In her head, Andrew being deaf just wasn't a big deal but of course it was for him. She'd told Ruby when she'd had no business sharing that with her. Andrew would be furious and quite rightly so.

'I wonder why Jacob didn't tell me about Poppy,' Ruby said.

'Probably because he knew you'd be really inappropriate about it,' Willow snapped and then regretted it. None of this was really Ruby's fault but she wished she would be a bit more discreet about it.

'What am I doing that's inappropriate?' Ruby said.

'You're staring at her like she's a freak.'

'I'm not. Oh my god, of course I don't think she's a freak, that's an awful thing to say. I just didn't even know Jacob had a niece until ten minutes ago and now I find out the poor girl is deaf and Andrew's deaf and—'

'Stop saying that. Christ. Andrew's really sensitive about it and I should never have blabbed it to you in the first place but you don't need to keep repeating it to the whole pub. And stop with the "poor girl" crap. Deaf people don't need or want our pity, they don't want to be labelled as an abnormality or different. They just want understanding, to have the same opportunities as us, to have access to the same stuff that we do. And sometimes that can be difficult for them but they want empathy not sympathy.'

Ruby stared at her. 'God, I am being inappropriate, aren't I?'

'Yes you are.'

'I'm sorry. It was just a surprise, that's all. I didn't mean to be an arse about it. I really should know better, what with Cal putting up with all that crap all his life, and I've just turned into one of those people who stare and make a big deal about something that really isn't a big deal.'

Willow nodded. She knew Ruby's brother, Cal, had lost his lower leg in a car accident when he was only a small child. He'd had his own battles to fight as he'd grown up. Although if anyone was a good role model for overcoming adversity, it was Cal. He was a Paralympian. Ruby really should know better.

'Right, I'm stopping now, I promise. I'll say no more about it.' Ruby picked up the menu decisively. Willow looked over to where Lottie and Morgan were sitting. Morgan and Poppy were engaged in a very animated conversation and Poppy kept laughing and giggling at what Morgan was saying to her. Lottie, however, was staring at Willow and she wondered if she had heard what she'd said. Willow thought back to what she'd said to Ruby, hoping that she hadn't said anything wrong or offensive. Andrew was right, she had no real understanding of what it meant to be deaf. She just hoped she had championed the cause in the right way.

She watched Morgan and Poppy continue to chat, the little girl had completely come alive. She didn't think she would ever be able to engage with Poppy as easily and fluently as Morgan was. Morgan was so good for her. It was no wonder Lottie liked her.

But she was going to master this and she was going to start this afternoon with Poppy.

~

Willow ended up leaving the pub at the same time as Morgan. Ruby was going to go back to sleep for a few hours as apparently she hadn't got much sleep the night before and Willow needed to get to work.

Willow held the door open for Morgan as she came out. Despite Morgan's frostiness with her before breakfast, Willow wanted her to know she took that part of Andrew's life seriously. For some reason she couldn't identify, she wanted Morgan's approval.

'You and Poppy seemed to be having the best conversation over breakfast,' Willow said. 'You're so good with her, she absolutely adores you.'

'That's because I understand her,' Morgan said rather testily. Evidently she was still pissed off with Willow.

'I want to learn sign language. I want to be able to communicate with Poppy properly and being deaf is a big part of who Andrew is, I want to be able to share that with him. Would you teach me a few things?'

Morgan clearly thought about this for a moment. 'OK, what do you want to know?'

'Well Poppy is coming to see the candle shop this afternoon, she loves candles. I'd love to be able to say to her something like, "Would you like to make some candles with me?"'

Morgan hesitated for a while. 'OK.'

Morgan demonstrated how to sign that sentence, slowly going through each action, and Willow copied it carefully. She repeated it a few times with Morgan correcting her if she went wrong until she had got it perfected.

'That's it and, look, I'll show you something you can say to Andrew tonight in bed.'

Morgan showed her some other sign language actions and Willow dutifully copied her.

'Perfect,' Morgan said.

'What did I just say?'

'Ah, I'll let Andrew translate that one for you, but I promise he will love it.' Morgan smiled, almost smugly Willow thought.

'Thanks so much,' Willow said and waved her goodbye as she walked into her shop.

It was a very small start but she couldn't wait to show Andrew and Poppy the sign language she had learned and how serious she was about getting to grips with that side of their life.

CHAPTER THIRTY-TWO

Willow was waiting nervously inside her shop for Andrew and Jacob to arrive with Poppy.

She had to talk to Andrew before anything else. She had to tell him that she had accidentally outed him to the whole village and she had no idea what his reaction to that would be. He had been angry enough that first day when she had discovered he was deaf, so how would he feel when he discovered that the whole village now knew? She only hoped that no one in the village had said anything to him, she wanted to be the one to tell him.

She was also nervous about getting the sign language right when she spoke to Poppy, but at least it would show Andrew she was willing to try.

She had all the equipment laid out ready to make some candles and she was hoping she and Poppy would have a fun afternoon.

There was laughter outside and she looked up to see Andrew and Jacob swinging Poppy between them, Poppy holding onto their hands as they swung her up into the air.

Willow rushed to the door of the shop. 'Jacob, could you just give me and Andrew a second to talk before you bring Poppy in?'

'Oh, sure,' Jacob said. He quickly signed something to Poppy and she nodded. He swung Poppy up onto his back and started prancing around outside giving her a piggyback that made her laugh.

'What's up?' Andrew said, stepping into the shop and giving her a kiss on the cheek. The affection he had for her shone from his eyes. Clearly he didn't know.

'Look, I'm really sorry, but...' She rested her hands on his chest. There was no easy way to say this. 'But I accidentally let slip to Ruby that you're deaf.'

He frowned. 'Oh.'

'And... she sort of blurted it out to the whole pub,' Willow cringed.

His eyebrows shot up in surprise and then slashed down into a furious scowl. He was definitely pissed off.

'So the whole village knows?'

'I'm so sorry, I really am. I asked Jacob if he would interpret for me this afternoon and Ruby was there and she wanted to know why he would need to translate for me and Poppy and I told her she was deaf and then I ended up telling her that you were deaf too and... I'm so sorry. I know you don't want anyone to know because you don't want to be treated differently and I've ruined that for you. That was never my intention.'

He didn't say anything, but his jaw was tense, his eyes were dark and none of the affection he had for her was there any longer.

'Are we all ready?' Jacob asked from the doorway as Poppy stood in front of him staring round at all the candles with wide eyes.

Willow looked back at Andrew and he stepped back away from her. 'We'll talk later, I have to get back to work.'

God this hadn't gone well at all but now, with Poppy eager to explore, it was really not the time to discuss it.

Jacob brought Poppy inside and Willow smiled slightly that she had brought that hideous doll with her.

'I'll catch up with you in a few hours,' Andrew said to Jacob. He knelt down to talk to Poppy. He started signing. *'I'll see you later and maybe we can go out for ice cream?'*

Poppy's face lit up and she nodded.

'You OK?' Jacob asked. Although his brother nodded, it was very clear that he wasn't.

Willow needed to show Andrew that she took this part of his life very seriously. So she quickly crouched down to talk to Poppy.

'Hi Poppy,' Willow said, and as Andrew watched she very carefully signed the sentence that Morgan had taught her, asking Poppy if she would like to make some candles with her.

'What the hell?' Andrew exploded.

Jacob let out a bark of a laugh but he was clearly shocked, which was worrying if even Jacob was shocked.

Poppy blinked and then burst out laughing.

Crap. She must have got it wrong. She signed the words again and Poppy's laughter got louder. Even Jacob joined in this time. The only one who wasn't laughing was Andrew.

'What the fuck was that?' Andrew practically yelled. 'Is that your idea of a joke?'

Willow stood back up. 'Wait, did I get it wrong?'

'You're damned right you got it wrong. Where did you learn that?'

'Morgan taught me,' Willow said. 'What did I say?'

'"You have a very small penis,"' Jacob said.

'WHAT?!' Willow said. 'Holy shit, I didn't mean to say that. I'm so sorry.'

God, she was going to scar the poor child for life.

Poppy signed something to Willow, in between laughing almost hysterically.

'She says that she doesn't have a penis, only boys have one of those,' Jacob said.

Willow suddenly realised that she'd got the two sentences Morgan had taught her the wrong way round and what she'd signed to Poppy had been meant for Andrew, although why the hell would Morgan teach her that? She decided to try what Andrew had taught her the night before, she shouldn't go too far wrong with that.

She carefully signed to Poppy.

Poppy's laughter got louder and Andrew rolled his eyes. With that he stormed out of the shop.

She turned to Jacob. 'What did I say now?'

He pulled a face. 'Best translation I can come up with: "Your doll is making candles with me."'

Shit. This was just getting worse. 'Can you show Poppy round the shop for a moment? I need to talk to Andrew.'

Jacob nodded.

Tears smarting her eyes, she ran out of the shop after Andrew.

He was standing out on the street pacing back and forth. She raced up to him.

'I'm so sorry—'

'You just told my six-year-old niece that she has a small penis, how inappropriate is that?'

'I would never do that deliberately—'

'You should never have tried to talk to her at all unless you know more sign language, who knows what else you could have *accidentally* said,' Andrew said.

'I shouldn't have tried to communicate with her? Are you serious? I did this because I wanted to be part of your life and hers. I know I screwed it up but at least I was trying to share that side of your life with you.'

'I never asked you to do that.'

'But I wanted to. I wanted you to see that I took that part of your life seriously and how important you are to me. And you're just throwing that back in my face. And in actual fact, Morgan showed me how to sign that to her so if you have issues with my signing you take it up with her.'

'Are you saying all this is Morgan's fault?' Andrew said.

'Yes… No,' Willow said, the fight going out of her. Because he wasn't really angry at her for messing up the sign language, they both knew that. This was about her telling the whole village he was deaf and that was all on her, no matter what Morgan had deviously tried to teach her.

'Don't you dare put this on Morgan,' Andrew said. 'She wasn't the one who just blabbed to the whole village that I'm deaf. Do you know how let down I feel about that? This is my home and now you've made it awkward for me to carry on living here.'

'These people love you and care about you, they would want to help you. Why not let them in?' Willow said.

'That wasn't your decision to make.'

'That's what Morgan said, you really are well suited.'

Andrew clearly ignored that. 'I don't need their help, or anyone's.'

'That's ridiculous. You've always said that you want Poppy to grow up being proud of who she is, yet what kind of example are you setting for her pretending to everyone that you're not deaf?'

'You have no idea what it's like to be deaf, how bloody hard it is. You couldn't possibly understand what it's like to have that label permanently hanging over your head.'

'Because you won't tell me, you won't share that part of your life with me. Every time I asked you about it, you shut me out. Yet you'll share all that with Morgan. The man you are now, the most incredible man I've ever met, is a product of the life you've led, the good, the bad, the ugly, the things you love, the things you hate. And one of the most significant influences on your life, for good or bad, is you being deaf. But you won't share that with me. On our first date you made a toast to getting to know each other but you didn't really mean that, did you? You just meant the shiny stuff, the best bits, nothing else. You said you wanted us to be honest with each other but you have closed down conversations, changed the subject and lied whenever I asked you questions about that part of your life.' She took a step away from him as the full realisation of this hit her. 'I guess I really wasn't enough for you if you couldn't share that with me.'

Andrew didn't say anything, just stared at her.

'I'm sorry, I truly am, for telling the village you're deaf. I'm sorry for letting you down.' She swallowed down the lump of burning emotion in her throat. 'But I can't go through the next few years of my life feeling like I'm not enough and you shouldn't be with someone who you can't be yourself with.'

With that Willow turned and walked away, tears streaming down her cheeks as her heart broke into a million pieces.

CHAPTER THIRTY-THREE

Andrew slammed the tray of chips down on the kitchen unit and they bounced so hard that some of them landed on the floor.

'Jesus! Let me do that before you break something,' Lottie said behind him as Poppy sat happily at the kitchen table playing with her toys. 'Go and sit down.'

Andrew sighed and stepped back out of the way, because he had already burnt himself on the oven twice that night; his mind was clearly elsewhere.

Poppy, by all accounts, had had a lovely afternoon making candles with Willow. Jacob had said that Willow had arrived back at the shop clearly upset but somehow managed to pull it together to spend a few hours teaching Poppy. His niece hadn't stopped telling him all about it since she'd arrived at his house earlier.

'I can't believe you and Willow broke up,' Lottie said, as she turned the chips over and returned them to the oven. 'Over nothing.'

'It wasn't nothing,' Andrew said.

'Oh yes, she accidentally let slip to her *best* friend that you're deaf. Best friends do tend to tell each other everything.'

'And Ruby then blurted it out to the whole pub.'

'And that's worth losing the love of your life over? I don't know why you're so insistent on keeping that part of your life secret anyway. You need to learn to let people in. Being surrounded by people who have an understanding of your needs, even if it's a limited understanding, has got to be better than being surrounded by people who are completely ignorant to it.'

She'd hit the nail on the head.

Andrew sighed as he sat down at the table with Poppy. 'I think that's more the real reason why we broke up. I've been shutting her out.'

Lottie shook her head in exasperation. 'And why is that?'

'I guess I don't want to appear... less.'

'Oh Andrew. You are not... less of anything. You are my favourite person in the world. Don't tell Jacob I said that.'

Andrew smiled slightly.

Poppy galloped a toy horse up his arm and he grabbed a pig and trotted it up her arm, making her laugh.

Lottie sat down with them. 'You should have heard what Willow was saying in the pub about deaf people. She was telling Ruby off for feeling sorry for Poppy, she said that deaf people need empathy not sympathy. I think she understands a lot more than you think.'

Poppy started signing something. *'I like Willow, she's funny.'*

He signed back. *'I like her too.'*

'She's not very good at sign language,' Poppy giggled.

He smiled sadly and shook his head.

'I can't believe she signed to Poppy that she had a small penis,' Lottie said.

'I can't believe you're not mad about that,' Andrew said.

'Why would I be mad? Firstly it's hilarious, secondly Poppy does know the names of all the body parts so it's not like it was something completely inappropriate.'

'Willow said Morgan taught her to sign that.'

'I can well believe it.'

Andrew could too, it wasn't the first time Morgan had taught someone the wrong thing to sign for a laugh.

'You said you liked Morgan,' Andrew said.

'I do but she was very annoyed with Willow for outing you to the village. She's very protective of you. It wouldn't surprise me if she did that to get her back. I think she likes you.'

Andrew sighed. 'I think so too.'

Poppy started signing again. *'You need to teach Willow how to sign properly. She really wants to learn it.'*

He swallowed the lump in his throat. *'I know.'*

Poppy continued to sign. *'Because she loves you.'*

Andrew rubbed his hand across his eyes because Poppy in her innocence had got to the heart of the matter. Willow wanted to share this with him because she loved him and if he loved her he needed to let her in.

'I need to see her,' Andrew said.

'Yes you do,' Lottie said.

'And say sorry for making her sad,' Poppy signed. *'And then bring her back here and we can share that tub of ice cream in the freezer.'*

He smiled and kissed her on the head. *'I'll be back soon.'*

Lottie gave him a nod of encouragement and he raced out of the door.

The sun was setting, making the whole world outside rose-coloured as he ran up the lane towards Sunrise Cottage. He burst through the gate and hammered on the door.

Willow answered it and it was quite obvious she had been crying.

All the words he wanted to say went straight out of his head as he stared at her, bathed in the rose-gold light of the receding sun. He loved this woman so much. He stepped forward and kissed her and for a few seconds she kissed him back, melting against him, a little sob escaping on her lips before she put her hands on his chest and stopped him.

'What are you doing here?'

'I've come to say I'm sorry.'

She shook her head and his heart dropped into his stomach.

'This isn't going to work between us,' Willow said.

Christ he was really going to lose her. 'I love you. You said you loved me.'

'We rushed into a relationship without getting to know each other, how could we really love each other, it's been just over a week. We didn't know each other at all.'

'That's bollocks, I know how I feel for you, I don't care how long it's been. You must have felt that too.'

'I know you made me happy,' her voice was choked. 'You made me laugh and smile a lot.' She frowned. 'I know you are kind, generous, silly, determined, protective, I know you are an amazing man, and yes I think I did fall in love with you, but it wasn't enough. There was something missing—'

'There was something missing because I didn't let you in. That was all my fault. I want to change that, I'll tell you everything, whatever you want to know,' Andrew said, desperately.

She stared at him and he knew he had to give her something.

'I was bullied incessantly in school. About my hearing aids, about being deaf, about being stupid. I think the hearing children thought I was rude or antisocial when it was just easier sometimes to not get involved in group conversations in the playground or in class, everyone shouting over everyone else and speaking so quickly, I struggled to keep up with it all. I found secondary school especially hard, being with so many different children and different teachers' voices and trying to learn and understand their lip patterns when I was lip-reading. It was hard to concentrate with the other noises and I didn't get the best grades because of it. I just felt I didn't belong sometimes and it made me feel weak. I didn't tell you these things because I didn't want you to think I was weak.'

She stepped up and cupped his face. 'You are not weak, you are the bravest, strongest man I know.'

He leaned his forehead against hers, tentatively wrapping his hands around her waist. She didn't pull away.

'There is a chance that by the time I'm fifty I will have lost all my hearing completely. It's slowly getting worse and if that happens my hearing aids might not be of any use to me. I might be able to get a cochlear implant, which will help a lot, but it's not a magic fix and I might not be suitable for it anyway. And that is something I haven't really discussed with anyone, not even my family. They know, but we don't talk about it, simply because I would rather bury my head in the sand than think about what it will be like to not hear anything any more, to lose the sounds I love the most. Your laugh is one of the most beautiful sounds I've heard, it fills my heart every time I hear it and I don't want to lose that.'

'You may not be able to hear me laugh but you will still be able to see me smile. You'll still feel my touch when we make love, my breath on your lips. You won't lose that.'

He looked her in the eyes. 'Won't I?'

Tears filled her eyes and she shook her head. 'I love you. I'm not going anywhere.'

'I swear, I'll tell you everything, my hopes, my fears, my frustrations and triumphs.'

'I need to learn sign language.'

'I'll teach you, every word. I love you and I want to share this with you.'

She smiled and leaned forward and kissed him and he sighed with relief against her lips.

They were going to be OK and for the first time in his life he felt like he'd found somewhere where he truly belonged.

CHAPTER THIRTY-FOUR

Willow came out of the castle ready for the big open day to start. They'd told estate agents and lettings agents that the village open day started officially at twelve and, as it was only quarter past eleven, they still had a short while before people started to arrive, although Willow suspected some people would come early.

The castle was going to have its official opening at the same time and she knew people in the local area were particularly curious about seeing it. The castle grounds were filled with knights and princesses who were going to engage with the visitors and there was going to be a big jousting display later.

Outside the castle walls, on the grassy slopes near the village entrance, the villagers had set up tables. They had all risen spectacularly to the challenge of providing Happiness gifts for everyone. There were cakes, toys, jewellery, plants, knitted things, sweets, biscuits, hand-painted bits of slate and pottery mugs. Even Ruby had set up a small stand with baubles hand-painted with the word 'Happiness' and pretty little flowers. They didn't look remotely Christmassy but, as Ruby pointed out, anything could look festive once hung on a Christmas tree.

Willow moved through the stalls admiring the different gifts and stopped at Dorothy's stall, picking up one of the hand-painted postcards Dorothy had painted of the village itself. Some of them were very similar to the poster that had brought Willow to the village in the first place, but this time there was nothing misleading about the picture. Thanks to all the work that Andrew, Jacob, and Jack and his team had done over the last two weeks, the village now shone. They had managed to complete twelve houses, inside and out, and repainted all the others. Willow had worked her magic by painting flowers, butterflies and other things around all the doors and painted all the shop signs too in preparation for their new owners. Willow was excited to see the visitors' reactions.

'These look fab,' she said, picking up one of the postcards that was of the beach.

'Thank you. I hope the visitors like them,' Dorothy said and it was clear she was anxious.

'They will love them.'

Dorothy let out a big sigh. 'Do you think it will work, all of this?' she gestured to the stands. 'Everyone is so nervous.'

Willow looked around as the villagers added the last touches to their stalls. They all wanted this to work as much as she did.

'I really do,' Willow said. 'I think the visitors will see the cute houses, the pretty flowers, but most importantly the amazing people who live here and this wonderful community spirit, and I think they will fall in love with the place. Everyone has come together and they will see that and hopefully want to be a part of it.'

Dorothy nodded. 'I hope you're right.'

Willow smiled and made a move to walk away.

'Thank you for my cake by the way,' Dorothy said.

Willow turned back. The last of the mystery gifts had been delivered the night before and she and Andrew had decided to be open about it, giving the presents to the villagers directly and finally letting them in on the secret, even though many of them had suspected her all along. People had been coming up to her and Andrew all morning and thanking them, although Willow had been quick to point out that they hadn't been the sole gift-givers in all of this.

'I hope you weren't too disappointed that it wasn't Joseph after all,' Willow said.

Dorothy looked over at Joseph, who had a stand a little further down, and he gave her a little wave. Dorothy visibly blushed. Their relationship had really blossomed over the last week or so and there was even talk that Joseph might pop the question soon. Mainly that talk had been from Dorothy herself, but she'd said she would say yes if he asked because 'When you find the one, why wait?' Willow completely understood that sentiment. It was probably a bit too soon for her and Andrew to be thinking of marriage just yet, but in her heart she knew that what they had was forever.

'The gift-giving brought us together, regardless of who sent the gifts, so no, I'm not disappointed at all. Thank you for what you did, Willow. I think you brought us all together.'

Willow smiled; Dorothy had finally got her name right. 'It was my pleasure.'

Willow moved on to Ruby's stand. 'Thank you for doing this.'

'Oh, no worries. Besides, as this is going to be my new home, at least for a year, I want to help if I can.'

Willow was beyond excited that Ruby had made that decision. She couldn't wait for Ruby to move in properly, but she had to wait for her own house in St Octavia to sell first.

'Well you know, Jacob is thinking of moving here too,' Willow said and watched Ruby's face light up briefly before it closed down.

'Well that will be nice for Andrew to have his brother closer,' Ruby shrugged, trying to pull off an air of nonchalance that she didn't quite achieve.

'I think he might be coming to see the fireworks tonight,' Willow tried again. Jacob had taken off the week before because he had an exhibition of his work in St Ives. Both Ruby and Jacob had insisted to her and Andrew that it had just been a one-night stand between them, well actually a two-night stand as it turned out, but Willow had the feeling that it had been more than that for both of them, though Andrew didn't agree.

'Is he?' Ruby said, clearly trying to suppress a smile as she focussed her attention on rearranging the baubles on her stall.

Willow smiled. 'Well I'll send him your way if I see him.'

'If he wants to see me, I'm sure he'll find me, the village isn't that big. But I won't hold my breath.'

Willow sighed. She wanted someone lovely for Ruby but she had to remember that not everyone was looking for the rose-tinted happy ending. Ruby seemed very happy without a man and just because Willow had found her happy ending didn't mean that her friend needed or wanted that particular conventional happy ending for herself.

She moved on to the start of the main high street and looked down the hill at the little whitewashed houses and the smartly painted shops. The gardening team had done a fabulous job of providing hanging baskets and troughs filled with overflowing flowers and, coupled with the fairy lights that were strewn across the street, the place looked magical.

She heard a vehicle trundle round the grassy slopes and she turned to see who it was. All the cars from the visitors were going to park in the large car park behind the castle but she smiled to see the words 'The Big Bang' emblazoned onto the side. This was the fireworks team and Andrew's friend Leo.

The van pulled to a stop by her side and a man with dark hair and a huge smile wound down the window.

'Hey, any idea where we're supposed to go with the fireworks?' the man asked. 'Andrew was supposed to be here to meet us but he's probably off somewhere with his new girlfriend.'

'Well, I'm the new girlfriend and he's not here. I think he might be round the back sorting out signs for the car park. Leo, right?'

His smile grew wider. 'Yes. So you're the mystery Willow, we've been dying to meet you.'

Leo got out and a woman climbed out the passenger side who was so heavily pregnant it looked like she was going to pop at any second. She was followed by a small, overexcited boy.

'This is my wife Isla and my son Elliot,' Leo said and to Willow's surprise, Isla immediately enveloped her in a big hug.

'We're so pleased to meet you,' Isla said. 'We've heard so much about you. Now that Andrew has finished most of the work here, you'll have to come round for dinner one night.'

'I'd like that.' She turned her attention to Elliot. 'Are you looking forward to seeing the fireworks tonight?'

'Yes and Daddy Leo says I can help set it all up today,' Elliot said, bouncing on the spot.

'Wow, that is exciting.'

'And the baby likes the fireworks too,' Elliot said.

'Yes, she wriggles constantly, but the only time she is still is when the fireworks are going off,' Isla said. 'I think I'll have to play firework noises in the nursery to get her off to sleep.'

Willow laughed.

'Look, we better get down there and get everything set up,' Leo said. 'Can you point us in the right direction?'

'Sure, just follow the road down to the very end and we were going to have the fireworks on the edge of the cliffs. But you set it up wherever you think is suitable.'

'Great. We'll catch up with you later.'

Willow waved them off. It was nice to meet some of Andrew's friends. She turned around and her eyes fell on Morgan. The screens had been finished two days before but Morgan had been tweaking tiny bits here and there and she was still there now, touching up one of the horses. She was definitely a perfectionist. Even Willow had to agree that the screens looked amazing.

Willow hadn't really spoken to her since the day she'd had that blazing row with Andrew. Not in any deliberately hostile way – there had been so much going on with the last-minute preparations for the open day, making her little candle gifts, making the lanterns for the parade that night and finishing off all the painting that there hadn't been any time, and Willow hadn't felt particularly inclined to seek her out anyway. She wasn't sure if Andrew had talked to Morgan about more than work, but she knew he wasn't happy with her.

But life was too short for bitter grudges and Andrew and Morgan had so much history. She didn't want him to walk away from that so easily.

Willow took a deep breath and walked over to talk to her.

Morgan climbed down the ladder as she approached and stepped back to look at her work.

'Looks fantastic,' Willow said.

Morgan turned round to look at her. She didn't say anything for the longest time and then she nodded. 'Thanks.'

They were silent for a while as Morgan wiped her hands. 'I'm sorry.'

Willow felt her eyebrows shoot up, she hadn't been expecting that. 'For what? For teaching me to sign to Andrew that he had a small penis which I accidentally signed to Poppy instead? Or for trying to cause trouble between us from the moment you arrived in the village?'

'Yeah, both of those things.'

At that moment Andrew appeared from the car park round the back of the castle. Willow hadn't seen him for most of the morning and at some point he had clearly gone home and changed into a suit. He looked sexy and suave.

She let out an ear-piercing wolf whistle and he looked over and laughed when he saw it was her.

She carefully signed. *'You look hot.'*

He laughed again and signed back. *'Elephant shoes.'*

Her heart filled with love for him.

'Elephant shoes?' Morgan said, in confusion.

Willow smiled, not taking her eyes off him as he took up his place near the gate. 'It's kind of our thing.'

Morgan was quiet for a while and then she spoke. 'You're good for him. I literally have never seen him so happy as he is when he's with you.'

'He's good for me too.'

Morgan sighed. 'I always thought we would end up together some day. Not in the kind of way where I was head over heels in love with him. I just thought… we fitted. When I heard he had a serious girlfriend, someone he had shared things with that he'd never shared with me, I was jealous. I suppose I was jealous that I was never that person for him.'

Willow smiled. 'I was jealous of you too, the history you

had shared, the friendship. The fact that you are fluent in sign language.'

'I haven't been much of a friend to him lately. But I want him to be happy. And he's found that with you.'

Andrew suddenly let out a whistle and Willow looked over.

'They're coming,' he shouted.

'I better go,' Willow said.

Morgan nodded as she quickly packed away her things and Willow raced over to her candle table. There was a last-minute flurry as everyone straightened their wares on their tables, and then suddenly the first car was pulling up at the gates.

Willow watched Andrew hand over a Happiness gift voucher to all the occupants of the car and then direct them towards the car park. As the car trundled off, it was replaced by another.

Willow took a deep breath and crossed her fingers behind her back. After everything they had done, this had to work.

Willow couldn't help but smile as she passed out the lanterns she had made to the visitors and they started making their way towards the end of the village. There was an excited buzz about the firework display from the visitors, many of whom had stayed the whole day.

The open day had been a big success. There had been quite a few visitors to the castle who had loved exploring the ruins and watching the jousting entertainment and most of them had then gone to investigate the village. But there had been almost two hundred people that had come to specifically look at the village itself. A few people had even reserved houses there and then. Kitty and Ken had been rushed off their feet taking down details from interested parties. Many of them might go away and decide Happiness was not for them but Willow was quietly confident the village would at least be half filled in a few months' time.

Everyone had been charmed by the little village and most of all its people who had made the guests feel very welcome, chatting to them and giving them their little gifts. The visitors were thrilled with their presents and it really helped to show Happiness in its best light.

She watched people walk past, the villagers mingling with the visitors, everyone happily chatting to each other. They had achieved something wonderful and really put Happiness back on the map.

Across the street, Willow could see Ruby and Jacob talking, standing very close to one another as the sea of visitors and villagers swarmed around them. Jacob whispered something in her ear and she smiled and nodded. Then he took her hand and together they marched off towards the pub. It seemed that they might miss the fireworks and Ruby didn't seem to care.

Willow smiled. She didn't know what the future held for the two of them but as long as her friend was happy, then Willow was happy for her.

Kitty and Ken approached and she gave them a lantern. There didn't seem to be anyone else coming down the high street towards them as all the visitors were already making their way to the cliff tops, so she grabbed one of the last lanterns for herself and joined them on the walk down.

'I think the day has gone off with a bang,' Willow said.

'It really has,' Kitty said, linking arms with her. 'All thanks to you.'

'Oh god no, everyone has worked so hard for today, you guys have been rushed off your feet and so much work has gone into getting the village ready. And the presents that everyone has made, I can't take credit for any of that.'

'But it was your idea,' Ken said.

'But it took the whole village to make it work. How many houses did you manage to fill today?' Willow said, quickly deflecting the attention away from her.

'Eight definites and six more that are going to let me know on Monday. But there were lots more that were really interested so we may hear from them once they've had time to think about it,' Ken said.

'It will be lovely to have some new faces here and some new shops too,' Willow said.

Just then she saw Andrew moving towards them through the crowds, a big smile on his face.

'Sorry,' he said, signing it at the same time. 'Just helping Leo make sure everything is ready for the fireworks.'

She watched his hands as he spoke and smiled. The biggest change in the village over the last week or so had been Andrew's attitude to his deafness. He had started teaching her sign language straight away and, although she was a long way off being able to sign whole sentences, she knew many key words now. He had started to sign almost every time he spoke so she would get used to it and that meant he would sign to her in the pub, out on the street, in her shop, where everyone could see it. The villagers had been interested in this change, of course, Willow had seen them watching him on several occasions, but beyond that no one had treated him any differently and they had quickly got used to it. As Dorothy said, most of the elderly villagers were deaf or hearing impaired too and there had been talk of offering a sign language class to the whole village which a lot of people were interested in. Even Ruby had said she wanted to learn it, which Willow liked after all the fuss she had made about finding out both Poppy and Andrew were deaf.

Because Willow didn't yet know the signs for *'Don't worry'* or *'No problem'* she leaned up and kissed him instead. Sometimes actions spoke louder than words.

They followed the golden glow of the lanterns out of the village and past the old ruined houses until they came to where hundreds of people were standing against the temporary barricade. It had been erected so no one could get too close to the fireworks but Andrew lifted the rope for her and tugged her underneath.

'Aren't we supposed to stay that side?' Willow said, looking back at the crowds who were watching them disappear into the darkness as they approached the cliff edge. She could see all the fireworks were ready to go in tubes pointing out towards the sea and Leo running around doing last-minute checks.

To Willow's surprise, Andrew led her to the top of the steps leading down to the beach.

'I thought we could watch the fireworks from down here, it's a better view without all the crowds,' he said.

'Oh, that's a lovely idea,' Willow said as they started picking their way down the steps. She was glad of the lantern she was carrying but it didn't throw out too much light and, as they stepped away from the lights of the rest of the village, Andrew pulled his mobile phone from his pocket and turned on the torch too.

When they reached the bottom, Willow could see the tide was out and there was a picnic blanket laid out on the sand, surrounded by tiny little solar lights.

'Oh, this is why you were late?' Willow laughed and Andrew grinned at her over his shoulder.

The picnic blanket was laid out with a hamper to one side and a bottle of champagne chilling in an ice bucket.

'This is lovely, thank you for doing this,' Willow said, sitting down on the blanket and using the sign for '*Thank you*' as she spoke.

'It's my pleasure. I've been so busy over the last few weeks and I want to spend some quality time with you,' Andrew said, uncorking the champagne and pouring out two glasses. He passed one to her and sat down next to her. 'It was here on this beach, as you ran off with my clothes and I could barely breathe I was laughing so much, that I knew I was going to marry you one day. I think I loved you even then, though I didn't want to admit it to myself. You have turned my life around and I love you so much.'

She smiled and leaned forward and kissed him. 'I love you too,' she whispered against his lips before kissing him again.

She put her champagne glass down in the sand and lay down on the blanket, staring up at the stars twinkling above them. Andrew lay down by her side and held her hand. They listened to the sounds of the waves for a while and beyond that there was silence. She had never felt so completely and utterly blissfully content in her whole life as she felt then lying next to the man she loved.

Andrew rolled onto his side and placed a kiss on her bare shoulder. 'You know, the last time we made a toast we toasted to making love under the stars?'

She laughed. 'Oh that's your game, bringing me down here? Is that picnic basket filled with condoms instead of food?'

Andrew sat up, opened the picnic hamper and pulled out a condom. She laughed loudly.

'There is food in there too,' he said. 'For after.'

She shook her head. 'You're so sure of yourself.'

'I am now. That's because of you.'

She smiled with love for him and as he lay back down next to her she kissed him, slowly undressing him as he removed her own clothes. He rolled over on top of her, still kissing her.

He moved back onto his knees as he ripped open the condom and a firework exploded in the night sky above them.

'Oooh,' Willow said as the sky glittered with gold.

Andrew leaned over her, bracing himself on his forearms as he positioned himself between her legs.

'You're going to miss the show,' Willow said, watching another firework send cascading silvery stars through the darkness behind Andrew.

'I've got something much more beautiful to look at. You can tell me all about it.'

As the fireworks exploded above them, one after the other, Willow signed the words for the different colours that sparkled above the sea. Although she stopped when she realised Andrew was just watching her, smiling.

'Did I get it right?'

'You are perfect, in every single way.'

He slid carefully inside and she wrapped herself around him. As the fireworks lit up the sky in a riot of colour he started to move against her, his eyes locked on hers the whole time.

'I never did give you a Secret Society gift, did I?' Andrew said. 'It doesn't seem right that you're the only one in the village not to get one. I'll have to rectify that.'

'But you did,' Willow said, reaching up and stroking his face. 'You gave me the gift of happiness.'

The End

A NOTE ABOUT ANDREW

When I started writing Andrew's character, I knew almost straight away he was going to be deaf. As vividly as I knew he had dark hair and blue eyes, I knew he was going to be deaf too. But then I got worried about doing his character justice. I'm not deaf, I have no deaf people in my family, could I really comprehend what it was like to be hearing impaired or to have no hearing at all? But a very good author friend said that if we are scared to write what we don't know, then when will it stop? Should I not write about men because I'm a woman, should I not write about children because I'm an adult, should I not write about dogs and cats because I'm a human? She said being fearful of misrepresenting a certain way of life could drive further wedges between our differences, keeping us apart rather than bringing us closer to a society of true understanding and equality. And I knew she was right and I had to write Andrew as I always envisaged him.

So then I researched the hell out of it, more so than I ever had before for any other character. I had a deaf friend at university and while we are not really in contact anymore, I remembered what she told me and some of that helped to shape Andrew's past. I spoke to a lot of people in the Deaf community who were more than happy to share their experiences of growing up deaf, using hearing aids, sign language and all the good and the bad stuff in between.

A lot of people obviously had very different experiences of being deaf. For example, one person said it would be very unlikely that a person that had been born deaf could be cured so well with hearing aids that they had no problem speaking, she said that it was more likely that Andrew had learned to speak and then went deaf when he was older. Other people I spoke to said it was fine that Andrew was diagnosed very early in his life before he could talk. So while for some, Andrew might not be a true representation of their experience of being deaf, he is a character made up of lots of people's experiences.

The one sticking point I had while telling the story was with British Sign Language (BSL). The language has its own structure, so for example when you're describing something you always start with the setting. 'There was a small boy called Rob standing on the bridge in the park,' would be signed something like, 'Park, bridge, small boy, Rob, standing.' I obviously couldn't have conversations like that in my book as the reader wouldn't understand what the characters were saying so I had to use a bit of poetic licence while interpreting the sign language.

I have to say that the research paid off, at least for me. While writing Andrew's character and trying to ensure he was as real as possible, I completely and utterly fell in love with him and I hope you did too.

THE GIFT OF HAPPINESS

CHAPTER ONE

Ruby Marlowe bumped her custard-yellow Mini along the country road, the headlights picking out the sparkling frosty leaves of the hedges but not penetrating much further than that through the velvet darkness. The moonlight lit up the sky, like a lighthouse welcoming her home, and, as she rounded a corner, she could see the turrets and towers of Harmony Castle silhouetted against the inky sky.

She pulled into the gates of the little village of Happiness and stopped in front of the castle, cutting the engine and listening to the complete and utter silence.

She peered through the steamed-up windscreen at the village that was going to be her new home. The start of the village was a little further down from where she was, the Christmas lights hanging above the street sending warm puddles of gold across the wet cobbles. There was not a soul in sight. It wasn't the warm welcome she'd been hoping for. But then what had she been expecting? It was two o'clock in the morning and everyone was tucked up in their beds.

Even her best friend Willow wouldn't be there as she'd gone to Paris with her boyfriend Andrew, although they were arriving back the next day. Or rather, later on that day. To be fair to Willow, Ruby was supposed to have moved to Happiness the month before, but last-minute complications with selling her home had caused a few weeks' delay, which was not ideal. As her job involved selling Christmas decorations and paraphernalia, December was her busiest and best time of the year. Moving into Happiness with just over a week until the big day didn't leave a lot of time to get her shop set up and some sales through the tills.

To make matters worse, there had been a flood in the shop she had been given. Kitty and Ken, the owners of the castle and the village, had promised her it would be fixed and cleaned up in a few weeks and assigned her a temporary shop in the meantime. It was double-fronted and one half was taken up by the artist Phoenix Blade who was apparently away at an exhibition. Kitty and Ken had been unable to contact him to ask if he would mind if Ruby moved into the other half for a short time but Kitty had assured her that Phoenix was lovely and probably wouldn't mind at all.

Probably.

That filled Ruby with all kinds of joy.

Kitty and Ken had offered free rent and accommodation for a year to anyone who could bring something to the rundown little village. They had been more than happy to give Ruby a shop to sell her Christmas decorations, which had been a dream of hers for a long time. But now, and not for the first time, she wondered whether she'd done the right thing. She played with the snowflake around her neck that Harry had bought her. He would laugh at her if he could see her now. Ruby had lived in the same town all her life, even after her parents had long since emigrated to the furthest shores of

Norway. Her brother Cal had toured almost every country of the world before his thirtieth birthday, but Ruby had stayed put. Harry used to tease her that she didn't do change. She had been stuck in a rut, professionally, geographically, personally and emotionally, for too many years to count and when her best friend, Willow, had packed up her worldly goods and moved across the country to the little village of Happiness, Ruby had found herself yearning for a change exactly like that too. When she'd visited Happiness to see Willow, she'd kind of fallen in love with the place.

And that had absolutely nothing to do with Jacob Harrington, Andrew's sexy older brother.

Just the thought of Jacob sent a twist of desire through her stomach. He had been this glorious one-night stand – well OK, it had actually been three nights – and yes it had been incredible and he'd been lovely and made her laugh, but she had drawn a line under it when she had returned to her own home in St Octavia. He had texted and phoned a few times but she hadn't returned his messages and, when Willow tried to bring it up, Ruby had told her she didn't want to talk about Jacob Harrington. She wasn't interested in a relationship with him or anyone.

Not anymore.

She supposed she would have to face him at some point; he was Andrew's brother and would be bound to visit. But maybe if she got enough warning from Willow, she could make sure she was out the way those days, or at least try to keep her head down.

She looked around her. On the slopes leading up to the great castle was a tall Christmas tree with baubles as big as her head. Tiny lights twinkled in the darkness as they danced around the tree. It was an impressive sight with the castle silhouetted behind it.

There also appeared to be a life-size nativity scene set up in front of it with a large open-faced barn. Mary and Joseph were kneeling around the manger where presumably baby Jesus was wrapped up like an Egyptian mummy. There was no sign of the wise men or the shepherds but, as Ruby peered through the darkness, there was something moving in front of the barn.

She climbed out of the car and realised there was a real donkey and two sheep grazing in a small paddock in front of the barn. Well, that was certainly taking the nativity scene very seriously.

She knew Willow had been heavily involved in the decorations, although she hadn't mentioned a real-life nativity scene. Perhaps she'd done it to appease the older, more traditional members of the village.

Feeling suddenly mischievous, she opened her boot and rooted around until she found the appropriate bag and then walked up to the paddock.

She knew donkeys could be quite unpredictable and that some people used them as guard pets, but as Ruby approached the paddock the donkey immediately ambled over to the fence. She stroked his velvety nose and he seemed quite happy with that.

She shoved her hands in the pocket of her coat for the chopped carrots she had bought as a snack from McDonald's on her way over here and held one out. The donkey whiffled it up. The two sheep looked over with mild interest at the prospect of something to eat rather than grass or hay but they didn't approach. She tossed the carrots over the fence in their direction but they seemed scared by this gesture and quickly retreated to the furthest corner.

Ruby looked around; as no one was about she climbed over the fence. The donkey was unperturbed and she approached the nativity scene. Mary and Joseph were huge. If they had been standing they would have been seven or eight feet tall, but as it was they were kneeling down, leaning over the manger, which looked tiny in comparison. They looked creepy rather than realistic, and the model of Mary had very large hairy hands. In fact, it even looked like she might have had a beard at one point, which had been hastily painted over. Also, on closer inspection, Joseph was sporting an eye patch, although you wouldn't have been able to see that from the road as his face was turned to the side. Ruby laughed out loud when she spotted the hook instead of a hand. It seemed Willow might have got a cheap deal and found a couple of models of pirates to use for the nativity instead. The models had been dressed in real clothes and headdresses to make them look more authentic, so maybe Willow had thought no one would notice the pirate origins.

Ruby glanced down at the baby Jesus, who thankfully was just a large doll covered in a blanket and not pirate-themed like his parents.

She quickly looked around one more time and then swapped Jesus for a cuddly snowman, complete with top hat. She tucked the snowman under the blanket. She knew Willow would get a big kick out of this. Ruby and Willow had been playing jokes on each other every Christmas for many years so it was good to get in first before Willow could get back and start her regime of practical jokes.

Ruby made a move towards the fence just as one of the sheep started making a weird choking noise. She turned round and could see bits of chewed carrot on the floor in front of the sheep as the animal continued to hack and cough.

Bloody hell. Kidnapping baby Jesus was one thing but killing one of the sheep within minutes of arriving in the village was a new low, even for her.

She moved over to see what she could do, wondering how she could do the Heimlich manoeuvre on a sheep. She'd done a first aid course a few months before and one of the sessions had been dog first aid and how to help a dog when it was choking – surely it would be much the same? The sheep didn't move away from her when she got nearer. It was quite a small animal so she moved behind it and wrapped her arms around its belly, squeezing upwards a few times, but it made no difference. She patted the sheep between the shoulder blades but still the animal was choking. She lifted the back legs up as if she was about to run a wheelbarrow race with the poor animal and somehow this did the trick. The piece of carrot fell out of the sheep's mouth and then the sheep gave Ruby a kick in the leg for her trouble.

Ruby staggered back a bit, rubbing her leg as the sheep continued to eat the carrots as if nothing had happened.

She glanced around and the donkey was watching her, almost as if it was afraid she would suddenly try to do the same manoeuvre on him. It was all rather embarrassing – her only saving grace was that no one had been around to see her manhandling the poor sheep.

She picked up Jesus and climbed back over the fence.

She watched the sheep for a few moments to make sure it wasn't going to choke on the carrots again, but it had now finished and had moved back over to a bundle of hay with its friend, who had barely looked up during all the fracas.

Ruby quickly hurried back to her car before she could get into any more trouble. She climbed back into the driver's seat and put Jesus carefully on the seat next to her, wiping the mud off his face from where she'd dropped him on the ground to try to save the sheep.

She looked at the map that Kitty had sent her marking where the shop was and where her cottage was. The village was laid out like a large triangle, with the only pub in the village, The Welcome Home, at the top. Her shop and cottage were on the main high street that led down towards the cliff tops and the steps down to the beach. Along the cliff to the right, about half a mile down the coastal path, was Willow and Andrew's cottage and a little track from there led back to the village and met the pub at the junction with the high street.

She drove her little yellow Mini down the high street, passing small thatched cottages that had stood there for many hundreds of years, and shops that seemed to offer everything from bread, cheese, knitting stuff to some more items of the arty kind. The place had changed so much since Ruby had been there in the summer. The village had been practically a ghost town then but it looked like it had come alive in the last few months. There were Christmas lights hanging from the houses and lampposts, and it gave her hope.

She looked up at them as she drove carefully underneath them. The lights were mainly laid out in vertical strings like icicles, forming a large curtain which was sort of triangle-shaped. She cocked her head and then slammed on the brakes. They weren't triangles at all, they were... knickers.

No, they couldn't be. But the more she looked at them, there was no escaping the fact these were illuminated knickers. In fact, the way the curtains parted in the middle made them look more like Y-fronts than knickers. Ruby sat there and stared at the Y-fronts that were hung incrementally all the way down the street and burst out laughing. She was never going to let Willow live this down. Nothing would top this.

But then she spotted the candles either side of the street. The candles had holly leaves and two large red berries at the candles' base, making them look like penises. Ruby was crying with laughter by this time. Penis and Y-front lights, these were the best lights ever!

Ruby carried on driving down the high street, chuckling to herself. She found the double-fronted shop quite easily; Phoenix Blade had his name in gold writing above one side of the shop. She was just going to dump some of her stuff in the shop and then crawl into her bed.

Ruby got out of the car and stretched. There was a freezing chill in the air and the windows sparkled with a heavy frost, her breath coming out in little puffs of steam.

She wrapped her purple woollen coat around her and checked under the flowerpot near the door where Kitty had said she would leave the key. Sure enough, it was there waiting for her.

She picked it up and let herself in, closing the door behind her against the cold. She fumbled around inside and found the light switch, illuminating the whole room. There was an archway between the two shops and her side was empty, apart from a few boxes which seemed to have strayed over from the other half of the shop. She couldn't see much of Phoenix's side, as that half was still in darkness, but it didn't look particularly tidy.

Most of her stock was arriving tomorrow, so it wouldn't take her long to unload her car. She'd just taken the delicate things she didn't trust the removal men with.

She went back outside into the cold and started shifting the boxes inside the shop, but as she went back to collect the last one, she noticed a light on in the flat above the shop. She hoisted the box under her arm, closing the boot, and saw there was a tall shadowy figure peering out the window at her.

It seemed that Phoenix Blade had returned from his travels. He disappeared from the window and she wondered if she was going to meet her new neighbour. It probably wasn't the best time to introduce herself when it was two o'clock in the morning and she had been driving for what felt like eight hours.

She hoped to god he was nice and had been told she was coming.

She went back inside and closed the door, plonking the box on top of all the other boxes as she heard footsteps coming down the steps at the back of the shop. She dusted her hands down her coat, tried to straighten her hair and plastered a big smile on her face. And then suddenly a man was standing in the room with her and if this was Phoenix Blade he was not what she'd been expecting at all.

She felt a jolt of desire and shock slam into her as she stared at the man in front of her. His hair was dishevelled as if he'd just climbed out of bed. He was topless, showing a broad muscular chest and a smattering of hair disappearing into pyjama bottoms. His intense blue eyes showed shock and confusion. But mostly, what she hadn't been expecting was that Phoenix Blade was actually Jacob Harrington, the man she'd had probably the best sex of her life with just a few months before. The man who had touched places inside of her that hadn't been touched for over twelve years. The man she had blocked all contact with because she had been scared by how he made her feel.

Jacob stared at her.

'Ruby Marlowe, you're the last woman I'd expect to see here.'

Ruby found she still had no words to describe what she felt about seeing Jacob again.

She swallowed. 'I wasn't exactly expecting to see you either.'

He frowned. 'You're standing in my shop.'

Oh crap. This was *his* shop? Wait, no, Kitty had told her

she was sharing a shop with Phoenix Blade, not Jacob Harrington. There must be some mistake.

'I was told the shop belonged to some artist called Phoenix Blade.'

'It does, and that would be me.'

He was serious. He was obviously living here in the village and now she was going to have to share a shop with him too.

'How was I supposed to know that was you?'

'It didn't come up in conversation between us?' Jacob asked.

'When you were giving me multiple orgasms, strangely not.'

A ghost of a smile appeared on his lips and she cursed herself. The last thing she wanted to mention was the magnificent sex they'd shared. She wanted to forget it had ever happened. In fact, she had spent the last four months trying unsuccessfully to forget those incredible nights she'd spent with this man, and now the memory hung in the air between them.

Her emotions fought a war inside her. There was a huge part of her that wanted to take him straight back up to his bed and rekindle that amazing connection they'd had a few months before. But her heart and her head knew better. If they were both living here now, she couldn't get involved with him again. That would lead to a whole load of complicated emotions and a road that she had no interest in going down.

'What are you doing here, Ruby?'

'Kitty didn't tell you?'

He shook his head. 'Well to be honest, I haven't checked my emails and I've been away so I haven't seen her.'

Surely Kitty could have phoned him. And why hadn't Kitty mentioned to her that Phoenix was actually Jacob? Why hadn't Willow told her? Although Willow had no clue that

Ruby had been given the other half of Jacob's shop for the next few weeks, she would have known he was living in the village. A little bit of warning wouldn't have gone amiss. Unless... There had been many villagers who had been rooting for Jacob and Ruby to get together when they'd both been there in the summer and anyone could see the chemistry between them. Had this whole flood debacle been part of a cunning plan to reacquaint her and Jacob again in a much more intimate setting than either of them would probably like?

'Well, I'm sorry to be the one to tell you this but you now have a roommate, at least until after Christmas,' Ruby said.

His eyes widened. 'You're living here?'

Ruby couldn't help but smile at the panic on his face. He probably had a whole harem of women he entertained on a regular basis and he was now worried how this new living arrangement would affect that lifestyle. Even though she had her own cottage further down the street, she decided to tease him.

'Yeah, that's OK, isn't it?'

He looked around as if wondering where to stash her. 'I guess. I mean I have a spare room; it has a single bed for when Poppy stays over, you could sleep in there.'

She was surprised by that generous offer and that he wasn't throwing her out already. After blowing him off a few months before, she didn't think he would be welcoming her with open arms.

He fixed her with a mischievous look. 'Unless you want to share my bed?'

Ruby laughed. 'And there's the Jacob I know.'

She glanced down at his pyjama bottoms which had cuddly snowmen in various sexual positions all over them. She shook her head with a smile. They were funny, sexy, sweet and suited him to a T.

'I'm only messing with you, come on, let me show you to your room,' Jacob said.

She smiled. He was a good man. She certainly didn't deserve this level of kindness from him. She wondered if she had hurt him when she cut him off in the summer. But this was a man who had probably slept with more women than she'd had hot dinners. It had been a very casual, no-strings-attached arrangement in the summer and they'd both known that so he had no reason to be upset when she walked away. She sighed. She probably should have texted him back. They'd had fun, he had been really nice, they had parted with a really sweet kiss goodbye, she shouldn't have just blanked him. Although that kiss had probably been one of the main reasons why she had.

'I'm only joking too. I'm just sharing your shop. You don't need to worry about me cramping your style. You can continue to sleep with all the women in the village, I'm not going to be in your way,' she teased.

'You make me sound like some kind of Casanova,' Jacob said.

She smiled. 'We both know you're much worse than that.'

He laughed. 'You were the one who didn't return my calls. So does that make you the female equivalent of Casanova? Cleopatra maybe.'

'Maybe. Perhaps I should have delivered myself to you wrapped up in a Persian carpet rather than arriving in my little Mini.'

'Well that would have been a treat.' His eyes appraised her for a moment. 'Ah Ruby, I've actually missed you.'

He moved towards her and before she could stop him he wrapped her in a big hug.

She wanted to tell him it was ridiculous for him to miss her; it had been sex and nothing more. But she couldn't find the words to dismiss what they'd shared. This hug was everything she did and didn't need right then. His scent, his warmth, his body against hers. She took it all back, this was the perfect kind of welcome. There was a little voice inside her that was shouting at her that this was a terrible idea but she ignored that because being wrapped in Jacob Harrington's arms was the most incredible feeling ever.

She slid her arms around his back and held him close. Her heart felt tight in her chest, a lump of emotion burning a hole in her throat. She didn't want this but she couldn't let him go either.

Eventually she pulled back away from him.

'Come upstairs,' Jacob said, still holding her shoulders. 'We can… talk.'

From the way he was looking at her, talk seemed to be the very last thing on Jacob's mind. She absolutely could not jump straight back into bed with him as if the months they'd been apart hadn't happened at all. This was a dangerous road to go down. She didn't want this.

'Jacob, I need to go to bed. It's nearly half two in the morning and I'm exhausted.'

He hesitated before he spoke and something told her he knew she needed to get away from him.

'OK.'

'I'll see you tomorrow.'

'Come for breakfast,' Jacob said.

She really didn't want him to get any ideas about that hug or anything else happening between them. And although her plan for facing Jacob had originally been to avoid him at all costs, now it seemed she would need to talk to him, to explain that nothing was going to happen between them again. So if they were going to work alongside each other for the next few weeks, it would be better to have that conversation sooner rather than later.

'Breakfast sounds good.'

She wasn't looking forward to that conversation.

He bent his head and kissed her on the cheek and she hated the way her heart leapt at his touch.

'I'll see you tomorrow then, Ruby Marlowe.'

She quickly hurried outside and locked the door, trying not to look at him as he watched her go.

She climbed back in her car and pulled off down the high street, bumping over the cobbles. The main shops fell away and out on the horizon the sea glittered under the moonlight. She could see a cluster of white cottages. She knew hers was on the right somewhere, so she slowed down and looked at the house names. Dragonfly Cottage, Butterfly Cottage, all with flowers painted around the door, which she knew had been done by her friend Willow's hand. And then she saw it. Christmas Cottage, with little holly leaves and red berries painted around the front door. She couldn't help but smile about that.

She quickly got out and looked at it. It gleamed in the moonlight. This was going to be her new home. She grabbed her suitcase, found the key under the mat and let herself in, stepping into the lounge. She switched on the light and looked around.

Ruby's heart filled to see the Christmas tree in the corner, tastefully decorated with a few baubles and tiny fairy lights. This would definitely be Willow's doing and she had left enough room for Ruby to add her own decorations. There was a gorgeous cherry-red log burner under a solid wood mantelpiece and a beautiful silver-grey rug on the floor that looked soft enough to sleep on.

She had a quick look at the kitchen before going upstairs

and walking into the bedroom. Thankfully Willow had worked her magic in here too, making up the king-size bed with a super-thick duvet and squishy pillows. She quickly got changed, brushed her teeth in the tiny en-suite bathroom and peeled the duvet back ready to get in. She leapt back when she saw there was an ugly black spider the size of her hand waiting for her. But as she stepped closer to it, she realised it was plastic and no doubt placed there by Willow. Ruby laughed, removed the spider and climbed into bed. She switched off the light and looked at the stars twinkling above her through the skylight.

Jacob Harrington.

God, of all the people she had casually dated over the last twelve years who had meant nothing to her, why had the one person who had meant something make his way back into her life?

She closed her eyes, knowing if she did manage to sleep that night, then he would feature very heavily in her dreams.

CHAPTER TWO

Jacob turned the sausages over and put them back under the grill. Ruby had texted him a while before and said she'd be over in half hour so he wanted to make sure that breakfast was ready for her.

It was somewhat ironic that that text was the first communication from her in around four or five months.

He'd read the emails from Kitty and Ken that morning explaining that Ruby was going to be in the other half of his shop until after Christmas. He wished he'd checked his messages before so he'd known to expect her. Although he still wasn't sure how he would have reacted if he had known.

He'd been here in Happiness for a week in the summer to help his brother, Andrew, get the dilapidated village ready for the open day and Ruby had been there at the same time. The connection between them had been instant, but she was only supposed to be a one-night stand and they both knew that. He'd never really had a serious relationship in his life and he was quite happy casually dating without any of the commitments or emotional attachments of a long-term relationship.

They'd spent two glorious nights together, which normally would be enough for him, but when he'd left to do an exhibition, he'd thought about her constantly. He'd come back a week later to see the fireworks on the night of the open day and they'd ended up in bed again, making fireworks of their own. There had been something about Ruby that had got under his skin. And although he certainly wasn't looking for marriage or forever, Ruby had made him want something... more. He wasn't sure what that *more* would look like, but he knew he hadn't been quite ready to say goodbye to her in the summer.

But she'd left, returning to her hometown of St Octavia, several hundred miles away. Well, three hundred and thirty-four to be exact. He'd checked.

He'd texted her a few times, even called her, but there had been no response and so he'd let things slide. He'd put their time down to a wonderful couple of days and tried really hard to forget about her, although he hadn't been particularly successful at that.

He had moved to Happiness a few weeks later and life was good, he loved the little village with its colourful characters.

And now she was back and here to stay by the look of things.

He couldn't help being a bit thrilled about that.

Not that it meant anything. He wasn't entirely sure Ruby wanted to pick up from where they'd left off a few months before. He'd gotten some very mixed messages from her last night. She had held him so tight when he had hugged her, as if she didn't want to let him go, but when he'd simply suggested she come upstairs to talk she'd practically ran out of there.

He suddenly heard footsteps on the stairs and turned to find her standing in the room with him.

God, he wanted to walk straight over and kiss her but he wasn't sure that was allowed.

She smiled and cocked her head on one side to look at him. 'Jacob Harrington, you're looking pretty bloody spectacular as always.'

He moved towards her and wrapped her in a hug. She hugged him back. 'It's good to see you, Ruby.' He pulled back, holding her at arm's length. 'You're looking pretty amazing yourself.'

Ruby smiled and then moved further into the flat, looking around. 'So you're living here now?'

He watched her, the winter sunlight catching her red hair. 'Yeah.'

'Funny that Willow never told me.'

'I believe she tried to bring me up in conversation with you several times but that you didn't want to talk about me.'

Willow had tried to defend Ruby's decision to not answer his texts and calls. She was obviously very protective of her best friend but in the end she'd told him that Ruby had her heart broken in the past and just wasn't looking for love anymore. It was more than a little sad that some asshole had destroyed Ruby's faith in men so much that she never wanted another relationship. But he wasn't looking for love either. He didn't want the big all-singing-and-dancing love affair so he wasn't sure why Ruby was shying away from him.

Ruby was clearly floundering at hearing this. 'That wasn't what it was, I was just busy.'

He made her coffee just as she liked it then dished up the breakfast and carried the plates to the little table by the window that had distant sea views. The fields were covered in a thick layer of frost that sparkled in the winter sun. She sat down opposite him.

He watched her tuck into her breakfast. 'So you're moving into Happiness?'

'For a year,' Ruby was quick to clarify.

'And then what?'

She shrugged. 'Maybe some travelling.'

'That does sound good.'

'Alone.'

He suppressed a smile at the distinction.

'And we're going to be roomies,' Jacob said.

'In the professional sense. We're just sharing shop space.'

She was clearly trying to warn him off.

'So what's going on with you, Ruby?' Jacob asked, getting straight to the point. 'You practically hotfooted it out of here last night when I suggested coming upstairs.'

'Because I didn't want to sleep with you.'

He couldn't help but smile. 'Who said anything about sex? I just wanted to talk.'

She laughed. 'You're such a liar.'

'So what is it? Do you have some weird disease I should know about?'

She laughed in outrage. 'No I do not.'

'I know what it is, you got a tattoo with my face on it and you didn't want me to see it.'

She laughed again.

He smiled and took a bite of his toast as they watched each other across the table. He loved having this banter with her. She was so easy to get on with and he enjoyed flirting and teasing her. There was obvious chemistry between them, it practically crackled in the air. He had really missed this. He'd just never had this connection with any of the other women he'd been with.

'So what's going on here? I'm not proposing marriage and babies or even any kind of serious relationship. We had fun the last time you were here. I'm happy to have no-strings-attached fun again.'

'Wow,' Ruby said, dryly. 'What an offer.'

'I'm not sure why you're protesting so much. If I recall, you seemed to have a pretty good time in the summer,' he teased.

She smiled and shook her head. 'You're so cocky.'

'And I was under the impression that you didn't want a relationship.'

'I don't,' Ruby said, far too quickly for his liking.

'Neither do I.'

She stared at him for a few moments, maybe weighing up what was on the table. She picked up her coffee mug and took a big sip.

'I think it's best if we're just friends,' Ruby said after a while.

'Just to clarify, are we talking friends with benefits or…'

She laughed. 'Just friends, no benefits. We're working alongside each other, we now live in the same village, I don't want things to be awkward between us. If we start jumping into bed with each other every night, well that's starting to sound a bit like a relationship to me and neither of us wants that. And then when it ends, which it undoubtedly will, we'll have all this awkwardness between us. We really are better off just being friends.'

He stared at her. There was something going on here but he clearly wasn't going to get any straight answers out of her today.

He pretended he was giving it some serious thought but in reality he liked Ruby, and if the only way he was going to have her in his life was to be friends then he was more than OK with that.

'I've never had a girl as a friend before,' Jacob said. 'How does that work?'

'In the same way that it does with *boys*,' Ruby said.

'But no kissing or sex?' Jacob teased.

Ruby laughed. 'No!'

'OK, OK, Ruby Marlowe. I'm just messing with you. If you want to be friends then that's just fine. But just so you know, the offer of no-strings-attached sex is always on the table.'

She shook her head with a smile.

'So what brought you to Happiness?' Jacob asked, taking a sip of his tea.

'Oh, lots of reasons.' She paused for a moment as she thought. 'I don't know if I ever told you, my brother, Cal, is a Paralympian.'

'No, you never told me that,' Jacob said.

'He lost his leg in an accident when he was a kid and he went on to become one of the world's greatest athletes.'

Recognition dawned on his face. 'Callum Marlowe?'

Ruby beamed. 'Yes, you know him?'

'He's amazing, he won gold in running and hurdles in the last Paralympics. He was incredible to watch, he just flew down the track,' Jacob said.

'My brother is pretty bloody special. He's touring America right now, giving inspirational talks, and I just look at him and look at my own life and I wonder what I've done. I've lived in the same town all my life, had the same job. I just wanted a change. I just feel like I've been stuck in a rut for so long and I wanted to do something different. Plus I missed Willow. When she lived in St Octavia, we'd see each other every day. The free rent is an attractive feature too, I can save some money for going travelling.'

'So I wasn't the reason you came back?' Jacob teased.

'You're so sure of yourself. It's not an attractive feature, you know,' Ruby said, although she was still smiling.

He focussed his attention on his food for a moment but when he looked up she was still staring at him.

'So you're Phoenix Blade?'

He nodded.

'I knew you were a scrap metal artist. I didn't know you went under a pseudonym.'

'Well that's where the name comes from. Phoenix as in something new from the old and Blade because of the metal.'

'Makes sense,' Ruby said.

'Jacob Harrington sounds a bit boring.'

'Trust me, there is nothing boring about Jacob Harrington,' she said, staring him right in the eyes.

He smiled. God, being *just friends* with her was going to be a lot harder than he thought.

'And what made *you* decide to move to Happiness?' Ruby asked. 'This place strikes me as a little bit too sleepy for you.'

He thought about that for a moment as he mopped up the last of the egg with his sausage. 'I grew up in Newquay. I've lived in Plymouth, London, Rome and Penzance. They were all wonderful places but none of them felt like home. This place feels like home.'

Ruby nodded. 'I know what you mean.'

'People look out for each other here, I like that. It feels like a good place to raise a family.'

Her eyes bulged; all humour now gone. 'Jesus Christ, is that what you want? I never thought I'd ever hear you say those words.'

'Oh no, I didn't mean me, just that there are lots of young families here now, and if Andrew and Willow have children it's a great place to raise them.' He felt like he was backpedalling and he sighed. 'I suppose one day I might want that.'

He surprised himself with that comment. Did he really want that?

She was still looking horrified so he decided to reassure her.

'You don't need to worry; I'm not talking about now. One day.'

'I'm not worried because I won't be the one marrying you.'

'Have you never thought about marriage, babies, the happy ending?' Jacob asked, realising how clichéd he sounded.

'Why does a happy ending have to include marriage and babies?' Ruby said. 'I'm very happy on my own. There are no arguments about what to watch on TV, my house stays tidy until I mess it up. I don't need to worry about shaving my legs for my boyfriend or husband. I can go out and do whatever I want without having to think about someone else. No drama or arguments, having the bed to myself. I have friends for company, and sometimes wonderful men to spend the night with. That sounds pretty bloody happy to me.'

He'd obviously touched a nerve. 'I think you're right. Society puts a lot of pressure on us to get married, settle down, have children, when that life isn't for everyone. You need to do whatever makes you happy.'

Ruby visibly relaxed. 'I used to think I wanted marriage and children, when I was younger. I'd watched so many romance films, read so many books, and I expected that life. But that fairytale of the happy ever after doesn't exist. You need to make your own happiness in this world, not rely on someone else to do that for you.'

'To a certain extent I would agree. But just as marriage and children are not for everyone, there are many people that are very happily married, or very happy with a lifetime partner. Just because you don't want that lifestyle doesn't mean that other people won't find their happiness that way. Look at

Andrew and Willow. I've never seen two people so utterly in love and completely happy as they are together.'

Ruby smiled. 'I know. They are the epitome of the fairytale ending. You are right that, for some, they need someone in their lives to complete them, but I'm not one of them.'

'Some might say that the right man wouldn't complete you but complement you.'

'I don't need to be complemented. I'm pretty bloody fabulous as I am.'

He smiled. 'That you are, Ruby Marlowe.'

Jacob watched her finish her breakfast. He wanted to ask her what had happened in her life to make her so cynical but he decided that could wait for another day.

'So do you need a hand with settling in or moving boxes?' he asked.

'That's very kind. You're taking this friend thing very seriously,' Ruby said.

'If a job is worth doing, it's worth doing right.'

'Well, the removal van is arriving later, so yeah if you can give me a hand with unloading stuff into the shop, that would be great.'

'I can do that.'

Ruby smiled at him and then held her coffee cup up. 'I think we are going to be very good at this friendship malarkey.'

He chinked his mug against hers. 'To friendship.'

CHAPTER THREE

Ruby left Jacob's flat and stepped out onto the street, pulling her flowered knitted hat onto her head. It was freezing cold and the weather report had even promised a smattering of snow later.

She was glad she'd had the chance to sort things out with Jacob before it had got awkward and actually she was now looking forward to working alongside him for the next few weeks rather than dreading it. He was a lovely man and she knew they were going to be very close friends.

She decided to have a little wander around the village to remind herself of where everything was – she hadn't had a chance to have a proper look the night before when she had been distracted by giant underpants and penis-shaped candles. She looked to the left where, further down the street, her cottage was tucked into the last cluster of houses before the village ended and then there was only sea stretching out for miles into the horizon.

She turned right and wandered into the main part of the village. Villagers, wrapped up against the cold, bustled from shop to shop, either carrying bags of shopping or probably just popping in for a chat, while small children chased each other up the street or followed their parents around. The place felt so alive.

Little shops were dressed for Christmas, some with trees in the windows, some with lights curled around the window displays. It all looked very pretty. She took a few pictures of the more arty displays for her Instagram.

This was what a traditional Christmas was supposed to be like. Her parents always flew over from Norway to spend Christmas with her and Cal, but this year they had opted to spend it on the warm beaches of Australia. They had invited her to come along of course, especially as Cal was likely to be working away from home over Christmas, but wearing shorts and flip-flops and having a barbeque on the beach just didn't feel Christmassy enough for her. And as the plan was to move to Happiness, she'd thought she'd try Christmas in her new home. Being here now, it felt like the right decision.

There was such an array of shops here, the practical grocery shops, bakeries, cafés, a chemist, interspersed with the more quirky touristy kind of shops with paintings in the windows, jewellery, pottery, and other arty things. It was the perfect mix.

Ruby peered into Willow's shop window, which was all in darkness now as she still hadn't returned from her holiday yet, but the Christmas candles in the window glittered prettily in the lights from the street.

She walked on a bit further and smiled when she saw the gold hand-painted sign above one of the empty shops. *The Happy Little Christmas Shop.* This was where her shop was supposed to be until the burst pipe had put an end to that, well at least for now. She peered through the window and could see the shelves all ready for her Christmas decorations. It was a shame that her temporary shop was further down the high street, she would have preferred to be in the thick of it all. But at least it was only for a short while.

She turned around and saw what looked like a wanted poster on one of the lampposts. In fact, she realised, they were on every lamppost.

She moved closer and read it.

STOLEN! Baby Jesus was taken from the nativity last night, somewhere between the hours of 6pm and 7am. Reward of £5 leading to his safe return.

Then there was a photo of the doll underneath. Ruby stifled a giggle. What had started as a joke for Willow's benefit had escalated very quickly. She would be appearing on *Crimewatch* next. As soon as Willow had seen the snowman in the manger, Ruby would have to return Jesus to his rightful home. She was sure Pirate Pete and his wife must be missing him.

She decided to go into the post office, which also sold all the basic groceries, to get a few things. She remembered this place from when she had been there in the summer; it was a whole emporium of everything anyone could ever need, from inflatable paddleboards to ironing boards, from saucepans to pasta sauces, and everything in between.

Up at the counter, Julia Dalton, the postmistress, was deep in conversation with two other elderly ladies who Ruby recognised as Liz from the cheese shop and Dorothy who ran the little painting shop selling her wonderful works of art. They all stopped talking when they saw her.

'Ruby! Welcome back,' Julia said, coming round the counter and giving Ruby a hug. 'Or should I say, welcome home.'

Ruby smiled as she hugged her. 'Thank you, it's good to finally be here.'

'We were just talking about you,' Liz said with no trace of

embarrassment. Ruby didn't know whether that was a good or bad thing. 'You're bunking with that gorgeous Jacob Harrington, aren't you? I think there's many a woman in the village that would like to be in your shoes.'

'I'm just sharing the other half of the shop with him, and only for a few weeks until my shop is ready. There's no bunking involved,' Ruby said.

'But it can't exactly be a hardship working alongside him every day,' Dorothy said, waggling her eyebrows mischievously.

Julia flapped her hands. 'Ignore these two, what can I help you with?'

'I was going to place a big food shopping order for later this week, and Willow has left me a few things in the house, so just a few basics to keep me going. Milk, bread, cereal, that kind of thing,' Ruby said, trying to ignore the beady eyes of Liz and Dorothy as they watched her astutely.

'No problem.' Julia handed her a little wire basket. 'Follow me.'

Julia marched down the aisles, tossing bread, milk, cheese, eggs, cereal, jam, butter, biscuits and bananas into the basket as Ruby hurried to catch up with her. She followed her into an aisle that was mainly toiletries and Ruby watched with amusement as shampoo, conditioner, shower gel, deodorant, razors, moisturiser and toothpaste went into the basket too.

'Thanks Julia, I think what we have there is more than enough, I really do just need a few basics,' Ruby tried.

'Of course dear, just the essentials,' Julia said, throwing in a few boxes of condoms and, to her surprise, a pair of fluffy handcuffs too. 'Just in case.'

Ruby suppressed a smile. 'The condoms really aren't necessary.'

'Oh, you need to be safe Ruby dear, safe sex is very important in this day and age.'

'I'm always safe, but I won't be having sex with Jacob Harrington or with anyone, so the condoms won't be needed.'

Julia nodded but didn't take the condoms back out. 'Of course not, but you never can tell when these moments might happen, those passionate, sex-up-against-the-wall, go-with-the-flow type moments. It's best to be prepared.'

'Who's having sex up against the wall?' Liz said, her eyes lighting up as they returned to the till.

'Ruby,' Julia said, simply.

'No I'm not,' Ruby laughed.

'But you plan to, judging by the number of condoms in your basket,' Dorothy said, picking up the fluffy handcuffs and giving Ruby a pointed look over the top of her glasses.

Julia started ringing up the purchases.

'Those were what Julia considered to be essential shopping.'

'Quite right too,' Liz said. 'You don't want to have a baby unless you're in a serious relationship. Bringing up a baby alone can't be any fun. I see all of these single mothers raising their children and they just look exhausted. It's better to have a man there to help you.'

Ruby gave Julia the money. 'Well, I don't need a man to help me do anything and, as I was saying to Julia, I won't be having sex with anyone so—'

'Nothing wrong with a bit of casual sex,' Dorothy said.

'No, sex is perfectly natural,' Julia agreed.

Ruby decided to change the subject. 'So the decorations in the village, they look lovely.'

'Oh they do, don't they,' gushed Liz.

'So pretty,' Julia agreed.

OK. Obviously only Ruby's depraved mind had made the

rude connection. She decided to move on before she started giggling about it again.

'And I see from the posters around town that someone stole Jesus last night. Seems a bit odd, doesn't it?'

'It's very odd,' Julia nodded. 'I went up there this morning to feed Minty, Tatty and the donkey, Wonky, and he was missing.'

'Maybe an animal took him,' Ruby said.

'And swapped him for a snowman?' Julia said, sceptically.

Ah, that had been a rookie error on Ruby's part. She should have just stolen Jesus, not left a replacement.

'A snowman?' Ruby said, innocently.

Dorothy narrowed her eyes. 'You wouldn't have anything to do with this, would you?'

'Me? Of course not. I was too tired when I arrived late last night to do anything, let alone start stealing members of the nativity. I just went straight to the shop to dump a few things and then to my cottage. It sounds like something kids would do, not a full grown, mature adult.'

'I said it was kids,' Liz said.

'Well, that's why I offered five pounds for a reward. If some kid has got it, I thought five pounds would be enough to get them to bring it back,' Julia said.

Ruby nodded but inwardly thought that most kids today would barely get out of bed for five pounds. She wondered if she could prolong this somehow, maybe ask for a ransom for extra effectiveness. Maybe send postcards from Jesus on his holiday. She almost laughed out loud as she thought about all the fun she could have with this.

Ruby took her shopping bag. 'Well thanks for all this and for the… illuminating talk about sex. I'll keep my eyes peeled for Jesus.'

'Yes, please. And if you need any other… bedroom paraphernalia…' Julia lowered her voice but still spoke loud enough for Liz and Dorothy to hear her. 'I have whips, blindfolds and sexy lingerie out the back.'

Ruby smirked and nodded. 'I'll keep that in mind.'

She hurried out of the shop before there was any more sex talk or any more kinky essentials were added to her shopping basket.

Life in a small village was certainly going to take a lot of getting used to.

~

Ruby had just finished unpacking the few bags of clothes she had brought with her when there was a hammering on the door.

She wondered if Jacob had changed his mind about just being friends and come to ravish her. She didn't know if she had enough willpower to refuse him if he had.

She went downstairs and opened the door and was met with a squealing whirlwind of brown hair. She smiled as Willow threw herself at Ruby and hugged her tight.

'I can't believe you're finally here,' Willow said.

Ruby hugged her back. 'It's good to see you too.'

Willow stepped back to look at her and then hugged her again. 'I'm so sorry I wasn't here to greet you.'

Ruby kissed the top of her head and ushered her inside. 'Don't be daft, you were in Paris, it wasn't your fault everything was delayed my end. Besides, you made my bed up for me, provided me with a Christmas tree and food in the fridge and cupboards. What more could I want?'

'Ah, it was the least I could do.'

'And thank you for the spider in my bed,' Ruby said.

Willow giggled. 'One point to me.'

Ruby smirked and decided not to tell her about stealing Jesus. She'd let Willow find that out for herself.

Ruby moved to the log burner and threw another log inside; the flames crackled and burned a welcoming glow of orange and gold.

'So what's going on with your shop? Andrew said there was a message left for him that there was some kind of flood?' Willow asked, throwing herself down on the sofa.

'Yes there was, but Kitty and Ken have temporarily rehoused me in a different shop, so Andrew doesn't need to bust a gut to get it fixed two seconds after he has come back off holiday.'

'Oh, you know what Andrew's like, always has to be doing something round here. And he has an assistant now, Lucas. He helps Andrew a lot. Anyway, which shop have they put you in, all the shops are filled?'

'I'm in the other half of Jacob's shop,' Ruby said and watched Willow's face light up. Then she frowned.

'God, that's got to be a bit awkward.'

Ruby thought again about the incredible time she'd had with Jacob in the summer, and the fact that she had gone back to St Octavia and completely cut him off. Being back here had the potential of being all kinds of awkward. He could have made things a lot more difficult for her, but in fact he'd been a complete gentleman about it.

'Actually, it wasn't as bad as I thought it would be. We talked it out and we agreed nothing is going to happen between us. We have to work alongside each other, live in the same tiny village, it'd just be awkward if it all goes wrong. Although, a little bit of warning from you that he was living here too wouldn't have gone amiss.'

'You didn't want to talk about him, I didn't think you would care,' Willow said, innocently.

'You mean you deliberately didn't divulge the information in case it put me off coming here,' Ruby said, sitting down on the sofa next to her.

'Maybe,' Willow said. 'So was there no spark between you two at all?'

'Oh there was plenty of spark,' Ruby said. 'I just don't think it's a good idea to pursue it. I think what we had meant something more to him than it did to me. He's talking about coming here, settling down and having babies, for goodness sake. How could I possibly fit into that picture? It's best to end it now, I don't want to hurt him by leading him on.'

'Oh, don't give me that crap,' Willow said. 'The way you looked at him, the way you talked about him when you were both here last. It was something very different to how you've been with previous men. You liked him.'

Ruby sighed, because there was probably more than an element of truth to that. She shook her head and pushed that feeling away. 'It was just sex, Willow. What we have between us is just lust, nothing else.'

'I don't think you're giving this a chance. What harm would it do to see where it goes? I'm sure if it doesn't work out you two can be mature enough about it to not let it turn weird between you.'

'I don't know if he really wants a relationship with me. Maybe he's saving the marriage and babies for someone else. He even said he was quite happy to continue with the no-strings-attached sex.'

'And what do you want?' Willow asked.

'I don't want a relationship either, you know that.'

Willow's face softened. 'Because of Harry?'

Ruby let out a hard breath. She didn't talk about Harry with anyone. Of course everyone in St Octavia knew, but they also knew better than to bring it up. The thing with Harry had happened before she'd met Willow but one drunken night at university she'd let it all pour out. Willow didn't bring it up very often but Ruby was glad she knew, it was too big a thing to keep inside. And at times like this of course Harry was going to come up. He had impacted on every emotional relationship decision Ruby had made for the last twelve years.

'Of course because of Harry. That asshole broke my heart, smashed it into smithereens, and I honestly don't think I've ever got over that. I couldn't go through that again.'

She was surprised she was still angry over it. In the beginning it had been grief and pain but that had eventually turned to anger. Harry had promised her forever and then he'd left.

'I cannot even imagine what it was like to go through that but you can't spend the rest of your life avoiding love in case it happens again,' Willow said.

'Why not? It's worked pretty well for me for the last twelve years. Don't fall in love, don't get hurt. It's pretty simple to me.'

'You can't not fall in love because it's inconvenient. The heart doesn't work like that. It falls in love without permission.'

'Well, that's why nothing else is going to happen between me and Jacob, and then I won't get carried away and fall in love with him.'

'You think by not having sex with him you won't develop any feelings for him?' Willow said in exasperation.

'Yes. If I'm not intimate with him then we can just be friends,' Ruby said, even though she knew it was ridiculous.

God, was this all a terrible mistake? She'd thought that she had cleared the air with Jacob, laid down the ground rules and that was that. She hadn't thought about what it would be really like to work alongside him every day, to laugh with him, chat with him.

OK, it was just until after Christmas, then she'd move back to her shop at the furthest end of the high street from his and she wouldn't have to see him at all... In a village the size of a postage stamp.

Ruby looked at Willow's doubtful face.

'It's going to be fine. Now Jacob knows that any kind of relationship or sex is off the table with me, he'll find some other woman to while away his time with.'

'And how would you feel about that?' Willow asked.

'I'd be absolutely fine with it,' Ruby said, knowing that she absolutely wouldn't be.

What was with this man, why had he affected her so much?

Willow squeezed her hand and Ruby looked down at the gesture, her heart suddenly leaping. 'Willow McKay, are you freaking kidding me, you're bloody engaged and you didn't think to mention it?'

'Oh.' Willow blushed, a huge smile spreading across her face. 'I just wanted to make sure you were OK first before I came in here and shouted my good news.'

'Tell me everything!' Ruby said, glad of the wonderful distraction.

Willow looked like she was going to burst with excitement. 'Oh god, it was so romantic, I had no idea Andrew was going to do it. It happened on our last night there. We went on a night-time river cruise of the Seine on this little boat and it was just me and him, and the driver obviously. The city lights were twinkling and we were cuddled up at the back under blankets and as we passed by the Eiffel Tower, lit up in all its splendour, he popped the question.'

'Did he use sign language to do it?' Ruby asked.

She knew Andrew was deaf, he could hear perfectly fine with his hearing aids in but not so much without them. Willow had been learning sign language so she could still communicate with him during those times, but when they had first met he didn't want to share that part of his life with her. As they had fallen in love, she had encouraged him to open up and trust her with it. If he had proposed with sign language Ruby knew that would be quite significant to Willow.

She nodded. 'He did. I wasn't sure at first what he was saying. I know most things now; I can hold a pretty decent conversation with him using sign language but I still struggle with a few words and phrases here and there. He asked me if I knew what this meant.' Willow signed something. 'And I told him I wasn't sure and then he did it again and said, "Will you marry me?"'

'This is amazing news, I'm so happy for you,' Ruby said, genuinely. Jacob was right, marriage wasn't for her, but she couldn't help but feel nothing but happiness at Willow's wonderful news. She hugged her and then pulled back to look at her. There was not an ounce of doubt that this was the right thing for Willow.

'I am so lucky to have found my soulmate,' Willow said. 'I love him so much. I just hope that one day you'll be able to find yours.'

Ruby smiled because now was definitely not the right time for her doom and gloom attitude to love.

'Maybe one day.'

Willow smiled at this and Ruby didn't have the heart to burst her bubble.

~

The van with Ruby's stuff arrived just after lunch. She couldn't wait to get everything into the shop and make the place into a magical Santa's grotto with all of her decorations.

Jacob was banging seven kinds of hell out of a piece of

metal next door as the removal men opened the back of the van and started unloading boxes. She didn't want to disturb him.

'Where do you want these, love?' the man asked.

'Oh, just inside the door on the left would be great,' Ruby said.

As they lifted one big box between them and took it inside, she was about to pick up one of the smaller boxes, when Jacob suddenly appeared at her side.

'Here, let me take that,' he said.

She passed him the box and took one herself.

'Is all of that Christmas stuff?' Jacob asked with theatrically wide eyes.

She laughed. 'Yeah, most of it is. All the boxes at the back are the ones for my house so I'll get them to drive down there when they're finished here.'

'You really like Christmas,' Jacob said, carrying the box into the shop.

Ruby followed him. 'Yeah I do, it's my favourite time of the year. I love the scents and the Christmas food. I love the Christmas films, the cornier and cheesier the better. I love silly Christmas jumpers and giving presents, but most of all I love the decorations, the Christmas trees, the twinkly lights, the streetlights. I love them all. I cannot wait to Christmassify this place. I'll do your shop as well if you want.'

'I'm not sure twinkly fairy lights wrapped around my metal sculptures are the best look but you're very welcome to help me decorate the flat,' Jacob said. 'My niece, Poppy, will be coming for Christmas so I need to make sure it's suitably festive for her.'

'Oooh, I'll take you up on that. I love nothing more than helping someone find their inner Christmas spirit.'

'I look forward to that,' Jacob said dryly.

'Actually, Poppy would probably like it more if she could help decorate your tree with you.'

He smiled. 'You're probably right, we could decorate it together, the three of us.'

Something like fear fluttered through Ruby's heart at that lovely rose-tinted family image.

They placed their boxes down.

'I'll leave you a box of decorations and order you a tree,' Ruby said, firmly. 'I'm sure Poppy would probably prefer it if it was just the two of you, she doesn't know me.'

'I can help you talk to her if that's what's bothering you,' Jacob said.

She knew Poppy was deaf and only communicated through sign language but Ruby definitely didn't want Jacob to think that was the reason she didn't want to decorate the tree with him.

'I've actually been learning a few words and phrases,' Ruby said and then regretted it when his whole face lit up.

'You have?'

'Yeah, it's not a big deal.'

He was smiling as if he thought it was. 'Why did you learn to sign?'

Ruby shrugged. She wasn't sure what had compelled her to learn sign language. She knew that it was partly to expand her skills and learn a new language and to be able to help understand people who might struggle to be understood. But she also knew that Poppy and Andrew had been in the back of her mind when she'd taken the course. She'd felt it was important that she could communicate with Jacob's niece and his brother, which was an odd thing to want to do since she'd never had any intention of seeing Jacob again. But with her best friend loved-up with his brother and Ruby moving to the village where they lived, she'd known she would cross paths with him again. Jacob had never introduced her to Poppy when she had been there in the summer – and why would he when they were only ever supposed to be a one-night stand? But if she was honest, she knew she wanted him to take her seriously and not just see her as a flaky person he'd slept with a few times. She wasn't sure why that had been important when she had insisted to herself and anyone who asked that nothing was ever going to happen between them again, but clearly her subconscious had thought otherwise.

He was still waiting for an answer.

'I just thought that as Willow was learning to sign for Andrew then maybe I should too. Being deaf can be so isolating and I know he can hear just fine when he has his hearing aids in, but that's not always practical is it? And Poppy relies on sign language entirely and it must be frustrating for her sometimes that she can't communicate with everyone. I just thought...'

He was staring at her in awe and she regretted saying anything. Time to get the conversation back on track.

'Anyway, the point is, I'm not saying no because of Poppy. Decorating a tree is the kind of thing you do with family or a girlfriend, not some woman you had casual sex with a few times.'

One of the removal men coughed, awkwardly as he came back in to drop off another box. Ruby blushed but Jacob was unfazed.

'What about friends? Is there some rule that says friends can't decorate a tree together?'

'Yes,' Ruby said, with exasperation, moving back outside to get some more boxes and to get away from him. How had this conversation turned so quickly? The last person she had decorated a tree with was Harry. God, it hurt to remember that.

'Decorating a tree is romantic and we agreed that nothing was going to happen between us.'

'OK,' he said, slowly, as he followed her.

She passed him a box and saw he was fighting a smirk. She knew her desperation to avoid anything romantic was silly but she knew she had to keep some distance from Jacob, emotionally if not physically.

'So we can't decorate a tree together, is there anything else we should avoid?' Jacob asked.

He wasn't taking this remotely seriously.

'I'll let you know if something comes up.'

He nodded. 'I'll make an anti-romance list.'

'You're so infuriating.'

He laughed. 'Sorry, let's change the subject. Are you ready for your welcome drinks in the pub this afternoon?'

She felt nothing but relief that he'd dropped it and she almost wanted to hug Jacob because of it.

'What welcome drinks?'

They stacked their boxes inside the shop and went back outside for some more.

'They always do it apparently, when there's a new resident. Well they started doing it after the big influx in the summer. I had mine a few days after I moved in. It's a nice way to meet all the villagers at the same time and for them to know who you are so you're not just some random walking around the village, although most of the villagers will remember you from the last time you were here. It starts at five, I think.'

'How do you know this?'

'It was on the village forum. It's where all the village info is, helps you keep updated with all the goings on. I'll show it to you.'

She stared at him. 'You have settled in here, haven't you?

The Jacob I knew wouldn't be seen dead attending a village meeting.'

'This place sucks you in pretty quickly.'

He grabbed another box as the removal men took some boxes in themselves.

'So everyone will just be staring at me?'

'I think most people will be too busy eating to do much staring and I'll be there to hold your hand if you need me to,' Jacob said.

'There won't be any need for that.'

'Fine. I'll hold my own hand.'

She laughed.

'Besides, you don't want to miss Liz's cakes, they are to die for, and you have to meet Julia Dalton, the postmistress. She knows everything that is happening in the village. I'm sure she'll know that you're here by now and what time you arrived last night,' Jacob said.

'Now that's a comforting thought, and not at all creepy. I've already met her actually, earlier today and in the summer, and I know exactly what you mean.'

'I wouldn't at all be surprised if there were rumours flying about that we'd already jumped into bed together.'

'I haven't even been here twenty-four hours.'

Jacob shrugged.

Ruby rolled her eyes – that would explain all the condoms Julia had made her buy earlier. Part of the reason she had left St Octavia was to escape from everyone knowing her business. And her past. She clearly hadn't thought moving to the little village of Happiness through.

Ruby placed the box down carefully. 'You're not that irresistible.'

'"The lady doth protest too much, methinks."' Jacob stacked his box on top of one of the others.

She smiled. She really bloody liked this man.

'Quoting *Hamlet* isn't going to impress me either.' Although the fact that he'd got it exactly right did impress her slightly.

'Would *Romeo and Juliet* do it for you instead?'

She wrinkled her nose. 'A romance that ends in joint suicide is hardly romantic.'

'Ah, do you see us more as Benedick and Beatrice?' Jacob asked.

She smiled. Of all of Shakespeare's couples, those two from *Much Ado About Nothing* were her favourite. And actually that Jacob knew of them rather than some of the more famous Shakespeare couples impressed her a tiny bit more.

'"Is it possible disdain should die while she hath such food to feed it as Jacob Harrington?"' Ruby quoted.

He laughed, not fazed at all by her words, and went out to get some more boxes. She watched him go. It shouldn't be this easy between them. They'd slept together three times, and then she had put the brakes on anything happening between them again. She was backpedalling away from anything remotely romantic and he was here, helping her move her boxes, laughing and joking with her and chatting to her as if they had been friends for years.

She just never expected it to be like this with Jacob. She thought it might be awkward and she'd thought that there might be some unresolved chemistry between them but she hadn't expected it to be so… friendly.

And in many ways that was worse.

She really was in trouble with this one.

CHAPTER FOUR

Jacob watched Ruby chatting with the removal men as he sipped the hot chocolate she had made for them all. She was so bubbly and animated when she talked he couldn't help but smile. She was wearing a dress with Christmas trees all over it today. She really was the epitome of the festive season. She sparkled.

There was something about her that he found so... compelling. He enjoyed spending time with her, talking to her. He could laugh with her and he'd never had that with a woman before. But there was something much deeper there too. And to find out that she had started to learn sign language so she could communicate with his niece and Andrew when he wasn't wearing his hearing aids, that meant more to him than she could possibly know.

He looked around Christmas Cottage at the boxes stacked along the walls. There certainly was a lot of stuff, although he wondered if half of it was Christmas decorations.

There were just a few more boxes on the van, so he drained his cup and, as the removal men grabbed some, Jacob picked up the last one. God this one was heavy. He slid it to the edge of the van, climbed out and hoisted it up in his arms, just as the removal men came out and were saying their goodbyes to Ruby. Jacob walked into the cottage and was just about to stack it on top of one of the other boxes when the bottom gave way and the contents spilled out onto the floor.

Crap.

He tossed the useless box on the floor and was relieved to see the contents were only books and not anything breakable.

He bent down and started stacking the books up but he stopped when it looked like one of the books was a photo album. It had fallen open and on the page was a photo of a much younger Ruby with a man… on what was obviously her wedding day.

His heart leapt. After her big speech about marriage and babies not being for her, how could she have forgotten to tell him that she had been married once? This couldn't be right, surely. He turned back to the front cover which had the words written in gold swirly writing, 'Our Wedding Album'. He turned back to the photos, Ruby with her bridesmaids, Ruby and the groomsmen, Ruby and her husband in various different poses. But one thing stood out in every single photo: how completely and utterly happy Ruby was. The love she had for her husband, and how much he clearly loved her, shone from the pages.

Ruby came in and shut the door behind her.

'Jesus, Jacob, you had one job to do and you can't even do that,' Ruby teased as she caught him crouching over the fallen books.

Should he tell her what he'd seen? Should he pretend he hadn't noticed anything? If she'd wanted to talk about her marriage she would have, but Christ he had a million questions right then. No, it was none of his business. He quickly closed the album and made to hide it under the other books, but she was suddenly standing right there.

'Oh,' she said, softly, seeing the album in his hand. She touched the snowflake she wore around her neck.

'I'm sorry, the books fell out the box and this fell open. I didn't mean to pry.'

She knelt down next to him and took the album from his hands.

'I haven't looked at this for over twelve years. I couldn't. I had it stashed behind some other books on my bookshelf and I suppose I almost forgot it was there. My brother helped me pack and I guess he shoved it in here and…' she trailed off.

She opened it on the first page, a grinning one of the bride and groom, hugging and laughing together. It wasn't a posed picture, just a natural snap of two young people very much in love.

'God, I looked so ridiculously happy,' Ruby said, stroking a finger down the man's face. 'Harry was handsome, wasn't he?'

Jacob stared at her. 'You were married?'

'Yes, I was very young. We both were. He was my childhood sweetheart. We'd dated since we were eleven, got married at eighteen. Everyone said we were too young. Maybe they were right.'

'What happened?'

She stared at the photo for the longest time. 'By the time I was nineteen it was over.'

'That didn't last long. Was it another woman?'

Ruby shook her head. 'No, Harry would never have done that. He went out to play football one day and never came home.'

'What? He just walked out on you? No explanation? Did you ever see him again?'

'I saw him, once. Called him every name under the sun. He didn't have a lot to say.'

'God, what an asshole.'

Ruby looked at him and smiled sadly. 'After, everyone always told me how wonderful he was, when all I could find in me was anger and hatred that he'd left me.'

'He doesn't sound wonderful to me,' Jacob said. What kind of dick left their wife just a few months after getting married?

'He was, in the beginning,' Ruby said, turning over the page. There was another of the two of them dancing by a Christmas tree. 'We got married just before Christmas, the twenty-third, because he knew how much I loved Christmas. The whole wedding was Christmas-themed; it was so beautiful.'

Jacob watched her as she reminisced. It sounded like she still had some feelings for him.

'So this is why you don't believe in marriage anymore?' Jacob asked.

Ruby nodded. 'When he left me, I was so utterly heartbroken, it physically hurt. I don't think I could go through that again.'

'But you can't let this… cockwomble ruin the rest of your life. You can't avoid any kind of emotional connection with a man because this dick didn't know what an amazing thing he had with you.'

She didn't say anything for the longest time as she turned over page after page of gloriously happy photos.

When she looked at him her eyes were filled with so much emotion it completely floored him.

She reached out and stroked his face, making his heart leap in his chest.

'I really like you Jacob Harrington, but I'd really like you to leave now so I can have a good cry over these photos without you coming up with new and ingenious ways to insult my husband.'

He didn't understand any of this.

'You mean your ex-husband?'

She shrugged. 'I suppose you could call him that.'

And then suddenly everything was crystal clear. Everything. Why she was so scared of falling in love again, why she'd never had a serious relationship since Harry, why she didn't believe in marriage and happy ever afters. He swallowed the emotion that was suddenly clogging in his throat.

'He didn't leave, did he?'

She stared at him and then shook her head. 'Not by choice. He had a heart attack. He'd just turned nineteen.'

He swore softly under his breath. 'Christ Ruby, I'm sorry.'

'It's OK. It's been over twelve years since he died. I'm over it.' A lone tear slid down her cheek and she let out a little laugh. 'Mostly.'

He wasn't sure how you ever got over something like that.

'Sometimes things like this bring it all back,' Ruby said. 'You should probably go, there's going to be a few more of these.'

'If you're going to have a cry, there's no way in hell I'm leaving you.'

'It's not going to be pretty.'

He got up from the floor and picked up the photo album, then he held his hand out for Ruby. 'Then we might as well get comfortable for it.'

She took his hand and he pulled her down on the sofa next to him. He grabbed a box of tissues from the nearby table and placed it on his lap, then he wrapped an arm round her shoulders and she leaned against him. As she flicked through the photo album once more he held her tight as she cried quietly into his chest.

Ruby stepped out of Christmas Cottage and wrapped her coat around her. It was only a five-minute walk up the hill to the pub, but the day was still bitterly cold. She wouldn't be surprised if it snowed soon, which would be nice. Everything looked far more Christmassy when there was snow on the ground.

Jacob stepped out the cottage too, closed the door behind him and then took her hand as they started walking up the high street.

She looked down at where their fingers entwined. She hadn't held hands with anyone since Harry had died. Of course there had been men that she'd seen casually or had a fling with but it had never been anything serious with any of them, so she had never really had the hugging and hand-holding with them that she would have had in a more intimate relationship. She wasn't sure how she felt about this hand-holding either. There was a part of her that recognised this was a little weird. She wasn't in a relationship with Jacob, she'd made that very clear to him, and she knew he was only holding her hand to offer some comfort and support after she had cried on him for the last hour. But there was also a part of her that felt there was something very lovely about doing this with him.

She looked up at him and he was smiling at her.

'You're not at all what I expected, Jacob Harrington,' Ruby said.

'What were you expecting?' Jacob said.

'Mostly, that we'd sleep together once and I'd never hear from you again.'

'Is that what you wanted?'

Ruby thought about that for a moment. 'Yeah, I've got

through the last twelve years with no commitments, no emotional attachments, and it's worked pretty well for me. But you're not at all what I imagined. You're…' she trailed off, not able to find the right word.

'Sexy?' Jacob teased. 'Amazing, the best sex you've ever had?'

She smiled. 'Lovely. You're lovely.'

'Ah god, don't tell anyone that, it'll ruin my reputation.'

'My lips are sealed. I wouldn't want to damage the good name of Phoenix Blade.'

'I wasn't talking about him; I was talking about me.'

She smiled. 'So what kind of persona does Phoenix Blade have? Is he dark, edgy, mysterious? Does he ride into his exhibitions on the back of a motorbike, dressed all in leather?'

'I hadn't really thought about making him into a character. Do you think I could pull off dark and dangerous?'

'I think you could. You have this bad boy look that all the women go for. We won't tell them the truth.'

'That I'm secretly lovely,' Jacob said.

'Yes, we'll keep that between us.'

She looked at the Christmas lights inside the shops and houses, twinkling in the receding light of the day. It looked magical.

'What should I expect from this meeting this afternoon?' Ruby said.

'There'll be mince pies and mulled wine, I expect, maybe some gingerbread men and other festive treats. Kitty and Ken will introduce you and you will generally be expected to give a short speech and then everyone will mingle.'

Ruby looked at him in alarm. 'What? Back up. A speech? Why didn't you mention this before?'

'I thought you knew. It's in the welcome pack.'

'Christ, I haven't read that yet. It was on my to-do list once I'd finished unpacking. What do I need to say in my speech?'

'Something about what you will bring to Happiness. I mean, it's not a big deal. Kitty and Ken just want people to fill the village but the whole *free rent for a year* thing is kind of on the proviso that you can bring something to the village. Kitty and Ken have already given you a home and a shop so it's not like this speech is some kind of test. They just want the villagers to know who you are.'

Ruby let out a big breath. 'What did you say in yours? Great sex to all who want it?'

He laughed loudly. 'I said that I offered diversity, that my art was something that could bring visitors to the village and that I was also pretty handy with bits of metal so, if anyone needed anything welding, I was their man. That and the great sex obviously.'

'God, what do I have to offer?' Ruby said.

'How about the joy of Christmas all year round.'

'OK, that's a start.'

Ruby wracked her brains for something else she could add.

'I know,' Jacob said. 'The village came together when Willow gave mystery gifts to everyone in the summer. Christmas is the time of giving. What about some kind of… advent calendar gift thing?'

'It's the eighteenth of December already, I've kind of missed that… But maybe I could do some kind of Secret Santa thing.'

'Yes, that could work.'

She thought for a few moments about how she could do it and then she noticed Willow and Andrew waiting for them outside the pub. They were still quite some way ahead and hadn't yet noticed her and Jacob.

'I might have to drop your hand now,' Ruby said. 'I will

never hear the end of it if Willow sees us together like this. She'll be buying a hat for the wedding before the end of the day.'

Jacob immediately let go of her hand. 'No problem. But if you need to, my hand is here to hold anytime.'

She smiled. 'Thank you.'

Willow moved to give her a hug as they drew close but stopped short.

'Have you been crying?'

Damn it. Ruby had washed her face and put on a tiny bit of make up to cover the red blotchiness, but of course Willow would spot it.

'A little. It's nothing.'

'Of course it's not nothing,' Willow said. 'What happened?'

'I found my wedding album amongst all my stuff as I was unpacking. I haven't looked at that for years.'

'Oh no, I hate the thought of you looking at that on your own.'

'I wasn't alone, Jacob was with me,' Ruby said.

Sure enough, Willow's eyes lit up at the idea of Jacob comforting her. But before Ruby could start to deny anything had happened, Jacob smoothly stepped forward.

'Welcome home by the way. I hear we're going to be family now, congratulations,' he said, hugging his future sister-in-law.

Willow's face erupted into a huge smile as she hugged him. 'I know, I can't believe it.'

'Yes, congratulations, Andrew.' Ruby hugged him. 'I'm sure you two are going to be very happy together.'

'Thank you,' Andrew said. It was clear to see he was as happy as Willow was.

Jacob clapped Andrew on the back. 'Good job little brother, I think you picked one of the good ones here.'

'She's the best,' Andrew said, fondly, kissing Willow on the head.

Ruby smiled. The two of them really were perfect for each other.

'Come on, let's get inside,' Jacob said. 'It's freezing and there's a mince pie in here with my name on it.'

He ushered them all inside the pub and Ruby gave him a grateful smile that he had managed to distract her friend from the fact that she had been crying and that he had comforted her. Although she didn't think for one minute that that would be the last she would hear of it from Willow.

The pub was rammed, young families, couples of varying ages and some of the older folk that had been the backbone of the village when she'd first visited in the summer. There was such a difference from how it had been a few months before. At that time the village had been largely in ruin and they had been having trouble attracting people to want to live there. Now it was a happy, buzzing, thriving place, and Ruby couldn't help but smile. There was a huge twinkling Christmas tree in one corner and a wonderful holly berry garland over the fireplace that had a welcoming fire roaring away underneath. It looked cosy and festive.

Willow led her over to Kitty and Ken, who she'd met briefly before when she'd been there in the summer. Kitty looked effortlessly glamorous with her platinum-blonde hair in gentle waves. Ken, with his white, walrus moustache, looked like he had come from the circus, and the bright red waistcoat adorned with satin green holly leaves he was wearing completed the look.

Kitty smiled when she saw her and gave her a big hug.

'Ruby, it's so lovely to see you again. I'm so sorry about your shop, we should have it fixed and cleaned out straight after Christmas.'

'It's no problem at all. Jacob has been very welcoming,' Ruby said.

Jacob smiled at her in a way that suggested he'd wanted to welcome her in much more interesting ways.

Kitty eyed the two of them and her face lit up. 'Well that's wonderful. If you want you can always stay in that shop.'

'No, no, I wouldn't want to intrude on Jacob's creativity longer than I have to and it would be nice to have my own space too.'

Jacob shrugged. 'I'm happy either way.'

Ruby couldn't imagine what it would be like to work alongside Jacob every day and still hold onto her willpower to not sleep with him. The next few weeks were going to be hard enough, especially as he was being so bloody lovely. She kind of would have preferred him to be a complete ass about it as then her decision to not let anything more happen between them would have been a hell of a lot easier.

'Well, I'm glad it's all working out,' Kitty said. 'I knew Jacob would be the perfect person to put you with.'

Ruby narrowed her eyes slightly. 'Oh, I did wonder about that. Why didn't you tell me I was sharing with Jacob instead of Phoenix Blade?'

Kitty blushed. 'Oh, erm… I wasn't sure if I was allowed to divulge his real name.'

'But I know Jacob.'

'Oh, yes, of course you do. I must go and say hello to Shannon and Pete. I haven't met their new baby yet.'

Kitty hurried off to the other side of the room where a collection of elderly ladies were all cooing over a new baby.

Ruby smirked. Not telling her she was going to be sharing with Jacob had definitely been deliberate. She wondered if the flood in the shop had even happened at all.

'Are you ready to do your speech, dear?' Ken said, interrupting her thoughts.

'Umm, sort of,' Ruby said.

'It's nothing to worry about, just say a few words about who you are, where you're from and what you will bring to the village.'

Ruby smiled. No big deal at all.

'Well, we're very glad you're here,' Ken said. 'I'm sure you will bring a lot to the village. One of the reasons we wanted you to come here was because of your love of Christmas and we wanted you to bring that magic to the village itself. We have put a lot of time and effort into organising the Christmas ball but we haven't really done a lot else to celebrate Christmas. If you could think of something else to help us mark the big day, that would be great. I know we only have a week until Christmas so nothing big, but maybe you could have a think about some little ideas that we can all take part in.'

Kitty flapped her hands at him as she rejoined them. 'Ken, the girl has only just got here. Maybe we should let her unpack first before we push her head first into village life.'

'Well, I did have one idea I was going to suggest in my speech. I'm not sure what the villagers will think of it, but it's something everyone can get involved with if they are willing,' Ruby said.

'I think people will,' Kitty said. 'The village has changed so much since we first came here. Everyone was so removed from the community but now everyone actively embraces it. They all want to be a part of it, help each other out, give something back. I think you'll fit in here just perfectly.'

Ruby smiled.

'Well, let's get the show on the road,' Kitty said. 'And then we can tuck into these glorious goodies that the villagers have made for us.'

Ruby looked over at the table that was almost bowing under the weight of mince pies, mini Christmas cakes, gingerbread men, fudge, chocolates, cookies and other snacks.

Kitty banged on the side of the cup with her spoon and the whole pub fell silent and looked over at her expectantly.

'Everyone, our little village has now been filled, every house, every shop has now been taken. And the last person to move in is our lovely Ruby here.'

Everyone cheered and clapped and Ruby gave a little wave.

'Ruby, do you want to say a few words?' Ken said.

Ruby cleared her throat.

'Hello everyone, my name is Ruby Marlowe. I'm from St Octavia which is... very far from here. I'm friends with Willow and Andrew.'

Jacob coughed theatrically and she smiled.

'And Jacob.' She couldn't help noticing Kitty and Ken exchanging smiles at that. 'My shop in the village is going to be called The Happy Little Christmas Shop which, as you might have guessed, sells Christmas decorations. I love Christmas, it's my favourite time of the year, and I will be bringing the joy of Christmas to the village all year round. And on that note, I wonder if some of you might be willing to take part in a Secret Santa? I know the gift-giving that Willow started in the summer was a huge success but Christmas is the perfect time to give a secret gift. Of course we can't all give gifts to everyone in the village, but maybe we can give just one. It doesn't have to be a present you will buy, but maybe you could make one instead.'

There were nods and murmurs of agreement around the villagers. She looked at Kitty and Ken and they were nodding their approval.

'Do we have any paper and pens?' Ruby asked them quietly.

Ken waved his notepad in the air and gestured to his pencil case. Clearly he came prepared to these meetings.

Ruby turned back to the villagers. 'If those that want to take part can please come forward and write their name on a piece of paper. We'll put all the names in a hat and then you can all pick a name out and that is who you have to give a present to. On Christmas Eve we can put all our wrapped presents under the tree here with a gift tag to say who they are to, but not who they are from, and then we can open all of our presents together. Just one rule, you can't tell the person you're giving the gift to that the present is from you. It has to remain a secret. How does that sound?'

There were more nods around the room and people started coming forward to write their names on a piece of paper.

'Fab idea, Ruby Marlowe,' Jacob said. 'But only one small problem.'

'What's that?'

'We don't have a hat.'

She laughed.

'I'll go and ask Tabitha if we can borrow a bowl from the kitchen,' Jacob said and disappeared through the crowd.

Ruby watched as everyone wrote their names on a bit of paper which Ken was temporarily storing in his empty mug. Everyone wanted to be a part of this and she liked that she had done something small for the village already.

Jacob came back with a bowl and slowly it started filling up with little bits of paper.

After it was clear that everyone had put their name into the bowl, Kitty banged her spoon on the side of the cup again to quieten everyone down.

'Has everyone who wants to take part put their name in the bowl?' Kitty asked and everyone nodded. 'Then can you all come forward to draw the name of the person you will be giving the gift to, but remember to keep it a secret.'

Ken mixed all the names up and slowly everyone came forward and took a name from the bowl. There were chuckles and gasps as people found out who they were giving gifts to. As the last few people came forward to collect their name, Ruby stepped forward and took a name from the bowl. She stepped away to see who she had to give a gift to. She didn't know most of the people in the village so it could be tricky. She unwrapped the ball of paper to read the name and smiled when she saw it.

Jacob Harrington.

She shook her head. Of course it was.

CHAPTER FIVE

Ruby went over to the table where the mulled wine was and poured herself another glass. This stuff was good and, coupled with the Christmas cake and gingerbread men, it felt like Christmas had definitely arrived.

A woman a few years younger than Ruby approached, carrying the new-born that everyone had been gathering around for the last hour. She poured herself a glass too.

'Hi, I'm Megan,' she said.

'Ruby, nice to meet you. And who's this handsome chap?'

'This is Toby, my sister Shannon's son.' Megan indicated the blonde in the corner, who was obviously retelling the dramatic events of the birth. Shannon looked altogether too neat and awake for someone who had given birth only a few days before.

'Toby's her third, so she's done this before,' Megan said, as if reading her mind.

Ruby nodded. 'I think I'd be on my knees sobbing from exhaustion if I'd just given birth.'

'I know, the amount of crying this one does, kind of puts me off having children for life,' Megan said.

Ruby looked at Toby who was fast asleep, his head resting on Megan's shoulder. He looked like butter wouldn't melt in his mouth.

She felt a pang of something inside her. She had wanted children; she and Harry had talked about having a big family. They'd even started trying for a baby. When he'd died, not only had he taken her dream of her happy ever after with the man she loved, he'd taken her hopes of having children too.

'So I hear you're sharing a shop with Jacob,' Megan said, interrupting her thoughts. Ruby pushed down the pain in her heart and focussed on Megan who was watching her with wide eyes, visibly hoping for some gossip. She wasn't the first person to bring up her new neighbour. The fact that Ruby was adamant that nothing was going to happen between them didn't stop the idle speculation of when and how she and Jacob might get together. 'It's set the cat amongst the pigeons, let me tell you.'

'I know, everyone wants us to get together,' Ruby said, wearily.

'Not everyone wants that, believe me,' Megan said, bouncing Toby gently in her arms.

Ruby looked at her. She was very pretty in that lovely soft, gentle way, caramel-blonde hair in waves, a fluffy red jumper, large blue eyes. She wondered if Megan would be Jacob's type. She was surprised by the jolt of jealousy that hit her at that thought.

'Oh, not me,' Megan said, she gave a little laugh. 'I've been single for about a year now and if he asked me out I think I'd probably die of shock. I mean, he's gorgeous and of course I'd say yes, but he's not really my type, at all. I think I'd be terrified if it got as far as the bedroom. I'd probably just sit in the bathroom and hyperventilate into a paper bag; I mean, look at him.'

Ruby looked over at Jacob and felt another surge of jealousy to see that a woman with sleek brunette hair and a very short dress was talking to him, tossing her hair around like a frisky pony. While Jacob didn't seem that keen, Ruby couldn't say that he wasn't interested. He was laughing at something the woman was saying. Jacob was ridiculously good-looking, he had those big arms that a lot of women went for, and with his dark hair, denim-blue eyes and that beautiful face, he could easily be a model. He had that rough edge to him as well, like he was dark and dangerous. She was sure that was an attractive feature.

'And look at me,' Megan went on, giving a little self-deprecating laugh.

Ruby looked at her. 'Megan, you're lovely, what man wouldn't want to go out with you?'

Megan looked briefly across the room at another man standing near Shannon and her husband, Pete. He was wearing a bright green knitted Christmas jumper with what looked like the Batman symbol in the middle and snowflakes around the top. Ruby smiled when he glanced over in Megan's direction and Megan quickly looked away.

'Anyway, I wasn't talking about me,' Megan said, nodding her head over to a gaggle of gorgeous women. Ruby hadn't had the courage to go over to them yet. She had overheard a few snide comments from them and, although she didn't think they were directed at her, it made her think they weren't the nicest of people. They were all staring at the brunette talking to Jacob with daggers. 'They all fancy their chances with Jacob. Lucy, the one with the pink top, knows him from when they both lived in Penzance. Apparently he had a different woman every week and he's some kind of god between the sheets.'

'Lucy knows that personally, does she?' Ruby asked.

Megan shrugged. 'I think so from the way she crows about it but I don't know for sure. I just listen to them talking when they're in the pub. I don't hang out with them.'

Ruby smiled. 'Not your type.'

Megan laughed. 'Exactly.'

Ruby looked back over to the pack of women. Lucy was undeniably beautiful. Ruby could imagine she would be exactly the type Jacob would go for. Of course she knew Jacob had been with lots of women so why did the thought of him with Lucy or any of her friends suddenly hurt so much?

'Apparently he's going through a dry patch,' Megan said.

'He is?' Ruby said, in surprise.

'He's been here three or four months, he moved here not long after I did. Well, he hasn't been with anyone from the village since he arrived.'

For some unknown reason, that made Ruby feel suddenly a bit happier.

'They all think they can be the one to bring him out of it.'

Ruby thought about this. Jacob was not the shy retiring type. If he was interested in any of these women, he would have made a move by now.

'Maybe he just doesn't want the awkwardness of sleeping with someone he has to see every day,' Ruby said.

'Maybe,' Megan agreed. 'He could totally be screwing around with every woman in the next village for all I know.'

Ruby's little bubble of hope popped.

'Yeah, I bet he is,' she said. She shrugged. She didn't care. She really really didn't care at all. She took a large swig of her mulled wine as she watched him across the room. She wasn't bothered in the slightest.

Just then the man in the green Batman Christmas jumper came over to them and Ruby smiled as Megan blushed. 'Meg, Shannon and Pete are going now, it's Toby's bath time.'

'OK. Ruby, this is Lucas, Pete's brother and Toby's uncle.'

Lucas smiled.

'Hi Lucas,' Ruby said.

'Hi, good to meet you.'

'You're Andrew's assistant, aren't you? I've been hearing all about how brilliant you are,' Ruby said.

Lucas blushed. 'Well, I, erm, that's very nice.'

Megan gave her a little wave as they both walked back across the room. Ruby diverted her attention back to Jacob who had managed to separate himself from the brunette and was now talking to Dorothy. He glanced over and saw her watching him and broke into a huge smile. He gave her a little wink which stupidly caused her heart to leap.

This man. He was infuriatingly likeable.

Jacob took a bite of his mince pie, savouring the potent fruits and spices mixed with rum or brandy or something else equally heady. Liz's pies were always amazing, it would be a shame when Christmas was over and he wouldn't get to have them anymore. He might have to get her to make him a batch that he could freeze and thaw out whenever the craving got too much.

He watched as Ruby made her way around the room, chatting and laughing with everyone who came up to her. She was definitely not the wallflower type, she was doing a really good job of mingling and introducing herself to everyone.

Julia Dalton, the postmistress, came up to him and took a piece of fudge from the buffet table.

'Mmm rum and raisin, my favourite.'

Jacob took a piece and popped it into his mouth. 'Mmm, this is good fudge, who makes it?'

'I do.'

Jacob laughed at the lack of modesty.

'I make lots of different flavours, but some of them are not so good,' Julia said honestly. 'I put them in different containers but I don't always label them up correctly so sometimes it's a bit of a surprise when I open them. It seems Ruby got the good stuff today.'

Julia leaned against the table next to him.

'I'm going to make your fan club jealous by talking to you,' she said, gesturing to Lucy, Saffy, Pippa and their friends.

He knew there was a bet between them on who could get him into bed first. He wasn't sure whether to be flattered or appalled by that. The old Jacob probably would have slept with all of them but the thought just didn't appeal to him anymore.

'We should kiss, that would really upset them,' Julia said.

Jacob laughed. 'Is that your game, you wily minx?'

'I don't mind you using me to make them jealous,' Julia said and he laughed again. 'I just overheard them talking, Lucy is going to ask you to the ball.'

'Thanks for the heads up.'

'Do you have a date?'

'Are you asking me out?' Jacob gave her a nudge.

'No, I'm just thinking if you needed an excuse not to go with Lucy, maybe you should ask someone else.' Julia tilted her head over in Ruby's direction. He looked over at her and watched Ruby as she laughed loudly at something someone said to her. He smiled at the not-so-subtle matchmaking.

'I like her,' Julia said.

'I do too.'

'This idea of Secret Santa is a good one, who did you get?'

Jacob smiled. 'Isn't that supposed to be a secret?'

'You can trust me, dear. The different parcels that come into the post office for the villagers,' Julia said with wide eyes. 'I could tell you a story or two, but I don't. That's confidential. Just because I know everything going on in the village doesn't mean that I tell anyone about it.'

Jacob wasn't sure he totally believed that. She might keep the post confidential but the village gossip was definitely a free-for-all.

'Who do you have?' he asked.

'I have Ruby. I thought you might want to swap.'

Jacob frowned in confusion. 'Why would I want to swap?'

'Because you haven't taken your eyes off her since you both walked into the pub over an hour ago.'

Jacob chuckled, running his hand through his hair. Was he really that obvious?

'I'm just…'

'It's OK, you don't need to explain yourself to me. I know what happened between the two of you in the summer.'

He shook his head incredulously. How could she possibly know that?

'And I know what's happening now,' Julia said.

'Nothing is happening now.'

'Really?' Julia leaned in a bit closer. 'You were in her house for an awfully long time this afternoon.'

Jacob couldn't help but laugh. Because he wasn't going to tell the truth about looking at Ruby's wedding album with her, he decided to tease Julia. 'Well I'll leave that to your imagination what we were up to.'

Her eyes widened excitedly and he regretted it instantly.

'So you were...' she gave a rude gesture and he laughed loudly.

'No, we weren't, I was just messing with you. Nothing is going on between us. What happened in the summer is in the past now. As we're both living here, we've decided to put it behind us and just be friends. We don't want things to be awkward between us.'

'It might be over for her, but I don't think this thing is over for you,' Julia said.

He shrugged. 'It is what it is. She doesn't want anything to happen and I respect that.'

'You're a good lad. So do you want her for the Secret Santa or not?' Julia held out the piece of paper with Ruby's name on it.

He stared at it. Ruby was definitely going to be easier to get a present for than Elsie, who he'd probably only said hello to a handful of times since he'd moved in. Besides, Ruby was his friend, he could do something nice for his friend.

'OK, sure.'

He took the name and swapped it for the piece of paper with Elsie's name on it. He smiled as he held Ruby's name in his hand. This was going to be fun.

~

After Ruby had finished talking to Kitty and Ken, she turned round to see that Julia, Dorothy, Liz and her brother Roger were seemingly waiting for her to join them. She knew they would want to talk to her about Jacob and there wouldn't be any escape from their matchmaking and thirst for gossip, so she decided to change the subject before it even started. She took a few steps to join the throng and then lowered her voice conspiratorially.

'So what's the deal between Megan and Lucas?' Ruby asked, nodding over to where the two of them were seated in a booth, chatting away happily. She felt bad about using them to deflect the attention away from herself and Jacob, but even though she didn't want romance in her life she wasn't opposed to a bit of matchmaking for others and maybe the villagers could help her.

'Oh I know. Look at the two of them, they're perfect together, but neither of them are prepared to do anything about it,' Julia said, with exasperation.

'He's crazy about her,' Dorothy said. 'You can see that from the way he looks at her.'

'So why hasn't he asked her out?' Ruby said.

'I suppose it's a bit weird now, they're family,' Roger said.

'Only by marriage. Lucas is her sister's brother-in-law, not hers,' Ruby said.

'Does that make him her brother-in-law-in-law?' Liz asked.

Dorothy shook her head. 'There's no such thing. Lucas is related to Shannon by marriage, not Megan. Anyway, I don't think that's what's holding them back. He's just too shy to ask her and she was hurt in her last relationship and is too scared to put herself out there again.'

Ruby took a sip of her mulled wine. She knew that feeling all too well.

'Is that what happened to you, dear?' Julia asked.

Ruby let out a breath. Bloody hell. Was Julia some kind of mind reader as well as post office mistress and emporium owner extraordinaire? And how had the subject turned back to Ruby so quickly?

'How are you settling in with young Jacob?' Liz asked, despite the fact that it had only been a few hours since she'd seen them all in the post office that morning.

'What she means is, have you used those condoms yet?' Dorothy asked bluntly.

'I didn't mean that at all,' Liz said. 'Well, OK, I did.'

'We know that Jacob was helping you unload the removal van and that he stayed in your house with you long after they'd gone,' Julia said. 'And then you came out holding hands, so we just wondered if...'

'He'd parked his car in your garage,' Roger said, eyebrows wiggling mischievously.

'What?' Ruby laughed.

'Had a bit of rumpy-pumpy,' Liz supplied helpfully, although Ruby didn't need the translation.

'Making whoopee,' Julia said.

'Had hot sex,' Dorothy said, getting straight to the point.

'I've not even been here a day,' Ruby protested.

'Well that didn't stop you last time,' Dorothy said.

Ruby blushed.

'Ah, there's nothing to be embarrassed about,' Roger said. 'We've all been there, those passionate, clothes-being-torn-off, having-sex-on-the-nearest-hard-surface kind of moments. And a man as fine as that Jacob Harrington wangling it in your face, well how could you say no.'

Ruby burst out laughing. 'There's been no wangling in my face, I can assure you. As I said to Julia earlier, we're friends and nothing is going to happen between us.'

'Maybe not yet,' Liz said.

'I'll give it to Christmas Eve,' Julia said.

'I agree with Ruby's approach,' Dorothy said. '*Treat them mean, keep them keen.*'

'That's not what I'm doing,' Ruby said, getting a bit frustrated now. 'I'm not playing a game with him. We just decided we were better off as friends. I know we have history but that's exactly what it is, it's in the past.'

They were all quiet for a moment.

'Sounds like she's trying to convince herself more than she's trying to convince us,' Roger muttered.

Ruby rolled her eyes but she knew Roger was right. Being just friends with Jacob was going to be very hard work indeed.

CHAPTER SIX

Ruby was dancing around her shop, Christmas tunes playing on the little CD player she'd brought with her as she unpacked her Christmas decorations and paraphernalia and started making the shop come to life. She'd already decorated two big trees that stood sentry either side of the door and she'd set up her collection of baubles in little boxes on the main table in the middle of the shop. Now she just had to work on the window display.

She was used to having a little market stand in a big hall filled with other stands selling everything under the sun. She'd put out different things each day on her table but it wasn't exactly a display. She did a better trade online but she got quite a bit of attention each day when she sat and handmade the different pieces. Her most popular items were her baubles, which were made in lots of ways; she had fabric ones, papier-*mâché* ones and plain glass baubles she'd bought and then hand-painted using a variety of different ways.

This was the first time she'd had a proper shop and she couldn't wait to Christmassify the whole place.

She peered through to Jacob's shop. It was very minimalist. There was a large peacock made entirely from spoons standing centre stage illuminated with spotlights that gleamed off the steel. There was a lizard made from bike chains crawling across the wall and in the window were a few smaller birds, frogs and dragonflies. There was nothing Christmassy in there at all.

Jacob had been working away on some piece at the back of the shop but he had disappeared upstairs to his flat a while before. She wasn't sure if he was coming back down or if he was done for the day. It was already gone seven o'clock and outside the road was dark, lit only by the streetlights and the twinkling Christmas lights that flashed and danced above them.

Still singing along to the Christmas tunes, this one 'The Fairytale of New York' by The Pogues, she grabbed a few bits and danced into his side of the shop. She draped a piece of blue tinsel round the neck of the peacock like a very dashing scarf, then moved over to the lizard and hung an emerald-green bauble from his tail. She hung some tiny fairy lights over the window display and plugged them in so they sparkled against the metal.

Suddenly she heard footsteps on the stairs and she quickly scampered back into her own shop, giggling to herself.

To her surprise, Jacob appeared in her shop with two plates of food.

'I made chicken stir-fry, I thought you might be hungry,' he said.

Ah, now she felt guilty. While he'd been upstairs doing something nice for her, she'd been down here causing mischief in his shop.

'That's really nice of you, thank you.'

He shrugged and handed her a plate and then pulled out

some knives and forks from his pocket. She watched him drop down onto the floor, placing his plate in front of him, and then start eating. His back was to his own shop so he hadn't noticed her *improvements.*

She sat down on the floor too, tucking in. She really was very hungry.

'This is wonderful, thank you.'

'No problem at all, it's been a busy day for you.'

And he had helped her through all of it.

'So any more events coming up on the village forum that I need to be aware of? I've still not had a chance to look at it,' Ruby asked.

Jacob nodded as he chewed and dug his phone out of his pocket. He pressed a few buttons and swallowed his food.

'There's not a lot going on actually. We have carols on Wednesday the twenty-second at the big Christmas tree on the green by the castle and then we have the ball on Christmas Eve.'

'Oh, a Christmas ball, how wonderful. Kitty and Ken mentioned it earlier but I was too focussed on my speech to pay too much attention. Are they having it up at the castle?'

'Yes.'

'But I thought the castle was in ruins?'

'It is, but the great hall is still intact enough to hold a do in there, and they've hired outdoor heaters to keep the place warm and caterers and a band. It's going to be quite the night. I think Kitty and Ken's focus has all been about that so they haven't organised any other Christmas events'

'Well, I bet that will be lovely.'

'Want to be my date?' Jacob said. 'I promise, no kissing, no sex, I won't even squeeze your bum.'

'There definitely won't be any sex, I can assure you of that.'

'But you don't mind the other two? That's fine as long as I know where the boundaries are,' he teased.

She shook her head fondly. 'You're incorrigible.'

He smiled as he ate. 'I'll be on my very best behaviour.'

'A handsome man like you doesn't have a date for the ball already?'

'Believe me, I've had to fight all those women off with a stick. Liz, Julia, Mary, Ginny, they all wanted a piece of me,' Jacob said, listing all the women in the village over the age of seventy.

Ruby laughed, playing for time for a few moments as she continued to eat. She knew she wanted to go with Jacob. He was lovely and made her laugh, but that would be sending him and the rest of the village some very mixed messages.

'I… I'll think about it.'

'Well, don't think too long or some octogenarian will have snapped me up.'

'I'm sure they will.'

She watched him eat for a while as she enjoyed her stir-fry too. She was actually surprised he didn't have a date. There must be several single women in the village or the surrounding areas who would jump at the chance to have a date with him; Lucy, and her gang, the pretty brunette, even Megan. He was sweet, funny, artistic, kind and sexy as hell. In fact he was exactly the sort of man that should have been snapped up and married years ago. When she had first met him she got the impression that he was a bit of a lad and liked playing the field, which had suited her just fine. But now, to hear him talk about one day settling down, she had to wonder why he hadn't chosen that life for himself before now.

'So why don't you have a date?' Ruby said.

'Ah, I'm a free spirit,' Jacob shrugged.

Ruby frowned as she finished off her stir-fry. There was something he wasn't saying here.

'So no stories of broken hearts?'

His eyebrows slashed down. 'I hope to god I haven't broken anyone's heart. Women know what they get with me, I never give them any false promises or pretend it's anything more than it is.'

She watched him and she got the feeling she had touched on a nerve. She waited to see if there was any more. He glanced up and saw her looking at him.

His face softened. 'I think, as you shared your demons with me earlier, maybe I should share some of mine. My dad walked out on us when we were kids. Lottie and Andrew were still so young when he left but I was old enough to see how much it broke my mum's heart. It utterly destroyed her. He'd had an affair, multiple affairs actually, and I think that was a lot worse than him just leaving. It made my mum feel she wasn't good enough if he had to go elsewhere for sex. Even as a boy, I could see the ramifications of another person's actions, how one person could ruin another person's life. I vowed then that I would never be that person. As I grew up, all the family and my parents' friends used to tell me how much like my dad I was, how similar I looked, acted, we were into all the same things, had the same mannerisms, told the same stupid jokes. And, to be honest, I was scared that maybe I'd be too similar. I've always enjoyed women's company, just like my dad. When I was a teen I had more girlfriends than I could count. I was worried that maybe one day I'd have a relationship with a woman and break her heart just like my dad. What if I couldn't remain faithful? I don't want to be like my dad and I don't want any woman to cry herself to sleep night after night because of me. So keeping my relationships with women casual seemed like the best thing. Then no one can get hurt.'

Ruby stared at him. That was very selfless. He cared more about the women than himself. 'So there's never been anyone that made you want to rethink that philosophy?'

'Not really. I've never been with a woman long enough to develop feelings for them. There was one woman who made me think that things could turn into something more but she didn't want that so nothing happened.'

'She broke your heart?'

'God no, it didn't get that far. My heart is completely intact,' Jacob said, quickly. Possibly too quickly and she got the feeling he wasn't being entirely truthful about that.

'But now you're here in Happiness, thinking about settling down,' Ruby said.

'No, I'm not thinking about that.'

'You said you wanted to raise a family one day.'

'I suppose I will one day, but not now,' Jacob said, seemingly backpedalling away from that lifestyle.

'OK, but how can you do that if you only want something casual?' Ruby asked.

'I came to realise something. When the right woman walks into my life, when I fall in love, I'll never need anyone else. When I love someone as much as Andrew loves Willow, I could never be unfaithful to them, I could never do anything to hurt them.'

Ruby nodded. 'You're in control of the kind of person you are, not genetics or your history. You can't let what happened in your past define your future. I think you'd make someone a wonderful husband one day.'

He smiled at her. 'I'm not scared of love anymore, Ruby. But I think the whole *don't let your past define your future* thing is *very* good advice.'

He fixed her with a look and she rolled her eyes with a smile. She'd walked straight into that trap.

'Marriage isn't for me, I tried it once, never again. But I'd be very happy to come to your wedding. I'll even wear a big hat.'

The thought of watching him getting married to someone else did something inside her she didn't like. She decided to change the subject.

'So are you going to the carol concert?' she asked.

'Of course, are you?'

'I can't sing.'

'Neither can I, but I think everyone in the village is going. Standing around that big tree. I think it will be quite special,' Jacob said.

'I need to go and see this tree; I only saw it briefly last night.'

'When you were stealing Jesus from the nativity.'

Ruby laughed. 'That wasn't me.'

'I found him hidden at the back of my shop. I nearly called the police but I thought harbouring a fugitive was much more fun.'

She laughed again. 'If we go down, we'll go down together.'

'Exactly.'

'I only did it to wind Willow up. I know she's responsible for the decorations, but now Julia has put up all those posters and it just makes me want to keep him a bit longer and wind her up even more.'

'Willow didn't do the nativity, Julia did,' Jacob said.

'Oh. Well, that explains it then. Do you think I should return him?'

He shook his head without hesitation. 'No, I think we could have some fun here.'

'Are you joining forces with a known criminal?'

'It looks like I am.'

She grinned.

'Oh, talking of the other decorations. Am I the only one who thinks they look like…'

'Penises and pants? Yeah, I thought that too. Although almost everyone else thinks it all looks wonderful.'

'What was Willow thinking?'

'I think she was given a really tiny budget and got the lights second-hand and really cheap, for obvious reasons. She was mortified when she saw them once they were up but no one else seems to have noticed.'

'I must go out and see them again, best laugh I've had in a very long time.'

'We can go and see them now if you want, pop down and see the tree too.'

Ruby looked around the shop. There was still much to be done but she figured she was probably finished for the night.

'OK, sounds good.'

'Great, I'll just grab my coat.' Jacob picked up the two empty plates and ran upstairs.

She stood up and pulled her coat on, found her hat in her pocket and put that and her gloves on too. Jacob reappeared with his long grey coat, a bright red scarf and a grey beanie hat covering his dark curly hair. He looked like he'd just stepped out of a Christmas movie in the role of the gorgeous hero. And to top it all off as they stepped outside, tiny snowflakes were dancing in the air.

'It's snowing,' Ruby said in surprise as Jacob locked the door behind him.

He turned round to watch the tiny flakes swirl around them. 'Oh, well that is romantic.'

'There's nothing romantic about snow at all.'

Jacob shoved his hands in his pockets as he fell in at her

side. It seemed they wouldn't be holding hands this time and she didn't know whether to be pleased or disappointed by that.

'For someone who is so in love with Christmas, you're a bit anti-snow,' Jacob said.

'I'm not. I love snow, but I don't think it's romantic. It's just... fluffy rain and no one thinks rain is romantic,' Ruby said, feeling like she was trying to backpedal away from him and doing a terrible job.

'I happen to think kissing someone in the rain is very romantic. So walks in the snow is also one of the things to avoid, along with tree decorating. I'll add it to my anti-romance list.'

She rolled her eyes. 'Will you stop with all the romance talk. I much preferred it when you were talking about no-strings-attached sex.'

'Well, we can definitely talk about that.'

She smiled and they walked on in silence for a bit. The street was deserted, everyone tucked up in their houses or sitting in the pub in front of that roaring fire. The Christmas lights danced and twinkled above them and she couldn't help but giggle again as she looked at them. They were utterly ridiculous and how people hadn't spotted what she had seen was beyond her.

She looked at Jacob as he walked next to her. In her heart she knew she was fighting a losing battle by keeping him at arm's length. Avoiding romantic situations was not going to help. There was no doubt in her mind that she was going to end up in bed with him again and he probably knew that too. The connection between them was too strong to try sweeping it under the carpet. And while that prospect was completely thrilling, she was more worried about the feelings she'd be trying to suppress if she was to sleep with him again. In reality that had been the reason she had blanked all of his calls and texts. Because she *had* felt something for him in the summer, it *had* been more than just sex. She really didn't want any of those feelings and she was going to do everything she could to keep them under lock and key.

They reached the end of the high street and there, in the middle of the green on the slopes leading up to the castle, was a towering Christmas tree glittering under the weight of the decorations. There were baubles of every colour the size of her head, interspersed with smaller ones. There were silvery ribbons blowing gently in the breeze and thousands of fairy lights that twinkled in the darkness.

'Oh, it's beautiful,' Ruby said softly. 'So many people just go for one colour when they have a big tree so it doesn't look too messy, but I think lots of different colours like this is a celebration of everything Christmassy.'

'I agree, the more colours the better,' Jacob said.

Ruby grabbed her phone from her pocket and took a picture for her Instagram.

She walked up to it and smiled when she could see her reflection in one of the huge glass baubles. She reached out and touched the branches, giving a small sigh of relief when she realised the tree was real.

'If there was a list for the perfect Christmas, having a real tree would be on it. I know I have artificial ones in my shop, they are easier and more cost-effective to display my things on, but in my own home it has to be real.'

She looked up at the very top and was suddenly hit with a memory.

'Harry took me to New York for our honeymoon, specifically so I could see the Rockefeller tree, one of the biggest Christmas trees in the world. New York really is spectacular at Christmas. He promised me we would travel the world to see all the big trees, the ones in Vienna, and the German markets. There is one in Italy that is a giant tree made of lights displayed on the side of Mount Ingino, it's over two thousand feet high. Obviously we never got to see them.'

'You know, I learned when I was young how fragile life is and you have to live it while you have it because it can end just like that.' Jacob snapped his fingers. 'And you know that too with what happened to Harry. To have these dreams of what you want to achieve in your life but never ticking them off because of what life has thrown at you is a little bit sad. If you want to see these things, if you want to go to Mount Ingino to see the world's biggest Christmas tree, then you should do it. I know it won't be the same without Harry, but Harry would never have wanted your life to stand still because of him, for you to miss out on the things you really want just because you can't do it with him.'

She stared at him. In her heart she knew he was right. The plan to see the Christmas trees was always something she and Harry were going to do together but in reality she had known he was doing it all for her. Would it be really wrong to go and see these things on her own?

'And I know it's scary, the thought of having another relationship again,' Jacob went on. 'But Harry wouldn't have wanted you to spend the rest of your life alone either. Sometimes you have to do the thing that scares you the most because the rewards far outweigh the risk. And I'm not talking about having a relationship with me, just that maybe one day you might be open to having that with someone again.'

She stepped back from the tree a bit to look at Jacob. He was watching her carefully. She didn't want to talk about this, mainly because she didn't want to admit that he was right.

'Let's change the subject, I don't want to burden you with all this. I never speak about him and now you've opened up a massive can of worms with finding that photo album earlier today. I promise I'm not going to cry again.'

'It's OK, I don't mind you talking about him.'

She pulled a face.

'Isn't it a bit weird, me talking about my ex-husband with my current…' She trailed off, not sure how she could define her relationship with Jacob.

'With your friend,' Jacob said, firmly. 'We're friends and we're supposed to talk about stuff like this with our friends. And even if we were more than friends, I still wouldn't mind you talking about him. So no, it's definitely not weird. What's weird actually is that you don't normally talk about him. He was a huge part of your life, you were married. You shouldn't just try to forget about that time, slam the lid shut on those memories. You should bring them out to look at now and again. Remember the good times you had with him. If he was as wonderful as he sounds, he deserves that.'

She stared at him, the tiny flakes of snow swirling around him, and she knew he was right. She had been trying to forget Harry and he was worth so much more than that. It was hard to know what she felt about him now. He had been gone for over twelve years so she couldn't say she was still in love with him, but she knew there would always be a tiny bit of her heart that belonged to him. She touched the snowflake necklace again.

'It was always easier to try to forget those memories. At first it was too painful and later, when I did try to talk about him, his family and friends didn't like it. It was always awkward talking to the grieving widow about her husband, I could see how uncomfortable they all were. Death is such a funny subject, it affects us all, but no one wants to talk about it. I suppose it became the norm to not talk about him at all. I talk about it with Willow sometimes – she never knew me when I was married to Harry so maybe it's easier for both of us.'

She reached out and touched one of the silver stars on the tree.

'When he died, I wanted to do something to honour his memory. His parents got a bench with his name on it in the park where he used to play as a kid. I don't know, it just felt so... wrong. A wooden bench didn't sum up Harry. He was so... active, so alive, so mischievous. He used to do so much for charity, sponsored fun runs, abseiling, parachute jumps. I had no idea what kind of memorial I could do for him that would honour him in the right way. So in the end I did nothing and I always regret that.'

'It's not too late,' Jacob said.

'It's been over twelve years.'

'So?'

'What could I do?'

Jacob turned his attention to the tree for a moment as he thought.

'You could do something for charity, just like he would have done. Organise an event in his memory. Raise money for the British Heart Foundation. A memorial doesn't have to be a static thing, a place to visit. You keep your memories of him in your heart, but if you want to honour him, then this might be a good way to do it.'

She looked up at the snow dancing in the inky darkness above them, feeling the tiny flakes pepper her cheeks.

'I think that is a wonderful idea.'

But what could she do? Whatever it was, it needed to be done before Christmas. Harry had loved Christmas almost as much as she did. She suddenly wanted to get back home and come up with some ideas.

'Come on, let's go,' Ruby said.

Jacob fell in at her side as they walked down the slopes of the green and she slipped her arm through his.

'Thank you.'

He looked down at her. 'For what?'

'For listening, and for just being so bloody lovely.'

'Ah god, there's that word again.'

'It's your own fault, Jacob Harrington. You're a man who's very hard not to like. It's quite annoying really.'

'Sorry about that.'

'Can you try harder to be horrible? It would make my "nothing is going to happen between us" edict a lot easier to stick to if you were.'

He smiled. 'I'm not sure that is great motivation but I'll do my best.'

'Thank you.'

They walked on in silence for a while, but it wasn't awkward, it was easy between them. Everything was easy with Jacob, including talking about her past. The only thing that wasn't easy was trying to ignore that incredible connection.

'So what else would be on your list for a perfect Christmas?' Jacob asked.

'Oh, I love Christmas food, mince pies, Christmas cake with that hard white icing on the top, gingerbread men. And hot chocolates with lashings of squirty cream and marshmallows melting in a goo on the top. There'd be lots of snow,' Ruby gestured to the sky. 'A lot more than this. I'd want a Dickensian kind of Christmas, with all the roofs and roads covered in at least a foot of the stuff. And then I'd make a big snowman outside my house, the traditional kind with a top hat, a red scarf, lumps of coal for the eyes and of course a carrot for the nose. Christmas Day would be with all the people I care about, we'd eat too much, play games and watch cheesy Christmas movies.'

'What's your favourite Christmas movie?'

'Ah, that's like asking me who is my favourite child. I love *Santa Clause: The Movie* and *Miracle on 34th Street* – the most recent one. I love *The Holiday* and *Elf*, but I also love the classics like *White Christmas* too. Do you have a favourite movie?'

'I like *Elf* as well; Poppy loves it so I've watched it several hundred times with her. It never gets old.'

'What about your perfect Christmas?' Ruby asked. 'What would be on your list?'

'Oh, I don't know. I suppose food, family, the usual.'

'Is that it?'

He grinned. 'I love Christmas, but I'm not in *love* with it like you are.'

'That's because you've obviously never had a *perfect* Christmas before so you don't know what to look for. Maybe we can change that for you this year.'

'I'll let you know when I find it.'

They reached his shop.

'Are you coming back in? We can have a drink, maybe toss some ideas around,' Jacob said.

'Not tonight,' Ruby said.

'OK, I'll walk you home.'

'There's no need.'

'Trust me, there's some pretty unsavoury types in the village.'

Ruby laughed as they carried on walking down the hill, knowing that was very unlikely. The snow was starting to settle now, dusting the tops of the roofs ahead of them and gathering at the edges of the road. It really was starting to look romantic.

She looked up at Jacob. She really liked this man and she knew it was more than just the romance of the snow.

They arrived back at her cottage and she opened the door and stepped inside, turning back to face him.

It was on the tip of her tongue to invite him in but she knew that was a terrible idea. Even still, there was a huge part of her that didn't want him to go. In the end he made the decision for her.

He leaned down and placed a kiss on her cheek. 'Goodnight Ruby Marlowe.'

She closed her eyes at the softness of his lips against her skin, her heart thundering against her chest at that simple tiny gesture.

He stepped back, gave her a smile and then turned and walked away.

She watched him go, wondering if he would look back. Just as she was about to go inside, he looked over his shoulder and saw her watching him. He gave her a wave before he disappeared into the snow-studded night.

She closed the door and leaned against it with a smile. It was going to be really hard to not fall in love with Jacob Harrington. But she knew things would be even harder if she did.

CHAPTER SEVEN

Ruby was just getting ready for bed when her phone rang. She smiled as she knew who it was. Only Cal, her brother, would be ringing her at this time of night as he was currently touring the US, so it wasn't late for him.

'Rubes, how's it going?' Cal said. It sounded like he was walking or maybe even running, he never stood still.

'It's going well,' Ruby said.

'Are you finally in Happiness?'

'Yes, I got here late last night.'

'I can't believe all that stress with selling your place meant it took all that time. Well, you're there now, that's what matters,' Cal said. 'So tell me everything, what are the neighbours like?'

Ruby climbed into bed. 'Lovely. Nosy, meddling, interfering, gossipy but lovely.'

Cal laughed.

'Willow's engaged.'

'Ah, that's fantastic, pass on my congratulations.'

'I will,' Ruby paused. 'Jacob's here too.'

There was silence from Cal for a moment and Ruby wondered if he remembered her mentioning him. When she had returned from Happiness in the summer, Cal had been staying at her house for a few days, and Ruby had been stupidly giddy about the time she had spent in the little village and her excitement about moving there, and of course Jacob had been mentioned. He had been a big part of why she had enjoyed her time in the village. When she had shared a bottle of wine with her brother, Jacob's name had come up on many occasions. It was possible she might have gushed about him. Cal had grilled her about him and over the next few days he had pushed her to take a chance with Jacob, to return his calls and texts, but Ruby had refused to even consider it. Cal had eventually given up pursuing it.

'Jacob Harrington?' Cal said.

Yes, he definitely remembered.

'Yeah, it's no big deal though. We're just friends. Nothing is going to happen.' How many times had she said that in the last twenty-four hours?

'Right, sure. Out of all the men you've been with over the years, Jacob is the only one you've told me about. What Jacob did, what he said. I feel like I already know him and we've never met.'

'He's a nice guy, he just came up in conversation,' Ruby said, knowing it was a lot more than that.

'So you're both living there now?' Cal asked.

'Yes. We're working together in the same shop.'

'And nothing is going to happen between you?'

'No.'

'You have no feelings for him at all?'

'Look, the man is sexy, there's no denying that and, yes, if I'm honest, I wouldn't mind a repeat of what we had in the summer. But what I feel for him is lust, there's nothing more to it than that. He makes me laugh and he's good to talk to. He's been really nice actually. We talked about Harry and he's been really supportive. But I don't *like* him, not in that way.'

'You told him about Harry? You never talk about him with anyone. Don't you think that's something significant?'

'He found out,' Ruby said. 'You don't need to make this into something when it's not. I've had enough meddling from the villagers without having that from you too.'

'That's because they can all see what you refuse to see. You like this man but you cling to your memory of Harry like a safety net and you won't let anyone in. Do you think Harry would have wanted this life for you where you spend the rest of it alone for fear of having your heart broken again?'

Only Cal could get away with pushing her like this. She thought about what Jacob had said about not giving up on her dreams, of living her life now because it could be gone in an instant. They were both right, but it didn't mean she could just forget the pain Harry's death had caused, she couldn't let go of that fear of it happening all over again.

'Tell me about your tour,' Ruby said, changing the subject because her heart and her head were at an impasse.

'Is that you closing the subject?'

'Yes, how's America?'

Cal sighed. 'I'm letting this go, for now, but we are going to talk about this again.'

'I know,' Ruby said, quietly because Cal was a determined, tenacious little bugger.

Cal started talking about his tour. As a Paralympian, when he wasn't in training for the next Paralympics or other sporting events, he toured around the world giving talks and inspiring hundreds and thousands of people. He had lost his leg in a car accident when he was a kid and it would have been so easy for him to give up on life there and then, put in the bare minimum. He couldn't play with his friends anymore, his dream of becoming a professional footballer gone in the blink of an eye, he'd been contained to a wheelchair for the first year or so after his accident, which he'd found beyond frustrating. But he was a poster boy for how to overcome adversity, for not letting the bad things in life define him. He had gone on to be one of the greatest Paralympian athletes, winning gold on multiple occasions in countries across the world. Maybe she needed to draw inspiration from him too.

~

Jacob was busy welding together bits of metal and cutlery the next day, in an attempt to make a large Christmas tree. He was more used to making animals than anything else, but he had been inspired to do something Christmassy by his lovely neighbour. He had come down to his shop that morning to find the Christmas additions that Ruby had left for him on his artwork the night before and had decided to try his own piece of festive art. He wasn't sure he was totally pleased with the way it had turned out, but he was sure Ruby would appreciate his efforts to get into the Christmas mood.

He hadn't been able to stop thinking about her all night. To lose her husband, the love of her life, at such a young age… he wasn't sure she could ever really get over that. At that age she would have been so idealistic, all those hopes and dreams of a happy ever after gone in an instant. Part of him understood her wanting to keep men at arm's length. She didn't want to fall in love and then have her heart broken again in the same way. But part of him wanted her to take that risk again because being in love had to be worth it. He had no idea what would happen between them and he was more than happy to just be her friend right now, but he hoped he could eventually get her to open her heart to a proper relationship, even if that relationship wasn't with him. Part of doing that was getting her to remember Harry properly, not locking that box of memories away never to be seen. Only when she had dealt with that loss could she really move on.

Just as he was attempting to create a star for the top of the Christmas tree out of several old forks, the woman herself arrived in his shop, shaking the snow that had been falling steadily all morning out from her hair. He lifted his face mask temporarily so he could say hello to her but realised straight away that she was bursting to talk to him. He switched off his welding torch and took off his mask.

'Good morning, beautiful,' Jacob said and she clearly stalled in what she was about to say.

'You promised that you were going to stop being charming,' Ruby said, taking off her coat and unwinding her scarf.

He grinned. 'I can't help it, charming is just the way I am. You'll just have to get used to it.'

'Smooth more like. You're just trying to get into my knickers.'

He laughed. 'No, just telling the truth. How was your night?'

'I've been thinking about what you said, and I've had some ideas. I think a charity event is a really good idea to celebrate Harry's life. I realise that most of the people round here are elderly and probably don't have that much money, and the young families probably won't either. But maybe we can come up with a few events that might charge a small entrance fee rather than asking for sponsorship. And maybe this can be something I can give to the village. You said yourself that there wasn't a lot going on for Christmas, and I know Kitty and Ken are hopeful that I might be able to do something. Maybe I can spread the joy of Christmas now. This time of year, families are always looking for ways to keep the children occupied. I don't imagine we would raise a lot, but a few hundred pounds would be nice. I'd like to do something this side of Christmas which, with only six days until the big day, doesn't give us a lot of time to organise.'

'Don't forget we have the carolling on Wednesday night.'

'Yes, I think we could do something in the day too. And some of these things could be spread over a number of days.'

'What do you have in mind?'

She smiled. 'I have quite a few ideas actually. But you were the inspiration for this first idea. I thought that we could have an Angel Festival and people can make angel sculptures out of anything they wish. It could be papier-*mâché* or old bits of wood or metal, maybe even last week's recycling. It doesn't have to be big or grand, it could just be something that families might enjoy doing together in the comfort of their own homes. We charge them a pound to enter the competition and then on the day people can position their sculptures around the village and choose their favourite by putting money in the jar next to the sculpture.'

'Well, I think that sounds like a wonderful idea and it's something that the villagers could easily do.'

'I also thought that we could have a Christmas Cookie competition and people can pay to enter. We'll get some plain biscuits and some icing and sweets and give them fifteen minutes or half an hour to decorate the biscuits as they see fit. Again we can choose a winner with the money in the jar, just a few pennies.'

'Again that's not a bad idea, it's something that anybody could easily do.'

'I'm going to offer a Christmas wrapping service too so people can bring along their presents and I will wrap them for a small fee.'

'I think you might be inundated with people wanting you to do that. I love buying presents for people but I hate wrapping them. I imagine lots of people feel the same way.'

She smiled. 'You've been very supportive but I don't think that you're going to be as encouraging about my next suggestion.'

He narrowed his eyes suspiciously. 'What's the idea?'

'How about a Polar Bear Plunge?'

His heart sank into his stomach. He couldn't think of anything worse.

'I have to say, I'm not liking the sound of that already. I hate the cold.' It was something much more than that but he wasn't going to tell Ruby that.

'You were the one who said the snow was romantic,' Ruby said.

'Yes, when I'm bundled up inside a hat and coat or watching it from inside. But swimming in minus temperatures is definitely not for me.'

'It's not minus temperatures, it's probably about ten degrees, that's practically tropical.'

'You're not going to convince me.'

'I thought it might be fun. We can all wear fancy dress and run into the sea. We don't have to be in there long. People can pay to enter and we can sell hot chocolate after to warm everybody up,' Ruby said.

'You do realise that a large proportion of people in the village are over the age of eighty? I would be worried about dodgy hearts giving out in the freezing cold water.'

She frowned and he felt suddenly sick. What a crappy thing to say when her husband had died from a heart attack.

'Shit. I'm so sorry,' Jacob said.

'It's fine, don't worry.'

'No, that was a really thoughtless thing to say.'

She smiled. 'There is not one single part of you that could ever be considered thoughtless. And you're probably right that a Polar Bear Plunge might not be suitable for a lot of people in the village.'

He shrugged. 'Maybe you give people the choice, let them make up their own minds.'

'Maybe we do a Polar Bear Paddle instead.'

He laughed at the compromise.

'Why don't you go on the village forum and write a post about all of your ideas? Tell them it's to raise money for charity and ask people to vote for what they are interested in doing. People can comment too and they might have some ideas of their own.'

'Great idea but will everyone have access to the forum? I imagine some of the older folk might not even have a computer.'

'You'd be surprised. It was Julia that set it up and she celebrated her seventy-fifth birthday last month. Everyone is on there as they can access it on their phones. They're all pretty active on it too.'

'OK, I might need you to show me how to log on to this thing.'

'Come on.'

She followed him to the computer. He spent a few minutes setting up her profile and then showing her how to add a post on the forum and then left her to it.

He was glad that she was doing this. She needed to remember her husband in the right way, not forget he ever existed. And hopefully this would help her to celebrate his life and to be more open about talking about him.

After a while she stood up.

'OK, that's all done. Now we'll just have to wait to see if people are up for it. Right, I must get on with some work in the shop. I'd like to open up tomorrow.' She made a move to walk through the archway but suddenly seemed to notice the Christmas tree he was making.

'Oh my god, that's amazing.' She hurried over to take a look, fishing out her phone to take a picture.

'It's nowhere near finished yet but I was inspired to be Christmassy by your lovely additions to my shop.'

She looked around. 'You didn't take them down.'

'Of course I didn't.'

'I thought you'd think it wasn't really in keeping with the minimalist arty atmosphere.'

'It looks great,' Jacob said, honestly. 'In fact, feel free to add some more.'

She smiled. 'You're going to regret saying that.'

He watched her disappear through the archway. Having her next door was going to be fun.

CHAPTER EIGHT

Ruby was busy decorating one of her trees with hand-painted glass baubles. The tree was nearly finished but she had so much stuff to do in the shop. She had promised Andrew she would pop up to her other shop later so she could see the damage and talk about plans for redecoration, then she was meeting Willow for lunch. There didn't seem like there was a lot of time left now and with less than a week until Christmas, she really wanted to open up tomorrow.

At a noise behind her, she turned to see Jacob walking in with two hot chocolates, topped with squirty cream and marshmallows.

She smiled as she took her mug. He had obviously been listening the night before when she had talked about her perfect Christmas. It had been small little gestures like this that she had really loved about Harry. She frowned and pushed away the comparison. Harry had been the love of her life. Jacob was a great friend who she'd had amazing sex with. There was a big difference. She did not have feelings for Jacob just because he had bought her a hot chocolate. That would be ridiculous.

She stared at the hot chocolate for a moment. The marshmallows were already melting into little lumps of goo in the heat of the drink. It really was the perfect cup of hot chocolate.

'Thank you,' Ruby said.

'My pleasure.' Jacob took a sip, leaving a blob of cream on his lip. She had a sudden overwhelming desire to kiss it off. God, that wasn't good.

His phone pinged in his pocket and he frowned. 'My phone has been beeping with notifications from the village forum ever since you went on there this morning. I'm guessing people are commenting on your ideas for Christmas.'

'Do you get notified every time someone comments about something? That could get tiresome.'

'Not normally. Usually I only get notified if I'm being tagged in something or if someone is replying to a post I've made.'

He pulled his phone out of his pocket as Ruby moved to the computer to see all the comments for herself. She'd asked people to vote if they were interested in taking part in an event. Lots of people were keen to do the Angel Festival and the Christmas Cookie Competition. There was also a lot of interest in Ruby wrapping presents for people.

'Oh god,' Jacob muttered behind her.

'What's that?' Ruby said as she scanned through the different comments. Everyone was being hugely positive about it all.

She scrolled down to the bit about the Polar Bear Plunge. Not surprisingly, no one had indicated they were willing to do it, but there were a ton of comments about it underneath. She clicked to open the comments and read a few people saying that it was too cold for them but that they were happy to sponsor someone else to do it. Then she saw a comment from Julia.

Julia: *I'll sponsor Jacob £50 if he does it.*

She burst out laughing. 'Have you seen what Julia has put?'

'Yes. Have you seen the other comments?' Jacob said.

She scrolled down a bit more.

Liz: *I'll also sponsor Jacob £50.*

Dorothy: *I'll add £100 to the charity pot if Jacob does it dressed as an elf.*

Kitty: *We'll add another £100 to the pot if Jacob does it.*

Tabitha: *The Welcome Home will also add a £100 for Jacob to do it.*

There were several more comments with people offering ten, twenty or fifty pounds if Jacob did it and Ruby couldn't help but laugh.

'It's OK for you, it's not you that's going to die in the freezing waters,' Jacob said.

She turned round to find him looking very grumpy about the whole thing. 'You don't have to do it. Everyone is just having a laugh. I don't think anyone really expects you to go through with it.'

'Oh, I'm doing it. The pot is currently at over seven hundred pounds. I'm not going to let you down. Of course I'm doing it.'

Ruby smiled, her heart filling for this man. He was making it really bloody difficult not to have feelings for him. She'd thought she'd be safe. Just friends, no sex, and those pesky feelings would just go away. But it hadn't worked out like that. He was too lovely. In fact, spending time with him, talking to him, laughing with him, getting to know him on a deeper level, the feelings she had for him were just getting worse and she didn't know what she could do about it.

Ruby let herself into The Happy Little Christmas shop as she could see Andrew busy working away inside.

He was on his hands and knees when she walked in and he looked up and grinned at her.

'Hey Ruby.' He stood up and wiped his hands.

'Hey,' Ruby said, noticing Lucas working at the back of the shop. 'Hi Lucas.'

He came forward. 'Hi Ruby.'

She had a sudden idea. Megan might not thank her for it but she was going to follow her gut on this one.

'So are you both looking forward to the ball?'

Andrew nodded and Lucas shrugged.

'I think everyone is in a last-minute panic to get dates for the ball. Do you have a date, Lucas?' Ruby said.

'Oh, I probably won't go.'

'Ah, that's a shame.' She turned to Andrew. 'I think Jacob is going to ask Megan to go with him.'

Andrew looked confused. 'Really?'

'What?' Lucas said, suddenly visibly alarmed.

'Yes,' Ruby nodded. 'I think he likes her. And I was speaking to Megan and she hasn't got a date yet, so I imagine she'll say yes. Unless she gets a better offer before Jacob asks, of course.'

Lucas frowned. 'I need to get some tools for this.'

He hurried out the shop and Ruby giggled to herself as the door closed behind him.

'Jacob's not going to ask Megan out, is he?' Andrew said.

'Not that I know of,' Ruby said. 'But I think she's keen on your new assistant. I just thought I'd give them a little nudge in the right direction.'

'That felt like a bloody big shove rather than a nudge.'

Ruby shrugged. 'If I'm wrong, I'm sure Megan will be brave enough to say no if Lucas actually asks her. If I'm right, well, only good can come of it.'

Andrew shook his head with a smile. 'How are you settling into Happiness anyway?'

'Good, my temporary shop is looking particularly festive. I'll probably be able to open the doors for business tomorrow and everyone has been very welcoming.'

Andrew smirked. 'Did my brother welcome you with open arms?'

Ruby smiled. 'He's been very… helpful.'

'I bet he has.'

'What's going on with him anyway? He's talking about settling down one day, getting married, having children. We went for a walk last night in the snow and he said how romantic it was. And aside from all of that, he's just been so bloody lovely. The Jacob I knew in the summer was very much a love-them-and-leave-them kind of guy. I never thought we'd have serious heart-to-heart conversations but we have. He's changed.'

'Jacob can do serious if he wants to, he's a good listener. I think he's a complete pain in the arse sometimes but he's loyal and kind. He's always had a lot of time for other people. And I don't know about him settling down and having children, he certainly hasn't mentioned that to me, but I guess it comes with age. He adores our niece Poppy and I've always thought he would make a great dad one day.'

Ruby thought about what Jacob would be like as a dad and knew Andrew was right.

'So he's never had a serious relationship before, never had his heart broken?'

Andrew hesitated before answering. 'In Jacob's case that's

two different questions. As far as I know, he's never had a serious relationship.'

'But he has had his heart broken?'

Andrew cocked his head. 'Maybe that's a conversation you should have with Jacob.'

Ruby thought about this for a moment.

'So do you fancy the job of Mrs Harrington?' Andrew said, changing the subject slightly.

'No, thank you. I'm fine staying Miss Marlowe. There's only going to be one Mrs Harrington round here and I think Willow will fill that role perfectly.'

Andrew grinned. 'I cannot wait for her to be my wife.'

Ruby smiled. 'Any thoughts about when the wedding will be?'

'We thought maybe February. It'll be something quite small here in the village or up at the castle.'

'That will be lovely, I can't wait to see the castle all done up for the Christmas Eve ball, I'm sure you could do something similar for the wedding.'

'Yes, we were going to talk to Kitty and Ken about having it there.'

'I bet they will be all over that idea. The first wedding in the castle.'

'I hope so.'

'So, you don't fancy taking part in the Polar Bear Plunge?' Ruby asked, hoping to gather together more people in the hope that Jacob might feel better about doing it.

'Hell no. I love to swim in the sea, but I'm a fair-weather swimmer. I only go in when the weather is hot.'

'I think Jacob feels the same,' Ruby said.

Andrew shook his head. 'He doesn't swim.'

'He can't swim?'

'Oh no, he can swim, he just never goes in the sea. He's not going to let himself be bullied into doing this Polar Bear Plunge, is he?' Andrew asked in concern.

'He says he's doing it. We're raising money for charity; he says he doesn't want to let me down.'

'Crap,' Andrew said.

'Why, what's wrong?'

He shook his head. 'There was an incident, several years ago… Look, I don't think it's my place to say.'

This sounded really serious.

'OK, you're going to have to tell me what happened so I know what I'm dealing with here.'

Andrew didn't say anything for a while but eventually he spoke. 'We grew up in Newquay, which is well known for its big waves and great surfing. Jacob loved to surf. One morning, when he was fourteen, he took his surfboard and went down to the beach. It was very early, before anyone else was up. The beach was deserted but it was a place he had surfed hundreds of times before and I suppose he felt safe.'

'Why do I get the feeling that this story doesn't end well.'

'Well it doesn't. Not really. He got caught in an undertow, he was dragged under the water and carried out to sea. I mean, I suppose he was lucky, he managed to get back to the surface, but he did get pulled out to sea quite far. He'd lost his surfboard so he had nothing to hold onto. He had already been surfing for an hour and he was knackered and he tried to fight against the rip tide which made him more exhausted. He didn't have the energy to swim back to shore and the tide carried him further and further away. No one knew he'd gone surfing so no one raised the alarm when he didn't come home. Mum just thought he'd gone out with his mates. No one saw him get swept away. He was finally found by some fishermen about eight hours after he'd been swept out. He was exhausted, he had hypothermia, he was in hospital for a few days. There was no lasting damage but… well, he hasn't been back in the sea since.'

'Are you kidding me?' Ruby said, incredulously.

Andrew shook his head. 'No, he had terrible nightmares about it for years after. We've been to the beach with Poppy but he won't go anywhere near the sea. You can see it completely freaks him out whenever he goes within sniffing distance.'

'Oh my god, why the hell is he going through with this?'

'Because he's a determined, stubborn sod,' Andrew said.

'I'll call it off,' Ruby said. 'It was a silly idea anyway.'

'You can't do that! Then he'll know I told you and he should be the one to tell you this. I thought you should know because if he freaks out and pulls out at the last minute, at least you'll understand why and won't give him any grief about it.'

'Of course I won't.' She sighed. 'What a mess.'

Andrew was silent for a while. 'Maybe it'll be good for him, help him get over that fear once and for all. But let him make that decision himself whether he goes ahead with it or not.'

She let out a heavy breath, hating that she had inadvertently put Jacob in this position. She had to find a way to talk to him about this without letting on that she knew.

'So, shall I show you the damage?' Andrew said. He was clearly trying to change the subject after having outed Jacob in that way, though Ruby knew he'd done it for the right reasons.

She nodded, her mind still on Jacob.

'Well, it's quite bad back here.' Andrew walked to the back of the shop and when she followed him she was shocked to see that there was a gaping hole in the ceiling. 'The water tank up in the loft had evidently been leaking for a while and the ceiling eventually gave way. Water has poured through and completely ruined the carpet. We have a new tank on order but I don't think it will be delivered now until after Christmas. In the meantime we are going to repair the ceiling, replace the carpet and redecorate where it's needed. So if there's anything you particularly want in here, or anything you want changing, now would be a good time to do it.'

Ruby looked around. It was smaller than the shop she shared with Jacob, narrower and let in less light. Location wise, this shop was in a much better position in the village but in the short time she had spent in her temporary shop, she had enjoyed having someone to talk to next door. In the market hall in St Octavia where she'd had her little Christmas stand, she had loved talking to the other vendors. They'd get each other cakes, sandwiches and hot drinks and watch their stands for each other if they needed to nip to the loo. Being in here felt quite isolated in comparison to what she was used to. And she liked the layout in the temporary shop with its little shelves and nooks to display her pieces in. It had character and this really didn't. She imagined sharing cups of tea with Jacob, chatting about village life, and she liked the idea of always having someone there.

She shook her head as she caught herself. That was the last thing she wanted. She didn't want to get cosy with Jacob, laugh with him, talk with him, because that would lead her to a road she didn't want to go down.

'What are you thinking?' Andrew said.

There was no way in hell she was going to tell him that she had been thinking about staying in the temporary shop with Jacob.

'Nothing, just… where I would put everything.'

'Well I can put some shelves up if that's helpful?'

'Yes, that would be great. Maybe a big low shelf in the window so I can have a proper window display and then some large low shelves or tables here and over there so I can show off my baubles. And a large table in the middle so I can make my decorations.'

'OK, no problem. Any particular colour you want the walls painted?'

'Oh, I'm not sure. I've never had walls to contend with before. I guess just something neutral like white or cream and then it won't clash with my brightly coloured decorations.'

He smiled. 'I didn't take you for a neutral kind of person. What about silver or gold instead? Those are pretty neutral.'

Ruby thought about it for a moment. 'Gold would be wonderful, thank you.'

'Gold it is.'

Gold was definitely one up on the shop she shared with Jacob and she got to redesign this one to however she wanted. This was definitely the better option. Definitely.

She'd have to keep telling herself that.

Ruby walked into the pub and looked around for Willow. It was quieter now than it had been the day before at her welcome drinks but it was still a lot busier than she'd seen it in the summer.

Willow waved to her from a table in the corner and she made her way over. Megan was at the next table, eating her lunch and deeply engrossed in her book.

Ruby gave Willow a hug and sat down opposite her.

'I ordered fish and chips for us both, I hope that's OK,' Willow said. 'Connor does great fish here; it's grilled rather than battered and always comes in this delicious sauce.'

'That sounds great, I'm starving.'

'I bet you are. I was walking past your new shop earlier; it looks amazing in there.'

'There's still a ton to do, but it will be ready for the grand opening tomorrow,' Ruby said.

'And how's the old shop? Andrew says the damage is pretty bad?'

'It is, but Andrew and Lucas are on the case.'

Ruby noticed Megan glance over at the mention of Lucas's name and smiled to herself. There was definitely something between those two. Hopefully her little bit of meddling would help to get them together.

Willow leaned in closer. 'Now, Ruby Marlowe, would you have anything to do with Jesus going missing from the nativity? Because that kind of thing has your name all over it.'

Ruby laughed. 'I only did it to wind you up because I thought you were responsible for the nativity. I didn't realise there were going to be wanted posters and a reward.'

Willow laughed. 'Are you going to give him back?'

'Not yet. Me and Jacob are going to have some fun with him.'

Willow grinned. 'I'm glad you have Jacob to... distract you.'

Ruby smiled; she knew exactly what Willow meant. She and Willow had been carrying out practical jokes on each other every December for years and Ruby knew it was her friend's way of distracting her from focussing on her wedding anniversary on the twenty-third. Ruby appreciated the sentiment and she did enjoy the jokes, but that day was always going to be hard, the day when she was meant to start her happy ever after.

'I have a gift for you,' Willow said, placing the box on the table between them.

Ruby eyed it suspiciously. 'Is this going to contain cockroaches or a poisonous snake perhaps?'

Willow pretended to be hurt. 'No, of course not, it's just a little welcome to the village present.'

Years of knowing her meant she didn't trust her as far as she could throw her, but Ruby carefully removed the lid anyway.

There was a small pop and Ruby saw stars, literally, as a cloud of glitter and sequins exploded out of the box, covering her and the table in a matter of seconds.

Ruby laughed as she shook her hair and her clothes and she could see Megan at the next table giggling quietly into her book.

'Well played,' Ruby said as Willow was almost hysterical with laughter.

Connor came over with the food. 'I hope you're going to clear that up,' he said, grumpily.

Ruby smirked. He hadn't changed, even if the rest of the village had.

'I actually brought a dustpan and brush with me,' Willow said, ever efficient.

Connor grunted and walked away.

Ruby shook her head. 'You know how to make a statement, Willow McKay. Oh, talking of which, what is going on with those street decorations?'

Willow blushed as she ate her food. 'Sshhh. Keep your voice down.'

Ruby laughed. 'It's not exactly a secret, it's out there for everyone to see.'

'But no one has spotted it yet, well apart from Jacob and Andrew who have ribbed me about it constantly. Everyone else thinks they are just really nice decorations.'

'You have penis candles and Y-fronts hanging over the main high street. How has no one else realised?'

'I don't know, maybe because their minds are innocent and pure, unlike yours.'

Ruby laughed, not the least bit offended by that. 'Where did you get them from anyway, Ann Summers?'

Willow laughed. 'One of the nearby towns was selling them cheap, said they were upgrading their lights to some new ones and just wanted to get rid of them.'

'Did you not think to ask what they were before you bought them?'

'Why would I? Why would I even think that I was getting something other than just normal run-of-the-mill Christmas lights?'

Ruby laughed again and tucked into her food.

'What's going on with this Polar Bear Plunge anyway?' Willow asked.

'Well at the moment, it's just Jacob doing it,' Ruby said, her heart sinking again as she thought about him doing something he really didn't want to do.

'I don't think it's a good idea,' Willow said, diplomatically.

Ruby watched her for a moment. 'Andrew told you too, didn't he?'

Willow nodded. 'We were talking about our wedding and I suggested we could do it on the beach. Andrew said he would prefer his best man not to be standing there freaking out the whole time and then he told me.'

Ruby sighed. 'It's so awful for him. It must have been so scary. But imagine having that fear all your life, and never being able to get past that.'

Willow stared at her.

'I know,' Willow said, deliberately. 'Imagine what it would be like to have a traumatic incident in your past and never moving on from it.'

Ruby scowled and focussed on her food. 'It's not the same.'

Just then Lucas walked into the pub. He saw Megan and

marched over. Ooh, maybe he was going to be brave enough to ask her to the ball.

'Megan, I'm glad I found you,' Lucas said and Megan put her book down to look at him.

'Lucas, hi,' Megan said, her cheeks colouring slightly.

'I just wanted to give you a warning.'

Well, that wasn't the romantic start to the conversation that Ruby had been hoping for.

'Jacob Harrington is planning to ask you to the ball,' Lucas said, seriously.

Megan's eyes widened. 'He is?'

'Yes, apparently. I just thought I should warn you so you can say no.'

Megan blinked. 'Why would I say no?'

Lucas clearly hadn't been expecting that. 'A man like Jacob Harrington is no good for you.'

'What does that mean?' Megan said.

'Oh, he's a nice enough bloke, but I know him of old. He's a complete womaniser. Had more girlfriends than you've had hot dinners. He'll break your heart.'

'He can only break my heart if I give it to him and I have no intention of doing that. But going to the ball with him could be fun.'

'Fun?'

'Lucas, I haven't been out on a date for over a year. If Jacob asks me to the ball, I can do my hair and make-up, wear a pretty dress, dance with a handsome man and maybe have a bit of fun afterwards. Why would I say no to that?'

This wasn't going according to plan at all. Ruby exchanged worried glances with Willow.

Lucas scowled. 'I didn't take you for that sort of girl.'

Megan stood up and shoved her book in her bag. 'What sort of girl is that? The sort that likes to wear a pretty dress occasionally, or the sort that would be more than happy to jump into bed with Jacob Harrington if he asked me to? It's been a year, Lucas, and no one else is asking me out or asking me to the ball.'

'I don't like it.'

Megan slung her bag over her shoulder. 'Well you know what to do about it then, don't you?'

She stormed out and Lucas was left standing there looking very confused.

Ruby wanted to go over and shake him for completely missing the point but she'd interfered enough for one day.

She turned back to Willow. 'Love is a complicated thing, isn't it?'

'Yes, but I promise you, it's definitely worth it.'

Ruby turned her attention back to her food. She wasn't convinced.

Ruby walked back into her shop a while later and called out to Jacob to let him know she was there.

'Hi honey, I'm home.'

She heard the bark of laughter and smiled to herself. She looked around the shop – there was still quite a bit that needed doing before she could open the next day. She frowned. One of her Christmas trees that she hadn't got round to dressing yet had decorations on. And by the looks of them, not any she had seen before.

She moved closer and then laughed out loud when she realised there were spoons of different colours and sizes hanging from the tree. It actually looked really effective.

She looked around to see if Jacob had made any more additions and giggled to see there was a garland of bike chains hung from a shelf and two small colanders had replaced the stars at the top of her trees near the door. Her collection of baubles, which she had displayed artfully in a small pyramid, had been changed to a pyramid of metal serving spoons and spatulas balanced precariously against each other.

She marched over to the archway and stood with her hands on her hips. 'Jacob Harrington!'

He looked up from the Christmas tree he was still working on, which now had various decorations hanging from the boughs, all made from different bits of coloured metal.

'What?' he asked innocently, though it was very clear he knew full well what she was protesting about.

She gestured theatrically to her shop and he grinned.

'I was just making some improvements.'

She laughed. 'I'll give you *improvements*.' She looked back into her shop. In all honesty it looked great and was a wonderful link with Jacob's shop.

'An eye for an eye,' Jacob said, gesturing to the peacock who was still proudly displaying his blue tinsel scarf.

'Oh, it's going to be like that, is it?'

He grinned at the challenge in her voice. 'I guess it is.'

'Listen, I've been thinking about Jesus and what we could do with him,' Ruby said. 'I think we should take photos of him around the village and post them on the village forum. Could we create an anonymous account so the villagers wouldn't know it was us doing it?'

'I love that idea and, yes, I'm sure we could. I created your account in the forum, it would be easy to create an account under the name of Jesus.'

Ruby laughed. 'Let's do it.'

Jacob walked over to the computer and started creating a profile on the forum. 'You know, I was thinking about you stealing him. Did you know there was a webcam on the nativity?'

Ruby's stomach leapt as she remembered manhandling the sheep. God, she didn't want the villagers seeing that.

'Are you serious?'

'Yes, it was put there mainly so the children could watch the animals anytime they wanted, but also so that Julia and Lucas could keep an eye on the animals and make sure they were OK. The animals have come from Lucas's home so I think he likes to keep an eye on them throughout the day, even if he's working.'

'Oh god.'

'I shouldn't worry. It's a live webcam. So unless someone was watching at two in the morning, no one would have seen it.'

'I'm not remotely techy, so if it's live, it couldn't record footage as well?'

'I don't know, I don't think so. But I wouldn't worry. If someone had seen the footage, you would know about it by now.'

That was certainly true. She would probably have been chased out of the village for being an animal abuser… or worse. What would anyone have thought if they'd seen her trying to give a Heimlich manoeuvre to a sheep? Would they even have believed her if she told them the sheep was choking? OK, there was no point worrying about it. Like Jacob said, if someone had seen the webcam footage they would have been banging on her door by now.

'Right, that's done, we've now created a profile on the forum called "Jesus". This is going to be fun.'

'OK, before you log out I need to put out a timetable of events for the coming week.' Jacob stood up and Ruby slid into his seat and started adding a list of all the events. 'I intend to open tomorrow so I'll be busy with that but the day after, Tuesday twenty-first, we could do the Christmas Cookie Competition. Wednesday twenty-second we could do the Angel Festival and we have the Christmas carols that night around the tree. And then we could have the Polar Bear Plunge on Christmas Eve morning, the Secret Santa thing in the afternoon and the Christmas Eve ball on Friday night.'

He nodded and she inwardly winced when she watched the smile fall off his face at the mention of the Polar Bear Plunge.

She wanted to talk about it but she had no idea how to dissuade him from doing it without bringing up what had happened in his past. But maybe she didn't need to get him to change his mind. Maybe she just needed to support him with whatever he decided.

'And I've been thinking about the Polar Bear Plunge,' Ruby said. 'I'm going to do it with you.'

He shook his head. 'God no, I don't want anything to happen to you.'

Her heart swelled a little at that protective statement. 'Nothing is going to happen to me, it's just a little dip in the sea.'

He brushed his hair from his face. 'Yes, I know.'

'This was my bright idea that got you stuck doing something you don't want to do so we'll do it together,' Ruby insisted.

A small smile appeared on his face. 'Like a date? Because I could think of far more romantic settings for our first date.'

'Not a date,' she said firmly. 'But I'll hold your hand if you like.'

He smiled. 'I'll hold you to that.'

CHAPTER NINE

Jacob hung the baubles he'd made from spoons onto the branches of the Christmas tree sculpture. Ruby was next door, dancing along to the Christmas songs as she finished off setting out her shop. It had been completely transformed in there since her arrival. It looked festive and inviting, rather than the cold empty room he'd used for storage for the last few months. He smiled as he watched her dance. It really was good having her next door.

He looked outside as fat snowflakes swirled in the air. It was coming down heavily out there. If it lasted another week, Ruby might get her wish of a white Christmas after all. The weather was certainly cold enough to keep snowing and, according to weather reports, it was only going to get colder. He shivered at the thought.

This Polar Bear Plunge was bothering him a lot more than it should. After what had happened years before, he hadn't been back in the sea since. He'd told himself he just wasn't bothered about going in but he knew there was a lot more to it than that. And this time of year was hardly the right time to dive back into the icy waves for the first time in twenty years. But he couldn't let the bad weather or his fears stop him. He wanted to support Ruby in honouring her husband and help her to raise some money. If the villagers had decided to part with their hard-earned cash in return for seeing him swim in the sea for a few seconds then he was damned well going to do it. He ignored the sick feeling of unease in his stomach.

The door of his shop opened and Lucy strode in. She was relatively new to the village as well, having been there probably only a month. He'd met her the year before in Penzance, or so she said, when he had slept with her best friend, Amy. He was sorry to say he had no memory of Lucy at all, which made him feel completely crap as she had vivid memories of him – or, more to the point, of what Amy had told her about their night together. And now it seemed that Lucy had set her sights on him too.

'Hi Jacob,' Lucy said, moving into the shop and looking around.

'Hello Lucy.'

'I just came to say hello to our new resident. I didn't get a chance to talk to her yesterday at the welcome drinks so I thought I'd come and introduce myself now.'

'Ah, I see,' Jacob said, wondering why she hadn't gone straight into Ruby's side of the shop rather than into his. 'Well, she's next door.'

'Oh yes.' Lucy looked over and he saw the tiny wrinkle of her nose as she took in all the glitz and over-the-top glamour of the grotto next door. 'How very festive.'

'It definitely is that.'

Lucy turned her attention away from Ruby's shop and moved closer to him.

'I bet having that next door has been a complete headache,'

she whispered, conspiratorially. 'It's hardly the quiet, inspirational environment an artist like yourself needs to work.'

'Having Ruby next door has actually been very inspiring,' he gestured to the Christmas tree.

'Well, that's very classy, almost elegant. But that,' she nodded towards Ruby's shop and giggled, 'most definitely isn't.'

He glanced over at Ruby, who happened to look up from the tree and see them watching her. She blushed and gave a little wave. Thankfully the music in her shop was too loud for her to hear what Lucy was saying.

'It's actually been a breath of fresh air.'

'Really?' Lucy said in surprise. She looked around his shop again. 'I've always thought this place was cool, sexy, unique, it had an edge. The perfect place for the great Phoenix Blade. It would be such a shame to lose that to…' she picked up the end of the blue tinsel scarf the peacock was wearing and let it drop '…commercialism.'

He glanced over at Ruby again, who was subtly watching them as she continued to decorate her tree. It occurred to him that the old Jacob might have flirted with Lucy to make Ruby jealous but he didn't need to do that with Ruby. He had no intention of doing anything to hurt her and he wasn't going to play games with her like that.

'Still, it's only temporary,' Lucy was saying. 'She'll be gone soon.'

Time to nip this in the bud.

'Lucy, Ruby and I are very good friends so this line of conversation really isn't sitting well with me. The people in this village have been very welcoming to me and to you, and I would really hope that *everyone* in the village would give the same courtesy to Ruby too.'

Lucy stared at him, her cheeks flushing bright red. Then

she laughed nervously. 'Oh Jacob, I'm only joking, you don't need to take me so seriously. I love Christmas as much as the next person. In fact, I came in here intending to buy some more decorations for my tree.'

'Well her shop isn't quite open yet, but I'm sure she'll be very appreciative of that tomorrow.'

'I'll pop by tomorrow then.' Lucy forced a smile onto her face. 'I do love all these Christmas additions to your shop. Do you have anything planned for the big day?'

'My sister Lottie and her daughter Poppy will be coming round. Andrew and Willow will be having dinner here too. It'll be a nice family thing.'

The thought occurred to him that Ruby would probably be on her own. He would have to make a point of inviting her along for dinner.

'And you?' Jacob asked. He could play nice if Lucy was.

'I'll probably go to my mum's. Are you looking forward to the ball on Christmas Eve?' She twisted a strand of hair round her finger.

'I am. It should be fun.'

'Do you have a date?' Lucy asked.

Oh god, what could he say? Julia had warned him Lucy was going to ask him but he hadn't prepared an excuse.

His phone beeped in his pocket and he seized on the distraction.

'Sorry Lucy, I just need to get this, I've been waiting for an email to come in from a client.'

He grabbed his phone and although he knew the beep was just a notification of someone else sponsoring him to do the Polar Bear Plunge, he scrolled through his phone while he played for time.

He had no interest at all in going to the ball with Lucy. He glanced at her. Why was that? It wasn't that he didn't find

Lucy attractive, she was very pretty in that classic kind of way, the kind you might see on a catwalk – tall, thin, long caramel-blonde hair that was so silky straight she must spend the whole morning straightening it before she stepped out of the house. She was always very well dressed too – tailored trousers, fitted tops or jackets, high heels with every outfit, the perfect accessories. She was flawless in every single way.

She was very different from Ruby, who was dancing around her shop next door in red sequinned Converse, leggings with Rudolph on and an oversized jumper that had a large Christmas pudding on the front with googly eyes. Her scarlet hair was wavy and curly and he got the sense that other than giving her hair a quick brush in the mornings she probably did very little to style it. He couldn't help smiling as he watched her dance, very badly, around the tree she was decorating.

He turned his attention back to Lucy. She was exactly the sort of person he would have gone for six months before, someone attractive he could have casual sex with. But he found himself not wanting that life anymore. He had slept with two people since Ruby, which for him was a record low, but casual sex just didn't seem to tick that box for him like it used to. There had been nothing wrong with the two women he'd been with – they'd been attractive, good in bed – but he hadn't felt that connection he'd shared with Ruby and he missed that. He wanted something more than meaningless sex, he wanted someone he could really talk with, someone he could have a laugh with just like he had with Ruby. He wanted sex with someone special. That realisation was like a slap around the face. He looked back at Ruby. She had ruined him for other women.

He realised Lucy was still waiting and put his phone back

in his pocket. 'Sorry about that, Lucy. You were asking if I have a date for the ball?'

She licked her lips. 'Yes, do you?'

He should just say no, go to the ball with Lucy and get over these silly thoughts of wanting a proper relationship once and for all. But he couldn't do it.

He cleared his throat. 'I'm afraid I've already asked Ruby.'

Lucy didn't need to know that Ruby still hadn't given him an answer yet.

'Oh.' Her face fell and then she let out a nervous laugh. 'I wasn't asking you out. I was just... making polite conversation. I have a date, of course I do. His name is Zayn. Lives in the next town. Anyway, I must dash, things to do.'

She edged to the door.

'Didn't you want to meet Ruby?'

'Oh, I don't want to disturb her if she's getting everything ready to open tomorrow. And as I said, I'll pop in at some point to get some more decorations.'

She gave him a little wave and left the shop.

Jacob didn't think Lucy would ever show her face next door.

Ruby leaned against the archway connecting the two shops. 'Friend of yours?'

He shook his head. 'Lucy, she lives in the village.'

'I think she likes you.'

'You might be right. I think she came here to ask me to the ball.'

'Oh... well you should go with her,' Ruby said, her voice suddenly unnaturally high. Was she jealous? Surely not.

'I'm not interested,' Jacob said.

'Why not? She's pretty.'

He stopped himself from saying, 'She's not you.' Frustratingly that was the truth.

'I don't think she likes Christmas,' he said instead.

Ruby gasped theatrically. 'What kind of weirdo doesn't like Christmas?'

'Exactly.'

'Well, I think you made the right decision there.'

She turned and disappeared back into her shop and he watched her go. He had turned down a date with an attractive woman which probably would have ended in casual sex because he wanted something real with a woman who had no interest in him at all. It certainly didn't feel like the right decision.

~

Jacob was just putting the finishing touches to the star that would go on top of his Christmas tree when Ruby came into his shop carrying Jesus, who was now dressed as a reindeer in a cute Rudolph onesie, complete with antlers.

He laughed. 'Where did you get that?'

'I actually bought these baby Christmas costumes a few months ago, thought I might sell them in my shop. I bought some outfits for dogs too. Anyway, I dug this out and I thought it would be perfect for us to dress up Jesus.'

'Isn't that a bit of anachronism?'

'Probably and maybe even sacrilege and blasphemous too. Anyway, shall we take Jesus for a walk around the village?'

'OK, but do you have a bag to hide him in? We're going to have to be really discreet about this. If anyone sees us, we'll be in big trouble,' Jacob said, knowing full well that wasn't going to stop them.

'Ah, the risks are always outweighed by the fun,' Ruby said, slipping Jesus into her rucksack and pulling on her coat.

Jacob grabbed his coat as well and they stepped outside. It

was still snowing heavily outside and settling nicely on the roads and roofs. The sun was just starting to set, lending a pinky glow to the twinkling carpet. There were a few people on the street but most of the villagers were tucked up in their homes or the pub.

As the last few stragglers disappeared out of view, Ruby propped Jesus up against the frozen fountain. She positioned the doll standing up with one leg sticking out behind him as if he was skating. Jacob laughed as she quickly took a picture.

'Where should we take him next?' Ruby asked and Jacob loved the spark of mischief and amusement in her eyes.

'Should we dare to take a photo of him outside the post office?' he suggested. 'Julia will have a fit if she knows Jesus was that close to her and she had no idea.'

'That's brilliant,' Ruby said.

They walked up the high street and stopped outside the post office, peering through the window at the Christmas display of cookies, sweets and chocolates while they waited patiently for the street to clear. Ruby giggled next to him and he loved the sound of it.

Jacob looked around and saw that for a brief moment they were completely alone. 'Quick, now.'

Ruby grabbed Jesus from her rucksack and positioned him outside the door in the snow, while Jacob kept a look-out. When she was happy, she stepped back and Jacob took a picture on his phone.

A movement inside the shop caught Jacob's eye and he looked inside. 'Quick, Julia is coming.'

Ruby grabbed Jesus and just about managed to stuff him in her rucksack before Julia opened the door.

'What are you two lovebirds doing out here?' Julia asked, her eyes wide with excitement at seeing them both together.

'Nothing,' Ruby giggled, zipping up her rucksack.

'Just looking at all your chocolates,' Jacob said.

Julia clearly wasn't buying any of this as she looked between them suspiciously. She stepped outside and closed the shop door behind her. She looked around and then spoke in a whisper. 'Are you here to buy more condoms? You don't need to be embarrassed if you are. I've seen it all, believe me.'

Ruby laughed. 'No, it's OK, we don't need condoms.'

'Some of that sexy underwear I was telling you about?' Julia asked. 'Whips, blindfolds. I have a whole catalogue of stuff like that if that's what you're looking for.'

Well this had suddenly taken a rather kinky turn.

'We don't need any of that,' Jacob said, with a wink. 'I have everything covered in that department.'

Julia swatted his arm playfully. 'Oh, I bet you do. Well if you're not here for that, what are you lurking outside here for?'

'We weren't lurking. Jacob was just showing me which chocolates he wanted for Christmas,' Ruby said.

'Yes, the white chocolate snowman,' Jacob said, pointing.

Julia's face fell. 'Well, that's a bit boring. Come on then, let's go get your snowman.'

Ruby tried to stop her with protests that she would come back later but Julia wasn't haven't any of it. A few minutes later, Jacob was walking up the street eating a chocolate snowman that Ruby had been forced to buy for him, chuckling to himself at how that had turned out.

'I don't know what was funnier, Julia trying to sell us the contents of her Ann Summers catalogue or the fact that I ended up with a free snowman.'

'Oh, you can laugh, you weren't the one that was forced to fork out for a snowman I'd had no intention of buying. You owe me a snowman, Mr Harrington.'

'Noted, but I think we got away without her seeing Jesus which is the main thing,' Jacob said.

'Yeah, let's get back and upload it onto the forum. I need to finish the shop ready for the grand opening tomorrow anyway.'

They walked back into the shop and Jacob watched as Ruby logged in to the Jesus profile on the forum. He smiled when he saw what she'd written.

Taking a break from the nativity scene for a while to explore the delights of Happiness village. Went ice skating and stopped at the post office to try Julia's lovely fudge. Had to go in disguise of course, I don't want to be recognised. But don't worry, I'll be back on Christmas Eve.

Jesus x

Ruby stood up and grinned at him.

'I love your sense of humour,' Jacob said. There was actually quite a lot of things he liked about Ruby Marlowe.

'Well, you bring out the best in me.'

He liked that.

'Or the worst,' Ruby said. 'Depending on which way you look at it. An upstanding decent member of the community would tell me to take Jesus back, not join in with the antics.'

'But where's the fun in that?'

She smiled. 'I like you, Jacob Harrington.'

Ruby walked back into her shop and he watched her go. He liked her as well, too damned much.

CHAPTER TEN

Ruby gave one last look around the shop. Everything was ready for the big opening tomorrow. And now the snow had settled and was continuing to fall outside, she couldn't have asked for a more festive start to her big open day. She switched off the lights and moved to the archway.

Jacob was busy sorting out cutlery into different piles, no doubt for his next project.

'I'm off now, I'll see you tomorrow.'

He looked up and smiled. 'Before you go, I have a present for you.'

She frowned. 'A present?'

He shrugged. 'Let's call it an opening day present.'

He stood up and grabbed a neatly wrapped shoe box from the side and brought it over to her.

'Should I open it tomorrow?'

'No, I think you should open it now. You might want to do something with it tonight.'

She smiled and eagerly lifted the lid. She stared at the contents for a second. A red scarf, some coal and a carrot.

Her heart leapt and she looked up at Jacob as he presented her with a grand-looking top hat.

'It's a snowman-making kit,' he explained.

'Oh my god, I love it.' Ruby threw her arms around him to say thank you and he wrapped his arms around her. She quickly pulled back before she could get too carried away. 'Thank you, this is amazing.'

'Well, you said I owed you a snowman and I thought you might want to make one tonight, outside your shop ready for the opening tomorrow.'

'That's a wonderful idea. Will you help me?'

'I'd love to. Let me just get my coat.'

He raced off upstairs and, as she heard him moving around, it occurred to her that making a snowman together was definitely a very coupley thing to do. But right now, there was no one in the world that she wanted to make a snowman with more.

He came back downstairs and into the shop all bundled up against the cold as Ruby pulled her own coat and hat on.

She grabbed the box and followed Jacob outside. It was still snowing but not quite as heavily as before. The whole street was covered in a thick blanket of white glitter, making it look magical. There was not a soul in sight and it was completely and utterly silent. It felt like they were the only two people in the world.

'It's so beautiful,' Ruby said softly.

'It is. Some might say it was romantic.'

She looked up at him and smiled. 'I think I'll have to give you that.'

He grinned, then looked around. 'OK, you're in charge, what shall we do first?'

'Right, we need a big bottom,' Ruby said, gathering snow together to make a ball and then beginning to roll it across the ground so it gathered more snow. Jacob started helping her, as it was getting heavier as it got fatter. 'God, I haven't made a snowman in so long.'

'Is it like riding a bike?' Jacob asked.

'Yeah, you never forget.'

They finished the bottom and packed snow around the ground to make it more solid and then smoothed off the sides.

'Now I don't know about you but I'm definitely a three-ball snowman kind of person.'

Jacob smiled at her, the snow catching on his beautiful long eyelashes. 'I have no preference either way when it comes to how many balls a snowman should have. Generally two balls are enough in most cases, but I'm happy to go with three on this occasion.'

'Are you being rude, Jacob Harrington?' Ruby laughed.

'No, I wouldn't dream of it.'

'OK, well you can make the middle ball and I'll make the top.'

She watched him for a moment, carefully rolling his ball. He was taking this very seriously.

Soon the three balls were finished and stacked neatly on top of each other, the edges were smoothed down and snow was packed between the layers.

She picked up the box and took out the red scarf, wrapping it around the neck of the snowman and tying it in a knot. Jacob placed the hat on its head and she set about adding the coal for the eyes and buttons. He passed her the carrot so she could add the final finishing touch. She carefully wedged it into the face until it was firmly in place and then stood back to admire their handiwork.

'He does look really rather splendid, doesn't he?' Ruby said, leaning her head against Jacob's shoulder.

He wrapped an arm around her. 'He really does.'

They stood there in silence for a while, admiring their snowman as the snow continued to fall around them in the inky darkness.

'Honestly, this is the nicest thing that anyone has ever done for me.'

'Ah Ruby Marlowe. You set the bar very low, if a carrot and a few lumps of coal can make you this happy.'

She laughed. 'I can't help it, anything Christmas-related and I'm sold. Thank you for doing this.'

'It was my pleasure.'

She looked up at the sign above Jacob's half of the shop. Phoenix Blade. The sign above her shop was currently blank, which looked a bit odd. It was almost as if he was waiting for his other half to be complete. Could she fill that gap? Professionally of course. Or maybe… something more?

She glanced up at him and he stared down at her. Their lips were now only inches apart and she could feel his breath on her cheeks. Her heart started racing, his eyes darkened. God, he was going to kiss her and she wanted that more than anything.

She straightened and stepped away. 'Well I better go; I need to make some gingerbread men for tomorrow and Willow is coming round to help me.'

He shoved his hands in his pockets and kicked the snow with his foot. He nodded and smiled sadly. 'I'll see you tomorrow.'

She gave him a little wave and hurried off into the darkness, not daring to turn around.

What was she doing?

~

Ruby carefully piped icing onto the gingerbread men she had made ready for the grand opening the next day, focussing all her attention on that and not what had nearly happened between her and Jacob.

'I saw your post on the forum from Jesus,' Willow said, with a grin. 'I think if you didn't want to make it into a big thing, you failed spectacularly. No one really cared before apart from Julia, now the whole village has got involved.'

Ruby laughed. The reaction and comments from the villagers about Jesus's holiday had been far better than she ever could have dreamed of. Every single comment had been about how hilarious it was and asking where Jesus was going to show up next. She barely needed any encouragement but she knew she'd have to up her game for the next post.

Ruby looked at all the gingerbread men. Some of them were wrapped, some were drying, others that were waiting to be decorated.

'Do you think I made too much?'

'No, I think they'll be very popular and you can always sell the ones that don't get taken in your shop or at the Cookie Competition the next day.'

'I hope people come tomorrow,' Ruby said as she passed the biscuit to Willow so she could add on the Smarties for the eyes and the buttons.

'They will, of course they will. It's a new shop so people will be curious to see what you're selling. And we are only just under a week away until the big day so everyone is feeling in the festive mood,' Willow said. 'Plus you have Jacob next door and he's very popular with all the ladies.'

And there he was. He was impossible to get away from, even when he wasn't physically in the room. Ruby tried to ignore the pang of jealousy that cut through her at those words.

'I bet he has loads of girlfriends,' Ruby said, trying to carry off an air of nonchalance. She focussed her attention on the gingerbread men so Willow couldn't see how much she was interested in her answer.

'If he has, I've certainly never seen him with one since he moved here. He might be with women outside of Happiness but he definitely hasn't played hide the sausage with anyone here.'

Ruby laughed loudly at that lovely image.

She carried on icing the gingerbread man. 'What about Lucy?'

'Oh, I don't think you have anything to worry about there,' Willow said, placing her finished man on the baking tray to set.

'She likes him.'

'I think they have history,' Willow said.

Ruby found her head snapping up to look at her. Megan had said the same thing.

'Oh, not like that,' Willow said. 'At least I don't think so. I think he just knew her before he came here.'

'*Knew her*?' She gave a hefty squeeze on the icing bag. As Jacob himself had said he didn't have any female friends, it was unlikely they'd had that kind of relationship. Willow was watching her reaction with interest. Ruby shrugged. 'Oh, I'm not bothered. He can do what he wants, see who he wants, I don't care.'

Willow took the gingerbread man Ruby was icing off her. He had been doused rather heavily with icing as she had been talking. 'It's OK to care.'

Ruby sat down on one of the bar stools in the kitchen and sighed because she did care and she didn't have any right to.

'So it's all going well with Jacob?' Willow asked.

'It's going very well, better than I could have hoped for actually,' Ruby said. 'I didn't think we could really be friends after what happened in the summer. I thought we might be polite to each other but it's been really lovely. I have loved working alongside him over the last few days. He makes me laugh, he is easy to talk to and he's just a wonderful man.' She cringed a little about gushing so much over him. But she could at least be honest with her best friend. 'We nearly kissed tonight.'

'What?' Willow stared at her; the gingerbread man forgotten.

'I told him yesterday that making a snowman would feature very high on my list of a perfect Christmas and that he had to have a red scarf, coal for eyes and a carrot nose. And tonight, as I was getting ready to leave, he gave me a snowman-making kit with those things in,' Ruby swallowed down the lump in her throat because it was ridiculous to get emotional about a few lumps of coal. 'And we made a snowman together and then… well there was snow and just the two of us and…' she cleared her throat, 'and then I ran away.'

'Oh Ruby.'

'He makes me feel things I don't want to feel.'

'But you can't just run away from that.'

'It worked pretty well tonight.'

'Come on, what are you going to do?'

Ruby grabbed another gingerbread man and iced a sad face onto its head.

'It's not as if sleeping with him would help to get him out of my system. I already know what that's like and it's bloody spectacular.'

'Well that sounds like something you should definitely pursue,' Willow teased.

If only it was that simple.

Willow frowned. 'You're not thinking of leaving, are you?'

'Why would I leave?'

'So you don't have to be around him.'

'But that didn't work, did it? After I saw him in the summer I didn't see him for four or five months and I come back and those feelings are still as strong as they were then.'

Willow's concern clearly didn't lessen any.

'I'm not leaving, this is my home. This thing between me and him is not serious,' Ruby said with more conviction than she felt. 'I might have feelings for him but I don't love him. And like eating chocolate every day, you can have too much of a good thing. I'm sure I'll soon get bored of him.'

'I don't think I could ever get bored of chocolate,' Willow said. 'Even if I did eat it every day.'

Ruby sighed because Willow was right. She didn't think she would ever have her fill of Jacob Harrington.

~

Jacob was watching TV when he heard someone letting themselves into the shop and then start walking up the stairs to his flat.

He wondered if it was Ruby and he quickly shot up and started tidying up, taking his dirty cups to the kitchen. Then he realised the footsteps on the stairs were a lot heavier than someone Ruby's size would produce.

Andrew appeared in the doorway and grinned at Jacob obviously mid-tidy.

'It's OK, I'm not Ruby,' Andrew teased.

'I could tell the difference with you galumphing up the stairs.'

Jacob flopped back down on the sofa and immediately grabbed the TV remote and switched on the subtitles. It was an automatic thing. Although Andrew could hear pretty well with his hearing aids in, it was still easier for him to follow what was happening on TV with subtitles on, even if he had no interest in the programme about the Ancient Greeks Jacob had been vaguely watching.

'So are you really going through with this Polar Bear Plunge?' Andrew said, as he helped himself to a beer from the fridge.

The mention of it gave Jacob a sick feeling in his stomach.

'I think I have to. I've been telling Ruby she has to face her fears. It'd be a bit hypocritical if I couldn't face mine,' Jacob said.

'It's a bit different, you nearly died.'

'I don't know if it's that different. She lost her husband; I cannot even begin to imagine the pain she suffered from that. The courage to face that fear feels... insurmountable in comparison to a twenty-second swim in the sea.' He took a swig of his beer, trying to get rid of the bitter taste in his mouth. 'Although it doesn't mean I'm happy about doing it.'

His brother clearly had more to say on the subject but Jacob cut him off before he could dwell on it any longer. He really didn't want to talk about it anymore.

'What do I owe the *pleasure* of your company tonight anyway?' Jacob said.

'Well, I thought, as the girls are probably occupying themselves with talk about us, we could hang out and talk about them.'

'I'm sure Ruby has better things to talk about than me,' Jacob said.

'Well, she came to her shop today while I was fixing it. You definitely came up in conversation.'

He wasn't going to rise to the bait. He grabbed the remote again and flicked through the channels.

Andrew took a long deliberate swig of beer.

'Do you mean, *you* brought me up in conversation?' Jacob said.

'I can't remember how you came up,' Andrew said vaguely.

Jacob sighed. 'Go on then, I'll bite. What did she say?'

'Well, she's a bit concerned by your plans to get married and settle down.'

'She's concerned because she thinks those plans involve her.'

Andrew stole one of the crisps that were in a bowl on the table. 'And do they?'

'Do I want to marry someone who is terrified of marriage? I don't think so,' Jacob said, knowing he wasn't being entirely truthful with his brother. There was something about Ruby that made him think about forever.

'It's not as simple as that though, is it?' Andrew said. 'She's not terrified of marriage because she has weird commitment issues. She's scared of falling in love again and having that person cruelly taken from her.'

'I know,' Jacob said, softly. It was a lot more complicated than any relationship he'd ever had before, if the casual flings could be called that. He had avoided any baggage or emotional drama quite successfully with the women he'd been with in the past. But, strangely, Ruby's issues hadn't put him off.

Andrew sat down; all humour gone from his face. 'You like her?'

Jacob continued flicking through the channels before he sighed and turned to face his brother. 'I do and for many reasons that don't just involve great sex. She makes me laugh and I can really talk to her. Did you know she's started learning sign language so she can communicate with you and Poppy?'

'Well, that's really nice. A lot of people wouldn't bother to do that.'

Jacob nodded. 'I think I fell a little bit in love with her because of that.'

Andrew let out a heavy breath. 'I didn't realise... I just thought you two would pick up the casual arrangement you had in the summer; sex, no commitments, no attachments.'

'You know, I realised something today. I don't want that life anymore. I look at what you have with Willow and I want that. I think I've reached a point in my life where I don't want lots of meaningless women to keep me company, I want someone special to spend the rest of my life with.'

He waited for Andrew to take the piss but for once his brother was showing no sign of his usual sarcasm.

'So this is something serious for you?'

'It's not,' Jacob said and then sighed. He took a swig from his bottle of beer. 'It's not because she doesn't want it to be.'

'But you'd like it to be.'

Jacob didn't speak for the longest time. 'I really like her. But she's locked that part of her heart away and I don't think she's ready to open herself up to that again. Part of me wants to help her deal with that grief properly. She never talked about it when her husband died, kept it all bottled up and then tried to forget all about it. I want to help her move on and find happiness again, even if that happiness isn't with me.'

Andrew sighed. 'You've been down this road before with Ella and it didn't end well for you.'

Jacob flicked the bottle top he was holding into an empty bowl. It bounced off the side and landed on the floor.

Ella Bradley. Christ, it had been a long time since he had thought of her. They had been best friends in their early twenties and she would come to him with all of her problems. He had been there for her through everything, including numerous failed relationships with boyfriends. He would hold her when she cried, patch her back up and give her some advice on how she could win her man back. He had been in love with her, but she had never looked at him in that way. Jacob would often tell himself, it didn't matter, he just wanted his friend to be happy. But really it did matter. When she'd got married, it had broken his heart. And if he was honest with himself that was a big reason he'd avoided all emotional connections with women ever since.

'This is different,' Jacob said.

'I'm not sure how, but OK.'

Jacob wasn't sure either. He was not going to get what he wanted out of this. The more time he spent with Ruby, the more he knew he was falling for her. But the closer they got, the more she looked like a deer in the headlights of a car. His feelings for her, and her feelings for him, were scaring her away.

Andrew took a swig of beer, contemplating this issue. 'When Willow first moved to Happiness, she didn't want a relationship either after just coming out of a crap one. But our connection was just too strong to ignore. If you two are meant to be together, it will happen.'

'Thanks for that oh so wise cliché,' Jacob said.

Andrew laughed and raised his beer. 'I can get it printed on a t-shirt if you like.'

Jacob sighed. 'I think the big difference between Willow and Ruby is that Willow pretty much fell in love with you from the first time she met you, no matter that she tried to deny it. Ruby, as far as I can tell, is still hung up on her husband. If she loved me, or had any feelings for me, surely it would be worth the risk.'

Andrew shrugged. 'Maybe you just need to give her some time to realise that.'

Jacob nodded. If time was all she needed, he would give her as much of that as she wanted. He just had to hope that was enough.

CHAPTER ELEVEN

Ruby looked round the shop to check for the twentieth time that everything was in its place. Every surface gleamed and sparkled, the fairy lights twinkled, the baubles and decorations shone. Willow had even given her some Christmas-scented candles to light in her shop. Currently she had a Christmas-cookie-scented candle burning happily in the doorway and a toffee-apple-scented candle burning near the back of the shop. She had homemade mince pies, gingerbread men, mulled wine and hot chocolate to give out to any customers who might come through the door. She even had chocolate gold coins for any children, although they probably wouldn't come until after school.

Everything was ready.

She looked up and saw Jacob watching her, leaning against the archway between the two shops.

'Does it look OK?' Ruby asked.

'It looks great.'

She looked around again. 'I was so excited about having

my own shop but now I'm just terrified. What if no one comes? What if I don't sell anything?'

'Firstly, everyone will come. I had the villagers coming in droves into my shop when I first opened.'

Ruby wondered if that had anything to do with Jacob being ridiculously good-looking and most of the women fancying him.

'Secondly, before the merry throngs come crashing through the door, I will be your first customer.'

Jacob pulled out his wallet from his back pocket and looked around.

'Stop it,' Ruby laughed. 'As if I'm going to let you buy anything. I'll give you whatever you want.'

'No, I want this to go through the till,' Jacob insisted. He moved around the shop and picked up a small giraffe with a Santa hat on. It was quirky and actually one of her favourite pieces. 'This little chap would be perfect in my shop.'

'Jacob, you don't need to buy it. You can have him.'

'No, how much is he?'

Ruby smiled at his insistence and walked over to the till. 'Two pounds fifty please.'

He handed her a fiver and she gave him the change then placed the giraffe in a little paper gift bag and passed it back to Jacob. She looked at this wonderful man and reached up and kissed him on the cheek. 'Thank you.'

He grinned. 'It was my pleasure. Now, what time is everyone coming?'

Her heart dropped into her stomach. Should she have arranged an official grand opening? 'Well… I… just thought that I would open and people would come in throughout the day.'

He rolled his eyes. 'You need to tell people, make it all official. I'll put something out on the forum. Go and open the door, I'm sure we'll have people coming shortly.'

She moved over to the door as he grabbed his phone from his pocket and started tapping away at it. She unlocked the door and peered outside into the cold, blustery street. It had been cold when she had walked to work earlier that morning but in the last few hours the wind had really got up. Although not as heavy as the day before, the snow was still falling and the wind was blowing the flakes in gusts across the street. An icy blast ripped through the houses and shops, rattling the shutters and bending the plants and bushes at odd angles. There was not a single soul in sight, everyone was probably tucked up in their homes and shops. No one was going to come all the way down here today.

She closed the door and sighed. So much for the grand opening.

She grabbed a gingerbread man and bit off one of his legs just as Jacob came back into her shop.

'Hey, don't eat all of them, the villagers are on their way.'

Ruby took another bite. She might get one or two customers later on if the wind dropped but she certainly wasn't going to get a big influx.

'It's OK,' she shrugged. 'At least I had one sale.'

She moved over to her desk and started getting out a few paints to decorate some of the glass baubles.

She was halfway through painting a holly leaf when she heard the shop door open and she smiled when she saw Julia wrapped up against the cold. She'd brought Dorothy and Liz with her, Roger was close behind and, as the door closed behind him, Tabitha and Connor from the pub pushed it back open again.

Ruby stood up and looked over at Jacob, who was grinning at her.

'What on earth did you write on that forum?'

'Only that it was your big opening and that everyone should come along.'

She watched as Mary and Ginny arrived in the shop, followed by a few others.

She looked back at Jacob, her heart filling up a little bit more for him. Whatever he'd written, it had worked.

She focussed her attention on her customers, offering them drinks and mince pies – anything to avoid the overwhelming feeling in her heart.

Ruby couldn't stop smiling. The place was heaving, it seemed like everyone in the village had turned up at some point that morning. The villagers had stayed, drank the wine and hot chocolate, ate the snacks and chatted like it was a party, with so many turning up at the start of the day that some of them had to stand in Jacob's shop. But amongst the party atmosphere, everyone had been genuinely interested in her baubles and decorations. Well, everyone except Lucy, who had walked in with a face like she'd sucked a lemon as she moved around Ruby's shop and looked at the different decorations.

Ruby still couldn't help wondering if something had happened between Lucy and Jacob, as Megan had said. She knew she had no right to care or be jealous but she did wonder why Jacob would go with someone like that. He was fun and kind and Lucy didn't look like that sort of person at all. Surely he wouldn't go to bed with Lucy just because she was attractive. Ruby shook her head. What did it matter who he slept with and why? They were friends, she had no claim to him beyond that. But … as his friend she wanted the best for him, someone nice who would appreciate how amazing he was and see him as more than just another notch on the bedpost. Someone like Megan perhaps. She ignored the punch of sadness she felt at the thought of him with *anyone* else.

She decided to bite the bullet and go and talk to Lucy. She'd been kind enough to come to her opening, after all.

Ruby walked over. 'Hi Lucy, thanks for coming. Has anything caught your eye?'

Lucy laughed and not kindly. 'I think the same thing that has caught the eye of most of the women in here.'

She gestured to where Jacob was holding court in the middle of a gaggle of women of all ages. There was even a little girl of around six years old staring at Jacob like he was a god.

Was that really the reason why most of the women had come that day, so they could fawn over Jacob? Ruby had kind of hoped that the excitement of a new shop and interest in her unique, handmade decorations would be enough of a lure. She felt her bubble of happiness at the success of the day slowly deflate like a balloon.

But she decided to play along in the interest of getting some information from Lucy.

'He's easy on the eye, isn't he?' Ruby said.

'He is that. And amazing in bed.'

Oh well, if Lucy was going to get straight to the point then so could she.

'So you knew Jacob before you moved here. Were you and he a thing?'

'Oh, I know Jacob very well,' Lucy said, with a smug smile, which wasn't exactly answering the question. 'I bet you think all your Christmases have come at once being put next door to him.'

There was something very blunt about that question.

'Jacob's lovely,' Ruby said.

'I wouldn't get your hopes up. I think a man like Jacob has very particular tastes, the sort that will drink the finest wines. He could have any woman he wanted, so he's only going to pick the crème de la crème.'

Ruby was astonished that someone could be so blatantly rude.

'Well, that's very flattering, isn't it Ruby,' Julia said as she squeezed past them to get to some gold baubles painted with glittery red poinsettias. 'He slept with Ruby several times in the summer, so if Jacob only indulges in the finest wines, that must make Ruby Champagne.'

Ruby smiled and she had to bite her lip to keep from laughing out loud. Lucy was obviously less than impressed.

'You and Jacob slept together?' Lucy said, aghast, just as Jacob walked past.

'Yes, and let me tell you, she was the best sex I've ever had,' Jacob said as he helped himself to another cup of hot chocolate.

Ruby smirked. God she really bloody liked this man.

'Did you want a hot chocolate, Lucy?' Jacob asked.

'I'm fine thanks.'

'Pity,' Jacob said. 'You look like you could use something sweet.'

Oh wow, he'd totally just called her out on her bitchiness.

He turned his attention to his hot chocolate for a moment, spraying squirty cream on the top before taking a long sip. He moved back towards his shop but he had cream on the top of his lip.

Ruby stopped him and without thinking leaned up and wiped the cream away with her thumb. His eyes darkened at her touch as he looked down at her.

'You had cream on your lip,' Ruby said.

He slipped his tongue out and licked round his lips.

Oh god.

'All gone?'

She nodded, because right then there were no words in her head at all.

'Come up to my flat tonight, once you close. I think we should celebrate your first day,' Jacob said and Ruby was aware of Lucy and Julia standing nearby watching and listening to their every word. Jacob must have been aware of it too.

She smiled. 'Just the two of us?'

'All the best celebrations are with two people; you don't need more than that.' He surreptitiously winked so that Lucy wouldn't see him and Ruby smirked.

'Sounds good.'

He gave her shoulder a squeeze and moved off through the crowds of people.

Ruby cleared her throat and looked at her small audience. Julia was standing there obviously absolutely delighted with this new turn of events. Lucy had a face like thunder.

She didn't want to break it to either of them that she would probably go up to Jacob's flat for a glass of wine and would more than likely be tucked up under a blanket on her own sofa, wearing her snowman pyjamas by six o'clock, probably reading her new book. Alone.

'Ladies, is there anything else I can help you with?' Ruby smiled brightly.

They both shook their head and Ruby turned and left them to it.

Ruby looked up from rearranging some of her displays. It was getting a bit quieter now, although there was still a good number of customers browsing her stock. She glanced over at Megan who had been hovering in her shop and Jacob's for the last few hours. It was lovely that Megan wanted to be so supportive, but the length of time she'd been here led Ruby to think she might have an ulterior motive. Ruby watched her as she glanced over in Jacob's direction as he chatted to some of the villagers. Her heart sank. After Ruby's meddling the day before, Megan was clearly here waiting for Jacob to ask her out and that wasn't going to happen.

Ruby took a deep breath and walked over to her. 'Hey Megan, how you doing?'

'Good. Good, thanks,' Megan said, eyeing Jacob again.

He wasn't looking at Megan at all and Ruby felt awful. She suddenly wanted Jacob to ask Megan out, even if that would make her green with jealousy. Jacob looked over and flashed Ruby a big smile.

Megan looked between the two of them and her shoulders slumped, her cheeks flushing bright red.

'He's not going to ask me to the Christmas Eve ball, is he?' Megan asked quietly, staring at her feet.

Ruby snagged her arm and pulled her to the back of her shop out of earshot of the other customers. 'I'm so sorry, Megan. This is all my fault. *I* told Lucas that Jacob was going to ask you to the ball.'

Megan stared at her. 'Why would you do that if it's not true?'

'Because I was hoping it might encourage Lucas to ask you instead.'

Her shoulders slumped even more. 'Lucas doesn't like me that way.'

'He does, anyone can see that. Why do you think he was so upset about Jacob asking you to the ball?'

Megan shrugged. 'Pete sees me as a little sister. Lucas probably feels the same. He was just being protective.'

'There was a lot more to it than that.'

'I thought if Jacob asked me to the ball Lucas would finally see me as someone who is desirable. I have this gorgeous dress and I thought if Lucas saw me in it, he'd finally see me as something more than just Pete's little sister-in-law.'

'The way he looks at you, I promise you there is nothing sisterly about that,' Ruby said. 'Look, if you like Lucas, why don't you ask him to the ball?'

'I couldn't do that. I have to see him at all the family events and get-togethers. If he says no, it would be so awkward.'

'But what if he says yes?' Ruby said.

Megan shook her head. 'If he liked me, he'd ask me out.'

'He probably thinks it would be awkward too, for the reasons you mentioned,' Ruby said.

Megan sighed. 'Why is it so complicated?'

Just as Ruby was trying to think of some way out of this. Jacob walked past. He saw them huddled into the corner and came over. 'Is everything OK?'

'We're just complaining about men and why they're so bloody hard to read,' Megan said.

'Ah, I see, I apologise for my gender,' Jacob said.

'I don't think you have anything to apologise for, you're pretty much an open book,' Megan said, with exasperation. 'You see something you want and you go after it.'

Ruby smirked. That was true. Jacob had made no secret of his feelings for her since she'd come back.

'Is this about Lucas?' Jacob asked.

'Oh my god, am I that obvious?' Megan said, her cheeks flushing bright red again.

'No, but he is. He came in here earlier and told me in no

uncertain terms that I was to keep my hands off you and if I was lucky enough to go to the ball with you then I was to treat you like a queen. He told me if I broke your heart, there'd be hell to pay.'

Megan stared at him. 'Are you serious?'

Jacob nodded.

Megan clearly thought about this for a moment. 'Well, that's pretty significant.'

Both Ruby and Jacob nodded encouragingly but then Megan sighed. 'We're not even speaking right now. How can I tell him that it's him I want to go to the ball with when he won't even talk to me?'

'Well, the cookie-decorating competition is tomorrow,' Ruby said. 'Maybe I should pull a few strings and make sure you're both on the same table. You'll have to talk to each other then. Even if you don't declare your feelings for him or ask him to the ball, at least you might spend enough time with each other to be friends again.'

Megan nodded. 'I'd like that. Look, I should go. I did actually come in here to buy something for my tree.' She moved forward into the shop and plucked a decoration off one of the shelves. She showed it to Ruby. It was of two snowmen hugging. 'I saw this but wasn't sure if it would be too optimistic.'

'Take it,' Ruby said. 'Give it to Lucas if you can't face telling him how you feel. He might actually get the hint.'

Megan smiled. 'Thank you. But let me pay.'

'No, I insist, after the damage I did interfering, it's the least I can do.'

'Thank you,' Megan said. Tucking the ornament carefully into her bag, she left the shop.

Ruby turned to Jacob. 'Did Lucas really say those things to you?'

'Yeah.'

'What did you say?'

'I told him, if he was so worried about me taking her to the ball, maybe he should ask her himself. He stormed off at that though, saying I didn't understand.'

Ruby frowned. 'I hope we haven't got this all completely wrong and sent Megan off to make a fool of herself.'

'He likes her. I can see it in his eyes,' Jacob said. 'Whatever reason he is holding himself back, it's not because he doesn't have feelings for her.'

Ruby sighed. She should never have interfered.

'And she was right about one thing,' Jacob went on. 'When I want something, I go after it.'

She smirked. 'Doesn't mean you'll get it though.'

He grinned. 'We'll see.'

~

Ruby turned the 'Open' shop sign to 'Closed' and locked the door. She'd had the most successful, profitable day ever with her till ringing almost non-stop. Her shop was looking more than a little depleted now and she would have to spend some time making and sourcing some more decorations, but she didn't care. Almost everyone in the village had turned up at some point in the day. Willow and Andrew had chosen all their tree decorations together, so they could decorate their first tree in their home. Even Kitty and Ken had turned up and bought decorations for all the tables for the Christmas Eve ball.

The day had been a huge success.

And now she was going to celebrate.

She jogged upstairs to Jacob's flat and found him pouring out two glasses of champagne. He looked up and watched her with a smile as she did a little excited jig on the spot, then she ran over and hugged him. He immediately wrapped his arms around her and hugged her back.

What had purely been a celebratory hug seemed to quickly escalate into something more. Even though neither of them had moved, there was this… spark between them. Truth be told, that spark had been there since she had arrived back in the village. She stood there listening to his heartbeat, relishing the warmth and comfort of his arms. She had firmly drawn a line under what happened between them in the summer, laid down the rules, but she had no desire to step away and neither, it seemed, did he.

After the longest time, she looked up at him and he was smiling at her.

God, she wanted to kiss him so much right then.

He brushed a hair from her face. 'I'm glad you've had a good day.'

'Thanks to you.'

'Not thanks to me at all. The villagers are all very welcoming and supportive, you'll learn that. All I put on the forum was that your shop was now officially open and it would be lovely to see everyone here.'

Ruby wasn't totally sure she believed him but, regardless of what he had said to get them there, and even if many of the women had come purely to see him, the villagers had bought the decorations of their own free will.

'Well, thank you,' Ruby said. He was still holding her and her arms were still wrapped around his back. 'For everything.'

'For what?'

'For being a great friend since I've been here. For listening to me, for helping me unpack, for making me dinner, for… just being there.'

'Always.'

'And thanks for the compliment too. Downstairs, with

Lucy,' Ruby explained when Jacob clearly didn't know what she meant.

'Oh, well it sounded like Lucy needed taking down a peg or two. Besides, I was only speaking the truth.'

Ruby gave a bark of a laugh. 'I'm the best sex you've ever had?'

'Yes.'

'How many women have you slept with?'

He pulled a face. 'A lot.'

'And I'm the best?' Ruby said, incredulously. 'I bet you say that to all the women.'

'Ruby, we had something special. I know you don't want to admit that but we did.'

Panic fluttered in her heart and she stepped away, shaking her head.

'And there it is,' Jacob said.

'There what is?'

'The look of fear you get every time you try to pretend you don't have feelings for me.'

'God, you're so arrogant, I don't have any feelings for you,' Ruby said, fear clawing at her throat. She couldn't face this. She moved away.

'I wish this was just my arrogance, because I could walk away from that very easily. But there's something between us and it's not just one-sided.'

She shook her head.

'I'm trying to help, I'm trying to fix this, but I feel every time we take a step closer, you take three steps away from me,' Jacob said.

'I don't need your help, I don't need to be fixed,' Ruby said, turning back round to face him.

'You think hiding away from any emotional connection for the last twelve years is perfectly normal. You think that being scared to fall in love again, pushing away the people you care about, is a healthy way to live?'

Ruby had no words to defend herself.

Jacob took a step closer. 'Last night, in the snow, we nearly kissed, but then you panicked and ran away.'

'I did not panic. I just didn't want to kiss you.'

'You're scared of letting me in, of getting close, you're scared to kiss me or sleep with me because you know that all those feelings you're keeping locked inside would come tumbling out.'

'That's rubbish. I could kiss you without feeling anything,' Ruby said, knowing the words were a complete lie.

'Really?' Jacob said.

'Yes, absolutely.'

Jacob bent his head and kissed her.

CHAPTER TWELVE

She hesitated for just a second before she was kissing him back. The kiss was angry at first but it quickly turned to something passionate and needful. She ran her hands down his shoulders, running them over the strong muscles in his back. His hands were at her waist where he suddenly hauled her closer.

God she wanted this man so much. She found her hands on the buttons of his shirt, desperately tugging them open as the kiss continued. He shuffled her back into his bedroom. Holy shit, they were really going to do this and there was not a single part of her that didn't want this. Greedy hands explored each other's bodies. He pinned her against the wall next to his bed, his shirt fell to the floor and still the kiss continued. She caressed his arms, his chest, his stomach. With one swift movement, he pulled her dress over her head and let that fall on the floor too. She reached for the belt on his jeans and fumbled to undo it. He kissed her again and she desperately pushed his jeans and his shorts down as he made quick work of the rest of her clothes so they were both naked.

'Condom,' she muttered against his lips.

'Not yet,' Jacob said.

She let out a groan of frustration but that groan quickly turned to one of pleasure as he placed kisses across her breast.

He slipped his hand between her legs, stroking and touching, that feeling was there but just out of reach.

'God, Jacob, please.'

But he was not to be deterred, he kept on stroking and slipped her nipple into his mouth. She cupped the back of his head, that feeling spreading inside of her so she felt like her whole body was on fire. She shouted out his name, trembling in his arms as he held her there against the wall.

She lifted his head and kissed him and she heard him fumble in his bedside drawers for a condom.

He pulled away from her for a few seconds while he slid it on and then he was kissing her again.

He lifted her and she wrapped her legs around him. He pulled back slightly to look at her.

'Are you sure you want this, Ruby?'

'It's not possible for me to want you more than I want you right now.'

'Is that a yes?' he teased.

'God, yes. Hit me with it.'

He laughed, loudly, and she could feel the vibrations of it through her body. 'I'm not going to hit you with it. I'm not sure what kind of sex you've been having, Ruby Marlowe, but that's not how this thing works.'

She giggled against his lips. 'Show me how it works.'

'My pleasure.'

He slid inside her in one exquisite move.

'God Jacob.'

He moved against her slowly, taking his time as he pinned her to the wall with his weight.

Nothing compared to this. Nothing ever would.

'I missed you so much,' she whispered.

'It's OK, I'm here now.'

She arched into him, pulling him tighter against her, and that glorious feeling started building in her again.

'I need this, I need you,' Ruby said, letting all her emotions tumble out.

'I'm here, always.'

She felt herself fall apart around him, as he moved against her harder and faster. She shouted out all manner of words and clung to him barely able to catch her breath as he carried her to the bed and collapsed down on top of her. He carried on moving against her, his eyes on her the whole time. She stroked down his back and he kissed her as he moaned against her lips.

He pulled back to look at her, his breath heavy, and as she stared into his beautiful blue eyes, she didn't think she had ever felt so complete in her entire life.

~

Jacob stroked his hand down Ruby's back. She was lying on his chest, presumably asleep or at least dozing.

He wasn't sure how he had ended up here, with this incredible woman in his arms. He had reconciled with himself that it was never going to happen again and yet here they were.

She stirred and looked up at him. They hadn't said a word since they'd had sex and he had no idea where he stood with her now or what would happen between them next. He didn't think he could handle just being friends again but he knew she would hardly be willing to jump straight into a proper relationship just because they'd had amazing sex.

'Hey beautiful,' he said, stroking her hair.

Something like fear flashed in her eyes and she scrambled out of bed.

'I should go. This was a mistake.'

He felt that like a punch to his gut. She thought sleeping with him had been a mistake when he had been so blissfully happy about it moments before.

She started gathering her clothes from where they were strewn around the room.

He swallowed. Nothing had changed. Yet it felt like everything had. She still liked him and during sex she had been unguarded with her feelings. She liked him a hell of a lot more than just two people having casual sex. But she was still running away. She wasn't ready to face those emotions yet.

'Why are you going?'

'Because we shouldn't have done this,' Ruby said, seemingly looking around for some item of her clothes.

'But we did and running away isn't going to change that,' Jacob said, carefully. He felt like he was dealing with a frightened animal.

'But this means more to you than it does to me. I can see that. This wasn't what that was. This was just two friends having incredible uncomplicated no-strings-attached sex, this was never going to be the next big love story of Happiness.'

He sighed. 'I know you would like to believe that was what it was but we both know it was a hell of a lot more than that.'

'I'm sorry, I really am. I never wanted to hurt you Jacob, that was the last thing I wanted, but I'm not looking for a relationship or love.' Ruby pulled her bra on.

'Just because you don't want to fall in love doesn't mean you can simply push those feelings away.'

'I don't have those feelings for you. I don't,' Ruby said and

Jacob got the feeling that she was trying to convince herself more than she was trying to convince him.

She reached for her knickers and he put a hand out to stall her. There was no way in hell he was going to let her go now that he had her.

'Look Ruby, I like you a lot, probably a lot more than I should. But if you just want no-strings-attached sex then that's absolutely fine with me.'

She paused for the longest time as if she was weighing it up. He used the opportunity to gently pull her back onto the bed and she didn't resist.

'You and I both know that being just friends wasn't working,' Jacob said. 'We wouldn't have ended up in bed together with the first kiss we've had in months if that was the case. It was torture for me to work alongside you and not be able to kiss you or take you to bed and I think you felt the same. Don't you think we should at least try the no-strings-attached route for a while?'

He had no idea why he was suggesting this. The last thing he wanted was casual, meaningless sex with her. But he couldn't walk away from her either. He knew she was scared of what she felt for him. Maybe the more time they spent together, the more willing she might be to take a risk on them.

'I don't want to hurt you,' Ruby said.

'I'm a big boy, I can look after myself. If we have no-strings-attached sex for the next few weeks and it comes to an end, or we have no-strings-attached sex for the rest of our lives with no emotional attachment or commitment, I'll be absolutely fine.'

She arched an eyebrow in amusement. 'No-strings-attached sex for the rest of our lives?'

He shrugged. 'If you want.'

'Exclusively?'

'Yes.' There was definitely not any room for negotiation on that point.

'That kind of sounds like a relationship,' Ruby said.

'Nope. Two friends having sex. That's it.'

She looked doubtful.

'Look, you end this whenever you want,' Jacob said. 'You call the shots.'

He placed a kiss on her shoulder and he felt her melt against him.

'I'm in charge?' Ruby said as he placed another kiss on her throat.

'Definitely.'

She shifted round and straddled him. 'And I can do whatever I want with you?'

'You have my full permission to use me however you see fit.'

He slipped her bra from her shoulders and then placed kisses over her breast.

She let out a sigh of contentment. 'Well, I could definitely get used to this.'

He stroked his hands down her back, caressing her hips, and she moaned softly as he continued to kiss across her breasts. She reached over to the drawers and grabbed another condom and ripped it open with her teeth. She rolled it on him, her touch almost unravelling him. She shifted over him and the next thing he was deep inside her. She kissed him hard as he moved his hands to her hips, holding her close. She wrapped her arms round his neck, stroking the hair at the back of his head. They moved in perfect sync with each other, stroking and caressing in the exact places where they knew the other liked to be touched.

He felt her breath change on his lips and he pulled back to look at her. The adoration for him in her eyes floored him.

There was no way this was just sex for her. And he was prepared to wait for however long it took for her to realise it too. He would be there for her in any way she wanted, he would slowly whittle away at her defences so her wall came tumbling down and maybe, just maybe, he could make her ever after a happy one.

~

Jacob woke with a start, his heart hammering against his chest, a cold film of sweat coating his body. It was dark and for a few panicky seconds he wondered where he was.

'Hey, are you OK?' Ruby said, gently, stroking his chest.

God, she was here and she was exactly what he needed right then.

He pulled her into his arms and held her tight while she stroked his back soothingly.

'I am now,' he muttered, feeling his heart rate slow.

It had been years since he'd had that dream, water pounding over his head, being dragged along the sea bed, fighting to get to the surface, his lungs screaming for much needed air and then finally breaking the surface and trying to get to the shore but being pulled further and further out to sea. The land disappearing from view and that desperate feeling of hopelessness that he would never be found. He shuddered in Ruby's arms and held her tighter.

'Are you sure you're OK?' Ruby said, stroking the back of his head. 'You were moaning in your sleep.'

'Just a bad dream,' Jacob said.

God, maybe Andrew was right. Maybe he shouldn't do this Polar Bear Plunge. Maybe his first reintroduction into the sea should be on a calm summer's day, not in the middle of a snowy cold winter. If he explained what had happened to

Ruby, she would understand. He pulled back to look at her and saw nothing but affection and concern for him shining from her eyes. He couldn't pull out now. He had to do this for her, not just to raise money for the British Heart Foundation, which he knew was important to her, but also to encourage her to face her own fears.

It was ridiculous for him to get so worked up over something that had happened nearly twenty years ago and it was time he got over that once and for all. He only hoped that one day Ruby would be able to move past her fears too.

CHAPTER THIRTEEN

Ruby woke the next day to the sound of someone moving around the flat. As Jacob was wrapped tight around her, she wondered who it could be. Andrew maybe? Who else would just let themselves into Jacob's flat? Although it was hardly likely to be a burglar in the sleepy village of Happiness.

Ruby disentangled herself from Jacob's arms, and started getting dressed. She watched Jacob sleeping as she pulled on her clothes. He was lying there, naked, with a huge smile on his face. She didn't know whether to be delighted or terrified by this 'no-strings-attached' arrangement. He was right, they couldn't just be friends; they'd tried it and it hadn't worked. But was friends with benefits going to work either? The last thing she wanted was to hurt Jacob and if he really started to fall for her she would have to end things between them before they went too far. If he was hoping she would fall in love with him, then he would be sadly mistaken. She liked him a lot but she was never going to fall in love with him. She touched the snowflake necklace Harry had given her. She had learned her lesson there.

She walked out into the living area of the flat, to find Jacob's sister Lottie and his niece Poppy busily decorating Jacob's flat for Christmas. Poppy was draping garlands of tinsel over everything and Lottie was tying baubles here, there and everywhere. As someone who liked things very minimalist in terms of décor, Jacob probably wouldn't be a huge fan of what they were doing now. Ruby couldn't help but laugh at this.

Lottie whirled round to see where the noise had come from and her eyebrows almost disappeared into her hairline at seeing Ruby standing there. Ruby had met Lottie a few times in the summer as she lived in the next town to Happiness and, while she'd probably not made the greatest first impression, Jacob's sister had started to warm to her towards the end of Ruby's stay.

She wondered how Lottie would take finding her here.

'Ruby, sorry, we weren't expecting anyone to be here. Jacob always goes over to Penzance early on a Tuesday, so we thought we'd surprise him with redecorating his home,' Lottie said.

Ruby felt a little kick of disappointment that Jacob wouldn't be there today if he was going off to Penzance. The Christmas Cookie Competition was taking place that afternoon and she had wondered if he would take part and maybe even if they could be a team. Although was that activity too… *cosy* for two people not in a proper relationship?

Lottie's eyes drifted up to Ruby's hair, which was probably showing the signs of a night of passion. 'I have to say, when Jacob mentioned you were working next door and living in the village now, I did wonder if you two would get together again.' She paused. 'He really likes you.'

Ruby didn't know what to say to that.

'I hope we didn't ... interrupt anything?' Lottie said.

'No, Jacob's fast asleep,' Ruby said honestly. There was no point lying about what she was doing there. Lottie certainly wouldn't appreciate that if and when she found out the truth, but Ruby didn't need to go into specifics about what she'd spent the night doing with Jacob. She'd leave that to Lottie's imagination.

Although she didn't know how she was going to explain her presence to Poppy. She glanced over at the little girl, who currently had no idea that Ruby was standing there.

Lottie followed her gaze and must have read her mind. 'I'm sure you can make something up.'

Lottie moved over to Poppy who was laying tinsel around the room in gay abandon and tapped her gently on the shoulder.

Poppy turned round and jumped a little to see Ruby standing there. Poppy waved hello and Ruby returned the gesture.

Poppy started signing, her little hands flying at a hundred miles an hour.

'She wants to know what you're doing here?' Lottie said, smirking.

'Yeah, I gathered that. I, umm... learned to sign. I understand a lot more than I can sign, so I might need a bit of help, but I can probably communicate fairly well with her.'

Lottie looked at her in surprise. 'You learned to sign?'

Ruby nodded. She turned her attention back to Poppy and carefully signed to her. *'Me and Jacob were working very hard and very late last night on my Christmas shop downstairs and I ended up sleeping here.'*

Poppy nodded.

'Your Christmas shop is beautiful,' Poppy signed, seemingly accepting that excuse completely.

'Thank you.' Ruby signed back. *'Are you here to make Jacob's home more festive?'*

Poppy nodded eagerly.

'Can I help?' Ruby signed and the little girl nodded again. *'I have more decorations downstairs in my shop. Give me a few minutes and I'll grab some stuff.'*

Poppy clapped her hands together excitedly and Ruby hurried off downstairs, selecting the brightest, craziest pieces she could get her hands on.

She returned to see Jacob had emerged from his bedroom wearing only his jeans, looking all sleepy and dishevelled and sexy.

He was chatting away to Poppy and obviously amused by the whole redecoration that was going on.

Jacob looked over at her as she walked back in and his whole face lit up. 'I thought you'd gone.'

'And miss out on a chance to Christmassify your home? Not a chance,' Ruby said, dumping her wares on the table. She turned back to Poppy and signed. *'Where shall I start?'*

'The kitchen,' Poppy replied.

Ruby nodded and then realised Jacob was watching her in awe, which wasn't good. She didn't need to give him any more ammunition to fall in love with her.

'When you told me you could sign a few words, I wasn't expecting this,' he said.

'I may have played it down.'

Jacob stared at her and then broke into a huge smile. 'Did anyone ever tell you, you're pretty bloody amazing?'

She smiled and picked up a brightly coloured string of Christmas stocking bunting and turned away. He made her feel so warm inside. This friends-with-benefits malarkey was going to get very complicated.

Jacob passed Poppy her hot chocolate with extra cream, marshmallows, sprinkles and even a flake on top and she plopped down on the sofa to drink it. He watched as she got cream on the end of her nose and smiled. Ruby would certainly appreciate a hot chocolate like that, it was a shame she'd had to rush off after they had finished decorating. He went back to the kitchen to get his and Lottie's drinks and then sat down next to his sister.

'Thank you for this,' Jacob gestured to his flat which now impossibly looked more Christmassy than Ruby's shop.

Lottie grinned at him. 'It was my pleasure.'

'Are you two going to hang around here for a few hours? There's a cookie-decorating competition this afternoon,' Jacob said, taking a sip. Poppy was focussing her attention on finding all the tiny marshmallows amongst the big dollop of whipped cream.

'Poppy will love that.'

'And we have the Angel Festival tomorrow. Everyone has to make a sculpture of an angel, using whatever you wish to use to make it, cardboard boxes, toilet rolls. I'm sure Poppy would enjoy doing that too.'

'Are we allowed to take part; we don't live here?' Lottie asked.

'Of course, the more the merrier, and we're raising money for charity so we want as many participants as possible. It was all Ruby's idea.'

'Along with the Polar Bear Plunge,' Lottie said.

He sighed. 'Andrew told you about it.'

'Yeah, I can't believe you're doing it.'

'It's not a big deal, not really, is it? It's just a ten or twenty-second splash in the sea. It's only an issue because of what happened in the past but maybe it's time I got over that.'

Lottie stared at him. 'While I applaud your *get back on the horse* mentality, is there another reason you're doing this after twenty years of never going in the sea?'

'It's for charity,' Jacob shrugged.

'You're doing this for Ruby, aren't you?'

He paused. 'I guess so.'

'You really like her, don't you?'

'We're... just casual. No strings attached. You know me.'

'I do know you, that's why I'm worried. I see the way you look at her and I don't think you're going to get what you want out of this.'

'You're probably right, but if it ends, it ends, I'll cope.'

He ignored the ache in his heart that said otherwise. He would be gutted if this thing didn't work out between him and Ruby. Was he setting himself up for a fall?

'I've seen how much hurt it can cause when one person is more into a relationship than the other,' Lottie said.

'Are you talking about your mystery man?'

Lottie smiled. 'He's not a mystery man.'

'But you won't tell me his name.'

'That's because he's a bit of a celebrity and you're about as discreet as a washerwoman when it comes to gossip. I'm sure he wouldn't appreciate anyone finding out he slept with some random woman who worked in the hotel he was staying at. I'm sure my boss wouldn't appreciate finding out I slept with one of the guests either.'

'From what you told me, it was a lot more than a one-night stand, at least for him,' Jacob said.

'It was more than that for me too and, yes, I think I broke his heart when I pushed him away and that kills me.'

Jacob knew Lottie was still hurting after her ex-husband had left and because of that she had been scared when she got involved with her mystery man. She had ended up pushing him away and he knew she had regretted it ever since.

'All I'm saying is, if this really is a casual arrangement between you and Ruby, then you can't let yourself fall in love with her, because you'll end up getting hurt. If you do feel something more for her, then I think you have to be brave enough to end it before it gets too far.'

Jacob sighed and nodded. He knew his sister was right.

Ruby sprinkled flour on the unit top and rolled out the biscuit dough so it was the same thickness all over. She had been busy making biscuits all morning and her arms were starting to ache from all the stirring and rolling.

Almost everyone in the village had signed up for the Christmas Cookie Competition that afternoon. It was lovely that everyone was so supportive but the logistics of doing such a big competition were not something she had thought through when she had offered it to the village. Kitty and Ken had agreed to using the great hall at the castle as they wouldn't be setting up for the ball until the afternoon the next day, but now Ruby had to provide all the cookies and they needed to be big enough to be decorated by the villagers too.

Ruby carefully cut out the biscuit circles and placed them on the baking tray.

Making the cookies did have the added advantage of not having to face Jacob. She just wasn't sure how to handle being around him right now. They hadn't kissed or even touched since the night before when they had agreed to this bizarre arrangement so he was keeping to his side of the bargain. They were friends who would have sex, nothing more. But even she could see this plan had flaws. Great big gaping ones. Could they really work alongside each other during the day, have no-strings-attached sex every night and not develop any feelings for each other at all? In reality she knew it wouldn't work like that. Her feelings for him had definitely intensified over the last few days. Sleeping with him on a regular basis would cement them in place.

They had spent an hour that morning with Lottie and Poppy making his flat look like a grotto. And despite her anti-romance rule, she had enjoyed being with his family and laughing and joking with him. He'd even asked her if she wanted to join him, Andrew and Lottie for Christmas Day and she'd said yes, though she wasn't sure why. If she was honest, the whole thing with Jacob was terrifying her. The thought of letting herself fall in love with this man and then losing him like she did Harry made panic grip her heart. And though the rational part of her brain said lightning wouldn't strike twice, she couldn't let go of that fear.

She sighed. This whole thing was a mess and she blamed Harry completely. If he hadn't upped and left her, she wouldn't be the emotional mess she was now.

She focussed her attention back on the cookies.

The other advantage of making the cookies was that she had something to share on her Instagram. She had created her profile, 'The Christmas Fairy', a year or so before and would share photos almost daily of the different baubles she had been making or any other Christmas activities she was doing throughout the year. Since coming here she had managed to post lots of photos; of her shop, of Jacob's metal Christmas tree, of the gingerbread men, the mulled wine, the tall Christmas tree outside the castle, some of the more … *appropriate* Christmas lights in the village. It all helped to direct people to her website where people could buy decorations online. Earlier that morning she had posted photos of the cookies she was making, explaining that it was for a Christmas Cookie Competition to raise money for the British Heart Foundation. She'd said that she needed to make two hundred cookies and had finished the post with *Send help* and *Send icing sugar, Smarties and sprinkles.*

She opened the oven and took out the biscuits that were golden brown, replacing them with the ones she had just rolled and cut out. Then she started mixing up a new batch of dough.

She had definitely bitten off more than she could chew with the Christmas Cookie Competition, the Angel Festival the next day and the Polar Bear Plunge on Christmas Eve. It didn't leave much time to actually be in her shop in her busiest time of the year. Maybe she should cancel something, the Polar Bear Plunge ideally. She thought back to the night before and Jacob's nightmare. Had that been related to the Polar Bear Plunge? The thought that this silly swim for charity was affecting him so badly made her heart sink. She hated the idea that he was worrying so much about this that he was having bad dreams. She could put a note on the forum that it was cancelled because of lack of interest. That was plausible. But she didn't want Jacob to think she was calling it off for him. And she got the feeling he needed to do this to conquer his demons once and for all.

There was a knock on the door and she sighed and dusted her hands down her apron and went to answer it.

Jacob was standing there and she couldn't help the flutter of excitement at seeing him.

He raised two bulging carrier bags. 'You said, send help, so I'm here to help.'

He stepped inside without waiting to be invited and kissed her on the cheek by way of a greeting, then moved through to the kitchen.

She stood there in shock for a moment, touching her cheek where his lips had been. Had they progressed to that now with their friends-with-benefits arrangement? She wasn't sure if she liked it. No, actually she knew she liked it. Too bloody much.

She closed the door and followed him through to the kitchen, still confused about what he was doing there. She hadn't told him she was going to be making cookies this morning. And wasn't he supposed to be in Penzance?

'What do you mean, you're here to help?'

'On your Instagram post, you said send help and send icing sugar, Smarties and sprinkles. So I brought them all.'

She blushed at the thought of him looking at her Instagram. She was always quite candid in her posts and she wouldn't be surprised if she'd put something up there about working next door to a sexy artist. She wracked her brains trying to remember. She'd certainly took a picture of him working away at the Christmas tree when he wasn't looking, but she wasn't sure if she'd got round to posting it yet.

'You've seen my Instagram?'

'You left it on my computer the other day, I've been cyber stalking you ever since. I like the idea of you being a Christmas fairy, sprinkling your Christmas magic over everything and everyone. Anyway, I saw your post about making cookies today so I thought I'd come and give you a hand.'

'I thought you'd be heading over to Penzance today?'

'It can wait for another day.' He moved over to the sink and washed his hands. 'What do you need me to do?'

She found herself smiling at him. He was here for her. As a friend. There was no agenda, he just wanted to help her out.

He grabbed some kitchen towel to dry his hands and she walked over and hugged him, her face against his back, her arms around his stomach.

'I really bloody like you, Jacob Harrington.'

He squeezed her hand. She wondered if he would say something back about how much he liked her but he didn't. Although he'd already proved that by coming here.

'Come on, shall I make the icing? After years of cupcake-making with Poppy, I reckon I know my way around a batch of buttercream or glacé icing.' He stepped away from her and started taking out the bags of icing sugar. 'Which one are we making?'

She watched him for a moment, that ache in her heart for him getting bigger. She cleared her throat.

'Buttercream, I think. You can pipe that on and get some good effects or spoon it on and it won't run,' Ruby said.

'I bought food colouring too so we can make different colour batches.'

'Good idea. You do realise you're going to have to make a ton of it?'

He shrugged. 'I have time.'

They worked together in silence for a while, though it wasn't uncomfortable. It was just two friends working side by side. Maybe they would be OK after all.

~

Cal phoned just after Jacob had left to deliver a car full of biscuits and icing to the castle. Ruby was busy cleaning the kitchen; the icing sugar had seemingly got everywhere. She put the call on loudspeaker as she wiped around the kitchen.

'How's it going out there, Cal?' Ruby asked, keen not to get onto the subject of her and Jacob again.

'All good. But I'm nearly done here. If I can get a flight out, I was thinking of coming down and spending Christmas with you.'

Excitement over seeing her brother again mixed with nerves at the thought of having Cal there interfering with her love life. She didn't need him there sticking his oar in, she could cock everything up quite well on her own. But she did want to see him again and it would be lovely to spend Christmas with him.

'That would be great.' She winced a little over what she was going to say next. 'I'm actually spending Christmas with Jacob and his family, but I'm sure you'll be very welcome to come along too.'

There was silence from Cal for a second and she thought the connection between there and the States had dropped out.

'You're spending Christmas Day with Jacob, a man who you have feelings for but refuse to let anything more happen between you? That doesn't sound like you're keeping your distance to me.'

'Well, actually we've made a bit of progress there.'

'Really?' Cal said, eagerly.

'We're trialling a friends-with-benefits arrangement,' Ruby said, knowing how pathetic that sounded.

Cal didn't say anything for a while. 'Right.'

'I thought you'd be pleased.'

'Pleased? How can I be pleased that my little sister is having meaningless sex with the only man who has meant something to her in twelve years?'

Ruby sighed but she knew that her brother was partly right.

'Look, we're both happy with this arrangement,' she tried.

'We're good friends, we get on well, we have great sex. It doesn't need to be more than that.'

'Maybe not for you.'

'This was Jacob's idea,' Ruby said.

'I think I might have to have words with Jacob Harrington.'

'Cal, I love you, I'm looking forward to seeing you at Christmas, but stay out of this.'

Cal was silent again but eventually he spoke. 'Ruby, when you were a kid, you were completely fearless. You'd climb the highest tree, ride your bike down the hill the fastest, learn all those scary skateboard stunts, do somersaults on the trampoline, stand up to the school's biggest bully. You were tremendous. What happened to that brave little girl?'

'She discovered what it was like to really get hurt, she discovered what real pain felt like,' Ruby said.

'And you've been hiding away ever since. It's time to be brave again, to take a risk. To live the life you want because this half-life is not the life you imagined when you were conquering dragons and fighting pirates. And this is not the life Harry would have wanted for you either. You might as well have died that day too if this is the life you're going to lead.'

'Cal, that's an awful thing to say.'

'I'm sorry but I hate to see you waste your life like this. If you don't want me to interfere then I promise, I won't say another word, but please just think about what I've said.'

'I will,' Ruby said, quietly.

'I'll keep you posted regarding flights and dates.'

'OK.'

'I love you, kid.'

'I love you too.'

And with that Cal was gone.

Ruby sighed. She remembered that euphoric feeling she'd

got as a kid, when she did something daring and bold, the wind in her hair as she raced her bike down the steepest hill. And although the risks of getting hurt were high, the sheer joy she got from those escapades always outweighed those risks.

Cal was right. After Harry's death she had closeted herself away, afraid to take those risks anymore. She had built a wall around her to protect herself from ever getting hurt again.

But Jacob had been pulling that wall down brick by brick, he had worked his way in. And sometimes, when she was with him, she would have those wonderful feelings of joy again and she liked that.

If she wanted that life she just had to reach through the wall and take it. But she had to find a shedload of courage first and she wasn't sure that brave little girl was in there anymore.

CHAPTER FOURTEEN

Ruby was delighted by how many people had turned up for the Cookie Competition. She'd figured it would just be something families with young kids would want to do, but it seemed that the whole village had turned up. Even Lottie and Poppy had hung around to take part.

The great hall in the castle wasn't quite set up for the Christmas ball yet apart from some of the beautiful Christmas decorations that adorned the ceilings and walls. Andrew had been working hard all morning to set up tables for the villagers to use for their cookie-decorating but there were so many groups now waiting to take part that many of them would have to share a table.

Ken was busy directing operations, doing what he did best. Jacob was running round giving everyone a jam jar so that people could put pennies in the jars of their favourite cookie, which would help to declare the winner and raise money for charity too. Willow was delivering bags of coloured icing to the tables and Ruby was collecting money at the door in return for a plain cookie and directing people to their places.

Lucas arrived at the door and handed over his money. She wasn't sure where things stood between him and Megan right now, whether they'd made up after their little spat or not, but as promised she was going to place Lucas with Megan so at least they could talk.

'Let me see where I can squeeze you in,' Ruby said, pretending to consult her clipboard. 'Would you mind sharing with the person on table eight?'

Lucas looked over and let out a little sigh, but he didn't protest and went over to join Megan. Megan glanced up as he arrived and then looked back down again at her cookie as if planning out what she was going to do. Obviously the air hadn't been cleared between them, but maybe this would give them the chance to at least become friends again.

When everyone seemed to be in their designated areas, Ken came over to Ruby with a microphone.

'These events are a wonderful idea,' Ken said. 'The Cookie Competition and the Angel Festival are something the families can all get involved in. Although I think the one event everyone is looking forward to the most is the Polar Bear Plunge on Christmas Eve. Everyone wants to see Jacob get wet.'

Ruby smiled, uneasily. This was such a big deal for Jacob and the thought that everyone was going to get a good laugh out of watching him do something that terrified him made her feel sick.

'I don't think he's looking forward to it,' she said, carefully.

'I'm not surprised, it's bloody freezing out there.'

Ruby couldn't tell him that it was so much more than that.

'Are you all ready to start?' Ken asked.

She looked around and nodded.

'Do you want to say a few words and explain any rules?'

'Sure,' Ruby said.

'Well, I'll introduce you and then pass the microphone over to you.'

He switched on the microphone and tapped it a few times to get everyone's attention. Silence fell over the great hall.

'Thank you all for coming to our first annual Christmas Cookie Competition,' Ken said. Ruby couldn't help but smirk that he had decided it was to become an annual thing rather than just a one-off, even though the event hadn't even kicked off yet. 'I'm going to pass you over to Ruby and she will explain how the whole thing is going to work.'

The villagers gave a small round of applause and Ken handed over the microphone.

'Thank you,' Ruby said to the villagers. 'You all have half hour to decorate your cookies, only using the sweets, sprinkles and coloured icing on the tables. Please do share the bags of coloured icing with other tables. We couldn't make every colour for every table – that would have been a lot of icing.'

Everyone laughed.

'After the thirty minutes is up, you will be able to walk around and see what everyone has made and you can put pennies or as much as you can afford in the jars next to your favourite cookie. As many of you are aware, we are raising money for the British Heart Foundation. Heart disease is one of the biggest killers in the UK and I myself lost someone close to me to a heart attack, so this charity is very important to me. So dig deep but have fun too.'

The villagers clapped loudly this time and Ruby passed the microphone back to Ken.

'Thanks Ruby. OK, without further ado, I declare the Cookie Competition open. You can start your cookies in three, two, one, go.'

There was suddenly a hive of activity as families, friends and couples all started working on their own cookies, making plans, squeezing the bags of icing, the children surreptitiously eating the sweets. Ruby didn't hold out any hope that any of the cookies would be great works of art but at least everyone was having fun.

She looked round and saw that Andrew and Willow were working together at one table and Lottie and Poppy were busily beavering away next to them.

She glanced over at Megan working alongside Lucas. Although they were working on their own individual cookies, it was evident they were at least talking, as something that Lucas said made Megan laugh.

Ruby looked around to see if there was a table spare so she could have a go but Jacob caught her eye and waved her over to join him.

She smiled and walked across to his table where there were two cookies waiting for them.

'Come on, I need a Christmas expert on my team if we stand any chance of winning this thing,' Jacob said.

'What about a little competition between ourselves?' Ruby said, moving to his side. 'You're an artist, I'm an expert in all things Christmassy, let's see who gets the most coins in their jar.'

He grinned at the challenge. 'OK, you're on. And what do I get when I win?'

She leaned up and whispered in his ear and took great pleasure in watching his eyes widen to comic proportions.

'Bloody hell, that's some incentive.'

'You won't win though, so don't get too excited,' Ruby said.

'What do you want *if* you win?' Jacob asked, picking up one of the bags of green icing.

She thought about this for a moment and decided to knock another brick from the wall, although it suddenly felt like a very big brick.

'I want you to make me a new necklace. Something Christmassy. I've had this snowflake for a while and maybe it's time I had something new.'

He stared at her for a moment. Had he detected a quiver in her voice when she'd suggested it? There was no way she was throwing Harry's necklace away, but maybe she could vary it with something different some days.

'You have yourself a deal,' Jacob said, seriously, but then he nudged her. 'You're not going to win though.'

'We'll see about that.'

'Twenty-five minutes,' Ken said over the microphone.

Ruby quickly grabbed a bag of brown icing and started carefully piping it onto the biscuit as Jacob got to work himself. She did the outline of the robin first of all and then coloured it in with long strokes so it looked like feathers.

She picked up the red icing and started creating the red breast. She glanced over at Jacob, who was clearly taking his time to get his design of a Santa just right.

'You're taking this very seriously,' Ruby said.

'There's a lot at stake.'

She laughed and picked up a bag of white icing as Jacob reached for it too, laughing and holding it out of his reach.

'Oh, is that your game, trying to hinder my creative process,' Jacob said. 'Well we'll see about that.'

He grabbed her around the waist with one arm, hauling her against him as he reached for the bag with the other. She squealed and tried to wiggle from his grasp. But then he was suddenly tickling her in the ribs, touching her in the exact spot that made her go weak. She brought her arms down in an attempt to protect herself and he swiped the bag from her hand and released her.

'That's not fair,' Ruby laughed.

He shrugged. 'If you can't take the heat, get out of the kitchen.'

'Oh, I can take the heat,' she said.

He fixed her with a dark look that gave her a punch of desire. 'Is that right?'

She shook her head with a smile and took a step away from him.

'Just get on with your biscuit.'

She turned her attention back to her own design, applying icing around the outside and then a pattern of sweets while she waited for him to finish with the white icing.

He passed over the bag and she carefully piped the white feathers at the bottom of the robin's belly. She had painted this design on baubles many times, so it wasn't really that different using icing instead.

Jacob started adding sweets round the outside as Ken began doing a countdown to the end of the competition. Everyone started joining in and there was a last-second flurry of activity from many of the tables.

'That's it everyone, your time is up,' Ken said, over the microphone.

Ruby licked a blob of icing off her thumb and wiped her hands down her jeans. She looked over at Jacob's cookie. It was surprisingly good. Although she shouldn't have had her doubts, he was a brilliant artist.

'That's very good, Ruby Marlowe,' Jacob said, studying her robin. 'But I don't think it will beat my Santa.'

'You're so cocky.'

He shrugged. 'We'll let the people decide.'

'Make sure your names are written on the jars so we can identify the winner,' Ken was saying over the microphone. 'And now please give donations in the jars next to the cookies you like the most.'

Jacob pulled his wallet out. 'Damn, I only have a twenty, I didn't bring any change.'

'Well, twenty pounds is a very generous donation,' Ruby teased. 'I'll put in for you if you tell me which cookie you like the most.'

'Thanks.'

People started walking around and Ruby moved between the tables, dropping a few coins in the jars here and there. Some of the designs were amazing, some were… more fun than artistic.

She moved to Willow and Andrew's table and smiled at the snowman cookie that kind of looked like the Stay Puft Marshmallow Man.

She turned around and bumped into Julia, who was eyeing her beadily.

'Julia, how did your cookie-decorating go?' Ruby asked, even though it was quite clear the postmistress wasn't there to talk about cookies.

'I was walking Colin and Rufus around the village last night around eightish and I noticed your cottage was in complete darkness. And then when I walked them later around ten, it was still in darkness and I thought perhaps you might have stayed at Jacob's last night to celebrate your first day in style.' Julia waggled her eyebrows mischievously.

Ruby wasn't exactly sure how to respond to being put on the spot like that.

'No, I—'

'And then I saw you leaving your shop around nine this morning wearing exactly the same clothes as you were wearing yesterday and my suspicions were confirmed.'

'Wow. That's… some good detective work,' Ruby said, not wanting to say that it was actually more than a little creepy.

'So are you two… making whoopee again?'

Ruby cleared her throat. 'Julia, sometimes a lady likes to be a bit mysterious and keep her secrets to herself.'

Julia looked delighted. 'That's a yes if ever I heard one.'

Ruby smiled and, as Julia looked around for Dorothy or Liz to spread the joyous news, she slipped away. She was sure that piece of gossip would be round the whole village within an hour. She really didn't have a chance of hiding something that momentous in a village so tiny it didn't show on any maps.

After Ruby had moved around all the tables, Ken came back on the microphone. 'Have you all now had a chance to put your money in the jar next to the cookie you like the most?'

There were murmurs of agreement from around the hall.

'Great. So can we have all the jars up here on the stage and we will count the money.'

Ruby grabbed a few nearby jars, bringing them over to the stage, and everyone else did the same.

'Well, it seems like we have a winner,' Ken said after a few seconds, which surprised Ruby. They couldn't possibly have counted all the money in all the jars already.

He held a jar aloft which quite clearly had a twenty-pound note stuffed inside, along with a few pennies. Ken tipped the jar into his hands and he quickly counted the coins.

'With twenty pounds and thirty-six pence, our winner is actually our very own Ruby Marlowe.'

Everyone clapped but Ruby frowned in confusion. There was no way she should have won; the robin was good but there were some real masterpieces out there. And then, suddenly, comprehension dawned on her. She whirled around to find Jacob and saw him standing by their table. He caught her eye and gave her a wink.

She made her way to the stage to collect the tin of chocolate biscuits which was her prize. Considering what she had promised Jacob if his cookie won out of the two of them, it would have been the obvious choice to stick his twenty pounds in his own jar, but he hadn't. He had made sure she'd won, which meant she was now going to get a new necklace.

She shook her head. This man really was going to be her undoing.

CHAPTER FIFTEEN

Jacob watched Ruby as she laughed with Willow up at the crowded bar. He couldn't drag his eyes away. She made him feel things he'd never felt before and he had no idea what to do about it. He wasn't sure whether this friends-with-benefits arrangement was going to be a great idea or a terrible one, though pessimistically he didn't think it was going to end well.

Andrew came over to join him, handing him a pint.

'Why the long face?' his brother said, sitting down on the sofa opposite him.

Jacob took a long sip of his beer. 'I think I've made a terrible mistake.'

'Well, rumour has it that Ruby stayed over at yours last night. Is that your terrible mistake?'

Jacob let out a heavy breath. 'Sleeping with Ruby was not the mistake. Suggesting that we could have a no-strings-attached-sex kind of relationship was probably one of the stupidest things I've ever done.'

Andrew stared at him for a few seconds. 'And why on earth would you suggest that when you like her so much?'

'Because it was that or nothing and I couldn't face nothing again.'

Andrew sighed. 'I don't think you're going to get what you want out of this. This is going to be like Ella all over again.'

Jacob nodded, knowing his brother was right. He had hoped that by being there for Ella she would eventually turn her affections in his direction, but she had never seen him that way and ultimately broke his heart. He thought Ruby had feelings for him but maybe he was only seeing what he wanted to see. As far as she was concerned, this arrangement could purely be about sex with a friend and nothing more.

'What do I do?' Jacob asked.

'I suppose you give her time initially. She likes you – anyone can see that –and she might eventually realise she likes you a hell of a lot more than friends. Although she might not. I guess, ultimately, meaningless sex can only last so long and at some point you're going to have to be honest with her about how you feel and hope she feels the same way. And if she doesn't I think you have to be brave enough to end it or it will only end in heartbreak for you.'

Jacob nodded and then let out a little laugh. 'I never thought I'd see the day when me and you have a proper serious conversation.'

'Ah, I'm practically a married man now, I suppose I had to grow up sometime.'

Jacob smiled. 'Well I think we better get back to telling fart jokes and talking about beer before our reputations are completely ruined.'

Andrew grinned. 'I'll do my best.'

Ruby looked around nervously. The pub was pretty packed so doing what she was about to do was a big risk. But when she'd returned from the bar with their drinks, she'd tucked herself away in the corner. Earlier she had enlisted Willow and Andrew to help her and Jacob. She had also changed Jesus's costume so no one would be on the look-out for a doll dressed as a reindeer. He was now dressed as an elf instead.

Andrew, Willow and Jacob were largely blocking her from view as Ruby sat Jesus on a bar stool, next to the pint she had just bought for Jacob. She quickly looked around and then took a picture, before bundling poor Jesus back into her rucksack again.

She looked around again to see if anyone had seen and locked eyes with Lucy. Her heart leapt. Had she seen, could she have seen Jesus from where she was sitting? Ruby had no idea but, judging from the smug smile slowly spreading on Lucy's face, she had definitely seen something.

God, if anyone could make trouble for Ruby, it would be her. She just had to hope Lucy had some kind of sense of humour.

Ruby pulled her coat around her tighter as she waited for Willow to unlock the door to her house later that night. Being stylish at Christmas with her purple velvet coat was one thing but being warm when living in a coastal village was probably more important. With the icy winds that were blowing in from the sea, Ruby thought she might need a coat made for Arctic explorers at this rate. Willow and Andrew's house was right on the cliff tops looking out over the sea, which made for some stunning views, but at this time of year it must be colder for them than if they lived a bit more centrally in the village.

Willow had invited her and Jacob round to watch Christmas movies, which was obviously code for Willow wanting to find out what was going on between her and Jacob. Ruby was happy to oblige though; Willow was sure to find out soon enough and Ruby would rather her friend heard it from her.

Willow pushed the door open and stepped back to let them in, Ruby rushed in and started building a fire, although it was very clear that the heating was on as well.

'Mulled wine OK for everyone?' Willow asked, shrugging out of her coat and heading for the kitchen. 'Or I can do hot chocolates. I'm having a hot chocolate so it's no bother.'

'Mulled wine is fine for me,' Ruby said, closing the log burner door.

'And me,' Jacob said.

'Mulled wine for me,' Andrew said, hanging all the coats up near the door.

'Ruby, why don't you give me a hand,' Willow said, meaningfully.

Ruby smirked as she ditched her coat and walked into the kitchen. Jacob winked at her as he flopped down on the sofa. He knew she was about to get the third degree.

Ruby watched as Willow poured the bottle of mulled wine into a saucepan. Where Ruby preferred to make her own from red wine and different spices, Willow had found a bottle of pre-spiced mulled wine that took away all of that hassle. She bought a few bottles of the stuff every year and Ruby had to admit the stuff was good, potent but delicious.

'So tell me everything,' Willow said eagerly.

Ruby smiled. 'There are certain things that even I don't want to share.'

'Ah come on, just give me a little bit. Did you…?' she trailed off, waving her hand in some kind of vague gesture. 'I heard lots of people say you had and although Lottie didn't say anything to anyone else, she did confide to me that she kind of walked in on you both this morning,' Willow said, as she started making herself a hot chocolate.

Ruby laughed. 'That makes it sound like she walked in on us in the middle of the throes of passion. She came into Jacob's flat early this morning when we were both fast asleep. I walked out of his bedroom with extreme bed hair and she made up her own mind about what me and Jacob had been doing all night. Although I'm sure whatever conclusion she came to was completely accurate.'

Willow turned around so fast she spilt hot chocolate powder all over the floor and didn't even notice. She let out a little squeal of excitement.

'Look, don't get too excited, we're not together, not in that sense.'

Willow frowned. 'What sense are you together?'

Ruby grabbed a dustpan and brush and started clearing up. She threw the chocolate powder in the bin and checked where Jacob was, but he was busy in conversation with Andrew.

Ruby took a deep breath. 'Casual, a friends-with-benefits arrangement.'

Willow couldn't have looked more disappointed if Ruby had told her Christmas was cancelled.

Ruby was starting to think it was a terrible idea too, not least because feelings were bubbling to the surface that she didn't want to face.

'This spark has been bubbling between us ever since I got here and I just thought, maybe, if we scratch that itch the need for each other will go away.'

'And did it work?'

Ruby shook her head. She sat down at the table, all the fight going out of her.

'I just need some time to get my head round all this. It feels so new and scary and terrifying. There's a huge part of me that wants this with Jacob, to say to hell with it and dive head first into a proper relationship. But then I remember Harry and...' she swallowed and touched the necklace he'd given her. 'We were supposed to be forever and then I lost him.'

Willow nodded and sat down at the table with her, holding her hand. 'I can't begin to imagine the pain you went through losing the only man you've ever loved. The thought of losing Andrew is enough to bring me to my knees. And I know this is easy for me to say, but you have to continue to live your life. You can't be too scared to get on a plane because it might crash, you can't be scared to go to Australia because you might get bitten by a poisonous spider and you can't be scared of falling in love again because you might get your heart broken in the worst possible way. Because getting on a plane or going to Australia could lead to the most amazing, beautiful adventures and falling in love, being loved in return, is one of the most glorious, wonderful, deliriously happy adventures we can ever go on.'

Ruby smiled at how happy Willow was with Andrew and she nodded. 'I know you're right. And Cal said pretty much the same thing, that I need to be brave. But I just can't rip the plaster off in one quick yank, I have to do it slowly. I need some time and I only hope Jacob is prepared to wait.'

Willow stood up and poured out three glasses of mulled wine, then added hot water to the hot chocolate. 'I think you two are perfect for each other, but just take it slow. I don't want to see either of you get hurt.'

Ruby nodded. 'I know. I don't want to hurt him either.'

Willow added some milk to her hot chocolate and then

grabbed a can of squirty cream and sprayed a big dollop of that on the top.

'Why are you not drinking the mulled wine anyway, you love that stuff?' Ruby asked just as Andrew walked into the room.

Willow blushed furiously. 'I just... fancied some hot chocolate.'

Andrew stared at her. It was her reaction to the question which made it obvious there was more to it than that.

'Oh my god, are you pregnant?' Ruby asked.

'No... I don't know,' Willow said.

'You're pregnant?' Andrew said.

Shit. Even he didn't know. Well this had suddenly got a little awkward.

'I don't think so. I'm not sure,' Willow said.

'Why didn't you tell me?' Andrew said.

Ruby wanted to leave them alone. This conversation was private but her friend suddenly looked close to tears and Ruby wanted to make sure she was OK.

'I wanted to be sure before I said anything. I'm a few days late, I don't think it's a big deal. I stopped using that new pill last month because it was giving me headaches and we've been super careful ever since then so it's really unlikely that I am. My body is probably still trying to sort itself out so it makes sense that I'd be late. But it's still too early to tell for sure and I didn't want to get your hopes up if it's just a... hormone thing.'

Andrew moved into the kitchen. 'Are *your* hopes up?'

Willow dashed tears from her eyes and laughed. 'A little. I mean, it's not the best time, we're not even married yet and I don't want to be the huge pregnant bride, but we have spoken about having children and I know it's something we are both looking forward to when the time is right. But yes, I am a little excited about the prospect I might be carrying your child.'

'Then why wouldn't you share that with me?' Andrew said.

'I only realised I was late this morning and, yes, I got stupidly excited for a few minutes when I thought about what that could mean. But it felt like buying a lottery ticket and then getting excited about what I'm going to spend the money on before the numbers had even been drawn. It felt silly to tell you I might be pregnant when the chances are I'm almost definitely not.'

'We made a deal, that we would always share our hopes and fears, our sadness and our triumphs.'

'OK, then. There is a very teeny tiny chance I might be pregnant. How do you feel about that?'

Andrew stared at her for a few moments and then took Willow in his arms. 'I feel... really excited.'

Willow groaned. 'But that's why I didn't want to tell you. I don't want you to be disappointed if I'm not.'

'But we'll share that disappointment together. If you didn't tell me, then when you found out in a few days' time that you're not, you'd be disappointed on your own and I don't want you to ever feel like you're alone in this relationship.'

Willow nodded and wrapped her arms around Andrew, leaning her head against his chest. 'OK.'

Ruby took the glasses of mulled wine and walked back into the lounge, leaving them to it.

'Is everything OK?' Jacob asked.

She passed him a glass of mulled wine and sat next to him on the sofa, cuddling into his side.

'I think it is now,' she said, leaning her head on his shoulder. He wrapped an arm around her and kissed her head.

Being part of a couple meant going through the good and bad times together, knowing you always had someone there to watch your back. Could she really have that with Jacob? Did she and Jacob really have that longevity to weather the storms, not just celebrate the sunshine? He had been there for her so much since she had arrived, but if she was going to enter into a proper relationship with this man, she had to trust that they would have that.

She looked up at him and he gave her a sweet kiss on the lips. She wanted to believe in that more than anything.

~

They had chosen to watch *The Holiday*. Not that Ruby had seen most of it. Willow and Andrew had come out of the kitchen, looking happy and loved-up. They'd sat down with Willow on Andrew's lap and probably ten minutes after the movie had started Willow was fast asleep, with her head on Andrew's shoulder and his arms tight around her. It was probably only another ten minutes after that that Andrew had fallen asleep too. Ruby and Jacob had spent most of the rest of the film kissing like teenagers on a first date. There was something gloriously wonderful about spending her evening like that, just kissing, because she really did like this man and it was quite obvious he was pretty keen too.

She was vaguely aware the film had finished and she pulled back to look at him.

She stroked his face, relishing the feel of his stubble against her fingers. 'I think we should go.'

He fixed her with a dark look. 'I think so too.'

She smiled and stood up. She watched Willow and Andrew for a moment; they looked so sweet together. 'Should we wake them?'

'Yeah, they'll be stiff tomorrow if they sleep here all night.'

Ruby moved over to them and gave Willow's shoulder a little shake. She opened her eyes blearily.

'Hey, we're off now.'

Willow looked around in confusion and at the credits rolling on the TV and Andrew snoring softly.

'Oh god, did the movie finish already? I'm so sorry, we're terrible hosts.'

'It's OK, I had a lovely evening.'

Willow stood up and Andrew carried on sleeping. She gave Ruby and Jacob a hug and then followed them to the door.

'I'll see you tomorrow,' Ruby said, as they pulled on their hats and coats.

Willow nodded sleepily and, as they stepped outside, she closed the door behind them.

Snow was still falling and the whole outside world was glittering under a layer of soft, white powder, making the night much lighter to walk through. The snow crunched under their feet and their breath escaped in small billows of steam.

'So Willow might be pregnant?' Jacob said.

'I didn't think you'd heard.'

Jacob laughed. 'The kitchen is right there.'

He linked hands with her as they walked up the little track back towards the village.

Ruby looked down at their joined hands. This seemed a bit too familiar for their friends-with-benefits arrangement but she liked it so she didn't pull away.

She focussed back on what he'd said.

'I'm sure they don't want anyone to know yet until they can at least confirm it,' Ruby said.

'You have nothing to worry about with me, but the whole village will know once she buys a pregnancy kit. In fact, I wouldn't put it past Julia Dalton to know already, she knows everything.'

Ruby laughed. 'I might have to buy one for her.'

'Oh great, then everyone will think I've gotten you pregnant just a few days after you've arrived,' Jacob said dryly.

She laughed. 'It will at least keep the attention off Willow and Andrew for a few days.'

'True.'

'So how do you feel about possibly being an uncle again?' Ruby asked as they followed a set of animal tracks through the snow. They looked like they might belong to a fox.

'Oh, I'm more than ready to play that role again. I love hanging out with Poppy, she's the funniest person I know. Besides, it would be good for Poppy to have a cousin to grow up with.'

They cut through an alley that took them to the village high street.

'I had Poppy quite often when she was little, took care of the stinky nappies, endured the sleepless nights,' Jacob said. 'Alex, Lottie's ex-husband, wasn't always around when Poppy was born, he was away a lot with work. Lottie found it hard to look after Poppy on her own so me and Andrew took her as often as we could. I'd do it all over again for Willow and Andrew.'

Ruby smiled. 'Does it make you think about having your own children?'

He grinned down at her. 'Is that an offer, Ruby Marlowe, because I'm not sure our casual sex arrangement covers that.'

She laughed.

'I never thought children were in my future,' she said. 'I never thought a serious relationship was in my future either but now…' she trailed off because it was unexpectedly sounding very serious and scary. 'Maybe… one day.'

God, that was a very big step all of a sudden for her to admit that she wanted that. She decided to try to lighten the mood a little.

'With the right person, obviously,' she teased.

Jacob was quiet for a while. They reached the main high street and they walked down it towards the shop.

'Oh look, someone else has built a snowman,' Ruby said, pointing to a strange-shaped snowman further down the street.

'That's outside Megan's house,' Jacob said.

Ruby looked up at him. 'Do you think it's from Lucas?'

'It might be.'

They drew closer and her heart leapt as she realised it was two people hugging.

'It's just like the tree decoration Megan bought from my shop yesterday. I bet she gave it to Lucas and he's done this.'

'Maybe, or Megan did it herself maybe as a massive hint for Lucas,' Jacob said.

'Well, let's hope he takes it. I really want those two to get together.'

'For someone who doesn't believe in the fairytale ending, that surprises me,' Jacob said.

'Maybe I'm coming round to the idea.'

She could see their snowman standing sentry by the shop door. Jacob had given her that. He had also given her a lot more than she'd ever dreamed possible.

'Why did you make sure I won the Christmas Cookie Competition? Why did you want to make me a new necklace rather than what I offered you?'

Jacob was silent for a while as he unlocked the shop door and then ushered her inside out of the cold.

'Harry gave you that necklace, didn't he?' Jacob said, rubbing his hands down her arms to get her warm.

She nodded.

'I thought as much. Every time you talk about him, or sometimes I can see you think about him, you touch that necklace. But I think it reminds you of the pain you felt when he died rather than the good times you shared.'

Wow, that was very insightful.

'And I never want to take away what the two of you shared, but maybe it's time you made some good memories for you to focus on instead. A new necklace could be the start of that.'

She smiled and reached up and kissed him. He held her against him, so she felt safe in his arms.

She pulled back to look at him. 'Take me to bed, you big beautiful man.'

He grinned and took her by the hand and led her up the stairs. He kissed her gently as he slipped her coat from her shoulders and she stroked his face and then started undressing him too. It wasn't fast and hurried this time, there was no desperate rush. Jacob was taking his time to treasure her, kissing her everywhere as he slowly removed her clothes. He moved his mouth to her neck and placed a kiss right where her pulse was hammering against her skin. It was so gentle and so completely unexpected it stalled her. He placed another soft kiss on her shoulder and another on her collar bone that was almost a whisper. He trailed his mouth to the other side, caressing her with his lips. She felt… adored.

He lifted her and laid her down on the bed as she removed the last of his clothes too.

He stroked her face. She ran her hands over his shoulders. He leaned forward and kissed her, wrapping his arms around her and bringing her close to his body. He didn't stop kissing her as he caressed her all over, stroking his fingers across her breast, down her ribs, over her stomach, and then slipping his hand between her legs.

God, this man. She loved his touch, his familiarity, the way he knew her body better than she knew it herself, the way he could bring her to the very edge with the simplest of touches. She moaned against his lips, felt her body shudder against his and still the kiss continued, his other hand in her hair stroking her, soothing her.

He reached out for a condom from the bedside drawers, shifted back a bit to put it on before he rolled back on top of her, settling himself between her legs. He stared down at her as he slid inside her and she felt her body almost sigh with relief.

He moved against her slowly, not taking his eyes from hers for a second. She wrapped her legs around his hips, bringing him closer as she stroked his face. That glorious feeling started spreading inside of her and she wanted to tell him how important he was to her. Words failed her as she stared up at this brilliant man. Her heart was full for him.

But instead, she kissed him. As she fell apart around him, as he moaned against her lips, shaking in her arms, she knew she wanted a chance at love again and she had to find the courage to take it.

CHAPTER SIXTEEN

Jacob bent to pick up another shell from the beach and put it in his bag.

He and Ruby had agreed they were going to make their angel for the festival later that day out of shells so he'd left her in bed and gone down to the beach to collect some. He was studiously ignoring the sea as it crashed onto the shore a few metres from where he stood. The tide was in but there was still enough beach left to collect the shells.

Fortunately, he had something else to focus on. He couldn't get the night before out of his head. Sex with Ruby had been magnificent because for the first time in his life it hadn't just been sex. It had been two people who cared about each other a great deal making love.

He'd never thought he would ever utter those words to describe sex. He had described it in many ways, sometimes in the crudest terms, but he'd never *made love* to a woman before. But he knew, in his heart, that he couldn't describe what he'd shared with Ruby any other way.

He had to believe that she felt that too. He just had to give her time to realise it as well.

He looked in his bag. It looked like he had enough shells to make a smallish hollow sculpture with perhaps chicken wire or paper and cardboard on the inside. He made a move to go back up the steps that would take him to the cliff tops but he hesitated.

He turned and faced the waves. Two days from now, on Christmas Eve, was the Polar Bear Plunge and he was going to go in the sea for the first time in around twenty years. He felt sick at the thought and he hated that it scared him so much. He had loved the sea as a child – growing up in Newquay he had been on the beach and playing in the waves almost every day of his life – and then one day had taken away that love completely. He needed to get past this and he needed to do this for Ruby.

He stared at the waves, watching as they crashed onto the shore and then were sucked back into the sea. He stepped closer, feeling the spray on his cheeks.

Suddenly he felt a hand in his and he turned to see Ruby standing next to him, all wrapped up against the cold. She looked adorable.

He leaned down and gave her a kiss on the lips, the taste of her a punch to the gut.

He pulled back to look at her, wondering if the night before had meant as much to her as it did to him. She smiled at him and stroked his face.

She gestured to the waves. 'Are you psyching yourself up for the plunge?'

He smiled, weakly. 'Something like that.'

'You don't have to do it, you know. You don't have anything to prove to me or to the villagers.'

'I am doing it. How much money have you raised for the Polar Bear Plunge?'

She hesitated. 'Eight hundred and forty-six pounds.'

'That's eight hundred and forty-six reasons why I will be doing it.'

She sighed. 'Jacob, I'm sure they would all still pay that money if I did it alone. And if they don't then they don't. I set up these charity events in the hope that I would raise a few hundred pounds and I've already raised a hundred and eighty from the Christmas Cookie Competition yesterday. I'm more than happy with that. I don't want you to do anything you don't want to do.'

Jacob shook his head. 'I need to do this.'

'Why?'

He studied her face but he couldn't tell her.

'I just do, but having you there, by my side, that will make all the difference.'

'I'll be here.'

He smiled and kissed her on the forehead. 'Come on, we have an angel sculpture to make.'

~

Ruby looked at the materials that Jacob had laid out for them on his desk ready to start making their angel sculpture. It didn't look promising. She had specifically banned him from using any metal as that was his specialist material and she didn't want him to have too much of an advantage over the children of the village using toilet rolls. Eventually she'd relented and let him use chicken wire, but she didn't think that really counted.

As per the instructions she had put up on the forum, the villagers could use whatever material and tools they wished, and they could spend as much time on the sculptures as they wanted, but all the finished angels had to be placed in the village by noon. Ruby had been busy in her shop all morning, replenishing the stock and getting ready for any last-minute shoppers who might pop in today and tomorrow before the big day, so with only one hour until their sculpture had to be placed out on the street, she didn't have much hope.

Jacob brought out two steaming mince pies with brandy ice cream drizzled over the top and passed her one. 'To help inspire us.'

She grinned and took a bite; it tasted divine.

'Come on, let's get started with our masterpiece,' Ruby said, swallowing another mouthful and then putting her plate to one side.

Jacob rubbed his hands together. 'This is where I shine. I'm definitely going to win this one.'

She smirked at his confidence. 'What did you have in mind?'

'Are we going for the typical angel image, long flowing dress, feathery wings?' Jacob asked.

'Yes, I guess so.'

'OK, so I suggest we use this plasticine to make the basic shape. I use this sometimes to make little maquettes of the sculptures I make, kind of a rough model, before I start. We'll get the basic shape from that, add the chicken wire around the outside of the wings, then we can add the shells to the wire to get that feathery look.'

'OK, sounds good.'

Jacob opened a large box with creamy white plasticine inside and plonked a large blob on the table. 'This is the fun bit.'

They started squeezing the plasticine between them,

moulding it into the shape of a dress and the top half of the angel with the arms, head and wings.

'This is nothing like building our snowman,' Ruby protested. Whereas Jacob was shaping something beautiful, Ruby was seemingly creating an angel that had been hit by a bus, several times. Jacob was having to do her parts of the sculpture again, though he didn't seem to mind.

'Our snowman was something special,' he said. 'We should have made our angel sculpture out of ice and snow instead.'

'I think sadly our angel would have melted in here if we'd done that.'

'Yeah, you're probably right.'

They worked alongside each other in silence for a while as their angel slowly took shape. Watching Jacob sculpt, shape and smooth was fascinating.

'What made you become an artist?' Ruby asked, as she watched him work. 'When did you decide you were going to be Phoenix Blade?'

'I just loved making stuff as a child. This kind of thing would have been right up my street when I was young, making things out of cardboard boxes or clay or papier-mâché. I always had little models everywhere when I was growing up. I used to make aliens and monsters because with them there was no limit to my imagination. An alien could be any shape, size or colour. It could have five arms or twelve eyes and no one could say it was wrong. When other kids were out on the street playing football, this was how I wanted to use my spare time.'

'So the hobby turned into a job?'

'My mum always wanted me to be a doctor; I think she was a bit disappointed when I told her I wanted to be an artist.'

He paused for a moment and Ruby didn't know whether he was focussed on the sculpture or whether he was trying to find the right words for what he wanted to say next. He looked suddenly uncomfortable.

'I had a bit of a near-death experience when I was a kid.'

Ruby knew he was talking about the day he nearly drowned but she couldn't tell him she knew. 'What happened?'

He was silent as he smoothed out a bit of the wing and then he shook his head. 'It doesn't matter. But I realised that life is short and fragile and I had to get out of it what I wanted, to do the things I love the most. So I pursued this life. Not the life my mum wanted me to take or the life that my teachers encouraged me to follow. I never wanted to look back on my life and wish I'd done things differently. You have to seek out the things that make you happy and then fill your life with them.'

She smiled. 'I think those are very wise words. Do you think you have everything you need in your life to make you happy?'

He stared at her for a moment. 'I'm working on it.'

Her breath caught in her throat and she wondered if he was going to say something else, but whatever it was slipped away.

Jacob focussed his attention back on the angel. 'I think maybe we should just use the chicken wire around the outside of the wings so we can attach the shells and leave the rest of the angel as it is.'

'OK, but she needs hair.'

'Yes, we can do that too.'

Jacob had already cut some of the chicken wire into strips and they set about securing it around the wings and then fixing the shells on with tiny strips of wire thread through the holes he had drilled through the shells earlier.

'So tell me, what is it about Christmas that you love so much? I mean, a lot of people love Christmas but to make it your job, that's a whole other level of love for the season,' Jacob asked.

She smiled. 'I don't know really. I loved it as a child and I suppose I never really grew out of that. I always hated it when the Christmas lights and decorations came down and that joy and celebration was forgotten for another twelve months. I vowed that when I grew up, I would keep the magic of Christmas alive all through the year. I think for me that magic was the thing that I loved the most. I used to love hearing the story of Santa Claus, travelling around the whole world in one night, and it seemed like that magic cast a spell over everyone. It felt like, at that time of year, anything was possible.'

'I like that.'

She focussed her attention on the shells for a moment. 'When I got married to Harry, we talked about our plans for the future and although it had been my dream to have my own Christmas shop, I thought practically that maybe I should do something else that had a bit more of a reliable income. But Harry encouraged me to follow my dreams and do it. When he died, I knew it was something I had to do. I went to university to study business studies so it wasn't just a hobby but something I was taking seriously. And I suppose all the festive activities and increased custom helps to keep my mind off our anniversary too, it gives me something else to focus on.'

She looked up at Jacob and he was watching her.

'I can understand that. And I don't think you should ever give up on your dreams. In fact, I wanted to talk to you about one of your dreams—'

They were both distracted for a moment by shouting and laughter outside as some kids walked past the window outside, struggling under the weight of a six-foot angel. It looked like it had been made out of their mum's clothes and stuffed with newspaper, with a football for a head and a tinsel halo glued onto it.

Ruby giggled and turned her attention back to Jacob. 'What were you saying?'

He shook his head. 'It doesn't matter, let's get this finished, we haven't got much time.'

They finished off their angel as quickly as they could and stepped back to look at it.

It had actually turned out really well, with longer shells towards the bottom of the wings and the smaller ones towards the top so it really did look feathery.

'She's beautiful,' Ruby said.

Jacob nodded. 'We make a pretty good team, Ruby Marlowe.'

She smiled. 'Yeah, we do.'

They bundled themselves into coats and Jacob carefully picked up the angel and carried it outside. They walked up the high street where there was quite a crowd gathering, some people placing their sculptures around the village, some walking around and admiring each other's.

Jacob placed their angel in between a sculpture made from cardboard boxes and another made from plastic bottles. It was quite obvious that some of these sculptures had taken hours to make.

Ruby noticed Willow and Andrew placing a small sculpture that looked like it might be made from wax. Lottie and Poppy were standing near what might have been their sculpture, made entirely out of tinsel and other Christmas decorations.

She looked around and saw Megan and Lucas putting a sculpture outside the pub, this one made from hay and straw like some kind of bizarre wicker man that looked a bit sinister. They were chatting and laughing together. Ruby didn't know if they'd plucked up the courage to ask each other to the ball yet but the important thing was they were at least friends again. Ruby had meddled enough there and it had made things worse so she wasn't going to try it again.

'Look, I have to go to Penzance for a few hours. Sneak this ten-pound note into Poppy's jar for her sculpture, will you?' Jacob said.

Ruby smiled and nodded.

He bent his head to give her a kiss on the cheek but she moved to hug him and he caught her on the corner of her mouth instead.

He pulled back slightly and smiled, his eyes going dark, and he leaned forward and kissed her properly in full view of everyone else. For a second, she worried about what people would say but with his mouth on hers she found she suddenly couldn't care less. His mouth was warm and sweet, his stubble soft as she stroked his face.

He pulled back and his smile was even bigger. 'I'll be back this afternoon.'

He gave her another quick peck on the cheek and moved off through the villagers.

Ruby cleared her throat and straightened her hair and then turned round to see how many people had noticed their very public display of affection. Sadly it seemed quite a lot, as Andrew, Willow, Lottie, Poppy, Julia, Dorothy, Kitty, Ken and several others were all staring at her, mostly with delight at this new turn of events.

Ruby decided she'd brazen it out and move around the village to look at the sculptures as if nothing had happened.

She moved over to Kitty's sculpture. She too had used chicken wire to get the basic shape but she'd also used holly leaves and poinsettias woven into the wire to decorate it. It looked stunning and was certainly getting a lot of attention from the villagers, judging by the amount of money that was in the jar. Ruby slipped a pound coin into the jar and moved on to Lottie and Poppy's sculpture. She could see Poppy walking around the village with Andrew and Willow but Lottie was hanging back as she was replying to an email on her phone. As she finished and shoved her phone back in her bag, she looked up at Ruby and smiled.

'This is great,' Ruby said, admiring their sculpture that really did look like an angel, through all the glitter and sparkle.

'Thank you, and your sculpture looks amazing,' Lottie said.

'Oh, you know I can't take any credit for that. It was pretty much all Jacob, he's very talented.'

'He is,' Lottie said, proudly.

There was silence then and Ruby got the sense that she wanted to say something else.

'He really likes you,' Lottie said.

'Oh no, it's not like that,' Ruby said automatically, knowing that it probably was exactly like that.

'No, he does. I've never seen him like this with anyone before.'

Ruby shook her head.

'Listen, there was a guy I met about six months after Alex walked out and left us. He was staying at the hotel I was working at in Penzance. We just clicked. He was funny and brilliant and great with Poppy. We spent a few days together and, god, I think I fell in love with him. But when his stay came to an end, I pushed him away. I was still hurting after Alex left and I wasn't prepared to risk my heart again. So he left and I never saw him again. I have always regretted that. Don't make the same mistake I did. Jacob won't hang around forever waiting for you. He has a whole life in Penzance, his shop is there, he has friends, women who he used to date. It would be very easy for him to move back there unless he has a really good reason to make him want to stay.'

Ruby stared at her. The thought that Jacob might leave hadn't even occurred to her. She'd thought that she had time to get her head and heart used to the idea of being in a relationship again but it wasn't fair on Jacob to drag this out forever, making him wait while she came to a decision about whether she wanted a relationship or not.

'I know this is scary for you, but you don't want to look back on your life and regret the things you didn't do. I see the way you look at him and I think letting Jacob walk away would be the biggest regret of your life.'

Ruby swallowed down the lump of emotion that was caught in her throat. She put the money that Jacob had given her in Poppy's jar. 'That's from Jacob.'

Lottie smiled. 'He's a good man.'

'I know. Look, I better go and…' Ruby waved with her hand '…circulate.'

Lottie nodded and Ruby moved away.

Maybe she needed to talk to Jacob about all of this, ask him to be patient and give her more time.

Or maybe it was time she was brave and took this chance once and for all.

CHAPTER SEVENTEEN

Sitting in the pub later with Andrew, Willow, Lottie and Poppy, and enjoying the general buzz of happiness from the other villagers, Ruby couldn't help but smile about how everything had turned out in the last few days. The Angel Festival had been a big hit with over a hundred sculptures dotted about the village. Everyone had enjoyed making the angels and seeing everyone else's sculptures. Kitty had won with her holly leaf and poinsettia angel and generously matched all the money raised that day. Ruby didn't know what the final total would be, but she knew they had raised over a thousand pounds for the British Heart Foundation.

The villagers had welcomed her with open arms and she felt she had really brought something to the village and spread a bit of Christmas magic. She felt like she could really make a home here and not leave after a year, as had been her original plan when she'd first moved here. Regardless of what happened with Jacob, she knew she wanted to stay.

Although Jacob was another great big plus point. Things were going great between them and for the first time in twelve years she thought she might even be ready to have a proper relationship. He was good for her, in so many ways.

Suddenly everyone's phones started beeping at the same time and all the villagers fell quiet as they looked around at each other in confusion. Then Ruby noticed Lucy climbing on a chair and banging a glass to get everyone's attention.

'I've just sent a video to you all via the village forum. It's something you all need to see. I'm sure we all would like to know who cruelly stole Jesus from the nativity and has then been mocking us with these photos of Jesus all round the village.'

There was stifled laughter; obviously a lot of people found this a lot funnier than Lucy did. But unease settled into Ruby's stomach. If there was a video of the event, would it show her manhandling the poor sheep?

'I had my suspicions that it was Ruby Marlowe, as Jesus went missing the same night she arrived.'

Other people started nodding but again not taking this remotely seriously. Even Julia was nodding and Ruby wondered if she had known all along.

'So as my company supplied the webcam for the animals, I did a bit of digging. Fortunately we had recorded the night of the theft. I expected to find evidence of who had stolen Jesus, but what I found instead was truly horrifying and I wanted you all to see it.'

People started pulling their phones out of their pockets and bags and clearly began watching the video. There were sudden gasps around the room.

Ruby quickly grabbed her phone, found the video and pressed play to see what everyone was watching. The camera didn't show the nativity scene at all, it was just focussed on the little paddock. Ruby didn't come into shot until that fateful moment when the sheep started choking, but it was painfully obvious that it was indeed her. Ruby watched as she approached the sheep, stood behind it, wrapped her arms around it and started squeezing its belly. There were gasps around the room as Ruby smacked the sheep between the shoulder blades and more gasps of shock as Ruby lifted the back legs up in the air and got kicked in the leg herself as soon as the sheep stopped choking.

Ruby was then seen running away and the video stopped.

Crap. That looked awfully damning. Ruby knew the reasons why she had been abusing the sheep, but no one else did.

Ruby looked up at the villagers who were all staring at her aghast. The only ones not finding it horrifying were Andrew and Willow who were giggling quietly as they watched the video but their giggles faded as they realised how everyone else was reacting to it.

Willow stood up quickly.

'Wait! Although many of you believe this to be Ruby, the video is not of good enough quality to prove it was her without any reasonable doubt—'

'It's OK, Willow, everyone knows it was me.' Ruby stood up too, ready to defend herself, but who was going to believe that she was trying to do the Heimlich manoeuvre on a bloody sheep? It sounded ridiculous even to her own ears.

'Well, I'm sure Ruby has a very good explanation for what we've all just seen,' Willow went on.

Ruby cleared her throat. 'It is true that I stole Jesus from the nativity and I've been the one responsible for taking photos of him around the village and all the posts on the forum. But it was never my intention for it to be cruel or malicious, I was just having a little joke.'

'What about the poor sheep?' Lucy shouted.

'While I was there, I gave some carrots to the donkey and

the sheep, and one of the sheep started choking on the carrots and… well, I was trying to help it,' Ruby finished, lamely.

'A likely story,' Lucy said, who was obviously in full swing now and enjoying every moment of her discomfort.

The villagers started muttering between themselves.

'There you go, Ruby was trying to help one of the sheep,' Willow said, over the noise of the villagers. 'I'm sure none of us would have liked to have seen Minty die and we all would have done the same thing in Ruby's shoes.'

The villagers didn't seem convinced at all.

Well, the perfect day had suddenly turned out to be not so perfect after all.

Ruby grabbed her bag and pulled out Jesus, who was dressed in a snowman outfit for some more photographs she'd planned to take later on. She placed him on the table. 'I'm really sorry.'

And with that, she left the pub and no one tried to stop her.

Jacob was on his way back from Penzance and had just stopped to get some petrol when his phone beeped with notification of the video. As he got back in the car he clicked on the video. He watched in surprise as Ruby gave one of the sheep the Heimlich manoeuvre and was impressed that she would go to those lengths for a sheep. He was also pretty impressed she knew how to do it. But then he realised that it was Lucy who had posted the video and he doubted somehow that she had done it to share Ruby's heroic actions with the rest of the village. Lucy could very easily twist this somehow. Many of the villagers probably wouldn't recognise Ruby's actions as the Heimlich manoeuvre and would be less than happy to see what she was doing to the sheep. God, he didn't want to give Ruby any ammunition to run, their relationship already felt tentative enough as it was, with Ruby looking like she was set to flee at any moment. If the villagers turned against her because of this, that could be all the reason she needed to pack her bags and go.

He quickly started the engine and drove down the road to the village. As he approached, he saw Lucas fixing one of the fences and he had an idea. He pulled over and wound down his window.

'Lucas, I need your help, will you come with me?'

Lucas looked at him suspiciously. 'Is this to do with Megan?'

'No, but if you come with me, I'll make it worth your while in that regard.'

Lucas clambered in.

Jacob drove off before Lucas had even put on his seatbelt.

'Look, I was never going to ask Megan to the ball.'

'Then why did Ruby tell me that you were?'

'Because she was hoping it might prompt you to ask Megan instead.'

Lucas flushed. 'Why would I do that?'

'Because you like her, anyone can see that, and she's crazy about you. So put the poor girl out of her misery and ask her. I guarantee she will say yes. In fact, I'll put my money where my mouth is and pay you a thousand pounds if you ask her and she says no.'

Lucas was silent for a moment. 'What did you want help with?'

Jacob decided to let the subject go. He'd done enough and he had more pressing things to attend to.

He handed Lucas his phone. 'Watch that video.'

Lucas was silent for a moment as he watched it. 'Christ, she saved Minty's life.'

Jacob had no idea how Lucas could tell the difference between the two sheep but he was just glad that Lucas had recognised the scene for what it was.

'Yes, Poppy made me watch a video once on how to do a Heimlich manoeuvre on dogs. That's what Ruby was doing, wasn't she?'

'Yes, thank god she was there.'

'Anyway, I doubt anyone in the village would understand what she was doing. Lucy posted it on the forum and you can bet it wasn't for nice reasons.'

'God, that woman is a cow,' Lucas muttered.

'Exactly. I need you to help me do some damage limitation here, explain to the villagers what Ruby was really doing.'

'I don't do public speeches.'

'Ruby saved Minty's life,' Jacob said. 'Are you really going to hang her out to dry?'

Lucas paused for a moment and then nodded. 'OK, fine.'

Jacob pulled up outside the pub, hoping there would be some villagers in there he could talk to. Otherwise he had every intention of marching Lucas round every house and shop to make sure everyone knew the truth.

The pub was quite full but there was no sign of Ruby. Or Willow and Andrew for that matter. But Lucy was holding court at a packed table.

'I think it's disgusting,' she was saying. 'And certainly not the kind of behaviour we want in our village.'

'I'm sure there is some reasonable explanation for all of this,' Kitty said. 'What did Ruby say?'

'Some rubbish that the animal was choking, a likely story.'

'It's true,' Jacob said.

'Of course you would say that,' Lucy said.

'No, it is true,' Lucas said. 'Trust me, when you work with animals long enough, you learn all sorts of ways to help them.' He flicked through his phone. 'This is a video on YouTube on how to give the Heimlich manoeuvre to dogs. You'll see a striking similarity to what Ruby was doing to Minty.' Lucas showed the phone to Kitty and then passed it round the table for others to see.

Lucy's face fell.

'Well there you go,' Kitty said, folding her arms and looking at Lucy. 'I have to say, *this* is certainly not the kind of behaviour we want in our village. You deliberately posted this video on the forum to turn people against Ruby. Why would you do that?'

'I… I didn't. I just thought people had a right to know what she did to the sheep. I didn't realise she was helping it.'

'Well you could have asked her first, instead of humiliating her in front of the whole village,' Julia said.

'But that wouldn't have had the same effect, would it?' Jacob said. 'What was this, revenge because I asked her to the ball and not you?'

Lucy's cheeks flushed. 'Of course not.'

Jacob looked around the table. Everyone had seen the truth of it, despite her denials.

'I would never have asked you, Lucy,' Jacob said. 'As you said before, I only go out with the finest, most attractive women. And while you might be quite pretty on the outside, there is certainly nothing attractive inside.'

'I agree,' Kitty said. 'What you did was ugly. And if that kind of attitude continues I will be looking for someone else to fill your house once the year is up.'

Lucy stared at them in shock. It was safe to say her cunning plan had totally backfired and everyone knew it.

Jacob had seen enough. He nodded his thanks to Lucas,

who was busy uploading the dog Heimlich video onto the forum for everyone else to see, and turned and left.

~

'Come back to the pub, I'm sure we can sort it all out,' Willow said.

'I'm not exactly winning any popularity contests right now,' Ruby said, grabbing some baubles to paint. She needed to focus on something else right now. She had ruined everything.

'It was quite obvious to me you were trying to help the sheep, I'm sure everyone else will see that too,' Andrew said.

'This is such a mess,' Ruby sighed. 'I shouldn't have stolen Jesus, none of this would have happened.'

'It was just a joke,' Willow said. 'People found it funny.'

The door was pushed open and in walked Julia and Kitty.

Ruby stood up from where she was working, wondering if this was it and she was about to be asked to leave.

'Julia, I'm so sorry,' Ruby said.

'What are you sorry for?' Julia asked.

'For stealing Jesus and—'

'I knew it was you – as soon as I saw that picture outside the post office, I knew,' Julia said. 'Biggest laugh I've had in ages watching these photos of Jesus pop up in various costumes around the village. I'm not sure which was funnier, that or the bizarre penis candles that Willow arranged to be hung over the village.'

'And the Y-fronts,' Kitty added.

'What, wait, you saw they looked like penises too?' Willow said.

'Yes, of course, the whole village has been talking about it for weeks. The whole thing is hilarious. But we didn't tell you because we didn't want to upset you after you went to all the trouble of arranging the lights,' Julia said.

'I thought no one noticed,' Willow muttered.

Julia patted her arm consolingly and then turned to Ruby. 'Now about this sheep.'

'Oh god, Julia, I really was trying to help it.'

'I know.'

Ruby paused. 'You do?'

'Lucas came into the pub not long after you'd left. He'd seen the video and recognised it for what it was. He showed us videos of Heimlich manoeuvres on dogs on YouTube and we all could see that you were doing exactly what was in those videos with Minty. You saved his life, you're a hero.'

Ruby stared at them. 'I don't know about that. If I hadn't been stealing Jesus from the nativity, if I hadn't given the carrots to them in the first place, none of this would have happened.'

'None of that was done maliciously,' Kitty said. 'It was unfortunate what happened but you dealt with it in the best possible way.'

'Everyone thinks you're amazing,' Julia said. 'There's even talk of erecting a statue in your honour.'

'I think that's a wonderful idea,' Willow giggled.

'I'll get right on that,' Andrew said.

Ruby laughed. 'That might be going too far. Just as long as I can stay in the village, then I'm happy.'

'Of course you can stay, you're exactly the sort of person we want in this village,' Kitty said. 'Now, Lucy on the other hand. I made it very clear to her that that kind of spiteful attitude was not welcome here in Happiness and if she was to continue acting like she did today, she wouldn't be welcome to stay here once her year was up. We have a very long waiting list of people who want to live here and it would be very easy to fill her shoes. I told her to watch her step.'

'I'm so relieved. I think I upset Lucy because I got together with Jacob. I'm sure she'll get over it.'

'That's what Jacob said,' Kitty said.

'Jacob's back?'

'Yes, he's just moving his car to the car park. It was parked rather illegally outside the pub and I told him he needed to move it. But he certainly came into the pub all guns blazing ready to fight for you.'

'He did?' Ruby smiled.

Kitty nodded.

'Now, about you and young Jacob,' Julia started. 'I think we need some kind of clarification of what is happening between the two of you—'

'Oh shush, we're not here for that,' Kitty said.

Ruby laughed as Kitty hauled Julia away before she could grill her with any more questions.

The door closed behind them but actually that was exactly what Ruby wanted to talk to Jacob about too.

~

Ruby glanced over into Jacob's shop. He had come back an hour before with a huge smile on his face, given her a kiss, explained his take on what had happened in the pub with Lucy and then disappeared into his shop where he had been banging, cutting and welding on a very small piece of metal ever since. She wondered if he was making her necklace.

She wanted to talk to him but she couldn't find the right words to even begin to cover all the emotion and worry in her head. She wanted to tell him that she was prepared to give having a proper relationship a go. She wanted to say that she had feelings for him that went way beyond friendship. But the words simply wouldn't come out. Saying them out loud kind of felt like a huge sign to the universe that she was happy again and then it would all be taken away.

Ruby's shop door opened and Willow burst in, pulling Andrew along with her.

'Right, we're doing it now,' Willow said.

'What are we doing now?'

'I'm taking a pregnancy test. It's safe to say that ever since I've declared that I might almost definitely not be pregnant we've thought about nothing else. Now, online information varies saying I shouldn't take a test until one week after I'm late and some websites say I can take it the day after, so I bought three different tests and we're going to find out once and for all.'

'You're doing it here?' Ruby asked in surprise as Jacob wandered into her shop.

'Yes. You two are the only ones that know, so you should be there when we find out,' Willow said.

'Yes, apparently taking a pregnancy test is a group activity,' Andrew said, dryly.

'There are some things I'm quite happy not sharing,' Jacob said.

'Oh shush, it's not like I'm asking you both to watch me do it,' Willow said. 'I just want you there after, for better or worse. And once we're done, we'll say no more about it. I bought these tests from out of town so no one in the village knows and I won't get loads of people coming up to me and saying how sorry they are if I'm not pregnant. Andrew and I have agreed that we're not going to be disappointed if we're not pregnant. It's not really the right time anyway when we're not even married yet and we'd both like a bit more time just for the two of us. If we are pregnant that's great, but if we're not then that's great too.'

It sounded like she was trying to convince herself more than she was trying to convince them.

'Well, my bathroom is free for you to use,' Jacob said, gesturing to the stairs like he was showing off a fabulous prize.

Willow ran up the stairs and they heard the bathroom door close.

Ruby, Jacob and Andrew followed her up and sat on the sofa. Jacob flicked the TV on, presumably to drown out any bathroom noises or maybe just to pass the time.

They all stared at the screen as some TV show demonstrated how to baste a turkey.

'Well it's safe to say this is not how I imagined spending my afternoon,' Jacob said.

'We just need to know,' Andrew said, quietly. 'It's driving us mad. She wanted you there because she didn't want to have to tell you she wasn't pregnant and have to deal with all that emotion a second time. Despite what she says, she'll be really disappointed if she isn't pregnant, we both would.'

Jacob nodded. 'Yeah, I get that.'

Willow emerged carrying three white plastic wands.

'They're clean, I promise, and you don't have to touch them, just look at them. Jacob and Ruby, your tests will be ready in three minutes. Andrew, yours will be ready in five,' Willow said, laying a white plastic stick in front of each of them.

Jacob pulled out his phone and swiped the screen a few times. 'Right, I've set two timers.'

'Now, we're going to talk about something else, anything but this,' Willow said, gesturing to the three tests which held so much weight with the answers they would soon tell.

'OK,' Ruby said. 'Tell me the worst Christmas present you ever had.'

Willow laughed. 'Mine would be from my ex, Garry with two Rs. He bought me a new ironing board cover.'

Andrew laughed. 'But you don't iron. I've not seen you iron a single thing in the whole time we're together.'

'I know, I don't. Life's too short for that kind of rubbish. When I was dating Garry I never told him that I don't iron, I just made up loads of excuses, lack of time, dodgy iron, crappy ironing board cover. I suppose he thought he was doing me a favour by buying me a new cover. I had to pretend to be delighted when I opened that on Christmas Day.'

'Well there was me worrying about what to get you for Christmas,' Andrew said. 'But I think anything I buy will be better than that.'

'What's yours?' Willow asked.

'Mine was from Jacob,' Andrew said.

'Of course it was,' Jacob said, dryly.

'When we were kids, Jacob had this cool Millennium Falcon which I always wanted.'

Jacob let out a bark of laughter; obviously he knew where this was going.

'He never let me play with it but he would take great pleasure in playing with it in front of me,' Andrew went on. 'Anyway, one day, our dog Barney found it and chewed it up. After that Jacob didn't want to play with it anymore, but that Christmas I got it in my stocking. This half-chewed, deformed plastic spaceship. I wasn't impressed.'

'I thought I was being quite generous,' Jacob said.

'What's yours, Jacob?' Ruby laughed.

'I was sort of seeing this girl just before Christmas one year. We'd met up twice before so it wasn't exactly the greatest love story. Anyway, we met up on Christmas Eve and she'd obviously thought she probably should buy me something and made a last-minute dash to the garage. She gave me a toothbrush and a car air freshener.'

They all laughed.

'What did you get her?' Ruby asked.

'I didn't. I'm not sure what was worse, me opening up that crappy present or me not giving her anything in return.'

Ruby got up and moved over to the kitchen area. 'Does anybody else want a drink?'

They all shook their heads. Ruby grabbed a glass. 'Mine was a Secret Santa thing we all did in the market hall where I worked. Except I ended up with someone else's present, at least I think I did. It was a pair of elephant underpants for men, with the trunk area where the… penis goes.' They all roared with laughter. 'I'm not sure what I was supposed to do with that.'

Ruby grabbed a bottle of juice and started pouring just as Jacob's phone went off to indicate that the three minutes were up.

They all fell silent. Ruby moved back into the lounge but she felt too nervous all of a sudden to go round and have a look at her test.

Willow took a deep breath. 'Go on then Jacob, tell me, are you about to become an uncle?'

Jacob looked down at his test and no one spoke, no one even breathed. He didn't say anything for the longest time as Jacob continued to stare at it. He looked back up at Willow and shook his head. 'I'm sorry, it's a negative.'

Willow let out a heavy breath and Andrew put his arm around her. 'Well, it's probably for the best,' she said, her voice shaky.

Ruby moved to sit back down on the sofa, suddenly feeling so disappointed for her best friend.

She glanced at her pregnancy test.

'We have the rest of our lives together to make hundreds of little babies. Now isn't our time, but our time will come,' Andrew said, gently.

'I know,' Willow said, quietly.

Ruby stared at the test, but there was no mistake. 'Um, my test says you *are* pregnant.'

Everyone turned to look at her.

'What?' Willow said.

Ruby passed her the test. 'See for yourself.'

Willow stared at it and showed Andrew. 'It says I am pregnant.'

'Or not,' Andrew said, gesturing to Jacob's test. He turned to Jacob. 'Are you sure you're reading it right?'

Jacob handed it over.

'That definitely says I'm not,' Willow said. 'So which is it?'

'I've heard that pregnancy tests can give out false negatives but not false positives. Although I'm not sure if that's true,' Ruby said.

'I guess the third test will be the decider,' Willow said.

They all stared at the test lying in front of Andrew. Jacob checked his phone. 'You still have one minute to go until it's ready.'

No one said anything. That minute that slowly ticked by was the longest of Ruby's life. She wanted this for Willow and Andrew so much.

The timer went off and Andrew picked it up. He let out a heavy breath but it was the huge smile on his face that confirmed his answer. 'We're pregnant.'

'Oh my god,' Willow said. 'Oh my god. We're going to have a baby.'

'Yes we are.'

Willow hugged him.

'Congratulations,' Ruby said.

'Thank you,' Willow said, wiping tears from her eyes. 'I can't believe this. We're going to be parents.'

'And brilliant parents at that,' Jacob said. 'Congratulations.'

Ruby couldn't help smiling. They had this perfect little future laid out in front of them and, for the first time since Harry had died, she suddenly wanted that future too and she wasn't afraid to take it.

CHAPTER EIGHTEEN

Ruby was waiting for Jacob in his flat while he got changed in his bedroom. They were going off to the carol service around the tree together. She was sure that everyone in the village would have some thoughts on that but she didn't really care. They could hardly keep their semi-relationship a secret.

Jacob came out of his room, dressed in a thick jumper and carrying what looked like a black watch box.

'I have your new necklace in here. I apologise for the box, but it was the only one I had.'

Ruby's heart fluttered at the prospect of wearing it and what that actually meant. 'You didn't have to put it in a box at all.'

'Well I did, because if you decide to wear it, I wanted you to have somewhere safe for your other necklace.'

She smiled at this lovely gesture. He knew what a big deal it was to take Harry's necklace off and replace it with his.

She swallowed. 'Well, let's see it.'

He opened the box and she stared at the beautiful silver

Christmas tree that shimmered in the light. The baubles were made from tiny pieces of coloured metal and on the top was a star that glittered with gold.

'Oh Jacob, it's wonderful, thank you so much.'

'You don't have to wear it tonight,' Jacob said.

She looked up at him. 'I want to.'

He paused. 'Are you sure?'

She nodded.

He moved round behind her and she lifted her hair. His warm fingers at the base of her neck was an incredible feeling. He unhooked Harry's necklace and Ruby pushed down the feeling of panic that started to rise in her. He moved back to the box, took out the Christmas tree and carefully laid the snowflake inside. Then he came back to her and fastened the Christmas tree around her neck.

She admired how it looked in the long mirror near the door. It was beautiful. 'Thank you.'

'It looks good on you. I've never made any jewellery before, so this one was a bit of a challenge.'

'Well you did a wonderful job.'

She carefully closed the lid on Harry's necklace. Baby steps.

'Let's go and sing our hearts out,' Jacob said, pulling his coat and hat on.

Ruby did the same. 'You'll regret saying that when you hear me sing.'

They went downstairs and left the shop. They started walking up the high street and Jacob slipped his hand into hers. She looked up at him and smiled. This felt so right. Tiny snowflakes were falling, the Christmas lights were twinkling and she was holding hands with the most wonderful man she had ever met.

She was scared, of course she was. She had successfully

avoided all relationships for the last twelve years, only ever seeing men casually, and now she had been in Happiness for only a few days and was on the verge of starting a proper relationship. They had something special and running away or denying those feelings was not the answer. She didn't know whether she'd be any good at being in a relationship but if they were really going to do it, she was going to give this her all.

They came to the end of the high street and there, on the grassy slopes leading up to the castle, villagers were gathering around the tree. It looked like something out of those old-fashioned Christmas cards with everyone bundled up in hats and scarves, the big tree in the middle, the snow glittering on the ground, children running around and chasing each other, the adults all holding their song sheets. The only anachronism in the scene was that Julia had wheeled out a large electric keyboard and a small generator and was currently practising a few chords while everyone got themselves ready to start. She spied them as they drew close and waved them over, holding out the song sheets.

'Come along, we're just about to get started,' Julia scolded.

Ruby reached out for the song sheet when Julia caught her hand.

'So you arrive here holding hands, you've spent the last two nights at his flat, we saw you kissing at the Angel Festival yesterday – are you two a thing now?' Julia waggled her eyebrows.

Ruby blushed, horribly aware that the villagers had fallen silent behind her. They all wanted to know too. Was nothing private in this place?

She looked at Jacob. They hadn't talked about whether or not they were going to tell people about their new 'friends-with-benefits' arrangement and things seemed to have moved on quite a bit since then, although they hadn't properly discussed that either. She didn't want all the villagers sticking their oar in – this was still so new for her and Jacob and they were quite capable of cocking it up on their own without outside interference. But there was a part of her that was very excited about this development and she wanted to shout about it. Jacob still wasn't saying anything, he was leaving it up to her.

'We're… trying it out,' Ruby said, lamely.

'Trying it out?' Julia said.

'Yes, like buying a new jumper or a pair of shoes,' Jacob said. 'If we don't like it we can take it back to the shop and exchange it for a different pair.'

The villagers tittered and Jacob took the song sheet and moved over to the villagers, disappearing to stand near the back.

Crap. Ruby had clearly pissed him off with her answer.

She took the song sheet and made her way over to the tree. Should she join him, should she not? God, this was all so complicated all of a sudden. She was saved from making that decision by Willow snagging her arm and pulling her into her side.

Her friend gave her a hug and Ruby held her tight.

'Are you OK?' Willow whispered in her ear before stepping back to look at her.

Ruby nodded. 'I really am.'

Willow smiled and linked arms with her as Julia started playing the first few bars of 'Silent Night'. The villagers turned their attention to their song sheets and started singing.

'So are you and Jacob…?' Willow said over the sound of the music.

'I'm not sure how you could define what we have right now. It seems more than what we had before but we're not there yet,' Ruby explained, knowing they weren't there because she wasn't quite ready yet. 'And evidently I'm making a huge success of it,' she gestured to Jacob grumpily staring at his song sheet.

'I shouldn't worry, he always has that face on,' Andrew said.

'You're out of practice,' Willow said. 'And what were you supposed to say when standing in front of the whole village like that?'

'I don't know,' Ruby sighed. 'I should go and see him.'

She kissed Willow on the cheek and walked over to Jacob. He glanced at her and she nudged him playfully. He smiled and wrapped an arm around her shoulders, kissing her head.

Well it seemed she was forgiven. She leaned into him and listened to the villagers sing their hearts out, some of them had wonderful voices.

The song ended and Julia moved seamlessly into 'We Wish You a Merry Christmas'.

Jacob started singing and she looked up at him in surprise. He had a beautiful voice, all deep and theatrical. He gave her a little nod of encouragement. He certainly wasn't going to be impressed in a minute.

She took a deep breath and, as the villagers started singing about figgy pudding, she joined in with great gusto. His eyes widened as he registered just how bad her singing voice was and then he laughed. Ruby carried on singing and Jacob hugged her closer to him.

'I really bloody like you, Ruby Marlowe,' Jacob said.

She smiled. She had a feeling that this Christmas was going to be a good one.

Ruby woke up with a huge smile on her face the next day. There was glorious sunshine outside the window, the snow had stopped falling but it had settled nicely in the street and on the roofs opposite. The sun made it sparkle and shimmer. It looked like a Christmas card scene outside. But the thing that was making her smile was Jacob Harrington wrapped around her; it really was the best possible way to wake up. However, much as she wanted to stay there with him for the rest of the day, there was probably tons to be done.

As she became more awake she realised what day it was. December 23rd. There was maybe two or three seconds when she didn't make the connection, when she was thinking of the day ahead, making some more decorations just in case there was some last-minute shoppers coming in before the big day, the Polar Bear Plunge the next day. And then as she woke up more fully, it hit her like a ton of bricks.

Today was her anniversary. Today, thirteen years ago, she'd got married to her best friend and the love of her life. She had woken up wrapped in Harry's arms on the morning of the wedding because they'd not held much stock in the superstition of not seeing the bride before the ceremony. They'd known they were forever; they didn't need to worry about silly little things like spending the night before the wedding apart. He'd kissed her, told her he'd loved her and then they'd made love. And then after, as he held her in his arms, he'd told her of his plans for their honeymoon – she'd had no idea what he'd been planning. They were to fly out to New York late that night to see the big tree at the Rockefeller Center and, after she stopped squealing in delight, they'd made plans to see all the big trees of the world. God, it still hurt when she thought about him and everything they had missed together.

It didn't feel right waking up with another man today,

almost as if she was betraying Harry's memory, which was ridiculous.

She wanted that future with Jacob but suddenly all those memories of the pain she went through when Harry died came flooding back, and that fear and panic of letting herself fall in love with Jacob and losing him slammed into her hard.

Jacob stirred next to her and she tried to push all these feelings away.

He smiled sleepily when he saw her and leaned over and kissed her.

'I love waking up next to you,' Jacob said. 'I love that kissing you is the first thing I do in the morning and the last thing I do at night. You make me smile so much.' He frowned as he stared at her. 'I never wanted forever before but I want that with you. I know we agreed no-strings-attached but I have to tell you, I love you.'

Panic ripped through her at those words.

'I was going to wait until Christmas Eve to give this to you as you're my Secret Santa, but I'd like to give this to you now,' Jacob said.

He leaned over and pulled out an envelope from the bedside drawers and handed it to her. She sat up in bed to open it. She slid out the contents and stared at them.

'It's two tickets to Italy. I thought you might want to finally go and see the largest Christmas tree in the world on Mount Ingino. We fly out on Boxing Day.'

God, it was happening all over again, the declaration of love, the trip to see the Christmas tree. What if what happened next was losing him just like she lost Harry?

'I need some air,' Ruby said, scrambling up from the bed.

She started throwing on some clothes and then moved out into the living area of the flat.

Everything was happening so quickly and she didn't like it.

She had arrived in Happiness not wanting another relationship and Jacob had got right under her skin. They had progressed from friends, to friends with benefits, to… whatever this was and she wasn't ready. Cal had said she was living this half-life, but she'd been relatively happy, she certainly hadn't had to deal with all this kind of emotional stress when she'd been free and single. She'd been content in her little bubble and at least she'd never get hurt.

Jacob followed her into the lounge.

'What's going on?'

'You, this,' she waved the tickets in the air. 'We agreed that we would have no-strings-attached sex, be friends with benefits, nothing more, and now you're telling me you love me and want to whisk me off to Italy,' Ruby said.

'We have something special Ruby, you know that. There are strings whether you want them or not.'

Ruby shook her head. 'No, I don't feel that way,' she said, knowing that she was saying things she didn't really mean out of panic.

But that was the problem. There *were* strings, tying his heart to hers, she could feel that and she knew how much it would hurt if those tethers were to snap.

He stared at her for the longest time.

'God, I'm so stupid,' Jacob said. 'I should have let you walk away the other day when we first slept together, when you said sleeping with me was a mistake. That hurt but letting myself fall in love with you and knowing you don't feel the same hurts even more. It hurts that you won't risk your heart on me, that I'm not considered worth the risk. I'm good for sex but not a lot else. I thought you might start to see things differently, that with time you might fall in love with me too, but that's not going to happen, is it?'

'I just…' Ruby trailed off, struggling to find any words to

defend herself. She wanted to ask for more time but was that fair? What if she could never give him that? She glanced over to the watch box which currently held Harry's necklace and she felt that pain and fear slam into her again.

'Jesus Ruby, I can't do this again.'

'What does that mean?'

'I've been here before, falling in love with someone who only ever saw me as a friend. I waited and waited and she never saw me like that. If you genuinely don't see us going that way, then I need to get out now before I fall in love too deeply.'

He was breaking up with her. She felt one of the tethers tying him to her break, and god that hurt. She was going to lose him and she couldn't help the sob that escaped her lips. But maybe it was better this way. Better to watch him walk away now than fall in love with him completely and lose him so cruelly again. Maybe this was the out she needed. She had been on an emotional rollercoaster since she'd arrived in the village and she suddenly wanted to get off.

'If you want that life, marriage, children, the happy ever after, then you need to find someone else,' Ruby said. 'I thought I could have that life, I tried, I really did, but I can't do it. You need to find someone that can.'

She ran from the room, went downstairs and out onto the street. She leaned against the wall, sagged to her knees and burst into tears. What the hell had she just done? She was supposed to feel free, relieved. She hadn't wanted a relationship and now she'd got what she wanted. But why did her heart feel like it had been smashed into smithereens again? She had been scared of losing him but she had lost him anyway. She put her head in her hands and sobbed. She didn't love Jacob, she didn't. So why did it hurt so much?

CHAPTER NINETEEN

Ruby knocked on the door of Willow's cottage. Snow swirled around her. It wasn't the slow dance of soft gentle snowflakes, but angry flakes of ice that whipped against her face.

Andrew opened the door, wearing only his jeans as he pulled a jumper on. It was clear he had only just woken up.

'Oh god, I'm sorry. I didn't mean to disturb you.'

'You didn't, you're fine. I need to get up anyway, I was just being lazy,' Andrew said.

She looked at her watch to see it was only half eight in the morning, hardly the greatest lie-in.

He gestured for her to come in and closed the door behind her. 'Willow's out, I'm afraid. She had some last-minute Christmas shopping to do, so she got up early and went to Penzance.'

'Oh,' Ruby said, feeling disappointed that her best friend wasn't there to hold her hand.

Andrew put a gentle hand on her arm. 'I can offer a shoulder to cry on if you need it.'

She smiled weakly.

'Let me make you a cup of tea,' Andrew said. 'And I could rustle up some pancakes if you're hungry. And if you feel like pouring out your heart to me, then I'm a good listener.'

Ruby nodded and followed him through to the kitchen. She wasn't sure if she should talk to Andrew or not. It didn't seem right talking to him about his brother. Although maybe he was the perfect person to talk to.

'So how's the shop going?' Andrew asked as he started making the pancake batter and mugs of tea. She smiled because she knew he was making polite conversation, to distract her.

'Good, the villagers seemed to like it. How are the renovations in the old shop going?'

'We're doing OK, but it will still be a couple of weeks before you can move back in.'

Ruby nodded. God, that was going to be awkward having to be next door to Jacob for the next few weeks now that whatever they'd had between them had ended so badly.

Andrew started cooking the pancakes and she felt the tears well in her eyes again.

How had it come to this?

Thirteen years ago today she was marrying the man of her dreams. Twelve years ago today she had been in pieces over Harry's death and now she was crying over another man.

She had thought she'd gotten over Harry's death – she certainly hadn't cried over him for many years – but being with Jacob made all these feelings and emotions bubble back to the surface. She knew that was because Jacob was the first man since Harry who had made her feel that way again and she remembered feeling that way before and then losing it all.

'Hey, come on,' Andrew said, placing down a plate of pancakes with chopped bananas and fruit on the side. 'Whatever my brother has done, I'm sure it can't be that bad. I'm sure he'll be banging on your door to apologise in the next hour or so.'

Ruby smiled, sadly, at Andrew's assumption that it must be Jacob's fault she was upset.

She pierced a bit of pancake on her fork and ate it. It tasted delicious but she was suddenly not very hungry.

'Your brother didn't do anything, other than tell me he loved me.'

'Ah, I see.'

'And then I told him I couldn't do it anymore, I couldn't be what he wanted,' Ruby said, tearfully.

'Oh crap.'

'Exactly. What kind of idiot says things like that to a wonderful man like Jacob when he tells her he loves her?'

'You're not an idiot, Ruby. You're just… broken. It takes time to heal and Jacob needs to realise that.'

'It's been over twelve years since Harry died. And the thing is, I can't even say that I'm still in love with him, even though a piece of my heart will always belong to him. It's just the pain of losing him I remember the most and that fear of letting myself fall in love with Jacob and it happening all over again.'

'That fear is not going to stop you falling in love with him, it will only stop you acting on it. But running away is not going to change those feelings for him,' Andrew said, kindly. 'And what happens if you keep pushing Jacob away and one day he starts going out with someone else, marries them, has children with them? You would have lost him anyway and it has nothing to do with the grim reaper.'

Ruby stared at him, knowing what he said made total sense. She'd lost Jacob now and it hurt so much.

'I'm not saying you should declare your love for him now and whisk him off to the nearest registry office this afternoon.

You need time to get used to the idea of being in a relationship again and Jacob needs to be patient enough to give you that. But if you feel even half what he feels for you then you need to give this a chance.'

'I don't want to hurt him.'

'But isn't it better to hurt him because you both gave it your best shot than hurt him because you gave up on him before it even started?'

Ruby pushed a piece of her pancake around her plate as she thought about this.

'That fear is never going to go away until you face it. It's like being scared of spiders or snakes or clowns, you can avoid them but the only way you can get rid of that fear is to pick one up and hold it in your hand.'

'I'm not holding a clown in my hand.'

Andrew laughed. 'No, fair point.'

'What if that fear never goes away? What if I hold the snake every day for the rest of my life and that fear of it biting me is with me every day?'

'It will get easier; I promise you that. It doesn't mean you won't worry about him, but surely a life with the man you love, if you do feel that way about him, has got to be better than a life without him.'

Ruby stared at her pancakes for a moment. She had lived most of her adult life without the man she loved. Over the last few days she had glimpsed what it could be like being in a relationship with Jacob and she didn't want to lose that. She couldn't. In many ways it would be like losing Harry all over again.

She stood up. 'I need to talk to him.'

'Go,' Andrew gestured.

'I'm sorry about the pancakes,' Ruby said, knowing that even if she stayed she still couldn't eat them.

Andrew picked up her plate and slid the pancakes onto his own. 'I am eating for two now.'

She laughed and bent down and kissed him on the cheek. 'Thank you.'

'It's my pleasure.'

Ruby smiled and left the house.

~

Jacob drove his car down the winding narrow lanes. He'd needed to get out so he didn't have to stare at the walls of his flat and replay that fateful conversation over and over again. Except now he was sitting in his car feeling sorry for himself and still replaying that bloody conversation.

He was an ass. He'd pushed her and she'd bolted like a frightened animal. He should have known better than that.

But the way she had easily thrown their relationship away hurt. When times got tough her answer was to run rather than face it and talk things through. How could they ever make a relationship work with that attitude?

Although what had she been supposed to say when he'd told her he needed to get out of their relationship now? That hadn't exactly been a loving and supportive attitude either.

He had no idea what he was going to do now. He wanted to fight for her but if they stood any chance of making this work she had to fight for them too.

He came to a stop at a little roundabout. He could go straight on towards Penzance or turn the car round and go back to Happiness.

He was still hurting because the sad reality was she didn't want him as much as he wanted her.

He put the car into first and drove straight on.

CHAPTER TWENTY

Ruby left her house and made her way down towards the beach ready to do the Polar Bear Plunge the next day. It was Christmas Eve but she wasn't feeling remotely festive. Tomorrow was Christmas Day and although Cal was coming later she couldn't get excited about that either. She had been looking forward to spending the day with Jacob but that wasn't going to happen now.

The day was bitterly cold, the wind hadn't abated from the day before, the clouds were a slate grey. It was not a good day to go swimming in the sea. But there were lots of villagers walking towards the beach ahead of her so she knew she had to do this. Entertainment was clearly thin on the ground round here and they all wanted to watch Ruby freeze her arse off in the cold sea.

She had spent most of the day yesterday looking for Jacob but when Julia had told her she'd seen him leave the village in his car, Ruby had returned to her shop to wait for him. She knew that even if he went straight up to his flat, he'd have to walk through his own shop to do that and she'd see him. But he hadn't come back. She had called and texted him but he hadn't returned any of her messages. Kind of ironic that she had done the same to him a few months before. And now it was looking pretty likely he wouldn't be there for the Polar Bear Plunge either and, after the way she had treated him the day before, she couldn't blame him. He hadn't wanted to do this Polar Bear Plunge anyway so he was probably as far away from here as possible right then.

She couldn't be angry at Jacob, none of this was his fault. He'd told her he loved her and bought her tickets to Italy to fulfil her dream to see the world's largest Christmas tree and she'd thrown it back in his face. She had to try and fix this but she had no idea how. The thought of entering into a proper relationship with him thrilled her and terrified her in equal measure but the part of her that wanted this now far outweighed the part that didn't.

She wrapped her coat around her tighter. The Mrs Claus costume she was wearing was skimpy and quite honestly completely ridiculous. Thankfully she was wearing her bathrobe and her coat over the top which she was only going to take off just before the swim, but she was still cold.

Ruby made her way down the steps that led to the beach, her heart heavy.

When she reached the bottom she could see that it was fairly crowded for a cold winter's day. The waves were crashing on the shore, big white foamy horses thundering onto the sand. Definitely not the best day to take a swim.

She looked around for Willow and found her next to Andrew, Kitty and Ken. Ruby wandered over to join them. Willow smiled at her as she reached them.

'Hello Ruby,' Kitty said. 'Are you ready to throw yourself into the icy waves?'

'Not really,' Ruby forced a laugh. 'But at least it will be over relatively quickly.'

Ken leaned round Willow and Andrew to talk to her. 'I've screened off the cave over there so you can get changed straight after into something warm. I've put some large towels in there too.'

Ruby nodded and held up her bag. 'Thank you. I have some spare clothes in here.'

'Why don't I go and take that into the cave for you,' Kitty said, taking the bag and walking off to a large cave cut into the cliff face

'Oh, there's Lucas. I'll just go and see if he managed to get me a loudspeaker,' Ken said, hurrying over to the steps where Lucas had just arrived.

Ruby turned her attention back to Willow and Andrew.

'Are you OK?' Willow said, giving her a hug. 'Andrew told me you and Jacob ended things.'

'We had a fight; it was my fault. I overreacted because yesterday was mine and Harry's anniversary.'

'I know, I told him that. His timing was awful.'

'You spoke to him? Is he OK?' Ruby asked.

That was the worst thing about all of this, that she had broken his heart with her stupid fears and inability to move on.

'Yes, I spoke to him about five minutes ago,' Willow gestured to the sea.

Ruby looked where she was pointing and her heart leapt.

Jacob wasn't hard to spot. Probably around six foot five and dressed in a bright green elf outfit with candy-striped socks, he actually stuck out like a sore thumb as everyone else was bundled up against the cold. He was standing near the sea, staring out over the waves.

God, he was here and he'd come for her. After everything

she'd said and done and knowing how much he hated and feared the sea, he was really going to do this just for her. He was an incredible man. Her heart filled with love for him. And then it hit her with the force of a bus. She was in love with this amazing man and it wasn't just this moment of clarity that made her love him. Truth be told, she'd had these feelings for him all along, she'd just refused to acknowledge them before.

But today Jacob was facing his fears, so it was about bloody time she faced hers too.

She started moving down towards the shore. Several people wished her good luck as she passed and she nodded and smiled, but her eyes were fixed on Jacob who was still staring out over the waves.

He was an impressive sight in his skin-tight costume. He hadn't lost any of his grandeur because of the ridiculous green jacket and shorts he was wearing. His strong back muscles stood out across his shoulders and the arms of the jacket bulged. The shorts were especially tight across the bum, something she couldn't help but appreciate as she drew closer.

She reached his side and he glanced briefly at her before returning his attention to the sea.

'I'm sorry I took so long to come back. Getting this elf costume was a lot harder than I thought.'

Oh god. Was that really what had kept him away?

He turned to face her. 'I'm very sorry about yesterday morning.'

'Please don't apologise, you didn't do anything wrong.'

'I did. You were very clear about having a friends-with-benefits arrangement. I shouldn't have tried to move the goal-posts. And I was an insensitive ass. I forgot it was your anniversary. I should have been there to support you and instead I just made things even more difficult for you.'

'I'm the one that needs to apologise. I overreacted. I woke

up and remembered my anniversary, remembered how happy I was that day marrying the love of my life and how much it hurt when it all came to a crashing end. And I got scared. Everything has been so lovely and perfect between us and I got scared of losing it all over again. Of losing you.'

'You'll never lose me, Ruby. I will always be here for you. As a friend.'

As a friend. Christ, that wasn't good.

He turned to look at the sea. 'Right, let's do this before I chicken out completely.'

And before she could say anything, he was suddenly running into the waves.

'Crap,' Ruby muttered.

He didn't hesitate as the sea crashed around him, he dived head first into the water and then started swimming through the surf, his powerful body pulling him easily through the waves.

Ruby watched him in awe for a moment.

She quickly ditched her coat and bathrobe on the sand and this caused a small cheer from the onlookers. She toed off her shoes and ran out into the sea, the icy waves crashing over her and knocking her backwards. The water was so cold, it actually hurt. She waded up to her waist, her legs going numb. The waves were so big she couldn't see Jacob at all, which was more than a little worrying.

Jacob's elf hat floated past her on the top of a wave and she grabbed it and looked around. Where the hell was he? It was ridiculous to suddenly feel scared for him but the thought of something happening to him out here filled her with dread.

A huge wave came thundering towards her and she tried to jump over it but mistimed it. It hit her hard in the stomach and sent her staggering backwards, she lost her footing and the wave crashed over her head. She fell back and landed on her bottom on the sand.

She coughed and spluttered and wiped the water from her eyes. She looked up and saw Jacob wading back out the water towards her and her heart soared with relief.

And although he was wearing a silly elf costume, he looked like a Greek Adonis, with his curly black hair and his ill-fitting clothes clinging to him *everywhere*, showing him in his magnificent glory.

He frowned when he saw her and knelt in front of her.

'Are you OK?'

She reached out and stroked his face. 'I am now.'

She needed to tell him how she felt, but not here, in front of everyone.

'How was it out there?' Ruby asked, playing for time and because everything she wanted to say was a jumble in her mind.

'It's a bit rough out there today,' Jacob said, running his hand through his hair but a small smile appeared on his face. 'It was actually really great to be back in the sea again after all this time.'

She grinned. 'I'm so glad you're OK. Are you going back in?'

He shook his head. 'I think we've done enough for one day.'

He stood back up and offered out his hand. She took it and he helped her to her feet. She scooped up her bathrobe and wrapped it around her. She offered out her coat to Jacob and he laughed and shook his head.

'I think that will fit me even less than this ridiculous costume.'

They walked back up the beach and people stopped them to congratulate them. They became separated and Ruby hurried up into the cave to get changed. She slipped behind the screen and started undressing and was standing there completely naked trying to get her clothes out of her bag when Jacob stepped inside the cave.

'Crap, sorry,' Jacob said, turning away slightly.

'Don't be daft. You've seen me naked before.' And hopefully would again.

Ruby grabbed one of the big towels and draped it around his shoulders. He turned to watch her. She shivered a little and he caught the ends of the towel and wrapped them around her, bringing her into his arms and holding her close against him.

'They say, if you're exposed to the cold, you're supposed to share body heat,' Jacob said.

She could feel his heart thundering against his chest.

'Is that what this is?' Ruby said, wrapping her arms round his back.

'I have no idea what this is. Are you wanting to go back to the friends-with-benefits arrangement again?'

'No, I definitely don't want that,' Ruby said. She swallowed and slid her hands up to his face. 'You are the most amazing man I have ever met. That you just dived into the freezing cold sea, when you haven't been in there for twenty years, and you did that for me…'

'You know about that?' Jacob said.

'Yes and I just…'

She had no more words to describe how he made her feel so she leaned up and kissed him briefly on the lips. She watched the spark of desire ignite in his eyes. He bent his head and kissed her hard.

The taste of him was sublime as he kissed her. He wrapped his arms around her tighter and a tiny moan of need fell from her lips. The noise seemed to spur him on, and he slid his tongue into her mouth, caressing his hands down her naked body. The towel fell to the ground and she wrestled his wet top from his body. He shuffled her back against the cave wall, barely taking his mouth from hers for a second. She hooked a leg around his hips, kissing him, touching him.

A child's laughter from outside brought the world back into focus again and she suddenly remembered where she was.

She put a hand to Jacob's chest and he stopped kissing her, searching her eyes intently.

They needed to talk but not here where people could hear them, not here where they couldn't celebrate their love for each other properly.

'Why don't we go back to mine to warm up?'

Jacob looked round the cave and nodded. 'I think that's an excellent idea.'

They quickly got dressed, which seemed slightly counter-intuitive considering her plans for getting warmed up.

They grabbed their things and left the cave only to be met with a big cheer. Ruby blushed, knowing what the villagers would have heard if she hadn't stopped it from going any further. She suppressed a smile when she saw Jacob holding his costume and towel discreetly in front of his jeans.

'Well done, you two,' Ken said. 'You've both raised a lot of money for a very worthy cause.'

'I think those congratulations are mainly for Jacob,' Ruby said. 'But I'm just very grateful to everyone for sponsoring us.'

'Well shall we all go off to the pub to celebrate? We have mulled wine and hot chocolate ready to warm everyone up,' Kitty said and there was another collective cheer of approval from the villagers and many of them started making for the steps, Ken leading the way.

'That sounds lovely…' Ruby said. Jacob cleared his throat. 'But I think I'm going to have a shower first to warm up.'

Jacob nodded his approval. 'That sounds like a good plan.'

Kitty's eyes slid between her and Jacob and she smiled. She obviously knew what was going to happen between the two of them. 'Well maybe you can come along later.'

Ruby nodded and Kitty gave her a squeeze on the shoulder.

They followed the villagers up the steps but it was very slow progress and she couldn't help looking at Jacob and giggling at how frustrated he was getting.

They reached the top and started making their way up the hill but the villagers in front of them were certainly in no hurry and many of them wanted to talk and congratulate them. She could see her house now ahead but it still seemed like a million miles away as they tried to circumnavigate around the villagers.

Finally they got there. She walked up to the front door and opened it, moving inside the warmth of her house. She held the door open and, without a second's hesitation, Jacob stepped inside and closed the door behind him.

CHAPTER TWENTY-ONE

She quickly made a fire and then she turned round to face him.

There were two seconds, maybe even three, when they stood and stared at each other before she stepped forward to kiss him. Or maybe he moved forward to kiss her. It didn't seem to matter because they were kissing, his large hands spanning her back, her arms round his neck, his body against hers.

She pushed his coat off his shoulders while he made short work of the buttons on her coat, dumping that on the floor too. She ran her hands down his sides, caught the hem of his jumper and t-shirt and slipped them over his head.

He yanked her jumper off and then he was kissing her neck, her shoulder, stroking his hands down her body.

He kissed her again. There was something so utterly wonderful about kissing this man. An immense sense of this was where she belonged.

He suddenly snatched his mouth from hers and groaned. 'Christ Ruby, I can't do this with you. I *really* wish I could but I can't have no-strings-attached sex with you anymore. You were right, it means more to me than it does to you and I can't do it. I thought about this a lot yesterday and I know I was a complete dick but breaking up was for the best. You got it right when you first came to the village, we really are better off being friends.'

God, this wasn't going at all to plan. She had to tell him how she felt.

'Wait, no, you don't understand. I love you.'

Jacob went very still.

'I love you Jacob Harrington. I think I always have. From the first moment we met, you got under my skin and I couldn't let you go. I wasn't ready to fall in love again but that didn't mean I didn't have those feelings for you. I kept pushing them away, told myself it was lust and nothing more. Told you nothing could happen between us. But you got it right, you knew. I was scared of how I felt and I was trying to run away from that. And yesterday I freaked out because it was my wedding anniversary, because I remembered what it was like to be so blissfully happy and then to have all of that snatched from me. But I'm not scared anymore. A life with you has got to be better than a life without you. You make me happy, Jacob, and I want that life with you. I want to fulfil our dreams and then make new ones together. I love you so—'

His mouth was on hers hard and she couldn't help the tears that were falling as he continued to kiss her. Clothes were removed in quick succession, his, hers, until they were both naked and he was shuffling her back onto the rug. She had enough time to snag the box of condoms that Julia had forced her to buy a few days before and threw it onto the rug and then she was on the floor and he was over her, kissing her again, touching, stroking, caressing everywhere until she was humming with need for him. He grabbed a condom from the box and tore his mouth from hers for just a second while he ripped it open and slid it on and was inside her a second later. He pulled back to look at her, trembling as she held him.

'I love you too, Ruby Marlowe. I probably should have mentioned that back there,' he gestured to the door where they'd been a few minutes before.

She giggled. 'Timing is everything.'

He moved against her slowly and she wrapped her arms and legs around him.

'I love you,' Ruby whispered against his lips.

She kissed him, stroking her hand round the back of his neck. She had never felt so blissfully happy before. Every fear, every doubt that this was the wrong thing, faded away. She had been given a second chance at happiness and this time she was going to take it.

~

Jacob walked up the high street towards the castle hand in hand with Ruby. He looked down and she flashed him a beautiful, happy smile. God, she filled him so much he felt his heart was going to burst. The Christmas Eve ball was something everyone was looking forward to, but the thing that he was most excited about was spending the rest of his life with the woman he loved.

They approached Megan's house and he could see Lucas waiting outside dressed in a tux. The door opened and Megan was standing there in a red velvet dress. Jacob felt Ruby slow down as they passed so she could watch. They heard Lucas say Megan was beautiful and suddenly Megan stepped forward, tugged the lapels of Lucas's jacket and kissed him. Ruby gave a little squeal of delight. Jacob hurried her on before she could stand there and gawk some more but he couldn't help looking back as Lucas hustled Megan back inside, his lips still against hers and kicked the door closed behind them. It seemed someone else was going to get their happy ever after tonight.

'I'm so happy they've finally got together,' Ruby said.

'I think when two people are meant to be together, love finds a way,' Jacob said.

Ruby grinned. 'Or tenacity.'

'That too.'

She leaned up and kissed him on the cheek. 'Thank you for being tenacious.'

He smiled. 'My pleasure.'

'I still feel bad that I never got you anything for the Secret Santa,' Ruby said as they walked past lanterns lighting their way towards the castle entrance. 'Everything has just been so busy the last few days.'

'You gave me your heart, Ruby Marlowe. Of all the crappy gifts that were being given out this afternoon at the Secret Santa, I definitely got the best one. Probably the best present I've ever been given.'

She smiled. 'I'm sure I can make it up to you later tonight.'

He grinned, feeling the punch of desire at that thought. He didn't think that need for her would ever go away.

'I'm looking forward to you meeting Cal tonight as well, he will love you,' Ruby said. 'His plane got in this afternoon, so he's on his way here now.'

'I'm looking forward to meeting him too,' Jacob said. 'I hope he approves.'

She looked up at him with a laugh. 'How could he not approve of someone who makes me so happy?'

He smiled.

They walked into the entrance and were met with an actual butler who offered to take their coats. Jacob knew that Kitty and Ken only had one housekeeper to cook and clean their tiny living quarters, so this butler was a step up, although he suspected it was just for tonight, along with all the other staff who were busy moving around, handing out champagne flutes and making everything run smoothly.

Ruby shrugged out of her coat and he got the chance to admire her dress again. She looked magnificent, wearing an emerald-green ball gown that clung in all the right places.

They moved down the corridor and stepped into the great hall, which really did look magnificent. There were several ornate-looking chandeliers dotted around the room that had been festooned with lots of holly, berries and other festive greenery. A large tree in one corner was dressed all in gold and a holly berry garland was draped across the spectacular fireplace, which had a huge log fire burning away. The tables, all covered in white tablecloths, looked spectacular with beautiful decorations in the middle that Jacob knew Kitty and Ken had bought from Ruby's shop.

He was well aware that many of the villagers were watching them as they walked hand in hand across the room to their table and he didn't care. Nothing could take away his happiness right then. They could stare and talk and whisper and point and his smile was still going to be permanently on his face.

He noticed Lucy in the corner with her friends. Clearly her date, if there ever had been one, was a no-show. Lucy looked well and truly fed up. While everyone was wandering around the tables and mingling happily, they were all giving Lucy's table a wide berth. But it was no wonder when she had a face like she'd just been told Christmas was cancelled. Jacob hoped that Happiness would thaw her out, and she would relax into having the kinder and more generous attitude that the rest of the villagers had, but he wouldn't hold his breath.

Julia came barrelling over before they'd even reached their table.

'It's nice to see you put that silly argument behind you,' she said. 'Are you two…' she gestured vaguely as if a simple gesture could even begin to cover what Jacob felt for Ruby Marlowe. Despite wanting to shout about their relationship from the rooftops, he would leave it up to Ruby to decide if she wanted to tell people about their new status or not.

'We're together,' Ruby said, proudly. 'Properly. He's my boyfriend and I love him.'

Jacob smiled and leaned down to kiss Ruby on the forehead.

Julia looked like she was about to burst with excitement. She immediately leapt forward and pulled them both into a big hug and then ran off to no doubt tell the entire village this exciting news.

'So it's official then, Ruby Marlowe?'

She grinned. 'I guess it is.'

He glanced over her shoulder and spotted Cal walking into the room, wearing a tux. He was a confident man, but not cocky, just someone who was very happy in his own skin.

He gestured to Ruby that her brother was here and she let out a little squeal and ran across the room to greet him. He watched her as she threw her arms round Cal's neck and he picked her up and swung her around.

Ruby linked arms with him and brought Cal back over to introduce them. This was it, the time he had to impress a Paralympian.

Ruby was whispering something to Cal as they drew near and Cal was smiling hugely.

'Cal, this is Jacob,' Ruby said. 'Jacob, this is my big brother.'

Cal squared up to him, which wasn't what Jacob was

expecting at all. 'I need a word with you, Jacob Harrington. Is it true you're sleeping with my little sister?'

Jacob had no idea how to respond to that. But then Ruby giggled and Jacob noticed the smile playing on Cal's lips.

'I'm totally messing with you,' Cal laughed, offering out a hand to shake. 'It's nice to finally meet the man who has put such a big smile back on my sister's face.'

Jacob sighed with relief but before he could speak, he heard a voice behind him.

'Cal?'

Jacob turned round to see that Lottie was standing there staring at Cal as if she'd seen a ghost.

Cal's face erupted into a big smile. 'Lottie.'

'Do you two know each other?' Ruby asked.

Jacob looked at the two of them, registering the way they were staring at each other, and suddenly he knew. This was the man his sister had told him about, the one she had pushed away because she'd got scared.

'Well, it seems I might need a word with you, Callum Marlowe. Did you sleep with my little sister?'

Cal laughed uneasily.

The band started to play and, because Lottie and Cal were still staring at each other, Jacob snagged Ruby's hand and whisked her onto the dancefloor.

'My brother and your sister?' Ruby said, watching them as Lottie moved towards Cal and gave him a tentative hug. Then Poppy came over and hugged his leg and Cal picked Poppy up and gave her a proper hug too.

'So it seems.'

Ruby leaned her head against his chest as he moved around the dancefloor with her in his arms.

'I love you,' Ruby said, looking up at him. 'You gave me a

future that I never thought possible, you made dreams come true that I stopped hoping for a long time ago.'

He bent his head and kissed her in full view of everyone else, not caring who saw or what they thought.

'You have given me happiness that I never knew I was looking for,' Jacob said, against her lips. He looked up for a moment at the tall Christmas tree and then back at Ruby and smiled. 'I think I've finally found what makes my perfect Christmas.'

CHAPTER TWENTY-TWO

Ruby was feeling completely stuffed. She'd had her fill of turkey, parsnips and roast potatoes and somehow still managed to find room for two mince pies with cream and numerous chocolates.

She looked around the room at the people she loved: Jacob, Cal and Willow and of course Andrew, Lottie and Poppy. The game of charades was well underway with Willow currently taking centre stage and prancing around waving her hands in the air. Andrew was watching her with complete love in his eyes as if her terrible rendition of *Mary Poppins* was the greatest thing he'd ever seen. Snow was falling steadily as it had been all morning. There were several snowmen outside their shop that they'd all spent the morning making.

It really was the perfect Christmas Day. But not for any of those reasons, but because she was spending it with the man she loved with everything she had. She was snuggled up against Jacob on the sofa, his arm around her shoulders. She looked up at him and watched him laugh at whatever Willow was doing. God, she loved him so much and, right then, she couldn't have been happier.

He noticed her watching him and looked down at her, his face lighting up into a beautiful smile.

'I love you,' Ruby whispered, although everyone was shouting out their guesses of what Willow was trying to act out so no one was really interested in what they were talking about. 'Have I told you that today?'

He grinned. 'Many times, but I don't think I will ever tire of hearing you say it.' He stroked a finger down her cheek. 'And I can't wait until tonight when I can show you how much I love you.'

She smiled. 'I'm so excited about going to Italy tomorrow. I know seeing the world's largest Christmas tree might not be your thing, but there'll be lots of other things we can do while we're there.'

'Ruby, your dreams are my dreams now. I will be more than happy watching you fulfil your dreams. Plus it's Italy, it'll be snowing, that sounds pretty damned romantic to me.'

'I think I'll have to give you that.'

'I knew I'd be able to change your mind about snow being romantic,' Jacob said.

She smiled. She wasn't going to admit that anywhere she was with him would be romantic in her eyes.

She turned back to watch Willow and decided to put her out of her misery. '*Mary Poppins*.'

'Yes, finally,' Willow said, flopping down on the sofa next to Andrew, exhausted.

Ruby stood up. 'Does anyone want a hot chocolate?'

There were nods of approval all around the room.

'Cal, why don't you give me a hand.'

He grinned and shifted Poppy off his lap, signing to her slowly where he was going. He had done the sign language course with her a few months before. It was funny to think they'd both been doing it to communicate with the same little girl.

Ruby walked into the kitchen and Cal followed her. She'd still not had a chance to talk to her brother properly yet since his arrival the night before. He'd spent most of the ball sitting with Poppy and Lottie and talking to them. They had slipped off early and arrived together at Jacob's flat a few hours before so something was definitely going on between them.

Ruby poured some milk into a jug and put it into the microwave. She turned round as Cal was getting mugs out the cupboard. She looked into the lounge and could see the game of charades was still going, with Lottie taking to the floor this time.

'So what's going on between you and Lottie and why did you never tell me about her before?' Ruby said.

Cal started adding hot chocolate powder to the mugs. 'I didn't tell you because it ended almost straight after it started so it was hardly a good advertisement for getting you back into the relationship saddle. And as to what's going on between us now… I don't know. We have a connection, I felt that the first time I met her. You know when you meet someone and you just know your life is going to change because of that person? That's what I felt when I saw her. We had chemistry. A ton of it. But it was so much more than that. That connection is still as strong now. She says she regrets pushing me away, I haven't been able to stop thinking about her since I left. And Poppy, I adore her.' He shrugged. 'Maybe we can make it work.'

Ruby grinned. She wanted that life for her brother. Now she'd had a taste of the fairytale, she wanted that for everyone. 'I hope so.'

'And what about you and Jacob?'

'I love him,' Ruby said, without a moment's hesitation.

He broke into a huge smile. 'You don't know how happy that makes me.'

'Thank you for pushing me, for helping me to be brave again.'

'I don't know if I can take any credit, you had to choose to take that step yourself in the end.'

'And he's one hundred percent worth it. There's not a single doubt in my mind that he is my forever.'

The microwave pinged and Ruby grabbed the jug and poured out the hot milk into the mugs while Cal added squirty cream and marshmallows to the top.

They took them out into the lounge and for a moment the game ceased as everyone snuggled up in their chairs and sofas to drink them.

Ruby sat next to Jacob and he put her arm around her. She looked around the room at Andrew cuddled up with Willow, his hand on her belly. She looked over at Cal, one arm around Lottie, the other wrapped around Poppy, and she couldn't help but smile. This really was the little village of Happiness.

EPILOGUE

Ruby hurried into the great hall to check everything was ready for her best friend. A Valentine's Day wedding for Willow and Andrew couldn't be more romantic and Ruby wanted to make sure that everything ran smoothly.

All the guests were waiting for the wedding to start, sitting in a big circle around the room. There were no 'his and hers' sides, no aisle, it was just going to be a day to celebrate their love for each other. Willow and Andrew had gone against almost every wedding tradition possible. She would not be given away, they were going to enter the circle together, equal partners in every way. Ruby liked that. Andrew had already had the wonderful delight of seeing Willow in her dress earlier that afternoon, a beautiful gold gown that sparkled and shimmered whenever she moved.

Purple flowers adorned the room, entwined with gold candles and fairy lights as Willow hadn't wanted the traditional red associated with Valentine's Day. They were making up their own rules today.

Ken had obviously got the memo about the colour scheme.

He was waiting in the middle of the circle ready to perform the marriage dressed in a splendid purple satin waistcoat which actually matched Ruby's own dress perfectly.

Lottie snagged her hand as she walked past. Cal was sitting next to her, holding her other hand with Poppy on his lap. The two of them had danced around their attraction for several weeks after Christmas, with Cal coming and going on several occasions, but eventually Cal had rented a flat just down the road from Lottie and now they were apparently taking things slow, although Ruby knew that their version of taking it slow was Cal spending almost every night round Lottie's place. They both seemed deliriously happy with this arrangement, as did Poppy. Ruby was enjoying having her brother so close again too.

'How's Willow doing?' Lottie asked.

Willow's morning sickness had started with a vengeance a few weeks before, but it seemed to have slowed and almost stopped over the last few days. Whether that had anything to do with Julia's secret recipe of ginger tea and peppermint biscuits, or whether it had just stopped on its own, no one knew, but it seemed that she would at least get some kind of reprieve from it today.

'I think she's OK, she's stocked up on those peppermint biscuits and she says she's doing fine. I think she's just too excited to even have time to be sick today.'

'And how's Andrew doing?' Cal said.

'I left them cuddled up on the sofa together and Andrew had the biggest grin on his face I think I've ever seen.'

'So we're all ready?' Lottie said.

Ruby looked around. 'I think so.'

'You better go and get Jacob, he's outside,' Lottie said, suppressing a tiny smirk.

Ruby moved to the door. Outside, snow was falling heavily, making the night seem so much brighter and magical. Little daffodils and tulips had already flowered and their heads were bowed against the unexpected snow. A large oak tree stood in the courtyard outside all lit up with tiny lights, glowing in the darkness. Jacob stood underneath its great boughs, holding what looked like a blanket. Her heart leapt at the sight of him.

She moved across the courtyard towards him and, as she got close, he wrapped the furry blanket around her shoulders.

'What are you doing out here? The wedding's about to start,' Ruby said.

'We have time.' Jacob gathered the blanket together and tugged her gently towards him, so he could kiss her. She melted against him and he held her in his arms.

'I love you,' Jacob said, against her lips.

She smiled. 'Jacob Harrington, you have changed my life completely. You make me so utterly happy every single day. I love you so much.'

'You're kind of stealing my lines here,' Jacob said, kissing her again.

And then she knew. Willow sending her downstairs to 'check everything was OK'. Lottie sending her outside. Jacob waiting for her in the snow, underneath the fairy lights with a blanket to keep her warm when in reality they both should have been inside waiting for the bride and groom. Her heart soared with happiness, as Jacob stroked her fingers and placed little kisses on her wedding ring finger.

'Ruby Marlowe. I wanted to do this somewhere Christmassy but I'll be damned if I'm waiting until Christmas. I thought that here with the snow and the fairy lights, it would be a close second.'

He took a deep breath and his hands shook as he held her.

'Jacob, if it's any easier, the answer's yes.'

He grinned. 'You're so impatient. You have to at least let me ask you first.'

'I just want you to know, there is not one single seed of doubt that this is the right thing for us. I'm not scared of that future anymore.'

'Some might say it's too soon for us,' Jacob said, his eyes clouding with concern.

'And they don't know what we have. We have something incredible; you know that.'

'I do. You are my entire world and I cannot wait to have you as my wife.'

'You have me, regardless of that ring you have in your pocket. What we have is forever.'

He smiled and pulled the ring from his jacket. Despite what she had just said, she couldn't wait to see it.

'Ooops, wrong ring,' Jacob said, pulling out Willow's wedding ring.

Ruby laughed, knowing Jacob had done that deliberately.

He put the ring back in his pocket with a wink and pulled out another ring box. He opened it to reveal a beautiful emerald.

'For all the Christmas trees we are going to see.'

'Oh Jacob, it's beautiful.'

'Shall I put it on?'

She nodded, tears in her eyes as he slid it onto her finger. She stared at it; her heart completely full.

'It's official, I'm going to be your wife,' Ruby said, tears streaming down her cheeks.

Jacob gently wiped them away and kissed her.

A noise above them broke the moment and Ruby turned round to see Andrew and Willow leaning out the window. 'Did she say yes?' Willow said.

'Of course I did,' Ruby said and then laughed to see half the villagers leaning out of doors and windows to watch the proposal too. They all gave a little cheer.

'Come on then, Ruby Marlowe, we have a wedding to watch, we might get some tips,' Jacob said.

He offered out his hand and she took it as they walked back inside.

'We don't need any tips, we've got this.'

And Ruby knew that was true. This was the start of their own happy ever after.

~

If you enjoyed *The Happiness Series*, you'll love my next gorgeously romantic story, *Sunrise over Sapphire Bay,* out in April.

STAY IN TOUCH…

To keep up to date with the latest news on my releases, just go to the link below to sign up for a newsletter. You'll also get two FREE short stories, get sneak peeks, booky news and be able to take part in exclusive giveaways. Your email will never be shared with anyone else and you can unsubscribe at any time
https://www.subscribepage.com/hollymartinsignup

Website: https://hollymartin-author.com/
Email: holly@hollymartin-author.com
Twitter: @HollyMAuthor

ALSO BY HOLLY MARTIN

Sunrise over Sapphire Bay

The Summer of Chasing Dreams

Sandcastle Bay Series

The Holiday Cottage by the Sea

The Cottage on Sunshine Beach

Coming Home to Maple Cottage

Hope Island Series

Spring at Blueberry Bay

Summer at Buttercup Beach

Christmas at Mistletoe Cove

Juniper Island Series

Christmas Under a Cranberry Sky

A Town Called Christmas

White Cliff Bay Series

Christmas at Lilac Cottage

Snowflakes on Silver Cove

Summer at Rose Island

Standalone Stories

Fairytale Beginnings

Tied Up With Love

A Home on Bramble Hill

One Hundred Christmas Proposals

One Hundred Proposals

The Guestbook at Willow Cottage

For Young Adults

The Sentinel Series

The Sentinel (Book 1 of the Sentinel Series)

The Prophecies (Book 2 of the Sentinel Series)

The Revenge (Book 3 of the Sentinel Series)

The Reckoning (Book 4 of the Sentinel Series)

ACKNOWLEDGEMENTS

To my family, my mom, my biggest fan, who reads every word I've written a hundred times over and loves it every single time, my dad, my brother Lee and my sister-in-law Julie, for your support, love, encouragement and endless excitement for my stories.

For my twinnie, the gorgeous Aven Ellis for just being my wonderful friend, for your endless support, for cheering me on, for reading my stories and telling me what works and what doesn't and for keeping me entertained with wonderful stories. I love you dearly.

To my lovely friends Julie, Natalie, Jac, Verity and Jodie, thanks for all the support.

To the Devon contingent, Paw and Order, Belinda, Lisa, Phil, Bodie, Kodi and Skipper. Thanks for keeping me entertained and always being there.

For Sharon Sant for just being there always and your wonderful friendship.

To everyone at Bookcamp, you gorgeous, fabulous bunch, thank you for your wonderful support on this venture.

To Kirsty Greenwood, thanks for answering all my questions with unending patience.

A huge thank you to Cath, Helen Edwards, Audrey Dickson for all your help. Thanks to BATOD, BDA, Action on Hearing Loss and the Royal Association for Deaf People for pointing me in the right direction.

Thanks to the brilliant Emma Rogers for the gorgeous cover design.

Thanks to my fabulous editors, Celine Kelly and Rhian McKay.

To all the wonderful bloggers for your tweets, retweets, facebook posts, tireless promotions, support, encouragement and endless enthusiasm. You guys are amazing and I couldn't do this journey without you.

To anyone who has read my book and taken the time to tell me you've enjoyed it or wrote a review, thank you so much.

Thank you, I love you all.

Published by Holly Martin in 2019

Cover design by Emma Rogers

Printed in Great Britain
by Amazon

49006569R00352